Felix Francis is the younger son of thriller-writing legend Dick Francis, with whom he co-wrote the Dick Francis novels *Dead Heat*, *Silks*, *Even Money* and *Crossfire*, with Felix taking an increasingly greater role in the writing. Sadly, Dick died in February 2010, but his work will live on through Felix. *Gamble* is Felix's first solo Dick Francis novel.

Felix trained as a physicist and spent seventeen years teaching A-level Physics before taking on the role of manager of his father, and then becoming an author. He lives in Oxfordshire.

GAMBLE

A Dick Francis Novel

by

FELIX FRANCIS

PENGUIN BOOKS

PENGUIN BOOKS

Published by the Penguin Group
Penguin Books Ltd, 80 Strand, London WC2R ORL, England
Penguin Group (USA) Inc., 375 Hudson Street, New York, New York 10014, USA
Penguin Group (Canada), 90 Eglinton Avenue East, Suite 700, Toronto, Ontario,
Canada M4P 2Y3 (a division of Pearson Penguin Canada Inc.)
Penguin Ireland, 25 St Stephen's Green, Dublin 2, Ireland (a division of Penguin Books Ltd)
Penguin Group (Australia), 707 Collins Street, Melbourne, Victoria 3008, Australia
(a division of Pearson Australia Group Pty Ltd)
Penguin Books India Pvt Ltd, 11 Community Centre, Panchsheel Park, New Delhi – 110 017, India
Penguin Group (NZ), 67 Apollo Drive, Rosedale, Auckland 0632, New Zealand
(a division of Pearson New Zealand Ltd)
Penguin Books (South Africa) (Pty) Ltd, Block D, Rosebank Office Park,
181 Jan Smuts Avenue, Parktown North, Gauteng 2193, South Africa

Penguin Books Ltd, Registered Offices: 80 Strand, London WC2R ORL, England

www.penguin.com

First published by Michael Joseph 2011
Published in Penguin Books 2012
This edition published 2014
001

Copyright © Dick Francis Corporation, 2011
All rights reserved

The moral right of the author has been asserted

Typeset by Jouve (UK), Milton Keynes
Printed in England by Clays Ltd, St Ives plc

ISBN: 978-1-405-92017-9

www.greenpenguin.co.uk

MIX
Paper from
responsible sources
FSC
www.fsc.org   FSC® C018179

Penguin Books is committed to a sustainable
future for our business, our readers and our planet.
This book is made from Forest Stewardship
Council™ certified paper.

For my granddaughter
Sienna Rose

With thanks to my cousin
Ned Francis
financial adviser

and the offices of
Calkin Pattinson and Company Limited

and to **Debbie,**
as always

I

I was standing right next to Herb Kovak when he was murdered. *Executed* would have been a better word. Shot three times from close range, twice in the heart and once in the face, he was almost certainly dead before he hit the ground, and definitely before the gunman had turned away and disappeared into the Grand National race-day crowd.

The shooting had happened so fast that neither Herb nor I, nor anyone else for that matter, would have had a chance to prevent it. In fact, I hadn't realized what was actually going on until it was over, and Herb was already dead at my feet. I wondered if Herb himself had had the time to comprehend that his life was in danger before the bullets tore into his body to end it.

Probably not, and I found that strangely comforting. I had liked Herb.

But someone else clearly hadn't.

The murder of Herb Kovak changed everyone's day, not just his. The police took over the situation with their usual insensitive efficiency, cancelling one of the world's major sporting events with just half an hour's notice and requiring the more than sixty thousand frustrated spectators to wait patiently in line for several hours to give their names and addresses.

'But you must have seen his face!'

I was sitting at a table opposite an exasperated police detective inspector in one of the restaurants that had been cleared of its usual clientele and set up as an emergency incident room.

'I've already told you,' I said. 'I wasn't looking at the man's face.'

I thought back once again to those few fatal seconds and all I could remember clearly was the gun.

'So it was a man?' the inspector asked.

'I think so,' I said.

'Was he black or white?'

'The gun was black,' I said. 'With a silencer.'

It didn't sound very helpful. Even I could tell that.

'Mr ... er.' The detective consulted the notebook on the table. 'Foxton. Is there nothing else you can tell us about the murderer?'

'I'm sorry,' I said, shaking my head. 'It all happened so quickly.'

He changed his line of questioning. 'So, how well did you know Mr Kovak?'

'Well enough,' I said. 'We work together. Have done for the past five years or so. I'd say we are work-friends.' I paused. 'At least, we were.'

It was difficult to believe that he was dead.

'What line of work?'

'Financial services,' I said. 'We're independent financial advisers.'

I could almost see the detective's eyes glaze over with boredom.

'It may not be as exciting as riding in the Grand National,' I said, 'but it's not that bad.'

He looked up at my face. 'And have you ridden in the Grand National?' His voice was full of sarcasm, and he was smiling.

'As a matter of fact, I have,' I said. 'Twice.'

The smile faded. 'Oh,' he said.

Oh, indeed, I thought. 'And I won it the second time.'

It was unlike me to talk much about what I now felt was a previous life, and bragging about it was even more uncharacteristic. I silently rebuked myself for my indulgence, but I was getting a little irritated by the policeman's attitude not only towards me but also towards my dead colleague.

He looked down again at his notes.

'Foxton,' he said, reading. He looked up. 'Not Foxy Foxton?'

'Yes,' I said, although I had long been trying to give up the 'Foxy' nickname, preferring my real name of Nicholas, which I felt was more suited to a serious life in the City.

'Well, well,' said the policeman. 'I won a few quid on you.'

I smiled. He'd probably lost a few quid too, but I wasn't going to say so.

'Not riding today, then?'

'No,' I said. 'Not for a long time.'

Had it really been eight years, I thought, since I had

last ridden in a race? In some ways it felt like only yesterday, but in others it was a lifetime away.

The policeman wrote another line in his notebook.

'So now you're a financial adviser?'

'Yes.'

'Bit of a comedown, wouldn't you say?'

I thought about replying that it was better than being a policeman but decided, in the end, that silence was probably the best policy. Anyway, I tended to agree with him. My whole life had been a bit of a comedown since those heady days of hurling myself over Aintree fences with half a ton of horseflesh between my legs.

'Who do you advise?' he asked.

'Anyone who will pay me,' I said, rather flippantly.

'And Mr Kovak?'

'Him too,' I said. 'We both work for a firm of independent financial advisers in the City.'

'Here in Liverpool?' he asked.

'No,' I said. 'The City of London.'

'Which firm?'

'Lyall and Black,' I said. 'Our offices are in Lombard Street.'

He wrote it down.

'Can you think of any reason why anyone would want Mr Kovak dead?'

It was the question I had been asking myself over and over again for the past two hours.

'No,' I said. 'Absolutely not. Everyone liked Herb. He was always smiling and happy. He was the life and soul of any party.'

'How long did you say you have known him?' asked the detective.

'Five years. We joined the firm at the same time.'

'I understand he was an American citizen.'

'Yes,' I said. 'He came from Louisville, in Kentucky. He used to go back to the States a couple of times a year.'

Everything was written down in the inspector's notebook.

'Was he married?'

'No.'

'Girlfriend?'

'None that I knew of,' I said.

'Were you and he in a gay relationship?' the policeman asked in a deadpan tone of voice, his eyes still on his notes.

'No,' I said, equally deadpan.

'I'll find out, you know,' he said, looking up.

'There's nothing to find out,' I said. 'I may have worked with Mr Kovak but I live with my girlfriend.'

'Where?'

'Finchley,' I said. 'North London.'

I gave him my full address and he wrote it down.

'Was Mr Kovak involved in a gay relationship with anyone else?'

'What makes you think he was gay?' I asked.

'No wife. No girlfriend. What else should I think?'

'I have no reason to believe Herb was gay. In fact, I know he wasn't.'

'How do you know?' The policeman leaned towards me purposefully.

I thought back to those rare occasions when Herb and I had spent any time together, sometimes in hotels where we would be staying overnight at financial conferences. He had never made any sort of pass at me, and he had occasionally chatted up the local girls and then boasted about his conquests over breakfast. It was true that I'd never actually seen him in a sexual situation with a woman, but I hadn't seen him with a man either.

'I just know,' I said weakly.

'Hmm,' said the inspector, clearly not believing me and making another note in his book.

But did I really know? And did it matter?

'What difference would it make, anyway?' I asked.

'Lots of murders have a sexual motive,' said the detective. 'Until we know differently, we have to explore every avenue.'

It was nearly dark before I was finally allowed to leave the racecourse, and it had also started raining. The courtesy shuttle service to the distant park-and-ride car park had long since ceased running and I was cold, wet and thoroughly fed up by the time I reached my Mercedes. But I sat for some while in the car before setting off, once more going over and over in my mind the events of the day.

I had picked Herb up from his flat at Seymour Way in Hendon soon after eight in the morning and we had set off to Liverpool in great good humour. It was to be

Herb's first trip to the Grand National and he was uncharacteristically excited by the prospect.

He had grown up in the shadow of the iconic twin spires of Churchill Downs racetrack, the venue of the Kentucky Derby and spiritual home of American Thoroughbred racing, but he had always claimed that gambling on the horses had ruined his childhood.

I had asked him to come to the races with me quite a few times before but he had always declined, claiming that the memories were still too painful. However, there had been no sign of that today as I had driven north on the motorway, the two of us chatting amicably about our work, our lives, and our hopes and fears for the future.

Little did we know then how short Herb's future was going to be.

He and I had always got on fairly well over the past five years but mostly on a strictly colleague-to-colleague level. Today had been the first day of a promising deeper friendship. It had also been the last.

I sat alone in my car and grieved for my new-found, but so quickly lost, friend. But still I had no idea why anyone would want him dead.

My journey back to Finchley seemed to be never ending. There was an accident on the M6 north of Birmingham with a five-mile tailback. It said so on the radio, sandwiched between endless news bulletins about the murder of Herb and the cancellation of the

Grand National. Not that they mentioned Herb by name, of course. He was just referred to as 'a man'. I assumed the police would withhold his identity until his next of kin had been informed. But who, I wondered, were his next of kin? And how would the authorities find them? Thankfully, I thought, that wasn't my problem.

I came upon the back of the traffic congestion just south of Stoke, the mass of red brake lights ahead of me shining brightly in the darkness.

I have to admit that I am usually an impatient driver. I suppose it is a case of 'once a racer, always a racer'. It makes little difference to me if my steed has four legs or four wheels, if I see a gap, I tend to take it. It was the way I had ridden during my all-too-short four years as a jockey and it had served me well.

But, that evening, I didn't have the energy to get irritated by the queues of near-stationary cars. Instead I sat quietly in the outside lane as we crawled past an upturned motor home that had spread its load of human and domestic clutter across half the carriageway. One shouldn't look at others' misfortune but, of course, we all did and thanked our lucky stars it wasn't us lying there on the cold tarmac receiving medical assistance.

I stopped at one of the motorway service areas and called home.

Claudia, my girlfriend, answered at the second ring.

'Hello, it's me,' I said. 'I'm on my way home but I'll be a couple of hours more at least.'

'Good day?' she asked.

'Have you seen the news?'

'No. Why?'

I knew she wouldn't have. Claudia was an artist and she had planned to spend the day painting in what she called her studio but what was actually the guest bedroom of the house we shared. Once she closed the door, turned up the music in her iPod headphones and set to work on a canvas it would take an earthquake or a nuclear strike to penetrate her bubble. I had been quite surprised that she had answered the phone.

'The National was cancelled,' I said.

'Cancelled?'

'Well, there's talk of them holding the race on Monday, but it was cancelled for today.'

'Why?' she asked.

'Someone was murdered.'

'How inconvenient of them.' There was laughter in her voice.

'It was Herb,' I said.

'What was Herb?' she asked. The laughter had gone.

'It was Herb who was murdered.'

'Oh my God!' she screamed. 'How?'

'Watch the news.'

'But Nick,' she said, concerned. 'I mean – are you OK?'

'I'm fine. I'll be home as soon as I can.'

Next I tried to call my boss – Herb's boss – to warn him of the coming disruption to business, as I was sure there would be, but there was no answer. I decided against leaving a message. Somehow voicemail didn't seem the right medium for bad news.

I set off southwards again and spent the remainder of the journey as I had the first part, thinking about Herb and wondering why anyone should want to kill him. But there were so many questions and so few answers.

How did the murderer know Herb would be at Aintree today?

Had we been followed from London and stalked around the racecourse?

Had Herb really been the target or had it been a case of mistaken identity?

And why would anyone commit murder with sixty thousand potential witnesses in close attendance when surely it would be safer to lure their victim alone into some dark, quiet alley?

I'd said as much to the detective inspector but he hadn't thought it particularly unusual. 'Sometimes it is easier for an assailant to get away if there is a big crowd to hide in,' he'd said. 'Also it can pamper to their ego to do it in a public place with witnesses.'

'But it must make it more likely that he would be recognized, or at least allow you to get a good description.'

'You'd be surprised,' he'd said. 'More witnesses often mean more confusion. They all see things differently and we end up with a description of a black white man with straight curly hair, four arms and two heads. And everyone tends to look at the bleeding victim rather than the perpetrator of the crime. We often get a great description of the corpse, but nothing about the murderer.'

'But how about CCTV?' I'd asked him.

'It appears that the particular spot behind the grandstand where Mr Kovak was shot is not in view of any of the racecourse security cameras and was also not visible from any of the cameras brought in by the television people to cover the event.'

The assassin had known what he was doing in that respect. It had clearly been a professional hit.

But why?

Every line of thought came back to the same question. Why would anyone want to kill Herb Kovak? I knew that some of our clients could get pretty cross when an investment that had been recommended to them went down in value rather than up, but to the point of murder? Surely not?

People like Herb and me didn't live in a world of contract killers and hit-men. We simply existed in an environment of figures and computers, profits and returns, interest rates and gilt yields, not of guns and bullets and violent death.

The more I thought about it the more convinced I became that, professional as the hit may have been, the killer must have shot the wrong man.

I was hungry and weary by the time I pulled the Mercedes into the parking area in front of my house in Lichfield Grove, Finchley. It was ten minutes to midnight and just sixteen hours since I had left here this morning. It felt longer – about a week longer.

Claudia had waited up and she came out to the car.

'I watched the television news,' she said. 'I can't believe it.'

Neither could I. It all seemed so unreal.

'I was standing right next to him,' I said. 'One moment he was alive and laughing about which horse we should bet on and the next second he was dead.'

'Awful.' She stroked my arm. 'Do they know who did it?'

'Not that they told me,' I said. 'What did it say on the news?'

'Not much, really,' Claudia said. 'Just a couple of so-called experts disagreeing with each other about whether it was as a result of terrorism or organized crime.'

'It was an assassination,' I said firmly. 'Plain and simple.'

'But who on earth would want to assassinate Herb Kovak?' Claudia said. 'I only met him twice but he seemed such a gentle soul.'

'I agree,' I said, 'and the more I think about it the more certain I become that it must have been a case of mistaken identity. Perhaps that's also why the police haven't yet revealed who was shot. They don't want to let the killer know he hit the wrong man.'

I walked round to the back of the car and opened the boot. It had been a warm and sunny spring day when we had arrived at Aintree and we had decided to leave our overcoats in the car. I looked down at them both lying there, Herb's dark blue one on top of my own brown.

'Oh God,' I said out loud, suddenly becoming quite emotional again. 'What shall I do with that?'

'Leave it there,' said Claudia, slamming the boot shut. She took me by the arm. 'Come on, Nick. Time to put you to bed.'

'I'd rather have a stiff drink or two.'

'OK,' she said with a smile. 'A couple of stiff drinks first, then bed.'

I didn't feel much better in the morning, but that might have had something to do with the few more than a couple of stiff drinks I'd consumed before finally going to bed around two o'clock.

I had never been much of a drinker, not least as a need to keep my riding weight down when I'd been a jockey. I had left school with three top grades at A level and, much to the dismay of my parents and teachers, I had forgone the offered place at the LSE, the London School of Economics, for a life in the saddle. So, aged eighteen, when many young men going up to university were learning how to use their new-found freedom to pour large amounts of alcohol down their throats, I'd been pounding the streets of Lambourn in a sweat-suit or sitting alone in a sauna trying to shed an extra pound or two.

However, the previous evening, the shock of the day's events had begun to show. So I had dug out the half bottle of single malt whisky left over from Christmas and polished it off before climbing the stairs to bed. But, of course, the spirit didn't take away the demons in my head and I had spent much of the night troubled and awake, unable to remove the mental image of Herb growing cold on a marble slab in some Liverpool mortuary.

The weather on Sunday morning was as miserable as I was with a string of heavy April showers blowing in on a bracing northerly breeze.

At about ten, during a break in the rain, I went out for a Sunday paper, nipping up to the newsagent on Regent's Park Road.

'A very good morning to you, Mr Foxton,' said the shop owner from behind the counter.

'Morning, Mr Patel,' I said in reply. 'But I'm not sure what's good about it.'

Mr Patel smiled at me and said nothing. We may have lived in the same place but we did so with different cultures.

All the front pages on the shelves had the same story: DEATH AT THE RACES read one headline, MURDER AT THE NATIONAL read another, GUN HORROR AT AINTREE ran a third.

I glanced quickly at them all. None gave the name of the victim and, to me, there appeared to be far greater coverage about the aggravation and inconvenience suffered by the crowd rather than any commiseration or condolence towards poor Herb. I suppose some conjecture was to be expected as the reporters had so little real factual information from which to make a story, but I was surprised at their apparent lack of sympathy for the target of the assassin.

One paper even went so far as to suggest that the murder was likely to have been drug related and then went on to imply that everyone else was probably better off with the victim dead.

I bought a copy of the *Sunday Times* for no better reason than its headline – POLICE HUNT RACE-DAY ASSASSIN – was the least sensational and the story beneath it didn't immediately assume that Herb had probably deserved to be killed.

'Thank you, sir,' said Mr Patel, giving me my change.

I tucked the heavy newspaper under my arm and retraced my tracks home.

Lichfield Grove was a fairly typical London suburban street of mostly 1930s-built semi-detached houses with bay windows and small front gardens.

I had lived here now for the past eight years yet I hardly knew my neighbours other than to wave at occasionally if we happened to arrive or leave our homes at the same time. In fact, I knew Mr Patel the newsagent better than those I lived right next to. I was aware that the couple on one side were called Jane and Phil (or was it John?) but I had no idea of their surname or what either of them did for a living.

As I walked back from the newsagent, I thought how strange it was that members of the human race could live here so cheek-by-jowl with their fellow beings without any meaningful reaction between them.

But at least it made a change from the rural village life I had experienced before, where everyone took pains to know every other person's business, and where nothing could be kept a secret for long.

I wondered whether I should make more of an effort to be more community minded. I suppose it would depend on how long I intended to stay.

Many of my racing friends had thought that Finchley was a strange choice but I had needed a clean break from my former life. A clean break – that was a joke! It had been a clean break that had forced me to stop race riding just as I was beginning to make my mark in the sport. The clean break in question was to my second cervical vertebra, the axis, on which the atlas vertebra above it rotated to turn the head. In short, I had broken my neck.

I suppose I should be thankful that the break hadn't killed or paralysed me, either of which could have been a highly likely outcome. The fact that I was now walking down Lichfield Grove at all was due to the prompt and gentle care of the paramedics on duty at Cheltenham racecourse that fateful day. They had taken great pains to immobilize my neck and spine before I was lifted from the turf.

It had been a silly fall, and I had to admit to a degree of carelessness on my part.

The last race on the Wednesday of the Cheltenham Steeplechase Festival is what is known as the Bumper – a National Hunt flat race. No jumps, no hurdles, just two miles of undulating rich green grass between start and finish. It is not the greatest spectacle the Festival has to offer and many of the large crowd had already made their way to the car parks, or the bar.

But the Bumper is very competitive and the jockeys take it very seriously. Not often do the jump boys and girls get to emulate Willie Shoemaker or Frankie Dettori. Judging the pace with no jumps to break up the rhythm is an art, and knowing where and when to make your final challenge to the finish can make all the difference to the outcome.

That particular Wednesday, just over eight years ago, I had been riding a horse that the *Racing Post* had rather kindly called 'an outsider'. The horse had just one speed – moderate – and absolutely no turn of foot to take it past others up the final climb to victory. My only chance was to go off fairly fast from the start and to try to run the 'finish' out of the others.

The plan worked quite well, up to a point.

At about half way, my mount and I were some fifteen lengths in front of the nearest challenger and still going reasonably well as we swung left-handed and down the hill. But the sound of the pursuers was getting ever louder in my ears, and six or seven of them swept past us like Ferraris overtaking a steamroller as we turned into the straight.

The race was lost, and it was no great surprise to me, or to the few still watching from the grandstands.

Perhaps the horse beneath sensed a subtle change in me – a change from expectation and excitement to resignation and disappointment. Or perhaps the horse was no longer concentrating on the task in hand in the same way that his jockey's mind was wandering to the following day's races and his rides to come.

Whatever the real cause, one moment he was galloping along serenely, albeit one-paced, and the next he had stumbled and gone down as if shot.

I had seen the television replay. I'd had no chance.

The fall had catapulted me over the horse's neck and head-first into the ground. I had woken up two days later in the neurosurgery and spinal-injuries department of Frenchay Hospital in Bristol with a humdinger of a headache and a metal contraption called a halo brace surrounding and literally screwed into my skull.

Three uncomfortable months later, with the metal halo finally removed, I set about regaining my fitness and place in the saddle only for my hopes to be dashed by the horseracing authority's medical board, who decided that I was permanently unfit to return to racing. 'Too risky,' they had said. 'Another fall on your head could prove fatal.' I had argued that I was prepared to accept the risk and pointed out that a fall on the head could prove fatal even if you hadn't previously broken your neck.

I had tried at length to explain to them that all jockeys risked their lives every time they climbed aboard half a ton of horse and galloped at thirty miles per hour over five-foot fences. Jockeys were well used to taking risks and accepted the consequences without blaming the authorities. But it was all to no avail. 'Sorry,' they said. 'Our decision is final.'

So that had been that.

From being the new kid on the block, the youngest winning jockey of the Grand National since Bruce Hobbs in 1938 and widely tipped to be the next Champion, I was suddenly a twenty-one-year-old ex-jockey with nothing to fall back on.

'You will need an education for when your riding days are over,' my father had once said in a last futile attempt to make me take up my place at university instead of going racing when I was eighteen.

'Then I'll get my education when I need it,' I'd replied.

And so I had, applying again and being accepted once more by the LSE to read for a combined degree in government and economics.

And hence I had come to live in Finchley, putting down a deposit on the house from the earnings of my last successful season in the saddle.

Finchley Central Underground Station, round the corner from Lichfield Grove, was just ten stops up the Northern Line from the LSE.

But it hadn't been an easy change.

I had become used to the adrenalin-fuelled excitement of riding horses at speed over obstacles when winning was the thing. Winning, winning, winning – nothing else mattered. Everything I did was with winning in mind. I loved it. I lived it. It was like a drug, and I was addicted.

When it was snatched away from me, I suffered badly from withdrawal symptoms. An alcoholic with the DTs had nothing on me.

In those first few months I tried hard to put on a

brave face, busying myself with buying the house and getting ready for my studies, cursing my luck and telling everyone that I was fine; but inside I was sick, shaking and near suicidal.

Another shower was about to fall out of the darkening sky as I hurried the last few yards along the road to my house with the newspaper.

In keeping with many of my neighbours, I had arranged, early on, to concrete over my small overgrown front lawn, converting it into an off-road parking space that was now occupied by my ageing Mercedes SLK sports car. I had excitedly bought the car brand new with my percentage from the Grand National win. That had been ten years and more than a hundred and eighty thousand miles ago and, in truth, I was well past needing a change.

I opened the boot and looked down at the two coats lying there. The previous evening the sight of Herb's blue cashmere had almost been too much for me to bear, but now it appeared as just an overcoat without a home.

I picked them both up, slammed the boot shut, and hurried inside as the first large drops of rain began to wet my hair.

I hung my coat on one of the hooks behind the front door and wondered what I should do with Herb's. He wouldn't be needing it now but I supposed it belonged to his family and would go back to them eventually.

In the meantime, I hung it up next to mine in my hallway.

I am not quite sure why I went through the pockets. Maybe I thought that he might have left his flat key there as he had been wearing the coat when he had locked his door the previous morning.

There was no key but there was a piece of paper deep in the left-hand pocket. It had been roughly folded over and screwed up. I flattened it out on the wall.

I stood there in disbelief reading the stark message written on the paper in black ballpoint:

YOU SHOULD HAVE DONE WHAT YOU WERE TOLD. YOU MAY SAY YOU REGRET IT, BUT YOU WON'T BE REGRETTING IT FOR LONG.

Did that mean Herb had been the real target? Had the assassin actually shot the right man? And if so, why?

2

I spent much of Sunday morning reading and re-reading the message on the paper, trying to work out whether it actually was a prediction of murder or just an innocent communication with no relevance to the events at the Grand National the previous afternoon.

YOU SHOULD HAVE DONE WHAT YOU WERE TOLD. YOU MAY SAY YOU REGRET IT, BUT YOU WON'T BE REGRETTING IT FOR LONG.

I dug out the business card that I had been given at Aintree by the detective: Inspector Paul Matthews, Merseyside Police. I tried the number printed there, but he wasn't available. I left a message asking him to call me back.

I wondered what it was that Herb should have done, what he had been told to do. And for what, and to whom, had he expressed regret?

I gave up trying to work it out and read the many reports about the murder in the *Sunday Times*. I thought again about calling my boss, but he would also read about it in the papers and he would find out soon enough that the victim had been his senior assistant. Why spoil his Sunday lunch?

I knew all too well from my time as a jockey that

one should never believe what one reads in newspapers but, on this occasion, I was surprised how accurate they were as far as the factual information was concerned. The *Sunday Times* correspondents clearly had good links direct to Merseyside Police headquarters, but not so good that they could actually name the victim. And they had little or no information about any motive but that didn't stop them from speculating.

'Such a clinical assassination has all the hallmarks of a gangland organized crime "hit".' It went on to suggest that a reason the name of the victim was being withheld was possibly because he was a well-known criminal and the police didn't want potential witnesses to feel it wasn't worth coming forward.

'That's rubbish,' I said out loud.

'What's rubbish?' Claudia asked.

I was sitting in our small kitchen with the newspaper spread out across the kitchen table while Claudia was baking a cake for her sister's birthday, her long black hair tied back in a ponytail.

'This in the paper,' I said. 'They're suggesting that Herb was a criminal and probably deserved to be killed.'

'And was he?' Claudia asked, turning round.

'Of course not,' I said firmly.

'How do you know?' she asked, echoing the detective inspector.

'I just do,' I said. 'I worked at the next desk to him for the past five years. Don't you think I'd have noticed if he was a criminal?'

'Not necessarily,' Claudia said. 'Do you think those

who worked next to Bernie Madoff realized he was a crook? And how about that doctor, Harold Shipman? He murdered two hundred of his patients over more than twenty years before anyone suspected him.'

She was right. She usually was.

I had met Claudia during my second year at the LSE. We actually met on the London Underground, the Tube, an environment not usually renowned for introducing strangers. That particular evening, nearly six years ago, I had been going into college for an evening event and I was sitting next to Claudia when the train came to a halt in the tunnel. Twenty minutes later the driver came through the train explaining that there was a signal problem at Euston due to an electrical fire. Another twenty minutes after that we moved slowly forward to Kentish Town, where everybody was required to leave the train.

I never did get to the evening event at the LSE.

Claudia and I went to a pub for supper instead. But it was not a romantic liaison, it was strictly business. I was finding life as a student far more expensive than I had budgeted for, and Claudia was in need of digs close to the Byam Shaw School of Art where she was studying.

By the end of the evening we had a deal. She would move into the guest bedroom in my house as a lodger and pay a contribution towards the mortgage.

By the end of the same month she had moved out of the guest bed and into mine as full-time girlfriend, while she still went on renting the guest bedroom as her studio.

The arrangement still existed although, since our student days, the rent she paid had decreased steadily to nothing as my earnings had risen and hers had remained stubbornly static at zero.

'Making your mark as an artist is not about commercial sales,' she would wail whenever I teased her about it. 'It's all to do with creativity.'

And creative she was, there was no doubt about that. Sometimes I just wished that others would appreciate her creations enough to write out a cheque. As it was, the third bedroom of the house had so many finished canvases stacked against the walls there was no longer space for a bed.

'One day,' she would say, 'these will all sell for tens of thousands and I'll be rich.' But the main problem was that she didn't actually want to part with any of them so she didn't even try to sell them. It was as if she painted them solely for her own benefit. And they were definitely an acquired taste – one I would call dark and foreboding, full of surreal disturbing images of pain and distress.

With the exception of a small life study in pencil, drawn during her Byam Shaw days, none of her work was hung on our walls and that was because I found them impossible to live with.

And yet, surprisingly, I was able to live happily with the artist.

For a long while I had worried about her state of mind but it was as if Claudia placed all her dark thoughts into her paintings, and there they stayed, leaving her to exist outside her work in a world of brightness and colour.

She herself had no real explanation for why she painted as she did and denied that it was due to the sudden death of her parents when she'd been a child. She said it was just how things turned out when her brushes stroked the canvas.

I had often thought of taking a selection of her weirdest paintings to be seen by an analyst to see if there might be some sort of psychological disturbance present but I hadn't liked to do so without her consent and I'd been too apprehensive to ask, in case she had objected.

So I had done nothing. I had always tried to avoid personal confrontation, not least because I had grown up with it all around me from my parents, who had fought each other tooth and nail for more than thirty years until they had finally divorced in their late fifties.

'But it says here,' I said to Claudia, pointing at the newspaper, 'that the murder had all the characteristics of a gangland killing. Now surely I would have known if Herb had been involved in that sort of thing.'

'I bet my friends have all sorts of skeletons in their cupboards we'll never hear about.'

'You're such a cynic,' I said, but she did have some strange friends.

'A realist,' she replied. 'It saves being disappointed.'

'Disappointed?'

'Yes,' she said. 'If I believe the worst of people then I'm not disappointed when it turns out to be accurate.'

'And do you believe the worst of me?'

'Don't be silly,' she said, coming over and stroking my hair with flour-covered hands. 'I know the worst of you.'

'And are you disappointed?'

'Always!' She laughed.

But I began to wonder if it was true.

I arrived at the offices of Lyall & Black on the fourth floor of 64 Lombard Street at 8.15 a.m. on Monday morning to find the door blocked by a burly looking police constable in full uniform complete with anti-stab vest and helmet.

'Sorry, sir,' he said in an official tone as I tried to push past him, 'no one is allowed into these offices without permission from my superior officer.'

'But I work here,' I said.

'Your name, sir?' he asked.

'Nicholas Foxton.'

He consulted a list that he had removed from his trouser pocket.

'Mr N. Foxton,' he read. 'Very well, sir, you may go in.' He moved slightly to one side while I passed, but then he stepped quickly back into his former spot as if expecting to prevent a rush from those not on his list.

The offices of Lyall & Black had never seen such activity so early on a Monday morning.

Both the senior partners, Patrick Lyall and Gregory Black, were in the client waiting area leaning on the chest-high reception desk.

'Oh, hi Nicholas,' said Patrick as I entered. 'The police are here.'

'So I see,' I said. 'Is it to do with Herb?'

They nodded.

'We've both been here since seven,' Patrick said. 'But they won't let us along into our offices. We've been told not to go beyond here.'

'Have they said what are they looking for exactly?' I asked.

'No,' Gregory said, sharply and with irritation. 'I presume they are hoping to find some clue as to who killed him. But I'm not happy about it. There may be sensitive client material on his desk that I wouldn't want them to see. It's highly confidential.'

I thought it was unlikely that the police would accept that anything was in the least bit confidential if it could have a bearing on unmasking a murderer.

'When did you find out he was dead?' I asked them. I knew that Herb's name had finally been included in the late news on Sunday evening.

'Yesterday afternoon,' said Patrick. 'I received a call from the police asking us to meet them here this morning. How about you?'

'I did try and call you on Saturday but there was no reply,' I said. 'I was actually with Herb when he was shot.'

'My God,' said Patrick. 'That's right. You were going to the races together.'

'And I was standing right next to him when he was killed,' I said.

'How awful,' Patrick said. 'Did you see who killed him?'

'Well, sort of,' I said. 'But I was looking mostly at his gun.'

'I just don't understand it.' Patrick shook his head. 'Why would anyone want to kill Herb Kovak?'

'Dreadful business,' said Gregory, also shaking his head. 'Not good for the firm. Not good at all.'

It wasn't too hot for Herb either, I thought, but decided not to say so. Lyall & Black, although very small, had risen to be one of the significant players in the financial services industry solely due to the single-mindedness of both Patrick Lyall and Gregory Black. Where Lyall & Black led, others usually followed. They took an innovative approach to their clients' investments, often recommending opportunities that more traditional advisers might classify as too risky.

All independent financial advisers are required to determine and grade their clients' attitude to risk. Low-risk investments, such as fixed-interest bank accounts or triple-A-rated government bonds, tended to give only a small rate of return but the capital sum was safe. Medium-risk might include stocks in major companies or unit trusts and mutual funds, where the return should be greater but there was a chance of losing some of the capital due to a drop in the stock market price. High-risk investments, including venture capital trusts and foreign currency dealings, gave the opportunity to make big returns but could also result in large losses.

Lyall & Black, however, also advised on investments for which the risk level could only be described as extreme, such as the financing of films or plays, buying shares in wine funds, in foreign property portfolios or in works of art. Returns could be vast, but so were the chances of losing everything.

It was the attitude that had first attracted me to them.

Kicking a horse hard in the belly to ask it to lengthen its stride, to make it right for a jump, was also an extreme-risk strategy that could so easily result in a crashing fall. An alternative, safer approach might be to take a pull, to ask the animal to shorten and to put in an extra stride. It may have been safer, but it was slower, much slower. A great deal better in my mind to crash to the turf trying to win than to be satisfied with second place.

'How much longer are they going to keep us waiting here?' Gregory Black demanded. 'Don't they realize we have work to do?'

No one answered.

One by one, all the other staff had turned up and the client waiting area was now full to overflowing. For the most part, they had only heard of Herb's demise as they had arrived, and the last thing they wanted to do was to start work. The two ladies who doubled as receptionists and admin assistants were both in tears. Herb had been popular and much loved, and not least because he'd been a change from the usual rather straight-laced, pin-stripe-suited City financier.

Herb had loved being the American abroad, turning up on the 4th of July with gifts of candy sticks and apple pie, hosting an office Thanksgiving lunch of turkey and all the trimmings in November, and drawling 'yee-haw!' at the top of his voice like a cowboy when he'd managed to lasso a new client. Herb had been fun, and life in the office was going to be a lot less cheerful for his passing.

Finally, around nine thirty, a middle-aged man in an ill-fitting grey suit came into the reception and addressed the waiting faces.

'Ladies and gentlemen,' he began formally. 'I am Detective Chief Inspector Tomlinson of the Merseyside Police. Sorry for the inconvenience but, as you will be aware, my colleagues and I are investigating the murder of Herbert Kovak at Aintree Races on Saturday afternoon. I expect we will be here for some time and I ask for your patience. However, I must ask you to remain here as I will want to speak to each of you individually.'

Gregory Black didn't look pleased. 'Can't we work in our offices while we wait?'

'I'm afraid that won't be possible,' replied the policeman.

'And why not?' demanded Gregory.

'Because I do not want any of you,' he looked around the room, 'having any access to your computers.'

'But that's outrageous.' Gregory was building up a head of steam. 'Are you accusing one of us of having something to do with Mr Kovak's death?'

'I'm not accusing anyone,' Chief Inspector Tomlinson replied in a more conciliatory tone. 'I just need to cover every avenue. If evidence does exist on Mr Kovak's computer then I am sure you will all understand that it has to be free from any possible contamination due to any of you accessing the files through the company server.'

Gregory was hardly placated. 'But all our files are remotely saved and can be viewed directly as they were at any time. This is completely ridiculous.'

'Mr Black.' The policeman turned to face him directly. 'You are wasting my time and the sooner I get back to work, the sooner you will be able to get into your office.'

I looked at Gregory Black. I suspected that no one had spoken to him like that since he was at school, if then. There was absolute silence in the room as we all waited for the explosion, but it didn't come. He just muttered something under his breath and turned away.

But in one respect Gregory was absolutely right: the restriction on using our computers was ridiculous. Our system allowed for remote access so that certain members of the firm could access the company files from their laptops when away from the office. If any of us had wanted to 'contaminate' the files since Herb's death, we'd had most of the weekend to have done so.

'Can we go out for a coffee?' asked Jessica Winter, the firm's Compliance Officer. The photocopy room, which also doubled as the small kitchen where we made all our hot drinks, was beyond the offices and hence currently out of bounds.

'Yes,' said the chief inspector, 'but not all of you at once. I will be starting the interviews soon. And if you do go, please be back by ten o'clock.'

Jessica stood up quickly and made for the door. Half a dozen more made a move in the same direction, including me. Clearly none of us exactly relished the prospect of being confined in close proximity to Gregory Black for the next half hour.

I had to wait until after eleven before I was interviewed and, much to Gregory Black's annoyance, I was second on the policeman's list after Patrick Lyall.

I don't know whether the policeman did it on purpose to further antagonize Gregory, but the interviews were carried out in *his* office and across *his* desk, with Chief Inspector Tomlinson sitting in the high-backed leather executive chair in which Gregory usually rested his ample frame. That wouldn't go down well, I thought, especially during a certain Gregory Black's interview.

'Now then, Mr Foxton,' said the chief inspector while studying his papers, 'I understand you were at Aintree Races on Saturday afternoon and were interviewed there by one of my colleagues.'

'Yes,' I replied. 'By Detective Inspector Matthews.'

He nodded. 'Have you anything further you wish to add to what you said in that interview?'

'Yes, I have,' I said. 'I tried to call Inspector Matthews yesterday. In fact, I left a message for him to call me back, but he didn't. It was about this.'

I removed from my pocket the folded piece of paper I had found in Herb's coat and spread it out on the desk, rotating it so the chief inspector could read the words. I knew them now by heart: YOU SHOULD HAVE DONE WHAT YOU WERE TOLD. YOU MAY SAY YOU REGRET IT, BUT YOU WON'T BE REGRETTING IT FOR LONG.

After quite a few moments, he looked up at me. 'Where did you find this?'

'In Mr Kovak's coat pocket. He'd left his coat in my car when we arrived at the races. I found it only yesterday.'

The chief inspector studied the paper once more but without touching it.

'Do you recognize the handwriting?' he asked.

'No,' I replied. But I wouldn't, the note had been written carefully in capital letters, each one very precise and separate.

'And you have handled this paper?' I assumed it was a rhetorical question as he had clearly seen me remove the paper from my pocket and spread it out. I remained silent.

'Did you not think this might be evidence?' he asked. 'Handling it may jeopardize the chances of recovering any forensics.'

'It was screwed up in his coat pocket,' I said in my defence. 'I didn't know what it was until I'd opened it up and by then it was too late.'

He studied it once more.

'And what do you think it means?'

'I've no idea,' I said. 'But I think it might be a warning.'

'A warning? Why a warning?'

'I've spent much of the night thinking about it,' I said. 'It's clearly not a threat or it would say "Do as you are told or else" and not "You should have done what you were told".'

'OK,' the policeman said slowly, 'but that doesn't make it a warning.'

'I know,' I said. 'But think about it. If you wanted to kill someone you'd hardly ring them up and tell them, now would you? It would do nothing except put them on their guard and make it more difficult for you. They might even ask for police protection. There is absolutely nothing to be gained and everything to lose. Surely you would just do it, unannounced.'

'You really have thought about it,' he said.

'Yes,' I said, 'a lot. And I was there when Herb was killed. There was no "You should have done so and so" from the killer before he fired. Quite the reverse. He shot so quickly, and without preamble that I reckon Herb was dead before he even knew what was happening. And that is not in keeping with this note.' I paused. 'So I think this might have been a warning from someone else, not from the killer. In fact, I believe that it's almost more than a warning, it's an apology.'

The chief inspector looked up at me for a few seconds. 'Mr Foxton,' he said finally. 'This isn't a television drama, you know. In real life people don't apologize for murdering someone before the event.'

'So you're saying I'm wrong?'

35

'No,' he said slowly, 'I'm not saying that. But I'm not saying you're right either. I'll keep an open mind on the matter.'

It sounded to me very much like he thought I was wrong. He stood up and went to the door and presently another officer came in and removed the piece of paper, placing it carefully into a plastic bag with some tweezers.

'Now,' said the chief inspector as the door closed. 'Do you know of anything in Mr Kovak's work that might help me understand why he was killed?'

'Absolutely not,' I said.

'Mr Lyall told me that you and Mr Kovak worked closely together.' I nodded. 'So what did he do exactly?'

'The same as me,' I said. 'He worked mostly for Patrick Lyall as one of his assistants but he also had some clients of his own. He –'

'Sorry,' said the chief inspector, interrupting, 'I'm a little confused. Mr Lyall didn't mention that Mr Kovak was his personal assistant.'

'But he wasn't like a secretary or anything,' I said. 'He assisted in the monitoring of the investments of Mr Lyall's clients.'

'Hmm,' he said, pausing and not appearing to be any the wiser. 'Could you describe to me exactly what you do here, and also what this firm does?'

'OK,' I said. 'I'll try.'

I took a breath and thought about how best to explain it so that DCI Tomlinson would understand. 'Putting it simply, we manage people's money for them.

They are our clients. We advise them where and when they should invest their capital and then, if they agree, we invest their money for them and then we monitor the performance of the investments, switching them into something else if we believe there is a better return elsewhere.'

'I see,' he said, writing some notes. 'And how many clients does the firm have?'

'It's not quite that simple,' I said. 'Even though we are a firm, the advisers are all individuals and it's they who have the clients. There are six qualified and registered IFAs here, at least there were before Herb got killed. I suppose there are now five.'

'IFAs?'

'Independent Financial Advisers.'

He wrote it down.

'Are you one of those?' he asked.

'Yes.'

'And you have clients of your own?'

'Yes,' I said. 'I have about fifty clients but I spend about half my time looking after Patrick's clients.'

'And how many clients does Mr Lyall have?'

'About six hundred,' I said. 'Apart from Herb Kovak and myself there are two other assistants that help look after them.'

'Are they also IFAs?'

'One is,' I said, 'although she's just recently qualified and has no clients of her own yet. And the other isn't.' I gave him their names and he found them on the list of all the firm's staff.

'How can you be *independent* if you work for a firm?'

It was a good question and one that I was asked often.

'Independent in this case means we are independent of any investment providers and we are therefore free to advise our clients about all investment opportunities. If you go to see your bank about investing some money, an adviser there will only sell you something from that bank's investment portfolio even if there are better products elsewhere. They may be excellent financial advisers but they are not independent.'

'So how do you make your money?' he asked. 'I'm sure you don't do this for free.'

'No,' I agreed. 'We make our money in one of two ways, depending on the client. Most of them nowadays opt to pay us a fixed fee, which is a small percentage of the total we invest for them, and others choose that we collect the commissions from investment providers on the products we advise them to buy.'

'I see,' he said, but I wondered if he did. 'How much money do you look after in total?'

'Lots,' I said flippantly, but he didn't laugh. 'Some clients have just a few thousand to invest, others have millions. I suppose the firm as a whole looks after hundreds of millions. Most of our clients are high earners or they have considerable family wealth, or both.'

'And these clients trust you with large sums of their money?' He sounded surprised.

'Yes,' I said. 'And they trust us because we have masses of safeguards and checks to ensure that none of it goes missing.'

'And do these safeguards and checks work?'

'Absolutely,' I said, trying to sound affronted that he should even question it.

'Could Mr Kovak have been stealing from his clients?'

'Impossible,' I replied instantly, but I couldn't help thinking about what Claudia had said the previous afternoon about not knowing if someone was a crook. 'Everything we do is subject to spot-check inspections by the financial services regulatory authorities, and we have someone called a Compliance Officer in the firm whose job is to scrutinize the transactions to ensure they are done according to the rules. If Herb had been stealing from his clients the Compliance Officer would have seen it, not to mention the regulator.'

He looked down at the staff list. 'Which is the Compliance Officer?'

'Jessica Winter,' I said. He found her on the list. 'She was the woman who asked you earlier if we could go out for a coffee.'

He nodded. 'How well did Mr Kovak know Miss Winter?'

I laughed. 'If you're suggesting that Herb Kovak and Jessica Winter conspired together to steal from his clients, you can forget it. Herb thought that our dear Compliance Officer was an arrogant little prig, and she thought he was a bit of a maverick. Jessica was the only person in the firm who didn't like Herb.'

'Maybe that was just a front,' said the detective, writing a note.

'My, you do have a suspicious mind,' I said.

'Yes,' he said, looking up. 'And it's surprising how often I'm right.'

Could he really be right? Could Herb and Jessica have been fooling the rest of us all this time? And could anyone else at the firm also be involved? I told myself not to be so silly. At this rate I would soon be distrustful of my own mother.

'And do you also think Mr Kovak was a bit of a maverick?'

'No,' I said, 'not really. He was just a flamboyant American in a business where people have a bit of a reputation for being boring.'

'And are you boring?' he said, looking up at me.

'Probably,' I said. I was certainly more boring now than I had been as a jockey. But maybe it was better being boring and alive than flamboyant and dead.

I returned to the reception area after my interview to join the other fifteen members of the firm squashed into the client waiting area that had been designed for just a small coffee table and two armchairs.

'What did they ask you?' Jessica said.

'Not much,' I said, looking at her and trying not to let her see in my face the questions about her that the chief inspector had triggered in my mind. 'They just want to know what Herb did here and why I thought anyone would want to kill him.'

'Surely he wasn't killed because of his work.' Jessica looked shocked. 'I thought it must be to do with his private life.'

'I don't think they have the slightest idea why he was killed,' said Patrick Lyall. 'That's why they're asking about everything.'

There was a slight commotion outside in the lobby as someone not on the company staff list tried to gain access. He was being barred by our rather overbearing uniformed guard. I could see through the glass door that the would-be visitor was Andrew Mellor, the company solicitor. Lyall & Black was too small to have a full-time company lawyer of its own, so we used Andrew who worked in a legal practice round the corner in King William Street.

Patrick saw him as well and went over to the door.

'It's all right, officer, Mr Mellor is our lawyer.'

'But he's not on my list,' said the uniformed policeman adamantly.

'It was I who provided that list and I forgot to add Mr Mellor.'

Reluctantly the policeman stood aside and allowed the visitor to enter.

'Sorry, Andrew,' said Patrick. 'It's all a bit of a nightmare here at present.'

'Yes, so I can see.' Andrew Mellor looked around at the sea of faces. 'I'm so sorry to hear about Herb Kovak. Unbelievable business.'

'And bloody inconvenient too,' interjected Gregory,

who had been mostly quiet since his altercation with the chief inspector earlier. 'But I'm glad you're here.' I wondered if Gregory had asked Andrew to come round to be present during his interview. 'We'll have to talk outside.' Gregory began to ease himself up from one of the armchairs.

'Actually, Gregory,' said the lawyer, putting up a hand to stop him, 'it's not you I have come to see. I need to talk to Nicholas.' Fifteen pairs of eyes swivelled round in my direction. 'Do you mind?' he said to me, holding out his arm towards the door.

I could almost feel the stares on my back as I went outside into the lobby with Andrew. We went past the lifts and round a corner so that the prying eyes in Lyall & Black could no longer see us through the glass door, and the policeman on guard couldn't hear our conversation.

'Sorry about this,' he said, 'but I have something to give you.'

He pulled a white envelope out of his jacket inside pocket and held it out to me. I took it.

'What is it?' I asked.

'Herb Kovak's Last Will and Testament.'

I looked up from the envelope to Andrew's face.

'But why are you giving it to me?' I asked.

'Because Herb named you in it as his executor.'

'Me?' I said, somewhat taken aback.

'Yes,' Andrew said. 'And you are also the sole beneficiary of his estate.'

I was astonished. 'Has he no family?'

'Obviously none that he wanted to leave anything to.'

'But why would he leave it to me?' I asked.

'I've no idea,' Andrew said. 'Perhaps he liked you.'

Little did I realize at the time how Herb Kovak's legacy would turn out to be a poisoned chalice.

3

On Tuesday I went to the races – Cheltenham Races, to
be precise. But this was no pleasure outing, it was work.

Racing can be a funny business, especially amongst
the jockeys.

Competition is intense. It always has been. Before
the advent in 1960 of the racing patrol films to aid the
stewards in catching the wrongdoers, stories abounded
of jockeys who would cut off a rival, giving them no
room and literally putting a horse and rider through
the wings of a fence in order to help their own chances
of winning. And riding whips have not always been
employed solely to strike the horse but have left their
mark on jockeys too. On one famous occasion at
Deauville in France, Lester Piggott, having dropped
his own whip, pinched one from another jockey actually during the race, to help him ride a tight finish.

But once the race is run, whatever the result, there
exists a camaraderie between these men and women
who risk their lives five or six times an afternoon for the
entertainment of others. And they look after their own.

Such it was with me.

My erstwhile opponents who, during my riding
days, would have happily seen me dumped onto the
turf if it meant that they could win a race, were the

first to express their concern and support when I'd been injured.

When I had been forced to retire at the ripe old age of twenty-one it had been a handful of my fellow jocks who had arranged a testimonial day for me at Sandown Park to raise the funds needed to pay my university tuition fees. And it had been the same individuals who had clamoured to become my first clients when I'd qualified as an IFA.

Since then I had acquired a bit of a reputation as horseracing's very own financial adviser. Nearly all my clients had some connection with racing and I had a near monopoly within the jockeys' changing room that I believed had much to do with a shared view of risk and reward.

So I now regularly spent a couple of days a week at one racecourse or another, all with Patrick and Gregory's blessing, making appointments to see my clients before or after, and occasionally during, the racing.

Cheltenham in April has a touch of 'after the Lord Mayor's Show' about it – rather an anticlimax after the heady excitement of the four-day Steeplechase Festival in March. Gone were the temporary grandstands and the acres of tented hospitality village. Gone, too, was the nervous energy and high anticipation of seventy thousand expectant spectators waiting to cheer home their new heroes.

This April meeting may have been a more sedate affair in the enclosures but it was no less competitive on the course, with two of the top jockeys still vying to be crowned as the Champion for the current season that concluded at the end of the month. Both were my clients and I had arranged to meet one of them, Billy Searle, after racing.

Part of the government's anti-money-laundering requirements was that financial advisers had to 'know their clients', and Lyall & Black, as a firm, reckoned that a face-to-face meeting with every client should occur at least annually, in addition to our regular three-monthly written communications and twice-yearly valuations of their investments.

I had long ago decided that expecting racing folk to come to a meeting in the London offices was a complete waste of time. If I wanted them as clients – and I did – then I would have to come to see them, not vice versa. And I had found that seeing them at their place of work, the racecourses, was easier than chasing after them at home.

I had also discovered that being regularly seen at the races was the best way to recruit new clients, which was why I was currently standing on the terrace in front of the Weighing Room warming myself in the midday April sunshine more than ninety minutes before the first race.

'Hi, Foxy. Penny for your thoughts? What a lovely day, eh? Did you see the National yesterday?' Martin Gifford was a large, jovial, middle-ranking racehorse trainer who always joked that he had never made it as a jockey due to his large feet. The fact that he stood more than six feet tall and had a waist measurement that a sumo wrestler would have been proud of seemed to have escaped him.

'No,' I said. 'I missed it. I was stuck in the office all day. I just saw the short report on the television news. But I'd been at Aintree on Saturday.'

'Bloody rum business, that was,' Martin said. 'Fancy postponing the Grand National just because some bastard got themselves killed.'

He had obviously been reading the papers.

'How do you know he was a bastard?' I asked.

Martin looked at me strangely. 'Because it said so in the paper.'

'I thought you knew better than to believe what you read in the papers.' I paused, deciding whether to go on. 'The person murdered was a friend of mine. I was standing right next to him when he was shot.'

'Bloody hell!' shouted Martin. 'God, I'm sorry. Trust me to jump in with both feet.'

Trust him, indeed. 'It's OK,' I said. 'Forget it.'

I was suddenly cross with myself for even mentioning it to him. Why hadn't I just kept quiet? Everyone in racing knew that Martin Gifford was a five-star gossip. In an industry where there were many who believed that there was no such thing as a private conversation or a secret, Martin was the past master. He seemed to have a talent for knowing other people's private business and passing it on to anyone who would listen. Telling Martin that the murder victim had been a friend of mine was akin to placing a full-page spread in the *Racing Post* to advertise the fact, except quicker. Everyone at Cheltenham would probably know by the end of the afternoon, and I was already regretting my indiscretion.

'So was the National a good race?' I asked, trying to change the subject.

'I suppose so,' he said. 'Diplomatic Leak won easily in the end but he made a right hash of the Canal Turn first time round. Nearly ended up in the canal.'

'Were there many people there?' I asked.

'Looked pretty full to me,' he said. 'But I watched it on television.'

'No runners?' I asked, but I knew he hadn't any.

'I haven't had a National horse for years,' he said. 'Not since Frosty Branch in the nineties and it was the death of him, poor fellow.'

'Any runners today?' I asked.

'Fallen Leaf in the first and Yellow Digger in the three-mile chase.'

'Good luck,' I said.

'Yeah. We'll need it,' he said. 'Fallen Leaf probably wouldn't win if he started now, and I don't rate Yellow Digger very highly at all. He has no chance.' He paused. 'So who was this friend of yours who got killed?'

Dammit, I thought. I'd hoped he would leave it, but I should have known better. Martin Gifford hadn't earned his reputation for nothing.

'He was just a work colleague, really,' I said, trying to sound indifferent.

'What was his name?'

I wondered if I should I tell him. But why not? It had been in all of yesterday's papers.

'Herbert Kovak.'

'And why was he killed?' Martin demanded.

'I've no idea,' I said. 'As I told you, he was only a work colleague.'

'Come on, Foxy,' Martin said in an inviting tone. 'You must have some inkling.'

'No. None. Nothing.'

He looked disappointed, like a child told he can't have any sweets.

'Go on,' he implored once more. 'I know you're holding something back. You can tell me.'

And half the world, I thought.

'Honestly, Martin,' I said. 'I have absolutely no idea why he was killed or who did it. And if I did, I'd be telling the police, not you.'

Martin shrugged his shoulders as if to imply he didn't fully believe me. Too bad, I thought. It was true.

I was saved from further inquisition by another trainer, Jan Setter, who was everything that Martin Gifford wasn't – short, slim, attractive and fun. She grabbed my arm and turned me round, away from Martin.

'Hello lover-boy,' she whispered in my ear while giving me a kiss on the cheek. 'Fancy a dirty weekend away?'

'I'm ready when you are,' I whispered back. 'Just name your hotel.'

She pulled back and laughed.

'Oh, you're such a tease,' she said, looking up at me beguilingly from beneath her heavily mascaraed eyelids.

But it was she who was the tease, and she'd been doing it since we had first met more than ten years ago. Back then I had been an impressionable eighteen-year-old, just starting out, and she was an established trainer for whom I was riding. I hadn't really known how to react, whether to be flattered or frightened. Apart from anything else, at the time she'd been a married woman.

Nowadays she was a mid- to late-forties divorcée who seemed intent on enjoying life. Not that she didn't work hard. Her stables in Lambourn were full with about seventy horses in training and, as I knew from experience, she ran the place with great efficiency and determination.

Jan had been one of my clients now for three years, ever since she had acquired a substantial sum from her ex during a very public High Court divorce case.

I adored her, and not just for her patronage. Perhaps I should accept her invitation to a dirty weekend away, but that would then have changed everything.

'How's my money?' she asked.

'Alive and kicking,' I replied.

'And growing, I hope.' She laughed.

So did I. 'How was the preview?'

'Fabulous,' she said. 'I took my daughter, Maria, and a friend of hers. We had a really wonderful time. The show was terrific.'

At my suggestion, Jan had invested a considerable sum in a new West End musical based on the life of Florence Nightingale set during the Crimean War. The true opening night was a week or so away but the previews had just started, and I'd read some of the newspaper reports and pre-reviews. They had been somewhat mixed but that didn't always mean the show wouldn't be a success. The *Wizard of Oz* spin-off musical, *Wicked*, had been panned by the *New York Times* after its opening night on Broadway, but it was still running there more than seven years and three thousand performances later, and it was breaking box-office records all round the world.

'Some of the pre-reviews are not great,' I said.

'I can't think why,' Jan replied with surprise. 'That girl that plays Florence is gorgeous, and what a voice! I think she'll make me a fortune. I am sure the proper reviews after the first night will be fabulous.' She laughed. 'But I'll blame my financial adviser if they aren't and I lose it all.'

'I hear he has broad shoulders,' I said, laughing back.

But it wasn't necessarily a laughing matter. Investing in the theatre had always been a high-risk strategy and fortunes had been lost far more often than they'd been won. Not that investing in anything was certain. It was always a gamble. I had known some seemingly cast-iron and gold-plated investments go belly-up almost without warning. Shares in big established companies were usually safe, with expected steady growth, but even that was not always the case. Enron shares had fallen from a healthy ninety dollars each to just a few cents within ten weeks, while Health South Inc., once one of America's largest health care providers, had lost ninety-eight per cent of its value on the New York Stock Exchange in a single day. Both those collapses had been due to fraud or dodgy accounting practices inflating their revenues and profits, but business catastrophes can have the same effect. BP shares fell in value by more than fifty per cent in a month when an oil platform exploded in the Gulf of Mexico, even though the costs associated with the explosion, and the subsequent oil clear-up, represented far less than half the company's assets.

Could such a calamitous loss have resulted in Herb's murder?

I couldn't believe it was possible.

Patrick Lyall held regular meetings, usually on a Monday, when investment plans for our clients were discussed. All his assistants were present and that had included Herb and myself. We were expected to research the markets and put forward investment suggestions – for example the new musical that I had recommended to Jan Setter – but the firm's rule was clear and simple: none of our clients' money could be invested in any product without the prior approval of either Patrick or Gregory.

Our exposure to BP losses had been mostly through personal pension schemes and, bad as it was, the risks had been well spread with no individuals actually losing their shirts, or even as much as a tie. Certainly not enough, I thought, to murder their adviser.

'You should come and ride out for me,' said Jan, bringing my daydreaming back to the present. 'First lot goes out at seven thirty on Saturdays. Come down on a Friday and stay the night. You'd enjoy it.'

Now, was that an invitation to a dirty weekend, or not?

And yes, I would enjoy it. The riding, that is. At least I think I would have, but I hadn't sat on a horse in eight years.

I could remember so clearly the devastation I had felt when told I couldn't be a jockey any more. I had been sitting at an oak table in the offices of the Jockey Club in High Holborn, London. Opposite me were the three members of the medical board.

I could recall almost word for word the brief announcement made by the board chairman. 'Sorry, Foxton,' he had said almost before we were all comfortable in our chairs, 'we have concluded that you are, and will permanently remain, unfit to ride in any form of racing. Consequently, your jockey's licence has been withdrawn indefinitely.' He had then started to rise, to leave the room.

I had sat there completely stunned. My skin had gone suddenly cold and the walls had seemed to press inwards towards me. I had expected the meeting with the Board to be a formality, just another necessary inconvenience on the long road to recovery.

'Hold on a minute,' I'd said, turning in my chair towards the departing chairman. 'I was told to come here to answer some questions. What questions?'

The chairman had stopped in the doorway. 'We don't need to ask you any questions. Your scan results have given us all the answers we need.'

'Well, *I* have some questions to ask *you*, so please sit down.'

I could recall the look of surprise on his face that a jockey, or an ex-jockey, would talk to him in such a manner. But he did come back and sit down again opposite me. I asked my questions and I argued myself hoarse, but to no avail. 'Our decision is final.'

But, of course, I hadn't been prepared to leave it at that.

I'd arranged to have a second opinion from a top specialist in neck and spinal injuries to help me win my case. But he only served to confirm the medical board's findings, as well as frightening me half to death.

'The problem,' he told me, 'is that the impact of your fall occurred with such force that your atlas vertebra was effectively crushed into the axis beneath. You are very lucky to be alive. Extraordinarily lucky, in fact. Quite apart from the main fracture right through the axis, many of the interlocking bone protrusions that helped hold the two vertebrae together have been broken away. Put in simple terms, your head is balanced precariously on your neck and the slightest trauma might be enough to cause it to topple. With that neck, I wouldn't ride a bike, let alone a horse.'

It hadn't exactly been encouraging.

'Is there nothing that can be done?' I'd asked him. 'An operation or something? How about a metal plate? I still have one in my ankle from a previous break.'

'This part of the neck is a difficult area,' he'd said. 'Far more complicated than even an ankle. There are so many planes and degrees of movement involved. Then there is the attachment of the skull, not to mention the inconvenience of having the nerves for the rest of your body passing right through the middle of it all, indeed the brain stem itself stretches down to the axis vertebra. I don't think a metal plate would help and it would certainly be another problem you could do without. In normal life, your muscles will hold everything together and your neck should be fine – just try not to have a car crash.' He'd smiled at me. 'And, whatever you do, don't get into a fight.'

For weeks afterwards I had hardly turned my head at all and, for a while, I'd gone back to wearing a neck brace to sleep in. I remember being absolutely terrified to sneeze in case my head fell off, and I hadn't even been near a horse, let alone on one's back. So much for being a carefree risk taker. The Health and Safety Executive had nothing on me when it came to my neck.

'I'd love to come and watch your horses work,' I said to Jan, returning once again to the present. 'But I'm afraid I can't ride one.'

She looked disappointed. 'I thought you'd love it.'

'I would have,' I said. 'But it's too much of a risk with my neck.'

'What a bloody shame,' she said.

Bloody shame was right. I longed to ride again. Coming racing every week was a pleasant change from spending all my time in a London office but, in some ways, it was a torment. Each day I chatted amicably to my clients as they wore their racing silks and I positively ached to be one of them again. Even after all this time, I would sometimes sit in my car at the end of a day and weep for what I had lost. Why? Why? Why had this happened to me?

I shook my head, albeit only slightly, and told myself to put such thoughts of self-pity out of my mind. I had much to be thankful for and I should be happy to be twenty-nine years old, alive, employed and financially secure.

But, oh, how I wanted still to be a jockey.

I watched the first race from a vantage point on the grandstand, the vivid harlequin-coloured jackets of the jockeys appearing bright in the sunshine as they cantered down to the two-mile hurdle start.

As always, the undiminished longing to be out there with them weighed heavy in the pit of my stomach. I wondered if it would it ever go away. Even though Cheltenham had been the scene of my last, ill-fated ride, I held no grudge towards the place. It hadn't been the racecourse's fault that I had been so badly injured. In fact, it was only due to their paramedics' great care after the fall that I wasn't paralysed, or dead.

Cheltenham had been the first racecourse I had ever known and I still loved the place. I had grown up in Prestbury village, right alongside the course, and I'd ridden my bicycle past it every morning on my way to school. Each March, as the Steeplechase Festival approached, the excitement surrounding not only the racecourse but the whole town had been the inspiration for me: first to ride a horse, then to pester a local trainer for holiday jobs, and finally to give up a planned future of anodyne academia for the perilous existence of a professional jockey.

Cheltenham was the home of jump racing. Whereas the Grand National was the most famous steeplechase in the world, every racehorse owner would rather win the Cheltenham Gold Cup.

The Grand National was a handicap so the better horses carried the greater weight. The Handicapper's dream was that all the horses would cross the finish line in a huge dead-heat. But it was a bit like making Usain Bolt run the Olympic 100 metres in wellington boots to even up the chances of the others. However, in the Cheltenham Gold Cup, other than a slight reduction for female horses, all the participants carried the same weight, and the winner was the true champion.

I had only ridden in it once, on a rank outsider that'd had no chance, but I could still recall the tension that had existed in the jockeys' changing room beforehand. The Gold Cup was not just another race, it was history in the making and one's performance mattered even if, as in my case, I had pulled up my horse long before the finish.

Away to my left, at the far end of the straight, the fifteen horses for the first race were called into line by the starter. 'They're off,' sounded the public address, and they were running.

Two miles of fast-paced hurdle racing with the clatter-clatter from hooves striking the wooden obstacles clearly audible to those of us in the grandstands. The horses first swept up the straight towards us, then turned left-handed to start another complete circuit of the course, ever increasing in speed. Three horses jumped the final hurdle side by side and a flurry of jockeys' legs, arms and whips encouraged their mounts up the hill to the finish.

'First, number three, Fallen Leaf,' sounded the public address system.

Mark Vickers, the other jockey in the race to be the Champion, had just extended his lead over Billy Searle from one to two.

And Martin Gifford, the gossip, had trained the winner in spite of his expressed lack of faith in its ability. I wondered if he had simply been trying to keep his horse's starting price high by recommending that other people should not bet on it. I looked down at my race-card and decided to invest a small sum on Yellow Digger in the third race: the other runner Martin had told me would have no chance.

I turned to go back to the Weighing Room, looking down at my feet to negotiate the grandstand steps.

'Hello, Nicholas.'

I looked up. 'Hello, Mr Roberts,' I said in surprise. 'I didn't realize you were a racing man.'

'Oh, yes,' he said. 'Always have been. In fact, my brother and I have horses in training. And I often used to watch you ride. You were a good jockey. You could have been one of the greats.' He pursed his lips and shook his head.

'Thank you,' I said.

Mr Roberts – or, to use his full title, Colonel The Honourable Jolyon Westrop Roberts MC OBE, younger son of the Earl of Balscott – was a client. To be precise, he was a client of Gregory Black, but I had met him fairly frequently in the offices at Lombard Street. Whereas many clients are happy to leave us to get on with looking after their money, Jolyon Roberts was one of those known to have a 'hands-on' approach to his investments.

'Are you on your day off?' he asked.

'No,' I replied with a laugh, 'I'm seeing one of my clients after racing, you know, the jockey Billy Searle.'

He nodded, then paused. 'I don't suppose . . .' He paused again. 'No, it doesn't matter.'

'Can I help you in some way?' I asked.

'No, it's all right,' he said. 'I'll leave it.'

'Leave what?' I asked.

'Oh, nothing,' he said. 'Nothing for you to worry about. It's fine. I'm sure it's fine.'

'What is fine?' I asked with persistence. 'Is it something to do with the firm?'

'No, it's nothing,' he said. 'Forget I even mentioned it.'

'But you didn't mention anything.'

'Oh, right,' he said with a laugh. 'So I didn't.'

'Are you sure there is nothing I can help you with?' I asked again.

'Yes, I'm sure,' he said. 'Thank you.'

I stood there on the grandstand steps for a few seconds looking at him but he made no further obscure reference to whatever was clearly troubling him.

'Right then,' I said. 'No doubt I'll see you sometime in the office. Bye now.'

'Yes,' he replied. 'Right. Goodbye.'

I walked away leaving him there, standing ramrod straight and looking out across the course as if in deep thought.

I wondered what that had all been about.

Mark Vickers won twice more during the afternoon, including the big race on Yellow Digger at the relatively long odds of eight to one, giving Mark a four-winner lead over Billy Searle in the championship race, and me a tidy payout from the Tote.

Billy Searle was not in the least bit happy when he emerged from the Weighing Room after the last race for our meeting.

'Bloody Vickers,' he said to me. 'Did you see the way he won the first? Beat the poor animal half to death with his whip. Stewards should have banned him for excessive use.'

I decided not to say that I actually thought that Mark Vickers had been rather gentle with his use of the whip in the first race, and had in fact ridden a text-book finish with his hands and heels to win by a head. Perhaps, in the circumstances it wouldn't have been very diplomatic. I also chose not to mention to Billy that Mark was a client of mine as well.

'But there's still plenty of time left for you to catch him,' I said, though I knew there wasn't, and Mark Vickers was bang in form while Billy was not.

'It's my bloody turn,' he said vehemently. 'I've been waiting all these years to get my chance and now, with Frank injured, I'm going to bloody lose out to some young upstart.'

Life could be hard. Billy Searle was four years older than me and he'd been runner-up in the championship for each of the past eight years. Every time he'd been beaten by the same man, the jump-jockey recognized by all as the best in the business, Frank Miller. But Frank had broken his leg badly in a fall the previous December and had been out of action now for four months. This year, for the first time in a decade, it would be someone else's turn to be Champion Jockey, but, after today's triple for Mark Vickers, it seemed likely that it wouldn't be Billy. And time was no longer on Billy's side. Thirty-three is getting on for a jump jockey and the new crop of youngsters were good, very good, and they were also hungry for success.

It was obvious to me that Billy was in no real mood to discuss his finances even though it had been he, not me, who had called the previous afternoon asking for this urgent meeting at Cheltenham. But I'd come all the way from London to talk to him, and I didn't want it to be a wasted journey.

'What was it that you wished to discuss?' I asked him.

'I want all my money back,' he said suddenly.

'What do you mean, back?' I asked.

'I want all my money back from Lyall and Black.'

'But your money is not with Lyall and Black,' I said. 'It's in the investments that we bought for you. You still own them.'

'Well, I want it back anyway,' he said.

'Why?' I asked.

'I just do,' he said crossly. 'And I don't need to tell you why. It's my money and I want it back.' He was building himself into a full-blown fury. 'Surely I can do what I like with my own money?'

'OK. OK, Billy,' I said, trying to calm him down. 'Of course you can have the money back, but it's not that simple. I will need to sell the shares and bonds you have. I can do that tomorrow.'

'Fine,' he said.

'But Billy,' I said, 'some of your investments were bought with long-term growth in mind. Just last week I acquired some thirty-year government bonds for you. If I have to sell them tomorrow, you are likely to sustain a loss.'

'I don't care,' he said. 'I need the money now.'

'All right,' I said. 'But, as your financial adviser, I have to ask you again why you need your money so quickly. If I had more time to sell you might get a better return.'

'I haven't got more time,' he said.

'Why not?'

'I can't tell you.'

'Billy,' I said seriously, 'are you in some sort of trouble?'

'No, of course not,' he said, but his body language gave another answer.

I could remember most of the details of the investment portfolios of most of my clients, and Billy Searle was no exception. His was rather smaller than one might imagine after so many years at the top of his profession, but Billy had always been a spender rather than a saver, driving expensive cars and staying in lavish hotels. However, as far as I could recall, he had a nest egg of around a hundred and fifty thousand growing nicely for his retirement, certainly more than he would prudently need just for a new car or a foreign holiday.

'OK, Billy,' I said. 'I'll get on with liquidating everything tomorrow. But it'll take a few days for you to get the cash.'

'Can't I have it tomorrow?' He looked desperate. 'I need it tomorrow.'

'Billy, that simply isn't possible. I need to sell the shares and bonds, have the funds transferred into the company's client account, and then transfer it to your own. Banks always say to allow three days for each transfer so overall it might take a week, but it will probably be a little quicker than that. Today's Tuesday. You might have it by Friday if you're lucky, but more likely it will be Monday.'

Billy went pale.

'Billy,' I said, 'are you sure you're not in any trouble?'

'I owe a guy some money, that's all,' he said. 'He says I have to pay him by tomorrow.'

'You will just have to tell him that's impossible,' I said. 'Explain to him the reasons. I'm sure he'll understand.'

Billy gave me a look that said everything. Clearly the guy in question wouldn't take excuses.

'I'm sorry,' I said. 'But I can't do it any quicker.'

'Can't your firm lend me the money until everything's sold?' he asked.

'Billy,' I said, 'it's a hundred and fifty thousand pounds. We don't have that sort of cash lying around.'

'I only need a hundred,' he said.

'No,' I said firmly. 'Not even a hundred.'

'You don't understand,' he said in desperation. 'I need that money by tomorrow night.' He was almost crying.

'Why?' I asked him. 'Why do you owe so much?'

'I can't tell you.' He almost screamed the words at me and the heads of a few other late-leaving racegoers turned our way. 'But I need it tomorrow.'

I looked at him. 'And I cannot help you,' I said quietly. 'I think I'd better go now. Do you still want me to sell your portfolio and liquidate the money?'

'Yes,' he said in a resigned tone.

'Right,' I said. 'I'll get the office to send you a written authority. Just sign it and send it straight back. I'll try and get the cash into your account by Friday.'

He was almost in a trance. 'I hope I'm still alive by Friday.'

4

I sat in my car in the members' car park and thought through my recent conversation with Billy Searle. I wondered what I should do about it, if anything.

As he had said, it was his money and he could do what he liked with it. Except that he clearly didn't like what he was doing with it.

He'd also told me that he owed some guy about a hundred thousand, and had implied that his life would be in danger if he didn't repay it by the following evening. I would have usually dismissed such a threat as melodramatic nonsense but now, after the events at Aintree the previous Saturday, I wasn't so sure.

Should I tell someone about our conversation? But, who? The police would probably want some evidence, and I had none. I also didn't want to get Billy into trouble. Jockeys who owe money would always be suspected of involvement with bookmakers. Perhaps Billy's need for urgent cash was completely legitimate. Maybe he was buying a house. I knew that estate agents could be pretty determined in their selling methods, but surely they didn't threaten murder to close a deal.

I decided to do nothing until I'd had a chance to discuss it with Patrick. Besides, I would need to inform him before I could start the process of liquidating Billy's assets.

I looked at my watch. It was already past six o'clock and the office would be closed. I'd have to speak to Patrick about it in the morning. Nothing could be done now anyway, the markets in London were also long closed for the day.

Instead, I went to stay with my mother.

'Hello, darling,' she said, opening her front door. 'You're far too thin.'

It was her usual greeting and one that was due to her long-standing pathological fear that I was anorexic. It had all started when I'd been a skinny fifteen-year-old who had been desperate to be a jockey. I'd never been very short so I had begun starving myself to keep my weight down. But it hadn't been due to anorexia, just willpower. I had always loved my food but it seemed that my body, and my mind, had now finally trained themselves to stay thin.

As a rule, I never really thought about food and, if left to my own devices, there was little doubt that I would have become undernourished through neglect. But my mother saw to it that I didn't. She would send food parcels to Claudia with strict instructions to feed me more protein, or more carbohydrate, or just more.

'Hello, Mum,' I said, ignoring her comment and giving her a kiss. 'How are things?'

'So so,' she replied, as always.

She still lived near Cheltenham but not in the big house in which I had grown up. Sadly, that had had to be sold during my parents' acrimonious divorce proceedings in order to divide the capital between them. My mother's current home was a modest whitewashed cottage, hidden down a rutted lane on the edge of a small village just north of the racecourse with two double bedrooms and a bathroom upstairs, and a single open-plan kitchen/diner/lounge downstairs, the levels connected by a narrow, twisting, boxed-in staircase in the corner, with a lever-latched door at the bottom.

The cottage was an ideal size for her enforced solitary lifestyle but I knew she longed still to be the charming hostess in the grand house, a role in which she had excelled throughout my childhood.

'How's your father?' she asked.

Her enquiry was a social nicety rather than a true request for information. She probably thought that I'd appreciate her asking.

'He's fine,' I replied, completing the duty. At least, I assumed he was fine. I hadn't spoken to him for more than a fortnight. We really didn't have much to say to each other.

'Good,' she said, but I doubt that she really meant it. I thought she would almost certainly have also replied 'good' if I'd told her he was on his death bed. But at least she had asked, which was more than he ever did about her.

'I've bought you some fillet steak for dinner,' she

said, turning the conversation back to my feeding habits. 'And I've made some profiteroles for pudding.'

'Lovely,' I said. And I meant it. As usual, when coming to stay with my mother, I hadn't eaten anything all day in preparation for a high-calorie encounter with her cooking and, by now, I was really hungry.

I went up to the guest bedroom and changed out of my suit and into jeans and a sweatshirt. I tossed my mobile onto the bed. As always, the closeness to Cleeve Hill, and the phone-signal shadow it produced, rendered the thing useless. But at least I'd have a rest from its constant ringing.

When I came down, my mother was standing by the stove with saucepans already steaming on the hob.

'Help yourself to a glass of wine,' she said over her shoulder. 'I've already got one.'

I went over to the antique sideboard that had once sat in the dining room of the big house and helped myself to a glass of Merlot from the open bottle.

'How is Claudia?' my mother asked.

'Fine, thank you,' I said. 'She sends her love.'

'She should have come with you.'

Yes, I thought, she should have. There had been a time when we couldn't bear to be apart even for a single night, but now that longing had seemingly evaporated. Perhaps that is what happens after six years.

'High time you made an honest woman out of her,' my mother said. 'Time you were married and raising children.'

Was it?

In spite of what had happened to my parents, I'd always believed that someday I would marry and have a family. A few years ago, I'd even discussed the prospect with Claudia but she had dismissed the notion, saying that marriage was for boring people, and that children were troublesome and not for artists like her who were busy pushing the boundaries of existence and imagination. I wondered if she still felt the same way. There had certainly been no recent hints about rings on the finger, or brooding over other people's babies but, if there were, would I still have welcomed them?

'But you and Dad are hardly a great advertisement for marriage,' I said, possibly unwisely.

'Nonsense,' she said, turning round to face me. 'We were married for thirty years and brought you into the world. I would call that a success.'

'But you got divorced,' I said in disbelief. 'And you fought all the time.'

'Well, maybe we did,' she said, turning back to the pans. 'But it was still a success. And I don't regret it.' I was amazed. She must be getting soft in her old age. 'No,' she went on, 'I don't regret it for a second because otherwise you wouldn't exist.'

What could I say? Nothing. So I didn't.

She turned back to face me once more. 'And now I want some grandchildren.'

Ah, I thought. There had to be a reason somewhere. And I was an only child.

'You should have had more children yourself, then,'

I said with a laugh. 'Not good to put all your eggs in one basket.'

She stood very still and I thought she was going to cry.

I placed my glass down on the kitchen table, stepped forward, and put my arm around her shoulder.

'I'm sorry,' I said. 'I shouldn't have said that.'

'It's all right,' she said, reaching for a tissue and dabbing her eyes. 'You never knew.'

'Knew what?' I asked.

'Nothing. Forget it.'

It clearly wasn't nothing if it reduced her to tears all these years later.

'Come on, Mum,' I said. 'Something's obviously troubling you. Tell me.'

She sighed. 'We wanted more children. We wanted lots. You were the first, although you were quite a long time coming as we'd been married for nearly eight years by then. I was so happy you were a boy.' She smiled at me and stroked my cheek. 'But something had gone wrong with my insides and we couldn't have any more.'

It was I who was almost crying now. I had always so wanted brothers and sisters.

'We tried, of course,' she said. 'And once I did become pregnant but the baby miscarried at three months. It nearly killed me.'

Again, I didn't know what to say, so, once more, I said nothing. I just hugged her instead.

'It was the real reason behind so much unhappiness in our marriage,' she said. 'Your father gradually became so bitter that I couldn't have any more babies, stupid man. I suppose it was my body's fault, but I couldn't do anything about it, could I? I tried so hard to make up for it, but . . .' She tailed off.

'Oh, Mum,' I said, hugging her tight again. 'How awful.'

'It's all right,' she said, pulling away from me and turning back towards the stove. 'It's a long time ago, and I'll overcook these potatoes if I don't get to them now.'

We sat at the kitchen table for dinner and I ate myself to a complete standstill.

I felt bloated and still my mother was trying to force me to eat more.

'Another profiterole?' she asked, dangling a heaped spoonful over my plate.

'Mum,' I said, 'I'm stuffed. I couldn't eat another thing.'

She looked disappointed but, in fact, I had eaten far more than I would have normally, even in this house. I had tried to please her, but enough was enough. Another mouthful and my stomach might have burst. She, meanwhile, had eaten almost nothing.

Whereas I had ploughed my way through half a cow, along with a mountain of potatoes and vegetables, my mother had picked like a bird at a small circle of steak, much of which she had fed to an overweight grey cat that purred against her leg for most of the meal.

'I didn't know you'd acquired a cat,' I said.

'I didn't,' she said. 'It acquired me. One day it just arrived and he has hardly left since.'

I wasn't surprised if she regularly fed it fillet steak.

'He sometimes goes off for a few days, even a week, but he usually comes back eventually.'

'What's his name?' I asked.

'I've no idea,' she said. 'He isn't wearing a collar. He's a visitor, not a resident.'

Like me, I thought. Just here for a good meal.

'Are you going to the races tomorrow?' she asked.

The April meeting at Cheltenham ran for two days.

'Yes, I'll go for the first few,' I said. 'But I have some work to do here in the morning. I have my computer with me. Can I use your phone and your broadband connection?'

'Of course you can,' she said. 'But what time do you plan to leave? I don't want to rush you away but I have the village historical society outing tomorrow afternoon.'

'The first race is at two o'clock,' I said. 'I'll be off around twelve.'

'Then I'll get you some lunch before you go.'

The thought of yet more food was almost unbearable. And I knew she would have bought the makings of a full English breakfast as well.

'No thanks, Mum,' I said. 'I'm meeting a client there for lunch.'

She looked sideways at me as if to say she knew I'd just lied to her.

She was right.

*

'I don't like it, but we have to do as he asks,' said Patrick when I called him at eight in the morning using my mother's phone in the kitchen. 'I'll get Diana on it right away.' Diana was another of his assistants, the one who had just qualified as an IFA. 'Are you at Cheltenham again today?'

'Yes,' I said. 'But I'll probably just stay for the first three.'

'Try and have another word with Billy Searle. Get him to see sense.'

'I'll try,' I said. 'But he seemed pretty determined. Scared, even.'

'All sounds a bit fishy to me,' Patrick said. 'But we are required by the regulator to do as our clients instruct, and we can't go off to the authorities every time they instruct us to do something we don't think is sensible.'

'But we have a duty to report anything we believe to be illegal.'

'And do you have any evidence that he wants to do something illegal with the funds?'

'No.' I paused. 'But I wonder if breaking the Rules of Racing is illegal?'

'Depends on what he's doing,' said Patrick. 'Defrauding the betting public is illegal. Remember that case at the Old Bailey a few years back.'

I did indeed.

'Billy told me he owed a guy some money,' I said. 'Seems he needs a hundred grand. That's a very big debt. I wonder if he's got mixed up with a bookmaker.'

'Betting is not illegal,' Patrick said.

'Maybe not,' I agreed, 'but it is strictly against the rules for a professional jockey to bet on horseracing.'

'That's not our problem,' he said. 'And if you do ask Billy any questions, for God's sake try and be discreet. We also have a duty to keep his affairs confidential.'

'OK, I will. I'll see you in the office tomorrow.'

'Right,' said Patrick. 'Oh, yes. Another thing. That policeman called yesterday asking for you.'

'He didn't call my mobile. It was on all day, although the damn thing doesn't work here. My mother lives in a mobile-phone-signal hole.'

'No, well, that wouldn't have mattered anyway because it seems he was rather rude to Mrs McDowd so she refused to give him your number. She told him you were unavailable and not to be contacted.'

I laughed. Good old Mrs McDowd, one of our fearless office receptionists.

'What did he want?' I asked.

'Seems they want you to attend at Herb's flat. Something about being his executor.' He gave me the policeman's number and I stored it in my phone. 'Call him, will you? I don't want Mrs McDowd arrested for obstructing the police.'

'OK,' I said. 'See you tomorrow.'

I disconnected from Patrick and called Detective Chief Inspector Tomlinson.

'Ah, Mr Foxton,' he said. 'Good of you to call. How are you feeling?'

'I'm fine,' I replied, wondering why he would ask.

'Is your toe OK?' he asked.

'Sorry?'

'Your toe,' he repeated. 'Your receptionist told me about your operation.'

'Oh, that,' I said, trying to suppress a laugh. 'My toe is fine, thank you. How can I help?'

'Was Mr Kovak in personal financial difficulties?' he asked.

'In what way?' I said.

'Was he in debt?'

'Not that I am aware of,' I said. 'No more than any of us. Why do you ask?'

'Mr Foxton, are you well enough to come to Mr Kovak's home? There are quite a few things I would like to discuss with you, and I also need you, as his executor, to agree to the removal of certain items from his flat to assist with our enquiries. I can send a car if that helps.'

I thought about my planned day at Cheltenham Races.

'Tomorrow would be better.'

'Of course,' he said. 'How about eight a.m.?'

'Eight tomorrow is fine,' I said. 'I'll be there.'

'Do you need me to send a car?'

Why not, I thought. 'Yes, that would be great.'

I'd have to develop a limp.

Billy Searle was in no mood to explain to me why he suddenly needed his money.

'Just put the bloody cash in my bank account,' he shouted.

We were standing on the terrace in front of the Weighing Room before the first race and heads were turning our way.

'Billy, for goodness' sake calm down,' I said quietly but determinedly.

It didn't work.

'And what the hell are you doing here anyway?' he shouted back. 'You should be at your desk getting my bloody cash together.'

More heads turned.

So much for Patrick's instruction to keep things discreet.

'Billy, I'm only trying to help.'

'I don't need your fucking help!' He curled his lip and spat out the words, spraying me with fine drops of spittle.

The racing journalists were moving ever closer.

I dropped my voice, leaned forward and spoke directly into his ear. 'Now listen to me, you little creep. You clearly need someone's help and I'm on your side.' I paused. 'Call me when you've calmed down. The money will be in your bank by Friday.'

'I told you I need a hundred grand by tonight,' he was shouting and almost crying. 'I need my money today.'

We were now the centre of attention for half the Cheltenham crowd.

'Sorry,' I said quietly, trying to maintain some level

of dignity. 'That's impossible. It will be there by Friday, maybe by Thursday if you're very lucky.'

'Thursday will be too late,' he screamed at me. 'I'll be fucking dead by Thursday.'

There was no point in us standing there arguing, with all the racing world listening to every word, so I simply walked away, ever conscious of the hacks gathering around us like vultures, their pencils now scribbling ferociously in their notebooks. At least there was no sign of Martin Gifford, the five-star gossip, but he'd no doubt know every detail by the end of the day.

'Why are you trying to murder me?' Billy shouted after me at full volume.

I ignored him and continued over towards the relative privacy of the pre-parade ring, where I called the office to check how the liquidation of Billy's assets was progressing.

Mrs McDowd answered. Patrick and Gregory didn't like automated telephone answering and faceless voicemail. 'Our clients need to know they are dealing with real people,' they said. Hence we employed Mrs McDowd and Mrs Johnson, to answer the telephones.

'What on earth did you say to that policeman?' I asked her. 'He's being uncommonly nice to me.'

'I told him you were having an ingrowing toenail removed.'

'Why?'

'Because he was bloody rude to me,' she said with indignation. 'Spoke to me as if I was the office cleaner, so I told him you couldn't be reached. The trouble was, he wanted to know why you couldn't be reached, so I told him you were unconscious having an operation. Seemed like a good idea at the time, but the damn man was persistent, I'll give him that. Demanded to know what you were having done so I told him it was an ingrowing toenail. I could hardly make it something more serious, now could I? Not with you up and about, like.'

'Mrs McDowd, if I ever need someone to make up an alibi, I promise I'll call you,' I said, never thinking for a second that I would need an alibi much sooner than I realized. 'Can I speak to Miss Diana please?'

She put me through.

The sale of Billy Searle's assets was progressing smoothly, albeit with a sizable loss on some of my recent bond purchases. But did I care? No, probably not. Billy deserved it. I chided myself a little for such non-IFA thoughts, but I was only human. I thanked Diana and disconnected.

'Hello, lover-boy,' said a voice close behind me. 'On the phone to my competition?'

'Please stop,' I said with mock indignation. 'People will talk.'

Jan Setter cuddled herself up to my back.

'Let them talk,' she said while giving me a tight hug, pressing her whole body against mine. 'I want you.' She said it into my ear, with passion.

This was the second time in two days she had made a pass at me in public, and there was nothing casual and light-hearted about this one. Perhaps she really was serious, and that could be a problem. I had always rather enjoyed my flirtatious friendship with Jan, but that was because I had believed we were both just having a bit of verbal fun with no prospect of any actual physical contact. Now, it seemed, the stakes had been raised quite a few notches.

I pulled her arms away from my waist and turned round.

'Jan,' I said firmly. 'Behave yourself.'

'Why should I?' she asked.

'Because you must.' She turned down the corners of her mouth like a scolded child. 'For a start,' I said, 'I'm too young for you.'

'Oh, thanks a lot,' she said crossly, stepping back. 'You really do know how to make a woman feel wanted.'

There was no mock indignation here, she was angry, and hurt.

'Look,' I said. 'I'm sorry, but I never intended this to get out of hand.'

'Nothing has got out of hand,' she said. 'Things are just as they have been before. Nothing has changed.'

But we both knew it had, and there would be no going back to as we had been before.

'Great,' I said.

She smiled at me ruefully. 'But you will let me know if you change your mind.'

'OK.' I smiled back at her. 'What do you have running?'

'Nothing,' she said. 'Most of mine have finished now

for the summer.' She paused. 'I only came today because I hoped you would be here.'

I stood silently for a moment and looked at her.

'I'm sorry,' I said.

'Yeah,' she replied with a sigh. 'So am I.'

Colonel The Honourable Jolyon Westrop Roberts MC OBE, younger son of the Earl of Balscott, was waiting for me in the same place on the grandstand where I had met him the previous day.

'Ah, Nicholas,' he said as I made my way up to watch the first race. 'I was hoping you might be here again today.'

'Hello, sir,' I said. In spite of calling himself plain Mr Roberts, I knew he liked his formality. 'How can I help?'

'Well,' he said with a slight laugh. 'I hope you can help. But there may be nothing to help about. If you know what I mean?'

'No, sir,' I said. 'I don't know what you mean. You haven't told me anything.'

He laughed again, nervously.

'As I explained to you yesterday,' he said, 'there may be nothing to worry about. In fact, I expect there isn't. I'm probably only wasting your time. And I wouldn't want to get anyone into trouble, now would I?'

'Sir,' I said with some determination. 'How would I know if you won't tell me? What is it exactly that is worrying you?'

He stood for a few seconds in silence looking out over my head towards the racecourse as if deciding whether he should go on.

'Gregory,' he said finally. 'I'm worried about Gregory.'

'What about Gregory?' I asked. At times we had all been worried about Gregory. He ate far too much and didn't do any exercise that we were aware of, other than to walk to the end of Lombard Street for a substantial lunch five days a week.

'It's probably nothing,' Jolyon Roberts said again. He stamped his feet and looked uncomfortable. 'Best forget I ever said anything.'

'Are you worried about Gregory's health?' I asked.

'His health?' Mr Roberts repeated with surprise. 'Why would I worry about Gregory's health?'

'Then what is it about Gregory that you are worried about?'

Jolyon Roberts drew himself up to his full six-foot three, the ex-Guards colonel who had won a Military Cross for gallantry as a young subaltern in the Falklands War.

'I'm worried about his judgement.'

My planned early departure from Cheltenham was put on hold as I steered Mr Roberts into a quiet corner of the seafood bar for a discussion away from the ears of others. When a client, especially one with such a large investment portfolio as the younger son of the

Earl of Balscott, questions the judgement of one of the senior partners, it is no time to hurry away home.

'Now, sir,' I said when we were each settled with a plate of prawns in Marie Rose sauce with smoked salmon. 'In what way do you question Gregory Black's judgement? And why are you telling *me*?'

'It's probably nothing,' he said again. 'He has been so good to me over the years, very good. In fact, I'm sure it's nothing.'

'Why don't you let me be the judge of that?'

'Yes,' he said slowly. 'I think you might be a good judge. You always were on a horse. It was me who recommended you to Lyall and Black in the first place, don't you know?'

No, I didn't know. And I was flattered. No wonder there had been such a welcoming open door when I'd applied for a job.

'Thank you, sir,' I said. 'I didn't know.'

'Oh, yes,' said Mr Roberts. 'I've had my eye on you since you were eighteen years old and won on my cousin's horse at Chepstow. Remarkable piece of riding. Told my cousin then that you would be Champion Jockey one day. Bloody shame you got injured.'

Yes, I thought once more, it was a bloody shame.

'But tell me about Gregory Black,' I said, trying to get back to the matter in hand.

'It's probably nothing,' he said once more.

'Sir,' I said. 'Colonel Roberts, you must see that you have to tell me now that you have questioned his judgement. I promise you that I will treat what you say in the strictest confidence.'

At least, I *hoped* I could treat what he told me with confidence. Independent financial advisers were governed by the financial regulator. We were expected to act in a manner that always reflected the highest principles of behaviour. I would not be able to suppress information of wrongdoing solely because it would embarrass another IFA, even if he were my boss.

He was still reluctant to start.

'Is it about one of your investments?' I asked.

Still nothing.

'Do you disapprove of something Gregory has asked you to do?'

He absent-mindedly ate some of his prawns, the cogs in his mind turning over slowly.

'He may be mistaken,' he said finally.

'Who might be mistaken? Gregory Black?'

Mr Roberts looked up at me. 'No,' he said. 'My nephew, Benjamin.'

I was becoming more confused.

'How might your nephew be mistaken?' I asked.

'He visited the site and he tells me there are no houses, no factory and no building work being done on it. In fact, he said it was just waste ground with a large amount of heavy-metal pollutants sitting there in stagnant pools. A local government official apparently told him that the cost of removal of the toxic waste would be far greater than the actual value of the land.'

'I'm sorry,' I said. 'But what has this to do with Gregory Black?'

'He advised me to invest in the project.'

'What project?' I asked.

'A Bulgarian property development project,' he said. 'Houses, shops and a new factory making low-energy light bulbs.'

I vaguely remembered the project being discussed several years ago at one of Patrick's weekly meetings but, as far as I could recall, it had been rejected as too risky an investment for us to recommend to our clients. But that didn't mean that Gregory hadn't thought it a sound investment. Patrick and Gregory may have had both their names on the company notepaper but they valued their independence, even from each other.

'Are you sure it's on the same site that your nephew visited?'

'He says so. He says there is no mistake. The site where there should be a factory and hundreds of new homes and shops is nothing but an industrial waste-land. There is even talk of it having being used as a dump for nuclear waste during the Soviet era.'

'How much have you invested in the scheme?' I asked him.

'Not that much,' he said. 'The family trust has invested about five million into the project as a whole. The factory is named the Balscott Lighting Factory after my father. I've seen pictures of the development. The project is designed to be a great social experiment for one of the most deprived areas of the European Union. A lot of EU money has gone into it.'

Five million may not be that much to Jolyon Roberts and his family trust, but it was a fortune to most people.

'Do these pictures show a factory and new homes?'

'Yes they do, and they show more houses under construction,' he said. 'Gregory Black showed them to me. But what am I to believe, the photos or my nephew?'

'There must be a simple explanation,' I said. 'Why don't you go and ask Gregory about it? I am sure he will have invested your money wisely.'

'I've already approached him and he just told me not to be so silly, of course the factory has been built. But Benjamin is adamant. He says that no Balscott Lighting Factory exists anywhere in Bulgaria.'

'So what do you want me to do?' I asked him.

'Find out the truth.'

'But why me?' I asked. 'If you think there is a fraud being perpetrated then you should go to the police, or to the financial services regulator.'

He sat and looked at me for a moment.

'Because I trust you,' he said.

'But you hardly know me.'

'I know you much better than you might realize.' He smiled. 'I've been watching your career every step of the way since you first rode that winner for my cousin. And I normally pride myself on being able to spot the good'uns from the bad'uns. That is why I am so concerned about this project. After all, it was me who persuaded my brother, Viscount Shenington, that the family trust should invest in something that appeared so worthwhile. I just need to know what is going on.'

'Sir,' I said. 'I am under an obligation to report it if I find that there is a fraud, or even if there is misrepresentation in advertising an investment.'

'Mmm, I see,' he said, stroking his chin. 'My brother and I are most concerned that the good name of the Roberts family should not be dragged through the courts. He is in favour of simply writing off the investment and saying nothing. However . . .' He stopped.

'You feel responsible?' I asked.

'Exactly,' he said. 'But I would prefer it if you could be very discreet. If this *is* a scam, well, to be honest, I would rather not have everybody know that I've been a fool.'

'Especially your brother.'

He looked me in the eye and smiled. 'Trustworthy, and wise.'

'But I will have to talk to Gregory about it,' I said.

'Can you not have a little look at things first without telling anybody? I am sure that someone with your keen nose for a good investment will be able to spot a rotten egg pretty quickly if there's one to find.'

I laughed. 'I think you have the wrong person. My nose isn't that keen.'

'Oh, I think it is,' Jolyon Roberts replied. 'I have a friend who's forever telling me about all the money you've made for her in films and theatre.'

'I've just been lucky,' I said.

'Yes,' he said, smiling. 'You and Arnold Palmer.'

I looked at him quizzically.

'You're too young,' he said, laughing. 'Arnold Palmer the golfer.'

'What about him?' I asked.

'When a reporter once asked him why he was so lucky in golf, he famously replied, "It's a funny thing, the harder I practice the luckier I get."'

But my luck was about to run out.

5

True to his word, Detective Chief Inspector Tomlinson sent a car to collect me from home on Thursday morning, and he was waiting at Herb Kovak's flat when I arrived at eight a.m. sharp.

'Ah, good morning, Mr Foxton,' he said, opening the front door and offering his hand. 'And how is your toe today?'

'It's fine,' I said honestly. 'It doesn't hurt at all.'

And I'd forgotten to limp.

'Nasty things, ingrowing toenails,' he said. 'Had one myself years ago. Hurt like hell.'

'Luckily, I'm a quick healer,' I said. 'Now, how can I help?'

He stepped to the side and I walked past him and into the hallway of Herb's flat. I still thought of it as Herb's flat although, I supposed, it was now technically mine, or it would be in due course.

'Are you certain Mr Kovak was not in personal financial difficulties?' the chief inspector asked while closing the front door.

'No, I'm not certain, but I have no reason to think he was. Why do you ask?'

He waved a stack of papers towards me.

'What are they?' I asked.

'Credit card statements,' said the chief inspector.

'So?'

'Mr Kovak appears to have had more than twenty credit cards and, according to these statements, at his death, he owed nearly a hundred thousand pounds on these cards alone.'

I could hardly believe it. Not only because Herb was in so much debt, but also because his debt was on credit cards. If anyone knew how expensive it was to borrow on plastic, then a financial adviser would. Even with interest rates historically low, the annual percentage rate on credit cards was typically between sixteen and twenty per cent, with some even as high as thirty. Borrowing money on credit cards was a mug's game. The interest charges alone on a debt as big as that would be around fifteen hundred a month. That was about half what Herb was taking home in salary, after the usual deductions for tax and National Insurance.

If Herb had owed nearly a hundred thousand on credit cards, then his flat must surely be mortgaged to the hilt. It certainly wouldn't end up being mine, more likely the bank's.

And yet he'd always had plenty of money in his pocket. He was extravagant, even, in his spending, always wearing new clothes and dining out as the norm. It didn't make sense.

'Can I have a closer look at those?' I asked the chief inspector, reaching out for the papers.

He handed them over and I skimmed through the first three or four statements. There was no doubt that the outstanding balance on each was very large and, in some cases, close to the maximum limit, but that did not show the full picture, not by a long way. I looked through the rest. They were all the same.

'Didn't you notice something unusual about these?' I asked.

'Notice what?' said the chief inspector.

'There are no interest payments from previous months. All these charges, on all of these statements, they're all new.'

I turned a statement over to look at the detailed breakdown and to see what Herb had spent a hundred thousand pounds on in a month and was shocked again. There were no purchases, as such, just payments to and from a plethora of internet gambling and online casino sites. Masses of them. I looked through all the statements and they were the same. Many of the payments were quite modest but one or two ran into the thousands. Quite a few of the betting sites had actually paid money back to the accounts, but most showed a deficit. Overall, Herb had been a loser not a winner, nearly a hundred-thousand-pound-a-month loser.

All the statements showed clearly that the previous month's balances had been settled in full by the due date. I mentally added them up. As well as still owing almost a hundred thousand, Herb had paid nearly the same amount in gambling debts to the cards during March alone. Where had he obtained that sort of money? And how on earth had he had the time to gamble on so many different sites with so many different credit cards while working full-time at Lyall & Black? It sure as hell didn't make any sense.

As Claudia had said, you never really knew what even your closest friends were up to. Could this compulsive online gambling somehow be the reason that Herb was killed? The totals may have been large but the individual entries on the statements were modest, and surely not big enough to initiate murder.

'There are some other things I would like you to have a look at,' said the chief inspector. 'You may be able to help me understand them.'

He turned and walked down the hallway, turning left through a door. I followed him.

Herb's living room was in true bachelor-pad fashion, with half of it taken up by a single deep armchair placed in front of a large wall-mounted flat-screen television. On the far side of the room was a large desk with a laptop computer, a printer and three piles of papers in metal baskets.

It was some of the papers that the chief inspector wanted me to look at.

'We need your permission, as Mr Kovak's executor, to remove certain items that we believe may help with our enquiries. These for example. But we would like your opinion on them first.'

He handed me two sheets of paper covered entirely on both sides by handwritten lists with columns of what appeared to be dates with amounts of money alongside, together with a further column of capital letters. 'Could they have something to do with Mr Kovak's work?'

I studied the lists briefly.

'I doubt it,' I said. 'They are handwritten and we do everything on computer. I think these could be amounts of money.' I pointed at the centre two columns. 'And these look like dates.'

'Yes,' he said. 'I worked that much out. But do you know what they are?'

'Do they correspond to the amounts on the credit cards statements?' I asked.

'No. I looked at that. None of the figures are the same.'

'How about last month's statements?' I said. 'Most of these dates are last month.'

'We have been unable to locate any statements other than those you have seen. But some of the dates on this list would have been for the statements we have, and none of the amounts match.'

'Then I'm afraid I can't help you,' I said. 'I don't recognize any of the amounts and, individually, most are far too small to be anything to do with Mr Kovak's work. We always work in thousands, if not tens of thousands. Most of these are hundreds.' I looked once more at the lists. 'Could that third column be people's initials?'

The chief inspector looked. 'It might be. Do you recognize any of them? For example, do they match any of your work colleagues?'

I scanned through the list. 'Not that I can see.'

'Right,' he said suddenly, as if making a decision. 'With your permission we will take these papers away, together with the credit card statements, Mr Kovak's laptop computer, and these other things.'

The chief inspector waved a hand towards a box on a side table near the door. I went over and looked in. The box contained various bits and pieces including Herb's American passport, an address book, a desk diary and a folder full of bank statements. It was all rather sad.

'It's fine by me,' I said. 'But you do know that his computer won't give you access to Mr Kovak's work files?'

'So I believe.'

'He would have been able to access the office files and e-mails through his laptop but no records of them would have been stored on it. The laptop would have merely been acting as a keyboard and a screen for the firm's mainframe computer in Lombard Street.'

'Nevertheless,' said the chief inspector, 'it is our policy to search through such a device for any correspondence that might have a bearing on his death. I trust you are happy with that.'

'Absolutely,' I agreed.

'Good,' he said, folding the computer flat and placing it in the box with the other things.

'But can I make copies of that credit card stuff before you take it away. I do know that one of the first tasks for executors is to close the bank accounts and pay the debts of the deceased but goodness' knows where I will get a hundred thousand to do that. How much did he have in the bank?'

'Not that much,' said the chief inspector.

'Do you mind if I look?' I asked.

'Not at all,' he said. 'I understand from Mr Kovak's lawyer that it will be yours anyway.'

I pulled the folder of bank statements out of the box and looked at the most recent ones. The balance was quite healthy but, as DCI Tomlinson had said, it didn't run to anything like a hundred thousand. More like a tenth of that. I unclipped the last statement from the folder and made a photocopy using the printer/copier on the desk. I then photocopied all the credit card statements, and both sides of the two sheets of handwritten figures, before handing them all back to the policeman.

'Thank you,' he said. 'I just need your signature on this form to give us permission to remove these items, and I have a receipt for them to give you.'

He handed me the form, which I signed, and the receipt, which I put in my pocket.

'Bloody paperwork,' he said, taking back the form. 'These days we have to be so damn careful to do everything exactly according to the book or some clever-dick defence lawyer will claim that any evidence we find is not admissible in court. I can tell you, it's a bloody nightmare.'

Although better, on the whole, I thought, than the police marching in anywhere they liked in their size-twelve boots taking away any stuff they wanted without permission, and for no good reason.

He packed his paperwork into the box along with the other things. 'Now, Mr Foxton,' he said, 'could you just wander around the flat to satisfy yourself that we have left the place in reasonable order, and also to check that nothing appears out of place or is missing.'

'I'm happy to have a look,' I said, 'but I've never been in here before so I don't know what it looked like before you arrived.'

'Please, anyway,' he said, putting his hand out towards the door.

He followed me as I went round the flat, looking briefly in each of the two bedrooms, the bathroom, and the well-fitted kitchen. Nothing to my eye appeared out of place but, of course, it wouldn't.

'Have you searched everywhere?' I asked.

'Not a proper forensic search,' he said. 'We haven't taken the floorboards up or knocked holes in the walls, that sort of thing. But we had a reasonable look around to see if there was anything that could assist us in determining why he was killed. Mr Kovak was the victim of the crime, not the perpetrator.'

'How did you get in?' I asked as we went back along the hallway. 'The front door doesn't seem to have been forced.'

'The key was in Mr Kovak's trouser pocket.'

I thought again about Herb lying silent and cold in some morgue refrigerator.

'How about his funeral?' I asked.

'What about it?' he said.

'I suppose it's my job to organize it.'

'Not before the coroner has released the body,' he said.

'And when will that be?' I asked.

'Not just yet,' he replied. 'He hasn't been formally identified.'

'But I told you who he was.'

'Yes, sir,' he said with irony, 'I know that. And we are pretty certain we know who he is because you told us, but you are not his next of kin and, to be fair, you have only known him for five years. He could have told you that he was Herbert Kovak while not actually being so.'

'You're showing that suspicious mind of yours again, Chief Inspector.'

He smiled. 'We are still trying to trace his next of kin but, so far, without success.'

'I know he lived in New York just before he came to England,' I said. 'But he was brought up in Kentucky. In Louisville. At least, that is what he said.'

Did I now doubt it?

'Yes,' said the chief inspector. 'We have been in touch with our counterparts in New York and Louisville but, so far, they have been unable to contact any members of his family. It would appear that his parents are deceased.'

'Can you give me any idea of when a funeral can be held?'

'Not at present,' he said. 'I imagine it won't be for a few weeks at least. Maybe his remains will need to be sent back to the United States.'

'Don't I decide that, as the executor of his will?' I asked.

'Maybe,' he said. 'Depends on the formal identification. But I'll leave that up to the coroner. In the meantime, if you think of anything else that might help us with our enquiries, please call me.' He dug in his inside pocket for a card. 'Use the mobile number. It's usually on all the time, and you can leave a message if it's not.'

I put the card in my wallet and Chief Inspector Tomlinson collected the box of possible evidence.

'Can I offer you a lift home?' he asked.

'No, thank you. I think I'll have a look around here first. I can catch the bus.'

'Don't overdo it with that toe,' he said. 'That's what I did with mine and it took weeks to get right.'

'I'll be careful,' I said with an inward smile. I would, in fact, be going in to the office and not home when I left here. 'Now, how do I lock up?'

'Ah, yes,' he replied, digging into his coat pocket. 'I had another key cut. We would like to hang on to one for the time being just in case we need to pop back to look through his things further.'

'Right,' I said, taking the offered key. 'Are you based down here, then? I thought you were Merseyside Police.'

'I am,' he replied. 'But I'm working on this case out of Paddington Green all this week. I will be going home on Friday.'

'And you'll let me know when I can start making funeral arrangements?'

'The Liverpool coroner will be in contact with you

in due course,' he said, rather unhelpfully, and then he departed, carrying his box of potential treasures under his arm.

I sat for a while at Herb's desk looking again at the credit card statements.

There were between twenty and thirty internet gambling or online casino websites on each statement. Half of them I didn't recognize but their names showed what they were. One was called www.oddsandevens. net and another www.pokermillions.co.eg. It didn't take a genius to work it out.

Not every statement had all the same sites, but some were on all of them, and all appeared at least half a dozen times. I started adding up. In total there were twenty-two different credit cards and five hundred and twelve different entries on the statements. The total owed was ninety-four thousand, six hundred and twenty-six pounds and fifty-two pence.

Some of the entries on all of the statements were credits but, overall, the average loss per entry was a fraction under a hundred and eighty-five pounds. I checked the actual amounts against those on the hand-written lists but, as the chief inspector had said, not one of them matched.

It wasn't so much the amount of money that amazed me, even though it did, it was the number of different entries. Again I wondered how Herb had had the time to play or gamble online with five hundred and twelve different log-ins. I did some more mental arithmetic. Without work, eating or sleeping, and spending every moment of the day for a whole month at the computer would have given him just an hour and a half on each account. It was impossible.

I stood up and went into the kitchen.

My mother always maintained that one could learn most about a person by looking in their fridge. Not with Herb. His fridge was starkly empty with just a plastic carton of skimmed milk and a half-full tub of low-fat spread. His cupboards were almost equally bare, with a couple of boxes of breakfast cereal and half a loaf bread, gone stale. On the worktop were a jar of instant coffee, and two round tins with TEA and SUGAR printed on their outsides and with some teabags and granulated sugar on their insides.

I filled the electric kettle and made myself a cup of coffee. I took it back to the desk in the living room and went on studying the credit card statements.

I spotted that there was something else slightly odd about them.

They didn't all have the same name or the same address at the top.

Some of them had this flat's address and others the Lyall & Black office's address in Lombard Street. Nothing too unusual about that. But the names on them also varied. Not very much, but enough for me to notice.

I looked through them again, carefully making two piles on the desk, one for each address.

There were eleven statements in each pile, and eleven

slight variations in Herb's name: Herb Kovak, Mr Herb E. Kovak, Herbert Kovak Esq., Mr H. Kovak, Herbert E. Kovak, Mr H. E. Kovak, H. E. Kovak Jr., H. Edward Kovak, Bert Kovak Jr., Herbert Edward Kovak, and Mr Bert E. Kovak.

No two statements had the same name and address.

Now, why did I think that was suspicious?

I heard the key turn in the door and thought that DCI Tomlinson must have forgotten something. I was wrong.

I went out into the hallway to find an attractive blonde-haired young woman struggling through the front door with an enormous suitcase. She saw me and stopped.

'Who the hell are you?' she demanded in a Southern American accent.

I'd been about to ask her the same thing.

'Nicholas Foxton,' I said. 'And you?'

'Sherri Kovak,' she said. 'And where's my damn brother?'

There was no easy way to tell Sherri that her brother was dead, but it was the nature of his death she found most distressing.

She sat in the big armchair and wept profusely while I made her a cup of hot, sweet tea.

In between bouts of near hysteria, I discovered that she had arrived early that morning on an overnight flight from Chicago. She had been surprised, and rather annoyed, that Herb had not been at the airport to meet her as he had promised, but she had eventually made her own way to Hendon by train and taxi.

'But how did you have a key to get in?' I asked her.

'Herb gave me one when I was here last year.'

Herb hadn't mentioned to me last year that his sister was visiting, or even that he had a sister in the first place. But why would he have? We had been work colleagues rather than close friends. He also hadn't mentioned to me that he was a compulsive online gambler.

I wondered if I ought to inform DCI Tomlinson that Herb Kovak's next of kin had turned up. Probably, but then he'd be back round here with a list of awkward questions when it was clear to me that, after a night of sitting upright on an aeroplane, what she needed most was a good sleep. I'd call the chief inspector later.

I found some fresh bed linen in an airing cupboard and made up the bed in the smaller of the two bedrooms. I then guided the over-tired and still-crying Miss Kovak from the living room to the bed, and made her take off her shoes and lie down.

'You sleep for a bit,' I said, covering her with a blanket. 'I'll still be here when you wake.'

'But who are you exactly?' she asked between sobs.

'A friend of your brother's,' I said. 'We worked together.' I decided not to mention to her, just yet, that her brother had left his entire estate to me and not to her. And I wondered why that was.

Sherri Kovak was almost asleep before her head reached the pillow. I left her there and went back to Herb's desk and the credit card statements.

It was gone nine o'clock and I called the office number on my mobile. Mrs McDowd answered.

'It's the man with the ingrowing toenail calling in sick,' I said.

'Shirker,' she announced with a laugh.

'No, really,' I said. 'I won't be in the office until later. Please tell Mr Patrick that I'm sorry but something has come up.'

'Trouble?' she asked.

'No,' I said. 'No trouble, but something that I need to deal with.'

I could almost feel her wanting to ask what it was. Mrs McDowd liked to know everything about the goings-on of her staff, as she called us. She was always asking after Claudia, and she seemed to know more about my mother than I did.

'Tell me, Mrs McDowd,' I said in a friendly tone, 'did you know that Herb Kovak had a sister?'

'Yes, of course,' she said. 'Sherri. She lives in Chicago. She and Mr Herb were twins. She visited him last summer.'

'Did you proffer this information to the policeman when he interviewed us all on Monday?'

'No,' she said firmly. 'I did not.'

'Why not?' I asked her.

'He didn't ask me.'

Mrs McDowd clearly didn't like the police very much.

'Please tell Mr Patrick that I'll see him later today,' I said.

'Right, I will,' she said. 'It's a good job you're not here now anyway. Mr Gregory is angry fit to burst.'

'What about?' I asked.

'You,' she said. 'He's absolutely livid. Claims you've brought the whole firm into disrepute. He wants your head on a stick.'

'But why?' I asked, rather worried. 'What have I done?'

'Don't you know?'

'No,' I said.

'Read the front page of the *Racing Post*.'

I went along the hall to check on Sherri. Her long blonde hair was obscuring her face so I waited in the doorway for a few seconds listening to her breathing. She was sound asleep. Best thing for her, I thought. Sadly, the horrors of real life would still be waiting for her when she woke.

As quietly as I could, I slipped out the front door and walked down towards Hendon Central in search of a newsagent.

I could see the problem even before I picked up the paper. The inch-high bold headline read:

FOXY FOXTON AND BILLY SEARLE IN £100,000 GAMBLE?

I bought the paper with shaking hands and stood reading it in the shop.

In addition to the headline there were photographs of Billy and me, mine taken during my racing days wearing racing colours and cap.

The article beneath was as damning as the headline:

Leading National Hunt jockey Billy Searle was observed in a heated argument at Cheltenham Races yesterday with former fellow jockey Nick (Foxy) Foxton. The topic of their acrimonious exchange? Money.

According to the Racing Post *correspondent at the course, the amount under discussion was in excess of a hundred thousand pounds, with Searle demanding instant payment of this amount, which he claimed he was owed by Foxton. At one point Searle was heard to ask why he, Foxton, wanted to murder Searle. Could this all be connected with Foxy's new job at City financial firm Lyall and Black, where he gambles daily with other people's money on the stock markets?*

Well-known trainer, Martin Gifford, stated that Foxton had informed him on Tuesday that Herbert Kovak, the man whose murder last Saturday led to the postponement of the Grand National, was Foxton's best friend and a fellow stock-market speculator who had also worked for Lyall and Black. Gifford implied that Foxton may have known more about the killing than he was telling.

Not surprisingly, people yesterday were asking if Foxton's argument with Searle could have had some sinister connection to the Aintree murder. The Rules of Racing clearly ban gambling by professional jockeys but no such restriction applies to former jockeys. The Racing Post *will endeavour to keep its readers up to date with this story.*

The article cleverly didn't actually accuse Billy Searle or me of any wrongdoing, it merely asked leading questions. But there was little doubt that the tone of the piece was designed to imply there was a criminal conspiracy between us, which also had something to do with the death of Herb Kovak.

No wonder Gregory Black was steaming round the office fit to burst.

I was surprised my phone wasn't ringing off the hook.

Bugger, I thought. What should I do now?

I called Patrick on his mobile. I didn't fancy using the office number just in case Gregory himself answered, as we all sometimes did if the receptionists were busy on other calls.

'Hello, Nicholas,' said Patrick. 'I thought I told you to be discreet. I hear that Gregory's after your blood. I'd keep your head down if I were you.'

'I will,' I said. 'But it's all a pack of lies.'

'You know that, and I know that. But, unfortunately, Joe Bloggs in the street will believe what he reads in the paper.'

'But they have completely distorted the truth. It's so unfair.'

'Tell that to the politicians.' He laughed. 'I have already told Gregory not to believe what he reads but he says, quite rightly, that you shouldn't have been having a public argument with a client in the first place. He's pretty mad.'

'It wasn't an argument,' I claimed in my defence. 'Billy Searle just started shouting and swearing at me for no reason.'

'Don't worry about it,' Patrick said. 'It'll all blow over in a couple of days.'

I wish he'd been right.

6

I walked back to Herb's flat hardly feeling my feet on the pavement.

What a bloody mess.

I could imagine that Billy Searle wasn't too happy about it either. I thought the last thing he'd want would be the racing authorities asking him questions about why he needed a hundred thousand pounds so urgently.

I let myself in through Herb's front door and went to check again on Sherri. She hadn't moved and was still sound asleep. I left her alone and went back to the living room, where I sat at Herb's desk wishing I'd brought my laptop with me. It was lying on the kitchen table in Finchley and I was tempted to go home to fetch it. Instead I called Claudia.

'Hi, it's me,' I said when she answered.

'Hi, you,' she replied.

'Could you bring my computer over to Herb's flat?' I said. 'His sister has turned up and she didn't know he was dead. She's sleeping now but I don't feel I can leave her for long. I'll stay and work here, but I do need my laptop.' I decided against mentioning, as yet, the unwelcome coverage in the *Racing Post*.

There was a slight pause.

'OK,' Claudia said in a slightly irritated tone.

'It's not very far,' I said encouragingly. 'Use the car. You won't need to park or anything, just drop it off.'

'OK,' she said again, lacking enthusiasm. 'But I was just going out.'

Bloody hell, I thought. It wasn't very much to ask.

'Where are you going?' I asked.

'Oh, nowhere,' she said. 'Just to have coffee with a friend.'

'Who?'

'No one you know,' she said evasively.

Probably one of her artist friends. I didn't know them, and I didn't really want to. Some of them were as weird as her paintings.

'Please, Claudia,' I said firmly. 'I need it here so I can do my job.' And to bring in the money so you can live rent free, I thought, but didn't say.

'OK,' she said once more, resigned. 'Where is the flat?'

I gave her the address and she promised she would bring the computer right over.

While I waited I went through the piles of papers on Herb's desk, those remaining after the chief inspector had taken his box away.

There were the usual clutter of utility bills and debit card receipts, interleaved with financial services' magazines, insurance documents and some personal letters. I glanced through them all but nothing gave any clue to who would want Herb dead, or how he came to gamble away a hundred thousand pounds a month on the internet.

I didn't expect them to. I assumed that the police would have removed anything of interest.

Next I went through the desk drawers. There were three on each side and the ones on the left contained such exciting items as a stapler with spare staples, various-sized brown envelopes, paper and ink cartridges for the printer, a pack of permanent markers in bright colours, a plastic tub of large paper clips, and a calculator.

Those on the right were only partially more interesting with a large pile of paid bills, various income tax papers, a copy of Herb's United States tax return, a rubber-band-bound stack of received Christmas cards, and a plastic folder containing monthly pay slips from Lyall & Black.

I was curious to see that Herb had been paid somewhat more than I was, no doubt due to his three years' prior experience at J.P. Morgan Asset Management in New York before moving to London. Now that I was Patrick's most senior assistant, I would have to have a discussion with him about a raise.

I flicked through the bills but there was nothing that appeared to shine out like a lighthouse to guide me to his killer, although I did notice that Herb had been what my mother always described as a 'free-spending spirit'. It was a term she used for those she considered to squander their money on lavish, unnecessary purchases instead of prudently saving it for a rainy day, as she had always done.

Two separate invoices from a local travel agent showed

that Herb's free spending had run to at least two British Airways first-class round-trip tickets across the Atlantic at eight thousand pounds each, one of them dated only the previous month for a planned, but not yet taken, trip in May. He may have been earning more than me but there was no way he could have financed those out of his income from Lyall & Black, even without the online gambling debts he had run up on the credit cards.

I wondered if he had inherited a large sum from his dead parents. I thought it unlikely as he had always claimed that his father had gambled away most of his family's money. But perhaps Herb had been busy spending and gambling away the rest.

But where had he kept it?

I looked again at the photocopy I had made of his last bank statement. I had only made it to have a record of Herb's account number and sort code. I would need them when I contacted the bank to inform them of his death. The latest balance was a little under ten thousand pounds but there were no entries on the statements that appeared to be payments for the credit card accounts, and certainly no eight thousand pounds to the travel agent the previous month.

Herb had to have had another bank account, but there was no sign of it anywhere in his desk.

I looked at my watch. I had called Claudia nearly half an hour ago and the journey should have taken her only ten minutes from Lichfield Grove, Finchley to Seymour Way, Hendon. I went to the door to see if she was outside somewhere but there was no sign of her, or the Mercedes.

I waited in the doorway for five further minutes with slightly increasing irritation. I didn't really want to call her again, but she was beginning to try my patience.

Once, I would have been so excited by the prospect of seeing her, I wouldn't have minded if she had been half a day late arriving. On one occasion I had been at Heathrow Airport at least two hours before her flight was due to land, just to be sure not to miss her arriving through customs.

But now, and not for the first time, I wondered if our relationship had run its course.

She finally arrived some thirty-five minutes after I had called. She stopped in the middle of the road and put down the passenger window. I leaned through it and picked up my computer from the seat.

'Thanks,' I said. 'See you later.'

'OK,' she said, and drove off quickly.

I stood in the road waving but, even if she could see me, she didn't wave back. There had been a time when we never parted without us waving vigorously until we were completely out of sight of each other.

I sighed. I had invested so much of my emotional capital in my relationship with Claudia and the thought of being single again, having to start out once more, did not fill me with any joy. And I wasn't at all sure I wanted it to end.

Claudia still excited me, and the sex was good, albeit somewhat rarer than it once had been. In fact, sex had been non-existent over the last couple of weeks with Claudia always making some excuse. So what had gone wrong? Why was she suddenly not so loving towards me?

I wondered if she was seeing someone else. But who? Surely not one of her artistic layabout friends from her time at art college. The thought of her being intimate with one of them was enough to make me feel ill, and not a little bit angry.

Miserably, I went back into Herb's flat and sat down again at his desk but, even with my computer, I couldn't concentrate on any work due to thinking about the article in the paper, and also about Claudia. After about half an hour I called her mobile but it went straight to voicemail. I didn't leave a message because I didn't know what to say.

Instead, I logged on to the internet through Herb's router and checked my office e-mails, many of which were junk from various finance firms offering rates of return that were well above the norm for the market.

Nestled amongst the trash were three work e-mails from this morning: one from Diana confirming the sales of all Billy Searle's assets and the impending transfer from the firm's client account to his bank, one from Patrick asking me to research a new personal pension plan being offered by one of the leading providers in the light of new pension legislation, and the third from Jessica Winter advising me to wear a bullet-proof vest if I was planning on coming into the office.

I thought it a particularly insensitive comment

considering what had happened to Herb only five days previously.

I looked again at all the junk mail.

If a promised return appeared to be too good to be true, then it invariably was just that, too good to be true.

I thought back to my conversation with Jolyon Roberts at Cheltenham the previous day. Had the promised return on the Bulgarian property development project been too good to be true? Not as far as I could remember. It had not been the level of return that had been the concern, rather the distance away and the potential difficulty in acquiring accurate and up-to-date information on the progress of the project. In fact, just the problem that Mr Roberts believed to be the issue.

I started to type 'Roberts' into the company client index but thought better of it. The office mainframe computer kept a record of all files accessed, so any of us could see who had been looking at each file. It wasn't particularly designed to spy on us or to prevent us accessing files, indeed it made it easy to keep a record of files visited. I could expect my files to be accessed by Patrick on a fairly random but regular basis, and the company files as a whole were regularly scrutinized by Jessica Winter, our Compliance Officer.

Whenever any of us opened a file it clearly showed, in the top right hand corner of the computer screen, a list of the five people in the firm who had accessed the file most recently, together with the date and time of their access.

As one of the IFAs, I had authority to look at any of the company files but I might have had difficulty explaining to Gregory why I had accessed those of one of his clients without his knowledge, especially a client as important as the Roberts Family Trust, and especially now.

I told myself that I should go straight to Gregory and Patrick, and probably to Jessica as well, and tell them about my conversation with Jolyon Roberts and get the matter looked at by them. But did I really want to go and accuse Gregory of misleading one of his clients, and on today of all days?

Then I would truly need that bulletproof vest.

Unlike in the United States where the Securities and Exchange Commission, the SEC, employs a prescriptive rule-based regime, the United Kingdom authorities had moved to a principles-based regulatory system. The onus was now on me to act in a manner that upheld the highest principles of honesty, openness and integrity, and to prove it.

It was difficult to decide which system was the better. Experience had shown that neither was fraud-proof. Indeed, the SEC had investigated Bernie Madoff several times without unearthing the biggest individual fraud in American history. Talk about the asylum being run by the lunatics, Madoff served three times as chairman of the NASDAQ stock market. And that was many years after he had started his fraud, and even after the first failed SEC investigation into his company's activities.

And he'd just had to be called Madoff, hadn't he? He'd 'made off' with sixty-five billion dollars – yes, billion. And all because he'd been able to fraudulently circumvent the fixed US regulatory rules. Whereas in the UK, it was not just the letter of the law I had to follow, but also its spirit.

But was I, in fact, following the spirit of principles-based regulation not to mention immediately to my superiors, and to the Compliance Officer, that a client of the firm was questioning the judgement of one of the senior partners?

Probably not.

And I would mention it to them, I thought, just as soon as Gregory had calmed down a bit. In the meantime, I would do a bit of discreet investigating just as Jolyon Roberts had asked.

First I tried 'Bulgarian development projects' in the Google search engine but this turned up some fifty-five million hits, the first two pages of which appeared to have nothing to do with the development project I was looking for. Next I tried 'Balscott Bulgarian development project' and this turned up just two hits but neither of them had any connection whatsoever with a low-energy light-bulb factory on either side of the Danube.

Next I tried 'Europa', the official European Union website, but that was more difficult to navigate through than the continent itself.

It was all a bit of a dead end without accessing the firm's Roberts Family Trust computer file to see with whom and where the contact had been made in Bulgaria or with the EU. And I daren't do that.

I decided instead that I'd try to have a quiet look through the paper records we kept at the office. Shares and bonds may have increasingly been bought and sold online but the digital deals were still all backed up with physical paperwork, and we were required to keep the papers for a minimum of five years. The office was consequently stacked high with boxes of transaction reports and somewhere amongst them would be the Roberts Family Trust paperwork for their five-million-pound investment in the Balscott Lighting Factory.

I sat back in the chair and thought about Claudia. I tried her mobile again but, as before, it went straight to voicemail without ringing. I wished now that I had told her about the article in the *Racing Post* when she had brought over my computer. I tried her number once more and, this time, I did leave a message.

'Darling,' I said. 'Could you please give me a call when you get this? Love you. Byeee.' I hung up.

I looked at the clock on Herb's desk. It was only a quarter to eleven. I had been here for nearly three hours but it seemed like much longer.

I wondered what Claudia could be doing at a quarter to eleven in the morning, and with whom, that required her to have her phone switched off.

I sighed. Perhaps I didn't want to know.

In my role as Herb's executor, I used the account number and sort code on his statement to send an e-mail to his bank informing them that Mr Kovak was deceased, and would they please send me details of all his accounts, and especially the balances.

Somewhat surprisingly I received a reply almost immediately thanking me for the sad news and advising me that they would need various pieces of original documentation before they could release the information I had asked for, including the death certificate, a copy of the will, and a grant of probate.

And how long would it take to get that lot?

I heard Sherri go along the corridor to the bathroom.

At least my troubles with Billy Searle were minor compared to hers.

I took the front cover sheet off the *Racing Post* and folded it up, as if not being able to see the damning words would in some way limit their damage to my reputation and career. I put the offending piece in my pocket and went to throw the rest of it into the waste bin under Herb's desk.

The bin had some things in it already and, I thought, as I've looked everywhere else, why not there?

I poured the contents of the bin out onto the desk.

Amongst the opened envelopes, the empty Starbucks coffee cups and the screwed-up tissues were lots of little pieces of paper about an inch square. I put the cups, envelopes and tissues back in the bin leaving a pile of the paper squares on the desk. It was fairly obvious that they were the torn-up remains of a larger piece so I set about trying to put them back together. It was a bit like doing a jigsaw puzzle, but one without the picture on the box to guide me.

I quickly established that the pieces had not been from one larger piece but three. I slowly built up the originals in front of me. They were each about six inches by four, printed forms with words written on them in pen, similar forms but each with different writing. I stuck the bits together with sticky tape.

'What are you doing?' Sherri asked from the doorway.

She made me jump.

'Nothing much,' I said, swivelling the desk chair round to face her. 'How are you feeling?'

'Dreadful,' she said, coming into the room and flopping down into the deep armchair. 'I can't believe it.'

I thought she was about to cry again. I wasn't sure whether the dark shadows beneath her eyes were due to tiredness or her tear-smudged mascara.

'I'll get you some more tea,' I said, standing up.

'Lovely,' she said with a forced smile. 'Thank you.'

I went through to the kitchen and boiled the kettle. I also made myself another coffee and took both cups back to the living room.

Sherri was sitting at the desk looking at the pieces of paper, so I sat down on the arm of the big armchair.

'Do you know what they are?' I asked her.

'Of course,' she said. 'They're MoneyHome payment slips.' She sipped her tea. 'One for eight thousand, and two for five.'

'Pounds?' I asked.

She looked at them.

'Dollars. Converted into pounds.'

'How do you know?' I asked.

She looked at me.

'I use MoneyHome all the time,' she said. 'It's a bit like Western Union only cheaper. They have agents all over the world. Herb sent me the money for my air fare via MoneyHome.'

'Are any of these slips from that?'

'No,' she said with certainty. 'These are the slips you get when you collect money, not when you send it.'

'So Herb collected eighteen thousand dollars' worth of pounds from MoneyHome?'

'Yes,' she said.

'When?' I asked.

She looked at the reconstructed slips carefully. 'Last week, but not all on the same day. Eight thousand on Monday, and five each on Tuesday and Friday.'

'Who from?' I asked.

'These only tell you which MoneyHome office it was collected from, they don't say who sent the money.' She drank more of her tea. 'What's all this about?'

'I don't know,' I said. 'I just found those torn-up sheets in the waste bin.'

She sat drinking her tea, looking at me over the rim of the cup.

'But why are you here, anyway?' she asked.

'I was a friend of Herb's, and a work colleague,' I said, giving her one of the business cards from my wallet. 'He made me the executor of his will.' I decided again not to mention that he had also made me the sole beneficiary.

'I didn't know he even had a will,' Sherri said, reading from my card, 'Mr Nicholas Foxton, BSc, MEcon, DipPFS.'

'He made it five years ago when he first arrived at Lyall and Black,' I said, ignoring her reference to my qualifications. 'Everyone in the firm has to have a will. The senior partners are always saying that we can hardly advise our clients to plan ahead if we aren't prepared to do the same. But I have absolutely no idea why Herb chose to put me in his. Maybe it was just because we sat at desks next to each other. He'd only just landed in the country and perhaps he didn't know anyone else. And none of us really expect to die when we're in our twenties anyway. But he should still have named you as his executor, even if you were in the United States.'

'Herb and I weren't exactly talking to each other five years ago. In fact, I'd told him by then that I never wanted to see or hear from him again.'

'Wasn't that a bit extreme?' I said.

'We had a flaming row over our parents.' She sighed. 'It was always over our parents.'

'What about them?' I asked.

She looked at me as if deciding whether to tell me.

'Our mom and dad were, shall we say, an unusual couple. Dad had made a living, if you can call it that, acting as an unlicensed bookie round the back-side of Churchill Downs. He was meant to be a groom but he didn't do much looking after the horses. He spent his time taking bets from the other grooms, and some of the trainers and owners too. Sometimes he won, but mostly he lost. Mom, meanwhile, had worked as a cocktail waitress in one of the swanky tourist hotels in downtown Louisville. At least that's what she told people.'

She paused, and I waited in silence. She'd say it if she wanted to.

'She'd been a prostitute.' Sherri was crying again.

'You don't have to tell me,' I said.

She looked at me with tear-filled eyes. 'I've got to tell someone,' she gulped. 'I've bottled it all up for far too long.'

Between bouts of tears she told me the sorry saga of her and Herb's upbringing. It amazed me that I had sat next to Herb for all those years without realizing the hurdles he'd had to overcome to be a financial adviser.

Herb and Sherri's father had been an abusive drinker who had seemingly treated his children as unpaid slave labour. Both of them had excelled at school but their father insisted that they drop out, aged sixteen, to go to work, Herb as a groom in the Churchill Downs stables, and Sherri as a chambermaid in one of the tourist hotels where her mother had plied her trade.

Herb had rebelled and run away to Lexington, where he had secretly applied for, and won, a free place at a private high school. But he'd had no accommodation, so he'd slept on the streets. One of the trustees of the school had found him there and offered him a bed. The trustee had been in financial services and hence Herb's career had been decided.

He'd stayed in Lexington after high school to attend the University of Kentucky on a scholarship, before landing the top graduate job at J.P. Morgan in New York.

I wondered how such a high flyer had come to move from one of the global-asset-management giants to a firm such as Lyall & Black, a relative tiddler in the financial pond. Had he somehow queered his pitch in New York?

Sherri, meanwhile, had been good at her job, and bright with it, and she had been spotted by the management of the hotel for further training. That was ultimately how she came to be in Chicago, where she was currently assistant-housekeeper in a big hotel of the same chain.

I didn't see how all this information was going to be of any use to me, but I sat quietly and listened as she unburdened her emotions.

'How come you and Herb fell out?' I asked in one of the frequent pauses.

'He refused to come home from New York for the funeral when Dad died. I told him he should be there to support Mom, but he refused and he said he wouldn't come to her funeral either if she dropped down dead tomorrow. Those were his exact words. And Mom heard him say them because she and I were in my car and the call was on speaker-phone.' She paused and more tears ran down her cheeks. 'I still think it's the reason why she did it.'

'Did what?' I asked.

'Swallowed a whole tub of Tylenol Extra. A hundred tablets.'

'Dead?' I asked.

She nodded. 'That night. I found her in the morning.' She sat up straight and breathed in deeply through her nose. 'I accused Herb of killing her, and that's when I told him I never wanted to see or hear from him again.'

'How long has it been since your parents died?'

'About six years, maybe seven.' She thought for a moment. 'It'll be seven years in June.'

'When did you change your mind?'

'What? About contacting Herb?'

I nodded.

'I didn't. It was he who contacted me, about two years ago.' She sighed. 'Five years was a long time not to speak to your twin brother. I had wanted to be in touch with him much sooner but I was too proud.' She paused. 'Too stupid more like. He wrote to me at the hotel company and we arranged to meet in New York. Then last summer he invited me to come to England and stay with him for a holiday. It was great.' She smiled. 'Just like old times.' The smile faded and the tears began again. 'I just can't believe he's dead.'

Neither could I.

I finally arrived at the office at twenty past one, a time when I reckoned Gregory should be just sitting down to his substantial lunch at the far end of Lombard Street. However, I approached number sixty-four from the opposite direction to the one he took to his usual restaurant in order to minimize the chances of running into him if he was late.

I ignored the lift, sneaked up the emergency stairway to the fourth floor, and put my head around the glass entrance doors. 'Has Mr Gregory gone to lunch?' I whispered to Mrs McDowd, who was sitting at the reception desk.

'Ten minutes ago,' she whispered back.

'And Mr Patrick?' I asked.

'Went with him,' she replied. 'Both gone for an hour and a quarter at least, probably longer.'

I relaxed and smiled at her. 'Maybe I'll just stay for an hour.'

'Very wise,' she said with a grin from ear to ear. 'Now, tell me, is it true what it says in that newspaper?'

'No, of course not,' I said.

She gave me one of her 'I don't believe you' looks. 'You must have done something or it wouldn't have been on the front page.'

'Mrs McDowd, it's nothing. I promise you.'

She curled down her mouth as if she was a spoiled child who had failed to be given an ice cream. I ignored her, walking past the reception desk and down the corridor beyond. As I passed by, I glanced through the ever-open door of the compliance office, but Jessica Winter was not at her desk. Jessica was one of those who always went out for her lunch hour, as Herb had done, though in his case it was not to eat but to work out at a local gym.

I went on and into my office, not that I had it completely to myself. There were five desk cubicles crammed into the small room, one of which was mine. Herb had been next to me, both of us close to the window, while Diana and Rory, Patrick's other assistants, occupied the two cubicles nearer the door. The fifth cubicle was no one's specific personal domain but was used by any visiting staff, usually an accountant for two days a week, and Andrew Mellor, the lawyer, if he needed a desk. Today it was empty.

Diana was out to lunch, as usual, while Rory was sitting at his desk typing with one hand on his computer keyboard while holding a half-eaten sandwich in the other.

'My God,' said Rory with his mouth full. 'The invisible man returns. Gregory's been looking for you all morning. You're in real trouble.' He sounded as if he was rather pleased about it, and I could see a folded copy of the *Racing Post* lying on his desk. It had probably been he who had showed it to Gregory.

'You haven't seen me, all right!' I said.

'Don't involve me in your sordid little affairs,' he said rather haughtily. 'I'm not putting my career at risk for you.'

Rory could be a real pain sometimes.

'Rory,' I said. 'When, and if, you ever qualify to be an IFA, you can then start talking about your career. Until then, shut up!'

Rory knew that I knew that he had failed his

qualifying exams twice and he was now in the Last Chance Saloon. He sensibly kept quiet.

I took off my suit jacket and hung it on the back of my chair. Then I sat down at Herb's desk and pulled open the top drawer.

'What are you doing?' Rory asked somewhat arrogantly.

'I'm going through Herb's desk,' I said. 'I'm his executor and I'm trying to find the address of his sister.' He wasn't to know that Herb's sister was in Hendon. Rory ignored me and went back to his one-handed typing.

There was no sign of Sherri's address but there were two more of the MoneyHome payment slips lurking in a drawer and, this time, not torn up into squares. There was also another of the sheets with handwritten lists on both sides, just like the one Chief Inspector Tomlinson had shown me in Herb's flat. I carefully folded them all up and put them in my pocket.

Apart from that, the desk was almost too clean. No screwed-up sweet papers or chocolate bar wrappers.

I wasn't surprised. In fact, I was amazed there had been anything at all. I would have expected the police would have stripped it completely bare on the Monday after his death.

I looked around me at the cubicle. Some of the staff personalized their noticeboards with family pictures or souvenir postcards sent by friends on holiday, but there had never been any such personal items pinned to Herb's, not even a picture of Sherri. There was only the usual mandatory internal company telephone directory and a small key, pinned to the board with a drawing pin. I looked at it closely but left it where it was. A key without a lock wasn't much use.

And there was nothing of interest in his waste bin either, which was completely empty. It would be. Even if the police hadn't emptied it, the office cleaners had been in since Herb had last sat at this desk on the previous Friday afternoon.

I walked along the corridor and put my head right into the lion's den.

Now Gregory, as a senior partner, did qualify for an office of his own but, fortunately for me, this particular lion was still out to lunch. I sat down in his chair and looked at his computer screen. As I had hoped, he hadn't bothered to log out from his session when he went to lunch. Most of us didn't. The office system was great when it was working, but it took so long to boot up that we all tended to leave it on all day.

I typed 'Roberts Family Trust' into Gregory's computer and it instantly produced the details of the file on his screen with the date of the original investment prominently displayed at the top. The access list in the right-hand corner showed me that Gregory himself had looked at the file only that morning, at 10.22 a.m. precisely, no doubt in a lull from searching the offices for me. I just hoped he wouldn't notice that his computer had accessed it again at 1.46 p.m.

However, it was one of the other names on the recent-enquiry list I found most interesting. The list showed that Herb Kovak had accessed the file just ten days previously. Now why had Herb looked at one of Gregory's client files? It would have been most improper, just as it was for me to be looking at it now. Perhaps Herb had also had some suspicions about the Bulgarian investment. I wondered what they had been. It was too late to ask.

I would have loved to print out the whole file but, unfortunately, the office server used a central printing system that recorded who had asked for what to be printed, and when. How could I explain away an apparent request from Gregory when he was out to lunch? More to the point, how would I explain away sitting at Gregory's desk and using his computer if he returned unexpectedly early?

I instinctively looked at my watch. It was ten to two. I reckoned I should be safe for at least another twenty minutes but I had no intention of being even half that long.

I flipped through the pages of the file trying to find the names of the Bulgarian agents involved in the project but it was a nightmare with pdf scans of the relevant documents all in the local Cyrillic script. It might as well have been in Chinese. I couldn't read any of the words, but I could read what I thought was a telephone number written in regular digits. I copied it down on the back of one of Herb's MoneyHome payment slips. It began +359, which I knew from looking at the internet earlier was the international code for Bulgaria.

I looked again at my watch. Two o'clock.

I opened Gregory's e-mail inbox and did a search for 'Bulgaria'. There were six e-mails, all from September two years ago. I glanced through them but nothing seemed amiss. They were about European Union money and they were all from the same source. I copied down the e-mail address of the sender uri_joram @ec.europa.eu, and also that of the recipient, dimitar .petrov@bsnet.co.bg. Gregory had been copied into the correspondence but there was no sign of any replies. I took a chance and forwarded the e-mails to my private e-mail address, then I deleted the forwarded record from Gregory's 'sent' folder. I wished I could have e-mailed myself the whole Roberts file but our security system wouldn't allow it.

I reluctantly closed Gregory's inbox and the Roberts Family Trust file and checked that the screen appeared the same as when I had first arrived.

I slipped out into the corridor and no one shouted a challenge or questioned what I had been doing in Gregory's office.

As everywhere in the offices, the corridor outside was lined with cardboard document boxes holding the paper transaction reports. I searched for the box containing those for the date at the top of the computer file.

Mrs McDowd may not have liked policemen very much, and she was definitely too nosey about the staff's lives and families, but she was very methodical in her filing. All the boxes were in chronological order with dates clearly written in thick marker pen on the ends.

I lifted up the box with the correct date and dug through its papers until I found the Roberts Family Trust transaction report and associated paperwork. I pulled them out, folded them, and stuffed them in my trouser pocket alongside Herb's MoneyHome payment slips, before putting the box carefully back in the same place I'd found it.

I glanced at my watch once more, twenty past two. Where had those twenty minutes gone? Time I was away. But why did I suddenly feel like a thief in the night? I'd done nothing wrong. Or had I? Maybe I should just go and see Jessica straight away when she returned from lunch. But the client, Jolyon Roberts, had specifically asked me to have a discreet look rather than initiate a possible fraud investigation that would, as he put it, drag the good name of the Roberts family through the courts.

Nevertheless, whatever else I might do, I didn't want to be in the offices when Gregory returned from the restaurant.

I went back into my office to collect my jacket.

'Leaving already?' said Rory sarcastically. 'What shall I tell Gregory?'

I ignored him.

As I walked down the corridor towards the reception area I realized with a heavy heart that I'd left it too late. I could hear Gregory and Patrick talking. I would just have to face the music.

'Ah, there you are, Foxton,' Gregory announced at high volume. 'I've been looking for you all morning.'

I was so mesmerized by Gregory that I hardly took any notice of a man standing to the side of him, next to Patrick, but the man suddenly stepped forward, right in front of me.

'Nicholas Foxton,' the man said. 'I arrest you on suspicion of the attempted murder of William Peter Searle.'

7

I spent the afternoon waiting in an eight-foot-by-six holding cell at Paddington Green Police Station not quite knowing what to think.

The man in the office had identified himself as another detective chief inspector, this one from the Metropolitan Police.

I'd missed his name. I hadn't really been listening.

I did, however, remember him advising me that I didn't have to say anything, with the proviso that it might harm my defence if I didn't mention something when questioned that I later relied on in court. I'd been too shocked to say anything anyway. I had just stood there with my mouth open in surprise as a uniformed policeman had applied handcuffs to my wrists and then led me down in the lift to a waiting police car.

William Peter Searle, the chief inspector had said when I was arrested.

That had to be Billy Searle.

So, Billy had been right about one thing.

Thursday had been too late.

I suppose I couldn't really blame the police for arresting me. Hundreds of witnesses had heard Billy shouting the previous afternoon at Cheltenham. 'Why are you trying to murder me?' had been his exact words, even if the *Racing Post* had distorted them somewhat.

I hadn't been trying to murder him, but I hadn't taken him seriously either.

But to whom could Billy have owed so much money? Clearly, someone who was prepared to try to kill him for non-payment by the Wednesday-night deadline.

I sat on one end of the cell's fixed concrete bed and went on waiting. But I wasn't particularly worried. I knew I had nothing to do with Billy's or anyone else's attempted murder and surely it would be only a matter of time before the police discovered that.

First Herb Kovak, and now Billy Searle. Could the two be connected?

Thursday afternoon dragged on into early evening, and I was left alone in the cell, still waiting.

For the umpteenth time I looked at my wrist to check the time and, for the umpteenth time, saw no watch.

It had been removed when I was 'checked in' to the custody suite by the custody sergeant, along with my tie, my belt, my shoelaces and the contents of my pockets, including Herb's MoneyHome payment slips and the transaction report from the box outside Gregory's office.

The cell door opened and a white-shirted policeman brought in a tray that held a covered plate and a plastic bottle of water.

'What time is it?' I asked.

'Seven o'clock,' he said without looking at his watch.

'How much longer am I going to be kept here?' I asked.

'The DCI will see you when he's ready,' replied the policeman, who then placed the tray down next to me on the concrete bed and went out. The door clanged shut behind him.

I looked under the cover – fish and chips – and quite good too.

I ate the lot, and drank the water. It took about five minutes.

And then I waited some more, counting the bricks in the walls of the cell in an attempt to alleviate the boredom. It failed.

The detective chief inspector finally opened the metal door long after the barred and frosted-glass window had turned from day-light to night-black.

'Mr Foxton,' he said, coming into the cell. 'You are free to go.'

'What?' I said, not quite taking it all in.

'You are free to go,' the detective said again, standing to one side of the door. 'We will not be charging you with any offence.' He paused as if not being quite able to say the next bit. 'And I'm sorry for any inconvenience that may have been caused.'

'Sorry!' I said. 'Sorry! I should bloody well think you are sorry. I've been treated like a common criminal.'

'Mr Foxton,' the chief inspector replied, somewhat

affronted. 'You have been treated exactly in accord-ance with the laid-down regulations.'

'So why was I arrested?' I demanded.

'We had reason to believe you were responsible for the attempted murder of the jockey, William Searle.'

'So what's happened that now makes you so sure I'm not responsible for it?' I was purposefully making myself appear angry. It might be the only chance I would have of asking the detective for some answers and I wanted to take advantage of his defensive position.

'I am persuaded that you could not have been pres-ent when Mr Searle was attacked. You have an alibi.'

'How do you know?' I said. 'You haven't asked me any questions.'

'Nevertheless,' he replied, 'I am satisfied that it was not possible for you to have committed the attack. So you are free to go.'

I didn't move.

'How are you satisfied that I couldn't have done it?' I asked with persistence.

'Because it is physically impossible for you to have been in two places at the same time. That's what hav-ing an alibi means. *Alibi* is a Latin word meaning "somewhere else", and you were somewhere else when the attempt was made on Mr Searle's life.'

'So where was this attack?' I asked. 'And when?'

The chief inspector looked uncomfortable, as if he didn't particularly like answering questions. No doubt he was more relaxed when asking them.

'Mr Searle was deliberately knocked off his bicycle

on the road outside his home in the village of Baydon in Wiltshire at exactly five minutes past seven this morning. He is currently in a critical condition at the Great Western Hospital in Swindon.'

'And how are you so sure I was somewhere else at five minutes past seven this morning?' I asked.

'Because you were at 45 Seymour Way in Hendon exactly fifty-five minutes later,' he said. 'You were interviewed at that address at precisely eight o'clock by Detective Chief Inspector Tomlinson of the Merseyside Police. There is no way you could have travelled the seventy-two miles from Baydon to Hendon in fifty-five minutes, and especially not at that time of the morning during the rush hour.'

'And why didn't you work this out before I was arrested?' I was beginning to sound rather self-righteous, even to my ears.

'We were simply acting on a request from the Wiltshire force,' he replied, neatly passing the blame elsewhere.

'Well, then they should have checked,' I said, trying to maintain a look of rightful indignation. 'Maybe I'll sue you for wrongful arrest.'

'I think, sir,' he said very formally, 'that you will find that attempted murder is an arrestable offence, and that we had reasonable grounds for an arrest. Just because it turned out that you couldn't have been the perpetrator doesn't give you grounds for claiming false arrest.'

'Hmm,' I said. 'So I am now free to go, just like that?'

'Yes,' he said.

'No questions? No police bail?'

'No, sir,' he replied. 'An alibi is a complete defence. It doesn't mitigate a crime, it proves innocence. So there would be no point in charging or bailing you. However, I am sure that the Wiltshire force will want to ask some questions about your argument with Mr Searle at Cheltenham Races yesterday. No doubt they will be making an appointment in due course. You are free to go home now,' he said. He waved a hand towards the doorway as if trying to encourage me on my way.

I'd had enough of this cell and I didn't need his encouragement to leave it.

The custody sergeant sneered at me as he returned my watch and mobile phone, my tie, belt and shoelaces, and the previous contents of my pockets. He clearly enjoyed booking prisoners in far more than letting them go.

'Sign here,' said the sergeant without any warmth, pointing at a form on the desk.

I signed.

'Thanks for the supper,' I said cheerily.

The sergeant didn't reply.

'Which way out?' I asked, looking around at various doors, none of them with a convenient 'EXIT' sign above it. Perhaps it was designed that way to confuse any escapees.

'That way,' said the sergeant, pointing at one of the doors. He pushed a button on his desk and the lock on the heavy steel door buzzed. I pulled it open and walked out into the police station reception area as the door closed automatically behind me with a loud clunk.

Claudia was waiting there, sitting on an upright tubular-steel chair that was bolted to the floor. She jumped up when she saw me and rushed over, throwing her arms round my neck and hugging me tight. She was crying.

'Oh, Nick,' she sobbed into my neck, 'I've been so frightened.'

'Come on,' I said, hugging her back. 'Let's go home.'

We walked out into the night, hand in hand, and hailed a passing black cab.

'I didn't think you'd be here,' I said to Claudia as we sat down.

'Why ever not?' she said. 'I've been here ever since I found out where they'd taken you. It's been bloody hours.'

'But how did you know I'd been arrested?' The police had allowed me only one call and I'd made that to the company's lawyer, Andrew Mellor.

'Rosemary called me,' Claudia said. 'She was in floods of tears.'

'Rosemary?' I asked.

'You know,' she said. 'Rosemary McDowd. She's such a dear.'

I had worked at Lyall & Black for five years and, for all that time, I'd had no idea that Mrs McDowd's name was Rosemary. The receptionists were always referred to as Mrs McDowd and Mrs Johnson, because that's what they called each other. Only the other staff had first names, Mr Patrick, Mr Gregory, Miss Jessica,

Mr Nicholas and so on, and we were only addressed in that way because, again, that was how the Mesdames McDowd and Johnson did it.

'How did Mrs McDowd have your number?' I asked.

'Oh, we speak quite often.'

'What about?' I asked.

Claudia didn't reply.

'What about?' I repeated.

'You,' she said.

'What about me?' I asked.

'Oh, nothing,' she said evasively.

'No. Come on,' I said. 'Tell me. What about me?'

Claudia sighed. 'I sometimes call her to find out what sort of mood you're in when you leave the office.'

More likely, I thought suspiciously, to check that I was actually in the office, or when I'd left it.

'So what did Mrs McDowd tell you today?' I asked, purposely changing the conversation's direction.

'Between sobs, she told me that you had been arrested by the police for attempted murder. I thought it must be to do with Herb Kovak but she said it was about someone else.'

I nodded. 'Billy Searle was attacked this morning. He was a top jump jockey, and also a client of mine.'

'What the hell's going on?' Claudia said.

That's what I wanted to know.

It had been nearly eleven o'clock by the time I'd been released and I'd asked the taxi driver to go to the newspaper kiosk on the Edgware Road, where I knew they received the early editions of the daily newspapers the night before.

Claudia stayed in the cab as I went to buy copies of all they had, including the *Racing Post*, which arrived in a van as I was paying for the rest.

If its previous day's front-page headline had been vague and set as a question, this one pulled none of its punches:

BILLY SEARLE ATTACKED – FOXTON ARRESTED
FOR ATTEMPTED MURDER

And the article beneath gave no comfort to me either:

Further to our exclusive report in yesterday's Racing Post *concerning a heated argument at Cheltenham Races on Wednesday between top jump jockey Billy Searle and ex-jock turned financial wizard Nicholas (Foxy) Foxton, we can exclusively reveal that Foxton was yesterday arrested for Searle's attempted murder.*

Billy Searle was taken to the Great Western Hospital in Swindon from the scene of an horrific incident in Baydon, near Lambourn, early yesterday morning when it appears he was deliberately knocked from his bicycle. Doctors at the hospital state that Searle's condition is critical with a broken leg and serious head injuries.

Foxton was arrested yesterday at 2.25 p.m. on suspicion of attempted murder at the Lombard Street offices of City financial services firm Lyall and Black,

and he is currently being held for questioning at Pad-
dington Green Police Station.

Remarkably accurate, I thought, except for the bit about currently being held at Paddington Green Police Station, and that had been right until about twenty minutes ago. Beside the article was another picture of Billy Searle, this time all smiles and wearing a business suit, and a photograph of the cordoned-off village of Baydon. Overlaid across the top right-hand corner of this photo was a smaller head-and-shoulders shot of me positioned, to my eye, as if to imply my presence in Baydon High Street.

Gregory was going to have a field day in the morning. It wouldn't just be my head he would have on a stick, it would be my career as well. Who would trust a financial adviser who was on the front page of a national newspaper having been arrested for attempted murder?

Not me, for one.

I climbed back into the cab with the papers and showed the *Racing Post* to Claudia.

'It so bloody unfair,' she said, reading the headline. 'How can they mention your name when you haven't even been charged? You should sue.'

'Over what?' I asked. 'They haven't said anything that wasn't true.'

'But why do the police give out names before they charge someone?'

I suspected that the information had not come from

the police but from a source much closer to home. The time and place of the arrest were too precise, and too accurate. The police would have only said something like 'A twenty-nine-year-old man has been arrested and is helping with our enquiries'.

My money would be on Rory to be the office mole, although what he hoped to gain by it was anyone's idea. He couldn't have my job without passing his IFA exams first, and even I didn't believe he would have murdered Herb for the cubicle close to the window. It would have been Diana's anyway.

I looked at all the newspapers before I went to bed and all of them had front- or back-page reports about the attack on Billy Searle. None of them had the full facts but each still managed to mention me by name and imply my guilt.

Oh, God, I thought, my mother would see them in the morning, and it was far too late to call and warn her now.

I switched on the television and watched the latest news on one of the 24-hour news channels. They had a report live from Baydon.

'It appears,' said the reporter, 'that the jockey Billy Searle was leaving his home to ride his bicycle to Lambourn as he did every morning. He was due to ride horses at morning exercise. He was being waved away by his girlfriend when a car, which had seemingly been waiting in the street, suddenly accelerated into the bicycle, knocking Searle violently to the ground, before being driven away at speed. Billy Searle was taken to hospital in Swindon where he is in a critical but stable condition with head and leg injuries. Police are asking anyone who may have any information concerning the incident to come forward. A man, who we believe to be the ex-jockey Nicholas Foxton, was arrested in connection with the attack but he has since been released without charge.'

'Well at least they said you'd been released,' said Claudia.

'I'd rather they hadn't mentioned my name at all,' I said. 'You watch. Most people will think I'm guilty. They will already have me tried and convicted in their minds. Being released will make little difference. What I need is for the police to catch the real attacker and for him to confess. Even then there will be plenty of people who'll still believe I did it.'

'It's so unfair,' Claudia said again.

Indeed it was, but complaining about it wasn't going to help. I just hoped that they arrested the real culprit soon.

Claudia and I went upstairs to bed but I couldn't sleep. I lay awake in the darkness going over and over everything in my head.

Last Saturday morning my life had been so settled and predictable, and my career path mapped out to success and riches, even if it was a little boring. But the last five days had seen so much change. I had witnessed one murder at close range and been arrested for attempting another; I'd begun to doubt my relationship with Claudia, even suspecting that she might be having an affair with someone else; and I'd gone behind the back of my superior at work to access his personal e-mails to try to determine if he was complicit in a multimillion-pound fraud.

Not to mention becoming the executor and beneficiary of someone that I hardly knew, who then turned out to have a twin sister. And then, to top it all, I'd been propositioned for sex by a woman nearly twenty years older than me, and I'd also discovered the real heartbreaking reason for my parents' unhappy marriage.

It was enough to keep even the most tired of men from sleeping.

I tossed and turned for hours as I mulled over what I should do next, and also over whether I would still have a job to go to in the morning.

I woke late after a restless night, the space in the bed next to me already empty and cold.

I rolled over and looked at my bedside clock. It was gone eight o'clock and I was usually on the Tube by now.

The phone beside the clock started ringing loudly. I decided I didn't want to talk to anyone so I didn't pick it up and eventually it stopped when Claudia answered downstairs.

I turned on the television for the news. Billy Searle's

attempted murder had been downgraded from the top story by a government U-turn on schools' policy, but it still warranted a report from Baydon village, and they still managed to mention me by name and show my picture, in spite of my release.

At this rate the whole bloody world would believe me guilty.

Claudia came into the room. 'It's your mother,' she said.

I picked up the phone. 'Hello, Mum,' I said.

'Darling,' she said. 'What the hell's going on? You're in all the papers and on the TV.' She sounded very upset, as if she was in tears.

'It's all right, Mum,' I said. 'Calm down. I didn't do anything and the police know it. Otherwise they wouldn't have released me. I promise you, all is fine.'

It took me about five minutes to calm my mother down completely. I knew when I'd managed it because she told me to get up and have a good breakfast. Eventually I put the phone down and laid my head back on the pillow.

'Aren't you going to the office today?' Claudia asked, coming back into the bedroom carrying two cups of steaming coffee.

It was an innocent enough question so why did I straight away wonder if she was checking on my movements in order to plan her own?

'I don't know,' I said, taking one of the cups from her. 'What do you think?'

'Things could be worse,' she said. 'You could still be

in that police station, or in court. Let's look on the bright side.'

'What plans do you have?' I asked.

'Nothing much,' she said. 'I might go shopping later.'

'For food?'

'No,' she said. 'I need a new dress for the show next week.'

'Oh,' I said. 'I'd forgotten about that.'

The thought of attending the opening night of a new West End musical with all the associated press coverage did not now fill me with great joy. Claudia and I had accepted an invitation from Jan Setter to join her at the star-studded event, and at the after-show party. I wondered if, after my clumsy brush-off at Cheltenham, Jan would now be so keen for me to be there, to say nothing of my subsequent arrest.

Look on the bright side, Claudia had said. Things could indeed have been worse. I could have still been stuck in that unwelcome cell, or I might have been lying in a Liverpool mortuary refrigerator like Herb, or in a Swindon hospital intensive care bed like Billy. Things could have been a lot worse.

'Right,' I said with determination. 'It's time to show a defiant face to the world. I'm going to get up and go in to work and bugger what anyone thinks. I'm innocent and I'm going to act like it.'

'That's my boy,' said Claudia with a huge grin. 'Bugger the lot of them.'

She lay down on the bed and snuggled up to me, slipping her hand down under the sheets in search of me.

'But do you have to go immediately? Or ...' She grinned again. 'Can you wait a while longer?'

Now I was really confused.

Had I been reading the signals incorrectly?

'Hmm, let me think,' I said, laughing with joy as well as expectation. 'Work or sex? Sex or work? Such difficult decisions.'

Not really.

Sex won – easily.

I didn't go into the office until after lunch but that was not solely due to having fun and games in bed with Claudia. It was because I went to Hendon on the way to check on Sherri and to collect my laptop that I'd left on Herb's desk.

'What happened to you?' she said, opening the door. 'I thought you were coming back yesterday afternoon.'

'I was,' I said. 'But I was detained elsewhere.' I decided not to elaborate. 'What have you been up to?'

'I've started going through Herb's things in his bedroom,' she said. 'I got fed up doing nothing, and it somehow seems to help.'

'Did you find anything of interest?' I asked as I followed her down the corridor to the bedroom.

'Only this,' she replied, picking up something from the bed. 'It was at the back of his wardrobe, hanging on a hook behind his coats.'

She handed me a small blue plastic box with a clip-on lid. Inside the box, all neatly held together by a rubber band, were twenty-two credit cards. I rolled off the band and shuffled through them. As far as I could tell, they matched the statements, right down to the variations in Herb's name.

'Why would anyone have so many credit cards?' Sherri asked. 'And why would they all be in a box hidden in his wardrobe? They all look brand new to me.'

And to me, I thought. Herb hadn't even bothered signing them on the back. These cards had been obtained solely for use on the internet. But I knew that. I'd seen the statements.

Underneath the cards were four pieces of folded-up paper similar to the ones that Chief Inspector Tomlinson had shown me the previous morning. I looked at the lists of numbers and letters. The first columns on each side were definitely dates but they were written in the American way with the month first and then the day so 2/10 was the tenth of February. All the dates on these pieces started 1, 2 or 12, so were from January, February or December.

Sherri was sitting on the floor busily looking through a chest of drawers, lifting out neat piles of T-shirts and stacking them on the bed. I left her and went out of the bedroom, along the corridor and into the living room.

The handwritten lists I had photocopied yesterday were still on the desk next to my computer along with the photocopied bank and credit card statements. The dates on those lists all started with a 3, for March.

I took them back to the bedroom.

On all of the lists, the second and third columns definitely looked like amounts of money. And the fourth column was a list of capital letters, possibly initials. I counted them. There were ninety-seven different sets of letters.

'What are you looking at?' Sherri said.

'I don't know exactly,' I replied. 'Lists of numbers and letters. Have a look.' I handed her the sheets. 'I think the first column on each side are dates and the next two are probably amounts of money.'

'In dollars or pounds?' she asked.

'I don't know,' I said slowly. Was that why, I wondered, the amounts on the credit card statements didn't match the amounts on the sheets. Were one lot in dollars and the other in pounds?

I left Sherri studying the lists while I went back to the desk for the statements and Herb's calculator.

'What's the exchange rate for the US dollar to the pound?' I asked coming back into the bedroom.

'About one-point-six dollars to one pound,' Sherri said. 'At least it was last week but it changes all the time.'

I multiplied some of the amounts on the credit card statements by 1.6 and tried to match the new figure against any on the handwritten lists. It was a hopeless task. I didn't know the exact exchange rate and there were over five hundred different entries on the twenty-two statements. Some of the amounts were close but none were exactly the same. The best I could say was that they might have been related.

'Do you recognize any of the initials on the lists?' I asked Sherri.

'Is that what they are?' she said.

'I don't know, but they look like it.'

She shook her head.

'Did you know that Herb liked to gamble?' I asked.

She looked up at me. 'Of course,' she said. 'Don't all men? Herb had always been one for an occasional flutter on the horses. Just like his father had been. It must be in the genes.'

'Did you know how much he gambled?' I asked.

'Never very much,' she said. 'He may have liked the odd bet but I know he believed that gambling had ruined our childhood. He would never have staked more than he could afford to lose. I'm absolutely sure of that.'

'And how much could he afford to lose?' I asked.

'What are you getting at?' Sherri said.

'Herb gambled a lot on the internet,' I said. 'A huge amount.'

She was shocked. 'Are you sure?'

I nodded. 'He must have spent hours every day gambling on internet betting sites and playing poker on the virtual tables in online casinos. And he lost. He lost big time.'

'I don't believe it,' Sherri said. 'How do you know?'

I held out the photocopies of the credit card statements to her. 'Herb lost more than ninety thousand pounds last month alone. And the same the month before.'

'He can't have done,' she said with a nervous laugh. 'Herb didn't have that sort of money.'

'Look for yourself,' I said, handing her the statements.

She looked at them for a moment but, I could see, she was crying again.

'Do you think that's why he was killed?' she asked.

'I don't know,' I said. But I thought it quite likely.

She cried some more.

'I wish he'd never come to England,' Sherri said sadly. 'Herb wouldn't have been able to gamble like that at home. Internet gambling is illegal in most of the United States.'

So it was.

I remembered reading about the head of an internet gambling website who'd been arrested when he'd arrived at a US airport and charged with racketeering, simply for allowing Americans to gamble on his website, even though it was based in England. It had all been about accepting credit card accounts with a United States address.

I looked again at the handwritten lists of dates, amounts of money and initials. And I pulled from my pocket the MoneyHome payment slips I had found in Herb's office cubicle.

Only last week, according to the torn-up payment slips I'd found in his waste bin, Herb had received three large amounts of cash, two equivalent to five thousand dollars and one to eight thousand.

Suddenly, all of it made complete sense to me.

It hadn't been Herb who had lost ninety thousand pounds last month, it had been the people whose initials were to be found on Herb's lists, the ninety-seven people who were responsible for the five hundred and twelve different entries on the credit card accounts. And I'd like to bet they were all Americans.

If I was right, Herb had been running a system to provide ninety-seven Americans with a UK-based credit card account in order for them to gamble and play poker on internet betting and casino sites.

But why would that have got him murdered?

8

To say my arrival at the offices of Lyall & Black about an hour after lunch caused a bit of a stir would be an understatement.

'Get out of these offices,' Gregory shouted at me almost as soon as I walked through the door on the fourth floor into the reception area, and he wasn't finished then. 'You are a disgrace to your profession and to this firm. I will not have you here contaminating the other staff.'

I had made the mistake of not sneaking in while he was at lunch.

Mrs McDowd looked positively frightened by the outburst. I probably did as well.

'Gregory,' I tried to say, but he advanced towards me bunching his fists. Surely, I thought, he's not going to hit me. He didn't, but he grabbed me by the sleeve of my suit and dragged me towards the door.

He was surprisingly strong and fit for someone whose only workout was the walk to and from the restaurant on the corner.

'Leave me alone,' I shouted at him. But he took no notice.

'Gregory. Stop it!' Patrick's deep voice reverberated round the reception area.

Gregory stopped pulling and let go of my sleeve.

'I will not have this man in these offices,' Gregory said. 'He has brought the firm of Lyall and Black into disrepute.'

Patrick looked at the reception desk, and at Mrs McDowd and Mrs Johnson who were sitting behind it.

'Let us discuss this in your office,' Patrick said calmly. 'Nicholas, will you please wait here.'

'Outside the door,' Gregory said, pointing towards the lifts and not moving an inch towards his office.

I stood there looking back and forth between them. Everyone in the firm knew of Gregory's temper, it was legendary, but I had rarely seen it laid bare and so raw, and at such close quarters.

'I will go out for a coffee,' I said. 'I'll be back in twenty minutes.'

'Best to go home,' Patrick said. 'I'll call you later.'

Gregory turned towards Patrick. 'I told you that we should never have taken him on in the first place.'

'In your office, please, Gregory!' Patrick said, almost shouting. He had a pretty good temper in him, too, although it was usually slow to rise.

I waited while Gregory reluctantly moved off down the corridor with Patrick. I would have adored being a fly on the wall during their discussion.

'You had better go,' said Mrs McDowd firmly. 'I don't want you upsetting Mr Gregory any more. His heart can't take it.'

I looked at her. Mrs McDowd, who saw it as her business to know everything about everyone in the firm. She probably knew Gregory's blood pressure, and his heart surgeon.

'Tell me, Mrs McDowd, do you think Herb gambled much?'

'You mean on the stock market?' she asked.

'On the horses.'

'Oh, no,' she said. 'Mr Herb didn't like betting on the horses. Too risky, he said. So much better to bet on a certainty, that's what he always told me.'

Death was a certainty.

Benjamin Franklin had said so: death – and taxes.

I did go home, but not immediately.

Before I left Hendon I had looked up the locations of MoneyHome agents near to Lombard Street. I was amazed at how many there were, at least thirty within a one-mile radius of my office, the nearest being just round the corner in King William Street.

'This didn't come from here,' said the lady sitting behind a glass screen. 'It hasn't got our stamp on it.'

I had somehow expected the MoneyHome agency to be like a bank, or a money exchange, but this one was right at the back of a convenience store.

'Can you tell me where it did come from?' I asked the lady.

'Don't you know?' she asked.

'No,' I said with declining patience. 'I wouldn't have asked if I knew.'

She looked at me through the glass, then down at

the payment slip. I had brought with me one of those I had found in Herb's desk rather than the torn-up squares, which were still at Herb's flat anyway.

'Sorry,' she said. 'I don't recognize the stamp. But I know it's not ours.'

'Can you tell who sent the money?' I asked.

'No,' she said.

'What do you need to produce in the way of identification to collect money from a MoneyHome transfer?'

'The recipient's name and the MTCN.'

'What's that?'

'There,' she said pointing at the payment slip. 'It's the Money Transfer Control Number.'

'And that's all you need to collect the money,' I said. 'No passport or driving licence?'

'Not unless it's been specially requested by the sender,' she said. 'Sometimes there's a question I have to ask and then you'd have to give the right answer. It's a bit like spies and such.' She smiled.

'So, in fact,' I said, 'you have no way of knowing who has sent the money, or who has collected it?'

'The recipient's name is on the slip.'

The recipient's name on the slip I had shown her was Butch Cassidy. The names on the others I had were Billy Kid, Wyatt Earp, Jessie James and Bill Cody.

'That isn't his real name,' I said.

'No,' she said, looking. 'I suppose not. But it's their money. As long as they've paid us our fee, it's not our business who they really are.'

'Does the amount make any difference?' I asked.

'MoneyHome's head office doesn't allow us to accept transfers of more than the equivalent of ten thousand US dollars as that breaks the money-laundering rules. Other than that, the amount doesn't matter, although we here have a payout limit of four thousand pounds without prior notice. You know, so we can get in the cash.'

'Are your transfers always in cash?' I asked.

'Yeah, of course,' she said. 'That's what we do. Cash transfers. Lots of the immigrant workers round here send cash home to their wives. Poles mostly. And we do a special deal on transfers to Poland, up to a thousand pounds for just twenty quid.'

Overall, it wasn't very helpful. Herb had clearly set up a system that would be difficult, if not impossible, to unravel. From what I could tell from the lists and the MoneyHome payment slips, it was clear that he'd received large sums of cash from multiple sources, money he must have then used to pay the monthly balances on the twenty-two credit cards.

Herb had collected eighteen thousand dollars' worth of pounds sterling only the previous week, five thousand of it just the day before his death. Some of that cash must still be hidden somewhere.

My problem was that, while I had the statements showing the ninety-four thousand pounds outstanding and, as his executor and beneficiary, I was liable for the debt, I hadn't yet found the stash of readies to pay it.

*

Claudia wasn't at home when I arrived back at three thirty. I tried her mobile but it went straight to voicemail.

I wandered round the house wondering what had gone wrong with our relationship.

I didn't really understand it. The sex that morning had been as good as ever but Claudia had been uncharacteristically quiet during, and afterwards, as if her mind had been elsewhere.

I asked myself what I really wanted. Did I want to continue or was it time to draw a line, and move on? Did I love her enough? How much would I miss her if she left?

Claudia and I had been together now for almost six years. I was twenty-nine, and she was three years my junior. Apart from my real concern about her weird paintings, I found the set-up comfortable and fulfilling. And I was happy as things were.

Was that the trouble? Did Claudia want something more from our relationship than I did? Did she perhaps now want that ring on her finger? Or maybe she had changed her view about children? But then surely she would have told me. I would have been delighted.

So, I concluded, it had to be me that was the problem. Claudia must have tired of me, and perhaps there was someone else already lined up to take my place. It was the only conclusion that made any sense.

I tried her mobile again but, as before, it went straight to voicemail.

The house suddenly felt very empty and I realized

that I was lonely without Claudia here. I wandered round looking at familiar things as if it was the first time I had seen them.

I went up to Claudia's studio and looked at the painting she was working on and also at two or three others leaned against the wall waiting for the paint to dry and harden.

As always, they were dark and, to my eye, somewhat disturbed. One of them was full of bizarre flying monsters with bird-like bodies and human heads, each head with a huge open mouth full of fearsome-looking pointed teeth.

I shuddered and covered the image with another painting, this one of several identical and very beautiful women all dressed in blue ball gowns. A pretty enough sight one might think, except these women had feet that were, in fact, eagle claws ripping apart the naked body of the man on whom they were standing.

Was the man meant to be me? And were the women all representations of Claudia herself? Was this how our relationship would end, with Claudia ripping me apart? I doubted it would happen quite so literally as in the picture, but emotionally, she had me half-way to the funny farm already.

Once again I asked myself how such a sweet girl could paint such strange images. And I was sure they had become more bizarre and much more violent in recent months. Was there a whole side to Claudia's character that I remained totally unaware of? But, on the whole, I believed that it was better for her to find an outlet for such strange thoughts than to keep them bottled up inside her head, with the pressure ever building towards explosive levels.

The house phone rang and I went through to our bedroom to answer it, hoping it would be Claudia.

It wasn't. It was Patrick.

'I'm sorry for Gregory's outburst earlier,' he said. 'He and I had a discussion, and he's now calmed down a lot. He was just upset by what had been written in the papers.'

Not as upset as me, I thought.

'So can I come back into the office?' I asked.

'Not today,' he said rather too quickly. 'Maybe on Monday, or later next week. Let the dust settle for a few days.'

'I'll work from home, then,' I said, 'using the remote-access facility.'

'Right,' Patrick said slowly. 'But I agreed with Gregory that you would not be representing the firm for the immediate future.'

'And how long exactly is the immediate future?' I asked.

'Until he and I agree,' he said.

'Are you telling me I'm fired?'

'No, of course not,' he said. 'Just that it might be better for you to take some paid holiday until the police sort out who really did try to murder Billy Searle.'

'What if they never do?' I asked.

'Let's hope that is not the case,' he said. 'I'll call you next week. In the meantime I must ask you not to use the remote-access facility, and not to contact anyone at the firm.'

Patrick disconnected without saying goodbye, no doubt pleased to have got through the conversation without me shouting at him.

I felt like shouting at someone. Everything that had been fine just a week ago was suddenly going down the tubes. I sat down on the edge of the bed feeling more miserable than I had since the day I had been told I couldn't ride again.

I decided that feeling sorry for myself wasn't going to achieve anything, so I went downstairs and sat down at the kitchen table with my laptop computer.

I spent a fairly unproductive half hour looking at the six e-mails that I had forwarded to my inbox from Gregory's, concerning the Bulgarian property development.

They were all from the same man, Uri Joram, and the first two were about the grants available to disadvantaged parts of the European Union for industrial developments that would assist in the regeneration of sites previously occupied by state-subsidized factories. Many such factories had quickly gone bust when the communist regime had collapsed and free-market competition had arrived in its place.

As far as I could make out from Mr Joram's rather poor grasp of written English, the EU money would only be forthcoming if there was some private investment in the project on the basis that two euros would be granted for each one euro invested privately. Jolyon Roberts had told me that his family trust had invested five million pounds so that alone could have attracted a further ten million from the European tax coffers.

But that was not all, not by a long way.

The four remaining e-mails were about funding for the homes to be constructed close to the factory to house the workers. This was to come from a different source, the EU Social Housing Fund, and required no similar two-for-one arrangement. It appeared that the new factory alone was sufficient to trigger the hundred per cent grant for the housing, which was in the region of eighty million euros.

If, as Jolyon Roberts's nephew had implied, no houses and no factory had been built in Bulgaria, then someone somewhere had likely pocketed nearly a hundred million euros, most of it public money.

I looked closely at the e-mail addresses. The e-mails had been sent by uri_joram@ec.europa.eu to dimitar .petrov@bsnet.co.bg with Gregory Black being copied in. The ec.europa.eu domain indicated that Uri Joram worked in the offices of the European Commission, probably in Brussels, and I could deduce that Mr Petrov must be in Bulgaria from the .bg extension.

It wasn't a huge help.

I also looked at the telephone number I had copied from the Roberts Family Trust file on Gregory's computer. I wondered if I should call it. But what good would it do? I couldn't speak Bulgarian and, even if whoever answered could understand English, they were most unlikely to give me any information that would answer my questions.

What should I do?

It may very well have been a simple mistake made by Mr Roberts's nephew. He might have gone to the wrong place in Bulgaria, with the factory and the houses existing elsewhere. Surely there would have been checks made by the European Union officials running the EU Social Housing Fund to confirm that their eighty million euros had been spent properly on bricks and mortar.

I decided that, having been asked by Jolyon Roberts to look into it, I couldn't just do nothing so I sent a short e-mail to Dimitar Petrov asking him to send me the names and addresses of the directors of the Balscott Lighting Factory, if he had them.

By the time I realized that sending the e-mail was possibly not such a good idea if Mr Petrov himself was one of those involved in the potential hundred-million-euro fraud, it was well on its way and there was no bringing it back.

It couldn't do any harm, could it?

I closed my computer and looked at the clock. It was a quarter to five so I made myself a cup of tea.

I couldn't help but notice that Claudia had left her latest mobile phone bill lying on the worktop right next to the kettle. And I also couldn't resist the temptation to look at it.

I suppose I was looking for numbers I didn't recognize that she had called regularly. There was one, with calls almost every day for the past two weeks, and often more than once a day.

Now what did I do? Did I call the number and demand to know who had been talking so often to my girl? No, of course I didn't. But I copied the number into my mobile phone, just in case I changed my mind.

Claudia arrived home at five thirty and I resisted the temptation to ask her where she had been, and why her phone had been switched off.

'Why aren't you at the office?' she asked.

'Patrick sent me home,' I said. 'Gregory seems to think I've brought the company into disrepute. Patrick thinks it would be best for me to have some time off, to stay away from the office, just to let the dust settle.'

'But that's ridiculous,' she said. 'The police let you go. You have a cast-iron alibi.'

'I know that, and you know that,' I replied crossly. 'But you know what most people are like, they believe what they read.'

'Those bloody newspapers,' she said with feeling. 'They shouldn't be allowed to give out people's names before they're charged.'

Or even convicted, I thought. But I also knew the police were secretly quite keen for the names of those accused to be released early so that potential witnesses would come forward.

'Patrick says it will all blow over in a few days,' I said. 'He thinks people will forget.'

'I hope he's right,' she said.

So did I.

'Did you get your dress?' I asked.

'What dress?' she said.

'Come on, darling,' I said, slightly irritated. 'You know. The one you were going to buy for the opening night on Wednesday.'

'Oh, that,' she said, clearly distracted. 'Perhaps I'll go tomorrow. Something came up this afternoon.'

I didn't like to think what, so I didn't ask.

'How long did Patrick say you had to stay away from the office?' Claudia asked into the silence.

'Maybe a week,' I said, wondering if she was asking for reasons other than worries over my reputation and career. 'Perhaps I'll go to the races instead.'

'Great idea,' she said. 'Give your mind a rest from all those figures.'

Perhaps it was time to start looking at figures of a different kind.

9

On Saturday afternoon I put on my thick skin and went to Sandown Park Races on the train from Waterloo.

'Bloody hell,' said Jan Setter. 'I didn't expect to see you here. I thought you'd been sent to the Tower.'

'Not quite,' I said.

I was standing on the grass close to the parade ring, near the statue of the horse Special Cargo.

'Did you do it?' Jan asked in all seriousness.

'No, of course I didn't,' I said. 'The police wouldn't have let me go if they still thought I'd tried to kill Billy. I have an alibi.'

'Then who did do it?'

'I don't know,' I said. 'But it wasn't me.'

'Blimey,' she said. 'Then there's still a would-be murderer out there on the loose.'

'Lots of them,' I said. 'Not just Billy's but Herb Kovak's too.'

'Who's Herb Kovak?' she asked.

'Chap who was shot at Aintree last Saturday,' I said. 'He was a colleague of mine at work.'

'Did you kill him, then?'

'Jan,' I said forcefully, 'I didn't kill anyone, or try to. OK?'

'Then why were you arrested?'

I sighed. People, even good friends, really did believe what they read in the papers.

'Someone told the police that Billy had shouted at me at Cheltenham demanding to know why I was going to murder him. They put two and two together and made five. That's all. They got it wrong.'

'So why did Billy shout at you?'

'It was to do with his investments,' I said.

Jan raised a questioning eyebrow.

'It's confidential,' I said. 'You wouldn't want me telling everyone about your investments, now would you?'

'No,' she agreed. 'But then I haven't been deliberately knocked off my bike.'

'That's a fair point, but confidentiality rules still apply,' I said. 'Severely injured or not, he's still my client.'

Mind you, I thought, there was a limit to confidentiality.

The Wiltshire Police had called me on Friday evening to make an appointment, and I had spent time with two of their number earlier, going over in minute detail all the events of Tuesday and Wednesday at Cheltenham Races with particular reference to Billy Searle's investments.

'Was it true that you owe Mr Searle over a hundred thousand pounds?' one of them had asked me as his opening shot.

'No,' I'd replied calmly. 'Not personally. I'm a financial adviser and Billy Searle is a client of mine, which means I manage the investment of his money. In total, he has about a hundred and fifty thousand invested through me and he told me on Tuesday that he urgently wanted all his money out in cash. He became very distressed and angry when I told him it would take a few days to realize the cash through the sale of his stocks and shares.'

'Why do you think Mr Searle needed such a large sum so quickly?' the other policeman had asked.

'He told me he owed some guy a hundred thousand and he needed to pay it back by Wednesday night at the very latest, or else.'

'Or else what?' they'd both asked in unison.

'Billy seemed frightened and, when I told him that his money wouldn't be in his bank until Friday, he said he hoped he would still alive by Friday.'

'Those were his exact words?'

'Pretty much,' I'd said.

'Did he give you any indication who this guy was?'

'None, but he was clearly terrified of him. Why don't you ask Billy?'

'Mr Searle is in a critical condition,' one of them had replied. 'He has severe head injuries and it is far from certain yet whether he will ever recover consciousness.'

How dreadful, I thought. Billy had survived all those racing falls over all those years, only to have head injuries due to someone knocking him off his bike. It didn't seem fair.

'I wouldn't have thought that knocking someone off their bicycle was a very sure way of killing them,' I'd said. 'How would someone know he would be riding his bike at that time?'

'Mr Searle rode his bicycle to Lambourn every day at the same time. Apparently it was part of his fitness regime, and well known. And the car seems to have struck him with considerable force.'

'Yes, but even so, it is not as certain as a shooting.' I had been thinking of Herb the previous Saturday. 'Are you sure it was attempted murder?'

'We are treating the attack as attempted murder,' one of them had replied rather unhelpfully.

Yes, I'd thought, but that didn't necessarily make it so.

'Can we go back to this man to whom Mr Searle owed money? Are you sure that Mr Searle gave you no indication who it was?'

'Positive,' I'd said. 'All Billy told me was that he owed the money to some guy.'

But why would you try to kill someone because they owed you money? Then there would be no chance of getting it back. Maybe the attack had been meant as a warning, or a reminder to pay up, and had simply gone too far. Or had it been a message to others: pay up or else – just as Billy had been afraid of.

'The *Racing Post* seems to have implied it was a bookmaker.'

'I think that was probably speculation on their part,' I'd said. 'Billy never mentioned anything like that to me. In fact he said that he couldn't tell me why he owed the money.'

'So why did he claim that it was you who was murdering him?'

'I now realize that he must have believed he might

be murdered because I couldn't get his money together by Wednesday night, and it would therefore be my fault if he was killed. But, obviously, I didn't think that at the time.'

The two policemen had then effectively asked me the same questions over and over again in slightly different ways, and I had answered them each time identically, with patience and good grace.

Eventually, after more than an hour, they had been satisfied that I had nothing else to tell them and had gone away, but not before they'd had a close inspection of my car to see if there were any dents or scratches caused by Billy Searle's bicycle. So much for my alibi.

As soon as they had gone, I had rushed away from home, just making it to Sandown in time for the first race. I'd had to endure a few stares on my way into the racecourse, together with a few indelicate and abusive comments but, even so, it felt good to be in a familiar environment, as well as free in the fresh air.

It would have been better still if I'd been riding.

'Do you have any runners today?' I asked Jan. At least I could be certain that, this time, she hadn't come to the races just to see me.

'One in the big chase,' she said. 'Ed's Charger. Not much chance but the owner insisted.' She rolled her eyes up into her head and I laughed. 'Still got your sense of humour, then?'

'Why shouldn't I have?' I asked.

'Seems everyone you talk to gets themselves murdered or attacked. I hope it doesn't happen to me.'

So did I. She might have indeed been just about old enough to be my mother, but she was still a very attractive woman. Had I been a tad too hasty, I wondered, in turning down her offer?

Jan went into the Weighing Room to find the jockey who was riding her horse, while I leaned on the rail of the paddock and looked up Ed's Charger in the racecard. I noticed it was to be ridden by Mark Vickers, my client, and now, with Billy Searle out of the running, the Champion Jockey in waiting.

Billy's attempted murder had certainly been convenient for Mark's championship ambitions but I didn't really believe that the attack in Baydon had been arranged for that purpose. True, there had been the infamous incident when one Olympic ice skater had allegedly arranged for the leg of her rival to be broken, so as to better her own chances, but attempted murder was surely a step too far, if indeed that was what it had been. And there was the unanswered question of the hundred thousand pounds and, in particular, to whom it had been owed by Billy, and why.

'Hi, Foxy. Penny for your thoughts?' said a voice behind me and I groaned inwardly. Martin Gifford was the last person I wanted to see.

I turned round and forced a smile at him. 'Just working on my next murder,' I said. 'Do you fancy being the victim?'

Martin looked really worried for a fraction of a second before he realized I was joking.

'Very funny,' he said, regaining his composure. 'Tell me, what was it like being arrested?'

'A laugh a minute,' I said. 'And you didn't bloody help by telling the *Post* you thought I knew more about the Aintree killing than I was letting on. And why did you tell them that Herb Kovak was my best friend when I specifically told you he was only a work colleague?'

'I only told them what I believed to be true,' he said self-righteously.

'Bastard,' I said. 'You made it all up, and you know it.'

'Now, come on, Foxy,' he said. 'You weren't being completely honest with me. The truth, remember, the whole truth and nothing but the truth.'

'Bollocks,' I said forcefully. 'We were not in court, and what makes you think you have a divine right to know everything about everybody, anyway? You're the most indiscreet man on a racecourse. You couldn't keep a secret if your life depended in it.'

I knew as soon as I'd said it that it had been a mistake. Martin Gifford was all I'd said he was, but he was also the sort of person one needed to keep on one's side, and I'd probably just lost him as an ally for ever. But I didn't care. I'd had my fill of him over the years, and I looked forward to him not coming up every time he saw me and offering me a penny for my thoughts.

'Well, if that's what you think,' he said haughtily, 'you can bugger off.' And, with that, he turned and walked away with his nose held high. It had been a fairly weak riposte but no less accurate for that.

Jan came back out of the Weighing Room and over the grass to where I was standing. I watched her walk towards me with slightly renewed interest. She saw me looking at her and wiggled her hips.

'Changed your mind, then, lover-boy?' she said quietly as she came up close to me.

'No,' I said. But had I?

'Pity,' she replied. 'Are you sure you won't come over to my place for a ride?'

'I told you I couldn't. I can't take the chance with my neck.'

'Not that sort of ride, silly.' She smiled. 'I'd give you a ride where it wouldn't be your neck that would have to take its chances.' She leaned forward suggestively over the paddock rail, rubbing her bottom up against my leg.

'Jan, behave yourself!' I said.

'Why should I?' she asked, laughing. 'I'm a rich divorcée remember. By definition we're not meant to behave ourselves. Fancy a fuck?'

'Jan!' I said. 'Please stop it.'

'My,' she said, abruptly standing bolt upright next to me. 'I do believe you're embarrassed. What an old-fashioned strange boy you are.'

I was certainly old fashioned, but was I really strange?

Maybe I was, but did that mean I wanted Jan as a lover?

No, I suddenly decided, it did not.

I wanted Claudia.

My real reason for coming to Sandown had been to see Jolyon Roberts.

According to the morning paper, one of the horses running in the third race was owned by Viscount Shenington, and I hoped it was one of those he co-owned with his brother.

I looked out for Colonel Roberts on the grandstand during the first and second races but, unsurprisingly, I couldn't see him. The fine weather had helped to bring out a good Saturday crowd at Sandown for one of the very few mixed meetings of the year, that is where both flat and jumping contests were scheduled side-by-side on the eight-race card. Indeed, the first race of the day was a special one-mile flat race where jockeys from both codes raced against each other in a sort of Flat versus Jumping championship.

I went down to the parade ring before the third race and, sure enough, Jolyon Roberts was there, standing on the grass in the centre with a group of three other men and two ladies, none of whom I recognized.

I manoeuvred myself next to a gap in the rails through which I assumed the Roberts party would eventually need to pass, and waited.

He saw me when he was about five strides away and, if he was shocked or surprised, he didn't show it.

However, I did detect a very slight shake of the head as he looked me square in the eye.

As a true gentleman he stepped to the side to allow the others in his party to pass through the exit first.

'Chasers Bar after the sixth,' Jolyon Roberts said quietly but distinctly, and straight at me as he went through the gap, not breaking his Guard's step. I stood still and watched as he caught up one of the ladies and took her arm. He didn't look back at me. His words may have been softly spoken but his message had been crystal clear – 'Don't stop me now, I'll speak with you later, in private.'

I was in the Chasers Bar well ahead of him. In fact I watched the sixth race on one of the wall-mounted television sets so as to ensure I could get a table discreetly situated in the corner furthest from the door, and away from the bar.

I sat watching the entrance with two glasses of wine in front of me, one red and one white.

Jolyon Roberts appeared, stopped briefly to look around, then strode purposefully over and sat down opposite me.

'Sorry about this, sir,' I said. 'But I had no other way of contacting you.'

'What do you have to tell me?' he said.

'Drink?' I asked, indicating the wine.

'No thank you,' he said. 'I don't. Never have.'

'Something soft?' I asked.

'No, nothing, thank you.'

'What a shame about your horse,' I said.

It had fallen at the second hurdle and broken a leg.

'These things happen,' he said. 'My wife was more upset about it than me. To be honest it solved the problem of what to do with the damn thing. It couldn't have won the race if it'd started yesterday.' He chuckled loudly at his own joke, a habit I found slightly irritating. 'Now, tell me what you've found.'

'Nothing much, I'm afraid,' I said, taking a large sip of the white wine. 'Except that, if it is a fraud, it's a much bigger fraud than either of us thought.'

'In what way?' he asked.

'The factory project would seem to be only the key to a much bigger enterprise,' I said. 'The factory was to have cost about twenty million euros with your family trust putting in just over six million and getting European Union funding at the rate of two euros for each one of yours.'

He nodded. 'That's right,' he said. 'It was about five million pounds.'

'Yes,' I said. 'But it was the funding of the factory that triggered the grant for the housing project. And that was a whopping eighty million euros, without the need for any further private finance. So it was your investment that was the key to it all.' I paused. 'How did you hear about the investment opportunity in the first place?'

'I can't really remember,' he said. 'But it must have been through Gregory Black. Almost everything the trust invests in, other than the family estate, is done through Lyall and Black.'

'So was the naming of the factory Gregory Black's idea?'

'Oh, I can't remember,' he said. 'What does it matter? The important thing is whether or not the factory exists. That's what I'm most concerned about.'

'I haven't yet managed to find that out. Is there any chance I could speak with your nephew?'

Mr Roberts looked doubtful.

'I'd just like to ask him where he went and what he saw, or not as the case may be.'

'He's up at Oxford,' he said.

'Oxford University?' I asked.

Jolyon Roberts nodded. 'At Keble. Reading PPE. Thinks he wants to change the world. Bit full of himself, if you ask me.'

PPE was philosophy, politics and economics. I'd thought of applying for it myself but had opted instead for a degree course at the LSE.

PPE at Oxford was often seen as the first step on the political ladder to real power, both in British and foreign governments, and elsewhere. Alumni included such diverse members as three UK Prime Ministers, including David Cameron, the Nobel Peace Prize winning Burmese pro-democracy campaigner Aung San Suu Kyi, the media tycoon Rupert Murdoch, and the convicted IRA bomber Rose Dugdale. Even Bill Clinton had studied with the Oxford PPE class for a while when he was at the university as a Rhodes Scholar.

If Jolyon Roberts's nephew wanted to change the world he was starting at the right place.

'Do you have a telephone number for him?' I asked.

Jolyon Roberts seemed rather hesitant. 'Look,' he said, 'I'd much rather he wasn't involved.'

'But, sir,' I said, 'he is involved. You told me he was the one who started your concerns in the first place by visiting Bulgaria.'

'Yes,' he said, 'but my brother, his father, has told him to forget it.'

'Does your brother have any idea you have spoken to me?'

'Good God, no,' replied Mr Roberts. 'He'd be furious.'

'Sir,' I said formally, 'I think it might be best if I left you to sort out any further questions you might have with Gregory himself. I have rather gone out on a limb here to find out the small amount I have but I think it's time to stop. The Roberts Family Trust is our client in this matter and your brother is the senior trustee. I really should not act behind his back.' Nor behind Gregory's, I thought.

'No,' he said. 'Quite right. I can see that.' He paused. 'Sorry. Should have realized. I'll give Gregory Black a call about it on Monday.' He paused again. 'Right, matter closed as far as you're concerned. I'll trouble you no further.' He stood up, nodded at me briefly and walked out of the bar.

I sat there for a while longer and transferred my allegiance from white wine to red.

Had I done the right thing?

Definitely.

I was a financial adviser not a fraud investigator.

But what if there really was a hundred-million-euro fraud going on? Had I not a responsibility to report it to someone? But to whom? Perhaps I should send an e-mail to Uri Joram at the European Commission. But did I care?

I finished the red wine and decided it was time to head home.

Going home to Claudia had always filled me with excitement, raising the pulse a fraction and causing things to stir down below. But now, I was hesitant, even frightened of what I might find, of what I might hear, of what I might see.

Claudia was at home when I arrived back, and she'd been crying.

She tried to hide it from me but I could always tell. The slight redness of the eyes and the streaky mascara were dead giveaways.

'You could have phoned me,' she said crossly as I walked into the kitchen. 'You should know better than to sneak up on a girl.'

I'd hardly sneaked up, I thought. This was my home and I was arriving back from the races at six thirty on a Saturday evening.

'You can't phone on the Tube,' I said.

'You could have phoned on the train from Sandown.'

That was true, but the reason I hadn't was because I didn't want my call to go straight to voicemail again. That alone sent my imagination into overdrive. It was much better not to know if Claudia's phone was turned off.

'Now, darling, what's the matter?' I said, putting an arm round her shoulders.

'Nothing,' she said, shrugging me off. 'Just my back hurts. I'm going up to have a bath.'

She walked briskly out of the kitchen leaving me standing there alone. She had complained of backache a lot recently. Probably from too much lying on it, I thought somewhat ungraciously.

I mixed myself a large, strong gin and tonic. Not really a great idea after two glasses of wine at Sandown, but, who cares, I wasn't trying to make a riding weight for the next day's racing, more's the pity.

I could hear her bath running upstairs and, quite suddenly, I was cross. Did she think I was a fool? Something was definitely not right in this household and, painful as it might be, I had a right to know.

I thought about charging upstairs and confronting her in the bathroom, but I was frightened. I didn't want to lose her. And I'm not sure I could bear it if she said she was leaving me for someone else.

I walked through into the sitting room and flicked on the television but I didn't watch it. Instead I sat in an armchair feeling miserable, and drank my gin.

In due course, I heard the bathwater drain away and, presently, Claudia came downstairs and went into the kitchen, closing the door.

I really didn't know what to do. Did she want me to go in to her or not? Not, I thought, or she would have left the door open.

I stayed where I was in the sitting room and finished my drink. According to the clock on the mantelpiece it was twenty past seven.

Was it too early to go to bed?

I sat in the armchair while some teenage stick insect warbled away on the screen in a TV talent show, going over and over in my head what I needed to say to Claudia. Doing nothing was no longer an option.

If our relationship was dead, so be it. Let me mourn. Anything was better than remaining in this state of limbo with my imagination running wild, and my emotions in turmoil. I loved Claudia, I was sure of it. But, here I was, angry and hurt, accusing her in my mind of deceiving me and sleeping with another. It was time for the truth.

When I walked into the kitchen she was crying openly and with no pretence this time that she wasn't. She was sitting at the kitchen table in her blue towelling dressing gown, her elbows on the table, a glass of white wine in one hand and her head in the other. She didn't look up as I went in.

At least, I thought, she's not leaving me with a dismissive wave of the hand and not a single glance back. This break-up was going to be painful for both of us.

I went over to the worktop beside the fridge and poured myself another stiff gin and tonic. I was going to need it.

'Darling, what's the matter?' I said, but without turning round.

Perhaps it would be easier for her to talk if she couldn't see my face.

'Oh, Nick,' she said, her voice quivering slightly. 'There's something I have to tell you.' She gulped. 'And you're not going to like it.'

I turned round to face her. Maybe I didn't want to make it too easy for her after all.

She looked up at me.

'I'm so sorry,' she said.

I could feel the tears welling up in my own eyes. All I wanted to do was to hug her.

'I'm so sorry,' she said again. 'I've got cancer.'

10

How could I have been so wrong? And so stupid?

'What?' I said.

'Cancer,' she repeated. 'I've got ovarian cancer.'

'How?' I said foolishly. 'I mean . . . when?'

'I've sort of known for about two weeks, but I found out for certain on Thursday.'

'So why didn't you tell me?' I asked.

'I was going to but, to start with you were so busy at work. Then I was going to tell you on the night of the Grand National but there was all that Herb Kovak business. I thought you had enough of your own troubles. Then on Thursday . . .' She gulped. 'Thursday was an awful day. When I left the hospital after the doctor confirmed everything, I was sort of numb, couldn't feel anything, didn't even know where I was going.' She paused and wiped a tear from her cheek with the sleeve of her dressing gown. 'It was while I was walking aimlessly down Tottenham Court Road that Rosemary called to tell me you'd been arrested. It was all dreadful. Then you were so angry at having your name in the papers that, somehow, I couldn't tell you that night and . . . well, yesterday seemed so fraught between us and I thought it best to leave it because you had so much else on.'

'You silly gorgeous girl,' I said. 'Nothing is more important to me than you.'

I went round behind her and put my hands on her shoulders and rubbed them.

'So what do we do now?' I asked.

'I've got to have an operation on Tuesday.'

'Oh,' I said. Suddenly this was very real, and very urgent. 'What are they going to do?'

'Remove my left ovary,' she said, choking back more tears. 'And they might have to remove them both. Then I'll never be able to have a baby.'

Oh, I thought. Too real, and too urgent.

'And I know how much you want to have children,' Claudia said. 'I'm so sorry.'

The tears flowed freely again.

'Now, now,' I said, stroking her back. 'Your current health is far more important than any future children. You always said children were troublesome anyway.'

'I've been desperate,' she said. 'I thought you'd be so cross.'

'Don't be so silly. The only thing I'm cross about is that you didn't tell me straight away. It must have been dreadful for you, bottling it all up with no one to talk to.'

'My doctor has been wonderful,' she said. 'He gave me the name of a cancer counsellor.' She produced a crumpled business card from the pocket of her dressing gown. 'And she's been an absolute rock. I've called her so many times now, I know her number by heart.'

I looked at the business card. The number was the

much-called one I had copied from her mobile phone bill.

How, I asked myself again, could I have got things so wrong?

'Tell me,' I said. 'What did the doctor say?'

'I first went to my GP because I didn't feel very well and I could feel that my tummy was bloated.' She smiled. 'I actually thought I might be pregnant, but I'm on the pill, and I'd just had my period.'

'And?' I prompted.

'He asked me if I had any back pain, and I said yes, so he sent me to see a cancer specialist who did some scans and other tests and they came back positive.'

Back pain.

I inwardly chastised myself for my earlier thoughts.

'So what is actually wrong with your ovaries?' I asked.

'I have a tumour in the left one,' she said. 'It's what is apparently called a germ cell tumour.'

'Is it malignant?' I asked, dreading the answer.

'Yes, I'm afraid it is,' she said. 'But it's fairly small, about the size of a peanut.'

That didn't sound that small to me. I thought whole ovaries themselves were not much bigger than that.

'And the oncologist is hopeful that it hasn't spread. But he will find out for sure about that on Tuesday.'

'Where are you having the op?' I asked.

'University College Hospital,' she said. 'It's where I've been seeing the oncologist and having tests all this last week. I was there most of the day yesterday having

MRI scans so they know exactly to the millimetre where the cancer is and how big, ready for the operation.'

With her phone turned off.

'Overall, I've been lucky they found it so soon. Apparently it's quite usual for such tumours to go undetected until it's too late because many GPs dismiss the symptoms or confuse them with other problems.'

'What can I do to help?' I asked.

'Nothing,' she said. 'Just be here.' She smiled. 'I love you so much.'

I felt a fool, and a charlatan. How could I have been so stupid?

'I love you so much more,' I said, kissing the top of her head. 'Do you need to go to bed?'

'I'm not feeling ill,' she said, turning and looking up at me with a smile. 'Or were you thinking of something else?'

I blushed. It must have been the gin.

'I wasn't,' I said. 'However, I could be persuaded. But, I mean, are you all right?'

'For sex?' she said. I nodded. 'Absolutely. The oncologist told me on Thursday that it wouldn't make any difference.'

It made a difference to me.

I lay awake in the dark of the small hours trying to get my head round this new problem.

I had feared so much the thought of losing her to

another man that the news of the cancer had almost been a relief, a reprieve. But this was now a much more serious battle with the unthinkable outcome of losing her altogether if the fight was lost.

Claudia had gone to sleep around ten o'clock and I had then spent the next couple of hours at my computer researching ovarian cancer on the internet.

My initial results had been far from encouraging.

Overall, ovarian cancer five-year-survival rates were only about fifty per cent.

That was not good, I thought. It was like tossing a coin. To live, you had to correctly call 'heads'.

However, Claudia had said that the oncologist thought that the cancer hadn't spread. For Stage 1a ovarian cancers, those that were confined within the affected organ and which hadn't spread to its surface, the survival rate was nearly ninety-two per cent.

That was better.

Throw two dice: score eleven or twelve and you die, anything else you live.

For germ cell cancer the rates were even better. Women with only Stage 1a germ cell tumours had a near ninety-seven per cent chance of survival at five years.

Throw those dice again: you are dead now only with a double-six.

Slightly worse than the statistical survival rate for a space shuttle flight (ninety-eight per cent), much better than for a heart transplant (seventy-one per cent at five years).

I could hear Claudia's rhythmic breathing on the pillow next to me.

Funny, I thought, how it often takes a crisis to reveal one's true feelings. Since coming home from the races I had been through the whole gamut from resentful anger to perilous joy, with apprehension, fear and overwhelming love coming in late on the side.

I was exhausted by it all, but still I couldn't sleep.

How close had I come to making a complete fool of myself?

Too close. Much too close.

Sunday morning dawned bright and sunny, both in terms of the weather and my disposition.

I looked at Claudia soundly asleep beside me and, in spite of the uncertainty of her future treatment, I thanked my lucky stars. True, I had been tempted by Jan's extraordinary behaviour, but I had resisted. In fact, it had been Jan's very behaviour that had strengthened my resolve to sort out a problem with Claudia that, in the end, hadn't existed.

Suddenly the other problem, the coming battle against the cancer, while not easy, somehow seemed now manageable. Especially as Claudia and I would both be fighting on the same side.

I got up quietly, leaving her sleeping, and went downstairs to the kitchen, and to my computer.

I pulled up the e-mails from Uri Joram onto the screen

and read them again. I wondered what I should do about them.

A hundred million euros was an awful lot of money but it was a mere drop in the ocean compared to the European Union total budget of more than a hundred and twenty-five billion. But if the European Court of Auditors, the body that had refused to sign off the annual audit of the EU budget for each of the past umpteen years, had themselves been unable to make a single major fraud charge stick, what chance did I have?

I decided that it simply wasn't my fight. Claudia and I now had more pressing things on our minds. If Jolyon Roberts needed to ask any further questions about his investments, then he'd have to speak directly to Gregory.

I, meanwhile, turned to other matters, in particular, the copies of the statements from Herb's twenty-two credit cards.

I sorted them into date order and noticed that four of them were due for payment in the coming week. I wondered what the law was on outstanding credit card debt at death. One thing I was absolutely certain about was that none of the banks would, out of the kindness of their hearts, cancel their debt. But it was the interest that I was most concerned about. Ninety-four thousand, six hundred and twenty-six pounds and fifty-two pence would, if left unpaid, attract a substantial interest charge each month, not to mention late-payment fees, and it might take many months before probate was granted and I was able to pay off the debts from other assets in Herb's estate.

I had to find the cash.

Even the eighteen thousand he collected from the MoneyHome agents the week of his death would not be enough to pay off the four most urgent ones.

And that would not be all.

The ninety-seven separate individuals who were using Herb's accounts for their internet gambling and casino playing probably didn't know Herb was dead. If their past form was anything to go by, they would be racking up further charges.

All gambling requires a degree of trust, but surely Herb must have required an upfront cash advance from each of the ninety-seven in order to allow them to operate the system. That meant the debt of ninety-four thousand, six hundred and twenty-six pounds and fifty-two pence that existed on the credit cards statements may have only been the start of it. How much more did he owe?

I had to find the cash.

I decided that the very first thing I had to do was to cancel the cards so that no more charges could be made on them.

Each of the statements had a phone number on the back and I set about calling them. Many of them did not answer because they were not open on Sundays, and those that did were mostly in India and, in truth, could have been more helpful.

As soon as I said that Mr Kovak was dead, they all

required me to contact them in writing enclosing an original death certificate.

'Fine,' I said to one man called Ashwin, making a mental note to ask the police chief inspector for twenty-two originals of Herb's death certificate. 'But could you, in the meantime, make a stop on any future charges?'

'Cut up the cards,' Ashwin said, 'and then there can't be any more charges, can there?'

How, I wondered, should I explain to him that the cards themselves hadn't actually been present when any of the charges on the statements had been made?

'There are some regular payments,' I said. 'Where the card is not actually present for the transaction. Can't you stop those?'

'You will have to contact the payee,' he said unhelpfully.

All five hundred and twelve of them, I thought.

Next I tried impersonating Herb to cancel one card, but this didn't work either as I didn't have the card – it was in Hendon – and I had no idea of the expiry date, or the pin number. Anyway, I was firmly told, I couldn't cancel a card until I had paid off the outstanding balance.

Dead end.

I just had to find that cash.

Claudia came downstairs in her blue dressing gown.

'What are you doing?' she asked.

'Oh, nothing,' I said, closing the lid of my laptop onto the credit card statements. 'Nothing for you to worry about, anyway.'

'Look here,' she said, putting on a stern face, 'I told you my troubles so now you have to tell me yours.'

'It's just something to do with Herb Kovak,' I said. 'In his will he appointed me as his executor.'

'And what does that mean exactly?' she asked.

'It means,' I said, 'that I have to sort out all his bloody affairs when I should be looking after you.'

'Quite right,' she said, coming over and sitting on my lap. She put her arms round my neck. 'Naughty boy.'

I smiled.

Life was back to normal – or almost.

During the afternoon I called Detective Chief Inspector Tomlinson on the mobile number he had given me.

'Hello,' a voice said, sounding sleepy.

'Chief Inspector Tomlinson?' I asked.

'Hello, yes?' he said, this time more alert.

'Sorry to wake you,' I said. 'This is Nicholas Foxton.'

'Just resting my eyes,' he said. 'How can I help you?'

'I think it's me who's going to help you,' I said. 'Herb Kovak's sister has turned up.'

'Really,' he said. 'When?'

'Well, actually, on Thursday morning not long after you'd left his flat. But so much has been happening since then that I forgot to tell you.'

'Yes,' he said. 'I did hear that you've been kept rather busy.'

'Yes,' I agreed. 'Thank you for giving me an alibi.'

'You don't have to thank me,' he said. 'I simply told

them there was no way, short of using a helicopter, that anyone could travel the seventy miles from Baydon to Hendon in fifty-five minutes at that time of day. Especially someone who'd just had an ingrowing toenail removed. I could hardly walk with mine for weeks.'

I stifled a laugh. Good old Mrs McDowd and her fertile imagination.

'Well, thank you nevertheless,' I said. 'Now, I have some other information for you.'

'Yes?' he said.

'I think I may have solved the riddle of the credit cards.'

'Go on,' he said.

'I think that Herb Kovak was allowing other people to use his credit card accounts to gamble on the internet, probably fellow Americans because it's illegal to gamble in most states over there.'

'What evidence do you have?' he asked.

'Not much,' I said. 'But I think I'm right. There are five hundred and twelve different entries on those statements. But there aren't five hundred and twelve different individuals because many of them bet or play on more than one internet site.'

'Do you have any idea who these people are?'

'No,' I said. 'But we do have ninety-seven different sets of initials. They're on those sheets you showed me. I think they refer to ninety-seven different people.'

'So you're saying that you think ninety-seven different people, who all live somewhere in the United

States, were using Herb Kovak's credit card accounts to bet on the internet.'

'Yes,' I said. 'And to play online poker. I found some MoneyHome receipts that show Herb collected large amounts of cash during the week before he died. I believe that cash was to pay off some of the credit card debts.'

'And are you telling me this has something to do with why he was killed?'

'Not necessarily,' I said. 'I have no idea why he was killed. I thought that was your job.'

He didn't rise to my bait. There was just silence from his end.

'I've been trying to cancel the credit cards,' I said finally, 'but they all need an original death certificate. Can you get me some? I'll need at least twenty-two.'

'No death certificate has been issued as yet,' he said. 'All unnatural deaths are subject to an inquest, and that would usually follow any criminal trial. The death certificate would be issued only after the inquest was complete.'

'But that will be months, if not years, away,' I said with a degree of exasperation. 'There must be some official piece of paper that shows that he's dead. I need something to show the damn credit card companies.'

'As his executor, you can apply for probate before the death certificate is issued.'

'How?' I said. 'I've got nothing to show he's even dead.'

'The inquest was opened and adjourned last Tuesday,' he said. 'The Liverpool coroner will issue you with a letter. I'll arrange it.'

'Thank you.'

'So where can I find Mr Kovak's sister?' the chief inspector asked.

'At his flat, I think. She was there on Friday afternoon.'

'Right,' he said. 'Does she know her brother was murdered?'

'Yes,' I said. 'I told her.'

'Good. I'll be in touch so she can make an official identification.' Poor girl, I thought. 'Anything else?'

'Yes,' I said. 'Have you any idea who killed him?'

'Not as yet,' he said.

'Any leads at all?'

'No. None. The gunman seems to have disappeared completely.'

At least he was honest.

'How about the note I found in Herb's coat pocket?' I asked.

'Nothing to go on,' he said. 'The paper was just common copy-paper available from any stationer or office supply store, and the only discernible finger-prints were either yours or Mr Kovak's.'

'How could you tell?' I asked.

'We checked yours against the sample set you gave me, and I arranged for Mr Kovak's to be taken from his body.'

I wished I hadn't asked.

'So where do you go from here?'

'I think I had better take another look at those lists,' he said. 'And I want to see those MoneyHome receipts. I'll arrange to have them collected from your office.'

'I may not be in the office this week,' I said. 'Can you collect them from my home?' I thought for a moment. 'In fact, I have two receipts here but the three from last week are still at Herb's flat.'

'I may need to go and see Mr Kovak's sister. I'll call you back later when I know my movements.'

'Sherri,' I said.

'What?'

'Sherri,' I repeated. 'Sherri Kovak. Herb's sister. They were twins.'

'Oh,' he said.

Somehow, being twins made it worse.

Claudia and I went out to dinner at Luigi's, a local Italian restaurant, and managed to spend the whole meal talking without once mentioning the 'c' word.

We both skirted around it on purpose, like a game, but it did mean we discussed all sorts of other things, many of which we had bottled up over the past couple of weeks.

'My mother sends her love,' I said.

'Oh, thanks,' Claudia replied. 'How is she?'

I wanted to say she was in need of grandchildren, but I didn't. My mother would have to take her chances on Tuesday with the surgeon's knife, like the rest of us.

'Fine,' I said. 'She loves her little cottage and she's been busy with the local village historical society.'

'Perhaps we can go down and see her together,' Claudia said. 'After.'

After the operation, she meant.

'I'd better call Jan Setter in the morning and tell her we won't be able to make the opening night on Wednesday.'

'You can go on your own,' Claudia said. 'You'll enjoy it.'

Sitting next to Jan in a theatre all evening, with her hands wandering all over me in the darkness? No thanks.

'No,' I said. 'I'll tell her that neither of us will be there.'

Claudia smiled at me. I knew it was what she really wanted.

'It saved me buying a new dress anyway.'

We laughed.

That was the closest we came all evening to discussing her operation and, presently, I paid the bill and took my girl home to bed.

She had to go into the hospital the following evening ready for the surgery on the Tuesday morning. Hence our lovemaking was passionate and full-on, as if we both realized that this might be our last time together with Claudia as a fertile woman.

11

At nine a.m. sharp on Monday morning I called Patrick in the office.

'Am I forgiven yet?' I asked him.

'Gregory's not here today,' he replied. 'He's been away for the weekend and isn't back until tomorrow afternoon or Wednesday. I think it best if you stay away a while longer.'

I wasn't going to argue. Not having to be in the office over the next couple of days suited me very well.

'Can I now use the remote-access facility?' I asked. 'Just to check that I'm not missing something that should be done today.'

The system allowed us to attach reminder notices to client files, for example to alert us to a maturing bond or a rights issue, so that we didn't miss an opportunity to invest the client's money most favourably.

'Of course,' Patrick replied.

Things had clearly mellowed over the weekend.

'So shall I plan on being in again on Wednesday?' I asked.

'Thursday might be better,' Patrick said, seemingly a little undecided. 'I'll speak to Gregory over lunch on Wednesday.'

'Thursday it is, then,' I said. 'Unless I hear from you sooner.'

'Right.' Patrick seemed rather distracted. 'There is a bit of a backlog with both you and Herb not being here. Diana and Rory will just have to cover everything until Thursday. I'll ask them to stay late.'

I smiled. I bet Rory wouldn't like that. There was no extra money for doing overtime in our job.

Detective Chief Inspector Tomlinson had called on Sunday evening to say he was travelling down from Liverpool, and to ask if could I meet him at Herb Kovak's flat at eleven the following morning. Yes, I'd said, I could.

In the end both Claudia and I went over to Hendon together in the Mercedes because she didn't want to be left alone, and I was delighted to have her with me.

The policeman was there ahead of us and he had been interviewing poor Sherri Kovak, who was clearly distressed by the experience. Her eyes were red from crying and she looked pale and drawn. Claudia went immediately and put her arm round Sherri's shoulders, even before they were introduced, taking her off into the kitchen.

'Thank you for coming,' the chief inspector said to me, shaking my hand. 'I'm sorry but I seem to have rather upset Miss Kovak.'

'How?' I asked.

'I told her that I needed her to come back with me

to Liverpool to carry out a formal identification of the body.'

I nodded. 'I feared you might. You would think it wouldn't be necessary to put people through such emotional trauma.' Especially, I thought, as one of the bullets that had killed him had entered through his face.

'I'm afraid the law takes little notice of people's feelings.'

'And you should know,' I said.

'Yes,' he said looking me in the eye. 'I certainly do.'

Claudia came back out into the hallway and I introduced her properly to Detective Chief Inspector Tomlinson.

'So, are you the man who arrested my Nick?' she asked accusingly.

'No, darling,' I said, springing quickly to the police-man's defence. 'This isn't the man who arrested me, this is the one who provided me with an alibi.'

'Oh,' she said. 'All right, then. You may live.'

The chief inspector smiled at her little joke, but he was there strictly on business.

'Now,' he said to me, getting down to it, 'where are these MoneyHome receipts?'

Claudia went back to Sherri in the kitchen while the chief inspector and I went through into the living room. I spread out the stuck-together little squares on Herb's desk. The chief inspector's eyebrows rose a notch.

'I found them torn up like this in the waste bin,' I

said. 'I stuck them together. There are three different payment slips here, one for eight thousand dollars and two for five thousand each.'

'And you say that Mr Kovak collected this money from a MoneyHome agent during the week before he was killed.'

'Yes,' I said. 'That's according to the stamps on them.'

'And do you know who sent him the money?'

'No,' I replied. 'MoneyHome apparently only require the recipient's name and something called the Money Transfer Control Number in order to pay out. The agent doesn't seem to know the sender's name.'

'These bloody money transfer companies,' he said. 'They seem to be absolutely determined to allow people to transfer money around the world completely anonymously. Cash in, cash out, no questions asked. They make it so easy for the villains, especially the drug dealers.'

'Can't you make them tell you who sent the money?' I asked.

'They probably don't know themselves,' he said. 'And if they do get a name it's probably false.'

'Butch Cassidy,' I said.

'Eh?'

'The recipient names on the payment slips,' I said. I added the two from my pocket to the three on the desk. 'Butch Cassidy, Billy Kid, Wyatt Earp, Jessie James and Bill Cody. It's not very difficult to spot they're false.'

'Were they the aliases used by Mr Kovak when he collected the money?' he asked, studying the slips.

'Yes,' I said.

I could see from his expression that the chief inspector immediately cast Herb as one of his villains.

'He wasn't a drug dealer,' I said. The chief inspector looked up at me. 'And he wasn't a crook. He was just allowing his fellow Americans to do what we in England can do quite legitimately every day.'

'Gambling is a mug's game,' he said.

'As maybe,' I agreed. 'But it's legal, taxed and, without it, there probably wouldn't be any horse racing. Certainly not the industry we have today.'

The policeman pursed his lips as if to say he didn't think it would be a great loss. I wondered if all policemen were born puritanical, or did it develop after several years in the job.

'Mr Kovak was still breaking the law.'

'Was he?' I asked. 'Whose law?'

'He was aiding and abetting others,' the chief inspector said with certainty.

I wasn't going to argue with him. I was pretty certain myself that, if the reports of the arrest of the CEO of the internet gambling site was anything to go by, Herb would have faced racketeering charges in the United States if they had known what he was up to.

I also showed the chief inspector the stack of unsigned credit cards but he seemed far more interested in the MoneyHome payment slips.

'So where do we go from here?' I asked.

'I will take these slips and try and get MoneyHome to at least divulge which of their offices the money was sent from. The transfer number should be enough to do that. Then we will have to painstakingly try to find out whose initials are on the sheets of paper.'

'You really think this must have something to do with Herb's murder?' I asked.

'Don't you?' he said. 'We've no other leads to go on. You never know, perhaps Mr Kovak was blackmailing one of his "clients", threatening to tell the US authorities about their illegal gambling. So they killed him.'

'There goes that suspicious mind of yours again, Chief Inspector.'

'Suspicion is all we have at the moment,' he said seriously. 'And there's precious little of that in this case.'

There was a heavy knock at the front door.

'That will be my sergeant,' the chief inspector said. 'He's come to drive Miss Kovak and me to Liverpool.'

Claudia and I watched them go.

'That poor girl,' Claudia said, holding my hand. 'Her family are all dead. She's alone in the world.'

At least she's healthy, I thought. How typical of my gorgeous Claudia to think of others when she had enough of her own troubles to worry about.

'Do you fancy going out to lunch?' I asked.

'Lovely,' she said.

'Luigi's again?'

'It's a bit unimaginative,' she said. 'But, why not? I like it there.'

I drove us home and we again walked round the corner to our favourite restaurant. On this occasion the proprietor, Luigi Pucinelli, was present.

'Ah, Signor Foxton and the lovely Signorina Claudia, *buongiorno*, welcome,' he said, being his usual effusive self. 'Table for two? *Bene*. Follow me.'

He showed us to our favourite table in the window.

'We don't often see you for lunch,' Luigi said in his Italian accent, adding an 'eh' to every word that ended in a consonant.

'No,' I said. 'It's a special treat.'

'*Eccellente*,' he said with a flourish, giving us the menus.

'*Grazie*,' I said to him, playing the game.

Luigi was no more Italian than I was. I had met his mother one night in the restaurant and she had told me with a laugh that Luigi Pucinelli had been born Jim Metcalf in a nursing home up the Tottenham High Road, not five miles away.

But good luck to him, I thought. The food and service at Luigi's were superb, and his restaurant thrived, authentic Italian or not.

Claudia chose the *antipasto* for us to share as a starter, with *saltimbocca alla pollo* to follow, while I decided on the *risotto al funghi*.

We ate the *antipasto* in silence.

'Speak to me,' Claudia said. 'This is not the last meal of the condemned, you know.'

I smiled at her. 'No, of course not.'

But we were both nervous.

Nervous of what tomorrow morning would bring.

I ordered a taxi to take us to the hospital that evening, at seven o'clock.

'Why do you need to go in the night before?' I asked Claudia as we made our way down the Finchley Road.

'Something about wanting to monitor me overnight before the operation so they have something to compare the readings with afterwards.'

'What time is the op in the morning?' I asked.

'The surgeon said it would be first thing, just as soon as he's finished his early-morning rounds.'

That meant it could be anytime, I thought.

In my experience, and I had plenty of it from my racing days, doctors and surgeons were about as good at time keeping as a London bus in the rush hour.

'At least we won't have to wait all day,' I said, smiling at her.

She gave me a look that said she would be quite happy to wait all year.

'It's better to get it done, and then at least we will know what we're up against.'

'I know,' she said. 'But I'm frightened.'

So was I. But now was not the time to show it.

'Everything will be OK,' I said, trying to sound reassuring. 'You said they've found it early, and I've researched everything on the internet. You're going to be just fine. You'll see.'

'Oh, Nick,' she said, grasping my hand very tight. There were tears in her eyes.

I pulled her close to me and we sat in silence as the taxi manoeuvred through Regent's Park and out onto the Euston Road.

It was a difficult evening, and night, for both of us.

Claudia was checked into the hospital by the admissions' staff, for whom it was a regular routine to be completed with brisk efficiency. They didn't mean to be uncaring but, quite a few times, they made us feel uncomfortable and even foolish.

I kept having to wait in the corridor outside her room as nurses and technicians came to perform some action or other. Swabs were taken from inside Claudia's nose and mouth, and others were then taken from more intimate areas. Blood was drawn for this, and urine was tested for that.

After a couple of hours they finally said that she was ready for the morning and they left us in peace. I turned off the bright overhead lights and dimmed the reading light to a much more subdued level. Suddenly everything did not look quite so stark and antiseptic. Much better.

I sat on a chair by her bed and held her hand.

'You ought to go home,' Claudia said. 'I'll be fine.'

'Unless they physically throw me out,' I said, 'I'm not going anywhere.'

Claudia laid her head back on the pillow and smiled. 'Good,' she said.

I still couldn't believe how badly I had read the situation between us. What a fool I had been, and what a greater fool I might have become. Just thinking about it brought me out in a cold sweat.

'You get some sleep now, my love,' I said to her. 'You'll need all the strength you can get for tomorrow.'

'This bloody bed is so hard. It makes my back ache.'

I spent a few minutes using the electric bed control, lifting the head or feet, trying to make her more comfortable. It didn't really work.

'Why can't they have bloody beds that are comfortable to lie on?' Claudia complained. 'You'd think that would be the first priority.'

I recognized what was happening. She was getting irritated by the slightest little thing. It was a sign of the nervous condition she was in. I would just have to smile gently and agree with her.

'Yes, darling,' I said. 'Please try and close your eyes and get some rest.'

'You try resting on this bloody thing,' she snapped, turning herself over once again to face away from me.

In the end she settled and, in time, I could tell from the sound of her breathing that she was asleep. I settled down into the chair and closed my eyes.

One of the nurses came into the room and snapped on the overhead lights.

'Time for your vitals,' she said loudly.

And so it went on through the night, with temperature, pulse and blood pressure being measured at two-hourly intervals, each time accompanied by the

Blackpool illuminations. Hospitals were clearly never designed for relaxation and recovery.

No one told me to go home, so I didn't, although I had to admit, it was not the best night's sleep I'd ever had.

Breakfast wasn't eaten by Claudia, or even offered, there being a large NIL BY MOUTH sign hanging on a hook by the door, so I went down to the hospital lobby at about six a.m. in search of a coffee and a bun for myself, while the patient had a shower.

At about eight thirty Mr Tomic, the surgeon, arrived wearing light blue scrub tunic and trousers, all set for the operating theatre. He brought with him some paperwork and a thick permanent marker pen, which he used to draw a big black arrow on the left side of Claudia below her belly button.

'Don't want to take out the wrong one now, do we,' he said.

It somehow wasn't very encouraging.

'What exactly are you going to do?' I asked.

'I will make two small incisions here and here.' He pointed to each side of Claudia's lower abdomen. 'I will then use a laparoscope to have a good look at all her bits, and then I'll remove the left ovary completely,' he said. 'I also plan to take a wedge biopsy of the right ovary.'

'And what is a wedge biopsy exactly?' I asked.

'A small sample that is removed, like a tiny bite, which is then tested to see if it's clear,' he said. 'Then I will sew everything up and Claudia will be back here before you know it. About two hours in total, maybe a fraction more.'

'And if the biopsy's not clear?' Claudia asked.

'If I can tell that straight away just by looking,' the surgeon said, 'then I'll have to remove that ovary as well, otherwise the biopsy will be sent to the lab for tests. There is a slight chance that I may also need to perform a complete hysterectomy if I find cancer cells attached to the uterus. But I think from the scans that that will be most unlikely.'

Claudia looked at me with rising panic in her eyes.

Mr Tomic spotted it. 'Claudia,' he said, 'I promise you I will do as little as possible. But we have to deal with this. It won't go away on its own. I have to tell you everything that might happen because I need your consent to proceed. You will understand that I can't wake you up half-way through the operation to ask your permission to remove your womb if I need to do it in order to save your life.' He smiled at her. 'But I really don't think it will come to that.'

'Can't you just remove the tumour?' I asked. 'Do you have to take the whole ovary?'

'The tumour will probably have taken over most of the ovary and it is the only way of ensuring it doesn't return.'

'If the second ovary is clear, does that mean it will remain so?' I asked.

'Let's cross one bridge at a time,' he said. 'We'll discuss the future after the operation.'

I took that to mean 'no', it probably wouldn't remain clear.

My mother's wish for grandchildren was not looking too promising.

'Right, then,' said Mr Tomic, 'I need you to sign here.' He pointed. 'And here. And here.'

Claudia looked at me in despair. I pursed my lips and nodded at her. She signed the papers. What choice did we have?

'OK,' said the surgeon, taking back the forms from her. 'I'll see you in theatre in about twenty minutes. Wait here, they'll come for you.'

I wanted to tell him to be careful with my girl, but I didn't. Of course he'd be careful. Wouldn't he?

If the previous evening had been bad, the next twenty minutes were intolerable.

Mr Tomic had left the door open and every time someone walked down the corridor outside, we both jumped.

What was there to say? Nothing. We both just watched the clock on the wall move inexorably round from eight fifty to nine o'clock, then ever onwards to nine five and nine ten.

Claudia held on to my hand as if her life depended on it.

'It'll be all right,' I said. 'You heard what he said, you'll be back in here before you know it.'

'Oh, Nick,' she said miserably, 'if I come out of this with only a tiny piece of an ovary left, let's use it to have kids.'

'OK,' I said. 'You're on.'

'Marry me first?' she asked.

'You bet,' I said.

It was an unusual proposal, but we were in an unusual situation.

At nine fifteen a theatre porter arrived wearing blue scrubs and a J-cloth hat.

'Please be careful with my fiancée,' I said to him as he wheeled her bed out of the room into the corridor. 'She's very precious to me.'

I went with her to the lift, where the porter said he was sorry, but I couldn't come any further. I looked at Claudia's frightened face until the closing lift doors cut off our line of sight, and all too quickly she was gone.

I went back into her room and sat down on the chair.

Never before had I felt so desperate, so helpless, and alone.

In truth, it was not a great start to an engagement.

Claudia didn't come back for nearly three hours, by which time I was almost crawling up the walls of her room with worry.

Sitting alone in that hospital room had been far worse than spending three times as long in a cell at Paddington Green Police Station.

I spent some time going over in my mind what must be happening downstairs in the operating theatre, mentally carving up the clock face into segments. First I tried to imagine how long it would take for Claudia to be put to sleep; then how long to make the incision in her body; next how long to remove the ovary, and so on. I had no idea if I was right or not, or even if I was close, but it seemed to help.

My mental calculations, however, had her coming back to the room in two hours and, when she didn't, my imagination went into overdrive, envisaging all sorts of horrors. While the clock on the wall went on ticking, as if mocking me. And still Claudia didn't return.

By the time I finally heard her being wheeled back along the corridor, I had convinced myself that the whole thing had gone horribly wrong and Claudia had died on the operating table.

But she wasn't dead, she was just cold, and shivering uncontrollably.

I was so pleased to see her but she was not a happy bunny, not at all. She was sore from the surgery and feeling nauseous from the anaesthetic. And she couldn't stop the shivering.

'It's quite normal,' said a nurse curtly when I asked about it. 'She'll be fine soon.'

'Can she please have another blanket?' I asked.

Reluctantly she agreed and, in time, the shivering did abate and Claudia relaxed and, eventually, she went to sleep.

*

Mr Tomic came to see us at about two o'clock while Claudia was still sleeping.

'I have some good news and not quite such good news,' he said to me quietly. 'Firstly, the good news is that I removed only one ovary and the other one looked perfectly fine, although I took a piece for a biopsy and it's currently being assessed in the path lab.'

'And the not-so-good news?' I asked.

'The tumour was not quite fully contained in the ovary as we had thought, and it had erupted on the surface. It's often difficult to tell precisely from the scans.'

'And what exactly does that mean?' I said.

'It means there is every likelihood that there will be some ovarian cancer cells present in the fluid within the abdominal cavity. We will know for sure when the lab tests are complete.'

'And?' I said.

'In order to be sure we've killed off the cancer completely, I think a course or two of chemo will probably be needed.'

'Chemotherapy?' I said.

'I'm afraid so,' he replied. 'Just to be sure.'

'Does that mean I'll lose my hair?' Claudia asked. Her eyes were closed and I hadn't realized she'd been awake, and listening.

'It might,' he said, 'although the drugs are much better than they used to be.' I took that to mean yes, she would lose her hair. 'But even so, it will grow back.'

Claudia's long, flowing, jet-black hair was her pride and joy.

'Does the chemo start straight away?' I asked.

'Within a few weeks,' he said. 'We'll give Claudia time to recover from the surgery first.'

'Will it affect the other ovary?' I asked. 'I read on the internet that some cancer drugs made women infertile.'

'The drugs used are very powerful,' he said. 'They work by attacking cells that divide rapidly, like cancer cells, but they do tend to affect everything in the body to some degree. Am I to assume that preserving fertility is a priority?'

'Yes,' said Claudia unequivocally, still not opening her eyes.

'Then we will just have to be very careful,' he said. 'Won't we?'

At three thirty in the afternoon I left Claudia resting in the hospital while I went home to change and have a shower, taking the Northern Line tube from Warren Street to Finchley Central.

'I won't be long,' I told her. 'About an hour and a half. Is there anything I can get you?'

'A new body,' she said miserably.

'I love the one you have,' I said, and she forced a smile.

The doctor had told us that she would have to stay in hospital for another night but she should be able to go home the following day, or on Thursday at the latest.

The sun was shining as the tube train rose from the dark tunnels into the daylight just before East Finchley

Station. It was always a welcome sign. It meant I was nearly home.

As I walked down Lichfield Grove I could see that there was a man standing outside my house with his finger on the doorbell. I was about to call out to him when he turned his head slightly, as if looking over his shoulder.

In spite of telling the police that I hadn't seen Herb's killer at Aintree, I knew him instantly. Here he was standing outside my front door in Finchley, and I didn't think he was visiting to enquire after my health.

My heartbeat at once jumped to stratospheric proportions and I stifled the shout that was already rising in my throat. I started to turn away from him but not before our eyes had made contact, and I had glimpsed the long black shape in his right hand: his trusty gun, complete with silencer.

Bugger, I thought.

I turned and ran as fast as I could back up Lichfield Grove towards Regent's Park Road.

Lichfield Grove may have been used as a busy shortcut during the rush hour but it was sleepy and deserted at four o'clock in the afternoon with not even any schoolchildren on their way home.

Safety, I thought, would be where there were lots of people. Surely he wouldn't kill me with witnesses. But he had killed Herb with over sixty thousand of them.

I chanced a glance back, having to turn my upper body due to the restricted movement in my neck. It was a mistake.

The gunman was still behind me, only about thirty yards away, running hard and lifting his right arm to aim.

I heard a bullet whizz past me on my left.

I ran harder and also I started shouting.

'Help! Help!' I shouted as loudly as my heaving lungs would allow. 'Call the police!'

No one shouted back, and I needed the air for my aching leg muscles. Oh to be as fit as I once was as a jockey.

I thought I heard another bullet fly past me and zing off the pavement ahead as a ricochet, but I wasn't stopping to check.

I made it unharmed to Regent's Park Road and went left round the corner. Without breaking stride I went straight into Mr Patel's newsagency, pushed past the startled owner and crouched down under his counter, gasping for air.

'Mr Patel,' I said. 'I am being chased. Please call the police.'

I didn't know why, perhaps it was because of his cultural background, but he didn't become angry or question why I had invaded his space. He simply stood quietly and looked down at me, as if in slight surprise at the strange behaviour of the English.

'Mr Patel,' I said again with urgency, still breathing hard. 'I am being chased by a very dangerous man. Please do not look down at me or he will know that I am here. Please call the police.'

'What man?' he said, still looking down at me.

'The man outside the window,' I said. Mr Patel looked up.

Suddenly I remembered that I had my mobile in my pocket. As I dialled 999 I heard the shop door being opened, the little bell ringing once.

I held my breath. I could feel my heart going thump, thump in my chest.

'Emergency, which service?' said a voice from my phone.

I stuffed the phone into my armpit, hoping that the newcomer into the shop hadn't heard it.

'Yes?' said Mr Patel. 'Can I help you, sir?'

The newcomer made no reply and I went on holding my breath, my chest feeling like it was going to burst.

'Can I help you, sir?' Mr Patel said again but more loudly.

Again there was no reply. All I could hear were faint footsteps.

I just had to breathe so I let the air out through my mouth as quietly as I could, and took another deep breath in.

I wished I could see what was happening in the shop. After a few seconds I heard the door close, ringing the bell once again, but was the gunman on the inside or the outside?

Mr Patel stood stock still above me giving me no indication either way.

'He has gone outside,' he said finally, without changing his position.

218

'What's he doing?' I asked.

'He is standing and looking around,' Mr Patel said. 'Who is he and why is he chasing you? Are you a criminal?'

'No,' I said. 'I am not.'

I remembered the phone under my arm. The operator had obviously got fed up waiting and had hung up. I dialled 999 again.

'Emergency, which service?' said a voice again.

'Police,' I said.

'Police incident room, go ahead,' said another voice.

'There's an armed gunman in the street on Regent's Park Road in Finchley,' I said quickly.

Mr Patel looked down at me.

'Mr Patel,' I said urgently. 'Please do not look down. The man might see you, and come back into the shop.'

'What number Regent's Park Road?' said the voice on the phone.

'Near the corner of Lichfield Grove,' I said. 'Please hurry.'

'Your name, sir?' said the voice.

'Foxton,' I said into the phone. 'Mr Patel, what is the man doing now?'

'He is walking away. No. He has stopped. He is looking back. Oh, goodness gracious, he is coming back this way.'

Mr Patel leaned down, grabbed some keys from a hook under the counter, and walked out of my sight.

'What are you doing?' I called after him urgently.

'Locking the door,' he said.

I didn't have time to think whether it was a good idea or not before I heard Mr Patel turn the key in the lock. Now the gunman would be sure where I was. And I could hear the door being shaken.

'Mr Patel,' I shouted, 'get away from the door. The man has a gun.'

'It is all right, Mr Foxton,' he said with a laugh. 'It is not him shaking the door, it is me. The man has gone past. I cannot see him any more.'

It didn't mean he wasn't there so I stayed exactly where I was. My heart rate may have come down a few notches but, as far as I was concerned, it was still no laughing matter.

'Now, Mr Foxton, why is a man with a gun chasing you? It is like a film, no?'

'No,' I said. 'This was very real life. He was trying to kill me.'

'But why?' he said.

It was a good question. A very good question.

I remained sitting on the floor behind Mr Patel's counter until the police arrived. It took them nearly forty minutes and I had telephoned 999 again twice more before two heavily armed and body-armoured officers finally made an appearance at the shop door. Mr Patel let them in.

'About time too,' I said, standing up from my hiding place.

'Mr Foxton?' one of the officers asked, his machine

pistol held at the ready position with his finger over the trigger.

'Yes,' I said. 'That's me.'

'Are you armed, sir?'

'No,' I said.

'Please put your hands on your head,' he said, pointing his gun towards me.

'It's not me who's the gunman,' I said, slightly irritated. 'It was the man who was chasing me.'

'Put your hands on your head,' the policeman repeated with a degree of menace. 'And you, sir,' he said, pointing his gun briefly towards Mr Patel.

We both put our hands on our heads. Mr Patel smiled broadly as if he thought the whole thing was a huge joke.

The second officer came forward and searched me, making sure he didn't get between my chest and the muzzle of his colleague's weapon. He then did likewise to Mr Patel. Then he went through the shop and out of sight through a plastic curtain into the room behind. He soon reappeared, shaking his head. Only then did they relax a little.

'Sorry about that, sir,' said the first officer, securing his gun across his chest with a strap. 'We can't be too careful.'

I put my arms down. 'What took you so long to get here?'

'We had to seal off the whole area,' he said. 'Standard practice when there's a report of a gunman.' He put his finger to his ear, clearly listening to someone on his personal radio earpiece. 'Now, sir,' he said to me, 'my superintendent wants to know if you have a description of this gunman.' His tone suggested that he didn't altogether believe that a gunman had been stalking the streets of Finchley on a sleepy Tuesday afternoon in late April.

'I think I may have better than that,' I said. 'Mr Patel, does your closed-circuit TV system have a recorder?' I had passed some of my time waiting for the police by looking up at the small white video camera situated above the racks of cigarettes.

'Of course,' Mr Patel replied. 'I need to have it to catch the young scoundrels who steal my stock.'

'Then, officer,' I said, 'please would you kindly inform Detective Chief Inspector Tomlinson of the Merseyside Police that we have the murderer of Herb Kovak caught on video.'

But how had he known where to find me? And why?

12

In the end, it was I who rang Chief Inspector Tomlinson, but not before the Armed Response Team had completed a full debrief of the events in Finchley.

'So you say you saw a man standing outside your front door?' asked the response team superintendent as we stood in Mr Patel's shop.

'Yes,' I said. 'He was ringing the doorbell.'

'And he had a gun?'

'Yes,' I said again, 'with a silencer.'

There was something about his demeanour that said that he, too, didn't really believe me. Mr Patel hadn't seen any gun nor, it seemed, had anyone else.

'He shot at me,' I said. 'As I ran up Lichfield Grove. He shot at least twice. I heard the bullets whizz past my head.'

A team was despatched to search and, in due course, one of them returned with two empty brass cases in a plastic bag.

Suddenly everything became more serious. They believed me now.

'You will have to come to the police station,' said the superintendent. 'To give a statement.'

'Can't I do it here?' I asked.

'I need to reopen my shop,' said Mr Patel anxiously.

'At my house, then?' I asked. 'I need to get back to University College Hospital. My girlfriend had an operation this morning and she's expecting me.'

Reluctantly the superintendent agreed to do it at my house and we walked down Lichfield Grove together. The road had been closed to traffic and about a dozen police officers in dark blue boiler-suits were moving up the road in line abreast, crawling on all fours.

'Looking for the bullets,' the superintendent informed me before I asked. 'Don't touch the door,' he said as we arrived at my house, 'or the doorbell.'

I carefully opened the door with my key and we went into the kitchen.

'Now, Mr Foxton,' the superintendent said formally, 'tell me why a gunman would come calling at your front door.'

It was the question I'd been asking myself for the past hour.

'I'm sure he was here to kill me,' I said.

'That's very dramatic. Why?'

Why, indeed, when he could have done it so easily at Aintree at the same time as he killed Herb. What, I wondered, had changed in the intervening ten days that meant that I needed to be killed now but hadn't needed to be then?

I told the superintendent all about the murder at the Grand National and it was then that I again suggested calling DCI Tomlinson.

'My goodness, Mr Foxton,' the chief inspector said

down the wire with a laugh. 'You seem to be making a habit of being interviewed by the police.'

'I can assure you it's a habit I intend to give up at the earliest opportunity,' I replied.

The two senior policemen then spoke together for some time and it was frustrating for me listening to only one half of the conversation. Mostly they spoke about the video tape that the superintendent had removed from Mr Patel's recorder. The superintendent and I had watched it on the small black-and-white screen in the storeroom behind the shop. Just seeing the grainy image of the man as he had come through the shop door made the hairs on the back of my neck stand upright. He had advanced a couple of paces in and stood there, looking around. Then he had walked down the length of the shop, putting his head through the plastic curtain into the storeroom behind. He then retraced his steps and went out of the door, closing it behind him. Unfortunately the angle of the CCTV camera didn't show what he did next. And none of the images showed his gun, which he must have been holding in his anorak pocket.

I shivered. How close had I come to hiding in the back room? Very close.

'Chief Inspector Tomlinson would like another word,' the superintendent said to me finally, handing over the phone.

'Yes,' I said.

'Can you think of any reason why someone would want you killed?'

'No, I can't,' I said. 'And, if they did, why wait until now? Why not do it at Aintree at the same time as killing Herb Kovak? Something must have changed since then.'

'But what?' he said. 'Have you been trying to find out whose initials are on those sheets?'

'No, I haven't. I did go into a MoneyHome agent and ask about the payslips, but that was last Friday.'

'Leave the investigating to the professionals, Mr Foxton,' said the chief inspector somewhat formally.

I think I was being told off.

'But if I hadn't,' I said in my defence, 'then you wouldn't know that it was other Americans who were gambling using Mr Kovak's credit cards.'

'We still don't know that for certain,' he said.

Maybe not, I thought, but I was sure I was right.

'So how are you going to catch this guy?' I asked him. 'And before he succeeds in killing me?'

'Superintendent Yering will issue an immediate alert to all stations, including the airports and ports, with the man's image from the tape. And we will be approaching the TV stations to run the video clip in their news broadcasts.'

It didn't sound sufficiently proactive to me.

'Haven't you got some mug shots or something for me to look at?' I asked. 'I have to tell you I don't feel very safe with this guy still out there on the loose.'

'You had better ask Superintendent Yering,' he said.

So I did but he wasn't very forthcoming.

'We have literally tens of thousands of mug shots,' he said. 'It would take you weeks to look through them all, and our man may not even be there. We need something else to point us in the right direction first, then it might be worthwhile. Perhaps we'll get a finger-print from your doorbell. Be patient, Mr Foxton. The video image is good and it should bear dividends when it's shown on the news.'

If I lived that long, I thought.

'Can't you provide me with some police protection?' I asked. 'In a safe house, or something?'

'MI5 might have safe houses but we don't,' he said with a smile. 'You've been watching too much TV.'

'But someone is trying to kill me,' I said in frustra-tion. 'Surely it's your job to prevent that. I need some protection.'

'I'm sorry,' he said. 'We simply don't have the man-power.'

They had the manpower, I thought, to have a dozen officers crawl along the road on their hands and knees looking for a bullet, but not enough to prevent a future murder. It was crazy.

'So what am I to do?' I asked him. 'Just sit here and wait to be killed?'

'Perhaps it wouldn't be sensible to stay here,' he conceded. 'Have you anywhere else to go to?'

My home and my office were now off limits. Where else?

'I'm going to go back to the hospital to see my girl-friend,' I said.

Some of the Armed Response Team agreed to wait in my house while I belatedly had a shower and changed my clothes. I then threw some things into a suitcase, including my computer, and set off for the hospital in the back of one of their police vans.

'It's the least we can do,' they said.

At one point I insisted that the police driver go right round the big roundabout at Swiss Cottage to make sure we were not being followed.

We weren't, of course. What sort of killer would follow a van full of heavily armed police? But what sort of killer would gun a man down with sixty thousand witnesses close to hand? Or try to kill someone on their own front doorstep?

I couldn't help but think of Jill Dando, the British TV personality, gunned down in exactly that way in a Fulham street.

And her killer has never been identified.

Claudia was still resting when I made it back to her room in the hospital. She was neither aware nor surprised that I had been away for nearly four hours, and not the one and a half I'd promised.

I had made it unmolested and alive from the police van outside the hospital main door to her room, but not without a nervous glance at every person I met on the way. I nearly had heart failure when, just as the lift doors were closing, a man jumped through the gap who slightly resembled my would-be killer.

If I went on like this I'd be a nervous wreck in no time.

I closed the door to Claudia's room but, of course, there was no lock on the inside.

It made me feel very uneasy.

I thought it unlikely that the gunman would give up just because he'd lost me once. I imagined he was a professional assassin and, like most professionals, he would take pride in completing his job.

Bugger the police, I thought. I felt so vulnerable. I believed absolutely that I needed some protection or else I'd wind up dead. Maybe I might be killed even if I had a bodyguard, but at least it would make me feel a little safer. However, Mrs Gandhi, the Indian Prime Minister, had been shot dead by one of her bodyguards so armed protection wasn't always the best policy.

What should I do?

I couldn't hide for ever. But what was the alternative? Perhaps I should buy a bulletproof vest.

My main objective had to be to find out who was trying to have me killed and stop them, or at least remove the need, as they saw it, for my life to be terminated.

Easy.

But why would anyone want me dead? It seemed a very extreme solution to any problem.

I must know something, or have something, that someone didn't want me to tell or show to somebody else. Hence I needed to be killed to prevent it.

So what was it that I had, or knew?

The police already had the credit card statements and the MoneyHome payment slips, so surely it couldn't be them. Was there something else I had inherited from

Herb that was so incriminating that murder was the only answer?

Claudia groaned a little and woke up.

'Hello, my darling,' I said. 'How are you feeling?'

'Bloody awful,' she said. 'And really thirsty.'

I poured some water from the jug on her bedside cabinet into a plastic glass and held it out to her.

'Just go easy,' I said. 'The nurse said to drink just small sips.'

She drank several large ones and then handed back the glass.

'I feel so sore and bloated,' she said.

'Mr Tomic said you might. It'll pass in a day or so.'

She didn't seem much reassured.

'Can you help me sit up a bit?' she asked. 'I'm so uncomfortable in this bloody bed.'

I did as she asked, but it didn't really improve matters. Nothing would, I realized, for as long as she was in pain.

'Let's get you some painkillers,' I said and pushed the nurse call bell.

They gave her an injection of morphine that deadened the pain but also sent Claudia back to sleep. It was probably the best thing for her.

I put on the television to watch the news, but I kept the sound down to a minimum so as not to disturb the patient.

The gunman in a London newsagent's was the lead story and, true to their word, the police had convinced the TV company to play the whole video clip of Herb's killer coming into the shop, looking around, and then leaving again. They even showed a blown-up still of the man's face as he had glanced directly up at the camera.

Just looking at his image made me nervous once more.

The news reporter then warned the viewers not to approach the man if they saw him but to report his presence to the police. The man is armed and very dangerous, the reporter said, but he didn't mention anything about Herb Kovak or the killing at Aintree.

Did the news report and the video make it safer for me or not?

I also wondered if it put Mr Patel at risk. After all, he was the one who'd had the best view of the gunman. I suddenly went quite cold just thinking about how much mortal danger I had placed Mr Patel in by hiding behind his counter. But what else could I have done? Stayed out in the street and been killed?

I switched over to another channel and watched the whole thing once more, trying my best to recognize the face staring out at me from the screen. I knew I didn't know him, other than at Aintree and in a Finchley street, but I tried to find some semblance or likeness. There was none.

Thankfully, Claudia slept soundly through both bulletins. She had enough worries on her own plate for the time being without being burdened with something else. After all, there was nothing she could do about it.

While she went on sleeping, I tried to work out

where I could spend the night. I wasn't going back to Finchley, that was for sure, but a second night sitting upright in the chair in Claudia's hospital room wasn't a very attractive proposition either.

As I still had the key in my pocket, I thought of going to Herb's flat in Hendon but I didn't want to turn up there late at night frightening Sherri after her traumatic trip to Liverpool. So, instead, I used my phone to find a cheap room near the hospital in a hotel located round the corner in Euston Square Gardens. They had plenty of availability so I didn't leave my name. I just planned to turn up there when I left the hospital. That somehow seemed safer.

One of the nurses came into Claudia's room to take, once more, her vital signs and to settle her for the night. I took it as my cue to leave.

'Night night, my darling,' I said. 'I'll be back in the morning.'

'What about your job?' she said sleepily.

'I'll call the office and tell them I'm not coming in,' I said. 'The work will have to wait.'

She smiled and laid her head back on the pillow. She looked very vulnerable with her pale face almost matching the slight greyness of the hospital linen. We had to beat this impostor within her body, this cancer that would eat away at our happiness. If chemotherapy was what was needed, so be it. Short-term discomfort for long-term gain, that was what we had to think, what we had to believe.

*

I checked in to the hotel using a false name, and I paid for the room in advance with cash that I had drawn from an ATM in Euston Station. As the superintendent had said, I'd probably been watching too much TV, and I didn't really believe for a minute that the gunman had access to my credit card accounts, but I was taking absolutely no chances.

I had left the hospital by the main door only because there were no dark shadowy corners as there were outside the back entrance, but not before I had stood for a while behind a pillar watching the road, checking for anyone lurking in wait for me with a silenced pistol.

And I hadn't left the building alone, but had waited for a group of cleaning staff going off duty.

No one had fired a shot or come running after me. But would I even know if they did? I was certain Herb had been dead at Aintree before he realized what was happening.

I locked my bedroom door and then propped a chair under the door handle for good measure. I then relaxed a little and ate the takeaway cheeseburger, fries and milkshake that I'd bought from a late-night burger bar in the railway station.

It was the first thing I'd eaten all day. My mother would not have been pleased.

I removed my computer from my bag and logged on to the internet to check my e-mails.

Amongst the usual bunch from various fund managers wanting me to contact them about their latest investment offering was one from Patrick expressing his disquiet over recent happenings both inside and outside the office.

It hadn't been addressed solely to me but had been sent to all the Lyall & Black staff, but it felt like I was the main target.

'Dear colleagues,' Patrick had written, 'At this time of seemingly major upheaval within the firm, it is important for us all to concentrate on why we are here. While we are, of course, greatly saddened by the tragic loss of Herb Kovak, it is our clients who we are here to serve. It is they who pay our salaries and we must not give them cause to look elsewhere for their investment advice. We need to conduct our personal affairs with the highest degree of probity, and not give them any reason to doubt our honesty and integrity. I am sure that you will be asked by clients to speculate concerning the reason for Herb's untimely death, as well as on the nature of it, and on the other unfortunate event that occurred in these offices last Thursday. I ask that you refrain from any comments that may in any way place Lyall & Black in a bad light. If in doubt, please refer the clients to Mr Gregory or myself.'

I assumed that the 'other unfortunate event' referred to was my arrest.

It made me wonder how Billy Searle was faring in hospital and whether the police had made any progress in finding his attacker. Claudia's cancer revelation and her operation, coupled with the minor matter of finding an assassin on my doorstep, had kept my mind somewhat occupied elsewhere.

I went on to the *Racing Post* website.

'Billy Searle,' it said, 'was reported to be making steady progress. In fact, doctors at the Great Western Hospital in Swindon are amazed by the swiftness of his recovery from what were thought to be life-threatening injuries.'

They shouldn't really be surprised, I thought. Jump jockeys were made tough, and a breed apart from normal human beings. Broken bones and concussion were accepted as normal hazards of their employment, to be endured and recovered from as quickly as possible. All jockeys were self-employed – no rides meant no pay. It was a powerful incentive for quick healing.

There was nothing in the report about his attacker other than the stated hope that Searle would soon be able to be interviewed by the detectives investigating the incident about the identity of his assailant.

I wondered, meanwhile, if Billy was getting police protection.

The night passed without incident although I lay awake for much of it half-listening for someone climbing the drainpipe outside my bedroom window with gun in hand, and murder in mind.

I also spent the time thinking.

In particular I spent the time thinking about the note I had found in Herb's coat pocket. I knew the words of it by heart.

YOU SHOULD HAVE DONE WHAT YOU WERE
TOLD. YOU MAY SAY YOU REGRET IT, BUT YOU
WON'T BE REGRETTING IT FOR LONG.

I had told DCI Tomlinson that I thought it hadn't
been so much a warning as an apology, even though
he'd pooh-poohed the idea.

However, it did mean one thing for certain: Herb
had known his killer, or at least he knew someone
who knew he was going to die. That was assuming
that the '*won't be regretting it for long*' did, in fact,
refer to him dying soon. It could, I suppose, have been
from a girlfriend who was dumping him for not doing
as he was told, but somehow I doubted it. Notes from
girlfriends are never written in stark capital letters
without a salutation of some kind, and a name.

What had Herb been told to do that he hadn't done?

Was it something to do with the gambling and the
credit cards, or was there something else?

I turned on the bedside light and wrote out the
words in full on a notepad:

YOU SHOULD HAVE DONE WHAT YOU WERE
TOLD. YOU MAY SAY YOU REGRET IT, BUT YOU
WON'T BE REGRETTING IT FOR LONG.

I studied it carefully.

Maybe Herb hadn't *not done* something that he'd
been told to do, perhaps he had *done* something that
he'd been told not to.

But to whom had he expressed regret for his inaction

or action? And why had he regretted it? Because it had been wrong, or because it had placed him in danger?

Still so many questions and still so few answers.

'Leave the investigating to the professionals,' the chief inspector had said to me. But how long would they take? And would I still be alive by then?

Maybe it was time for me to start poking a few hornets' nests, and hope not to get stung.

I went into the hospital just after seven thirty on Wednesday morning. Claudia was so much improved, sitting up in her uncomfortable bed without as much as a murmur about backache, and she was eating a breakfast of muesli and natural yoghurt.

'Well, look at you,' I said, smiling broadly. 'You obviously had a better night than me.'

'Why? What was wrong with your night?' she asked.

'Lumpy hotel bed,' I said.

'Why didn't you go home?'

Ah, I thought. Careless. Now what do I say?

'I wanted to be nearer you, my darling.'

'But what a waste of money,' she said with mock disapproval of my profligacy. 'If I have to stay in here another night, I insist you go home. I'll be fine.'

Little did she know that there was no way I was going home, and neither was she. It was far too risky.

'You look well enough to run a marathon,' I said. 'I'm sure they'll chuck you out just as soon as Mr Tomic's seen you.'

'The nurse says he's usually here by eight.'

I looked up at the clock on the wall, the one that had driven me mad the previous day when Claudia had been in the operating theatre.

It was ten minutes before eight.

As if on cue, Mr Tomic swept into the room. He had the blue scrubs on but, this time, wore a doctor's white coat over them.

'Good morning, Claudia,' he said, and he nodded at me. 'How are you feeling?'

'Much better than last night,' Claudia replied. 'But I'm rather sore.'

'Yes,' he said. 'That's normal. I had to make incisions in the abdominal wall. They were only small but still painful. Do you think you are up to getting up?'

'I have been,' she said, almost in triumph. 'I went to the loo last night and again this morning.'

'Good,' he said. 'Then I think you can go home today. I'll see you in ten days to check on everything and take out the stitches. Until then, take it easy.'

'Great,' I said. 'She will. I'll see to that.'

'And,' he went on, 'we've had the first results from the tests.'

'Yes?' Claudia said. 'You can tell me.'

'The right ovary seems clear but, as I feared, there were some cancer cells in the peritoneal fluid. Not many, but enough.'

We were all silent for a moment.

'Chemotherapy?' Claudia said.

'I'm afraid so,' said Mr Tomic. 'But maybe just one

course. Two at most. I'm sorry, but it's the best way forward.'

He left us digesting that not-so-tasty morsel, rushing off, no doubt, to cut out bits from another desperate cancer patient. It was not my idea of a fun job.

'Let's look on the bright side, my darling,' I said finally. 'The right ovary is clear.'

'That's true,' Claudia replied, trying to be a little enthusiastic.

'So we might still have kids,' I said.

'If the chemo doesn't make me infertile,' she replied gloomily.

Even the thought of being discharged from hospital didn't cheer her up much, especially when I told her we weren't going home but to my mother's house in Gloucestershire.

'Nick, you've got to be kidding?' were her exact words.

'Nope,' I said. 'And Mum is so looking forward to it.'

'But I want to go home,' Claudia whined. 'I want my own bed.'

'But how would I look after you there when I have to go to work tomorrow?'

'And how, pray,' she asked dryly, 'are you going to go to work tomorrow from Cheltenham?' She paused briefly. 'Come on, Nick, please, let's just go home.'

Now what could I say? I could hardly tell her I was worried we might get murdered on our own doorstep. She probably wouldn't have believed me anyway.

I was convinced that Lichfield Grove was far too dangerous for us, and there was no way I was knowingly going to place my new fiancée into jeopardy. I'd been lucky last time, very lucky, and I'd had to run for my life. There was no way that Claudia would be able to run after having had two incisions through her abdominal wall. And who was to say I'd be lucky again?

And, to live, I had to be lucky every time.

My best chance, surely, was to be where the assassin wouldn't be, and to remain where he couldn't find me. He only had to be lucky once.

So, I decided, returning to Lichfield Grove was completely out of the question.

'My mother is so looking forward to it,' I said. 'And you yourself said it would be nice to go down to see her after the operation.'

'Yes,' she replied, 'but I didn't mean straight from the hospital.'

'Oh, come on, darling,' I pleaded. 'If your mother were still alive we would probably go and stay with her.'

It was a low blow, well beneath the belt, and to someone who was in no state to receive one.

We rarely, if ever, spoke of Claudia's parents. They had left her, aged eight, to spend the day with her grandmother, but they had never come back. Their Ford Escort had been driven off the cliff at Beachy Head straight down to the shingle beach some five hundred feet below.

The inquest had, apparently, returned a misadventure verdict rather than one of suicide. There had been some doubt as to which of the two had been driving at the time, or whether some malfunction of the car had been the cause. But, either way, Claudia blamed them both absolutely for leaving her alone in the world.

I thought it was quite likely the true reason behind all her weird paintings, but it was a topic that I raised rarely, and then with great care and tact.

'Nick, that's hardly fair,' she said crossly.

'I'm sorry,' I said. 'But I do want us to go straight to Mum's.'

'But what about my things?' she said.

'You've got many of them here with you,' I said. 'And I collected a few more yesterday from home.'

'And I definitely can't go to your mother's without my make-up,' she said defiantly.

'I've collected that too,' I said, trying not to sound too triumphant.

We went to my mother's, but not before I'd received another tongue-lashing over my extravagance in hiring a car for the trip.

'And what's wrong with our Mercedes?' Claudia had asked angrily.

'I thought you'd rather have a bit more space after your op,' I said, all sweetness and light. 'The SLK is so cramped for the passenger.'

And rather conspicuous, I thought.

The man at the Hertz car rental centre had tried to get me to hire his 'Car of the Week', a bright yellow Audi convertible with shiny chrome wheels. 'It would suit you, sir,' he'd said eagerly. 'Your sort of colour. Makes a big statement.'

I had opted instead for a bog-standard, four-door, blue saloon with not so much as a 'go-faster' stripe down the side. I wanted to blend into the background, not stand out from it.

I'd make my big statement in another way.

I'd told Claudia that my mother was looking forward to having us to stay, and she was, but only after I had talked her out of going to her regular Wednesday-afternoon whist drive in the village.

'Mum,' I'd said on the telephone, having woken her at ten to seven in the morning, 'I just need to get us away for a few days.'

'But why, darling?' she'd replied. 'What's so sudden that you can't come tomorrow?'

'Please, Mum,' I'd said to her in a tone like a seven-year-old trying to get his reluctant parent to buy him a coveted toy.

'Oh, all right,' she'd said. 'But I'll have to go shopping for some food. And I really don't like letting down the other players.'

'They'll understand,' I'd said. 'Just tell them your son is coming and bringing his fiancée home for the first time.'

She hadn't been able to speak for a few moments. I had waited.

'Oh, darling,' she'd said eventually, her voice full of emotion. 'Is it really true or are you just saying that?'

'It's really true,' I'd replied.

Hence, when we drove down the lane to her cottage, my mother was already outside to welcome us, in tears and almost unable to speak with joy. She hugged Claudia like she'd never done so before.

'What did you say to her?' Claudia asked me quietly as we went inside.

'I told her we were engaged,' I said. 'We are, aren't we?'

'Yes,' she said, smiling. 'Of course we are. But what else did you tell her? You know, about the cancer?'

'Nothing,' I said. 'I'll leave that for you to decide.'

'I think not,' she said. 'Not yet.'

'Fine,' I replied.

We went into the open-plan kitchen/diner/lounge and Claudia sat down gingerly on a chair.

'What's the matter, my dear?' my mother asked with concern. 'You look like you're in pain.'

'I am, Dorothy,' Claudia said. 'I've just had an operation. A hernia. But I'll be fine soon.'

'My dear,' said my mother, 'come at once and put your feet up on the sofa.'

She fussed around her future daughter-in-law like a brooding mother hen and soon had Claudia propped up on a chintz-covered sofa with multiple pillows.

'There,' my mother said, standing back. 'How about a nice cup of tea?'

'That would be lovely,' Claudia said, and she winked at me.

I left them to their bonding session while I took our

things upstairs to the guest bedroom, negotiating the narrow, twisting staircase with our bags.

I sat on the bed and called the office using my mother's cordless phone. Gregory should have returned from his long weekend away by now and, with luck, Patrick would have convinced him over lunch not to hang, draw and quarter me, and even perhaps to let me back into the offices.

Mrs McDowd answered.

'Lyall and Black,' she said in her usual crisp tone. 'How can I direct your call?'

'Hello Mrs McDowd,' I said. 'Mr Nicholas here.'

'Ah, yes,' she said curtly. 'Mr Patrick said you might ring. But it's not your number.'

Mrs McDowd, I decided, was sitting on the fence with regards to me. She was being neither friendly nor hostile towards me. She would clearly wait to see how I fared with the senior partners before committing to an allegiance either way.

'Are Mr Patrick and Mr Gregory back from lunch yet?' I asked.

'They didn't go to lunch,' she said. 'They've gone to a funeral. They'll be gone for the rest of the day.'

'That was rather sudden,' I said.

'Death often is,' she replied.

'Whose funeral is it?' I asked.

'A client of Gregory's,' she said. 'Someone called Roberts. Colonel Jolyon Roberts.'

13

'What?' I said. 'What did you say?'

'Colonel Jolyon Roberts,' Mrs McDowd said again. 'Mr Patrick and Mr Gregory have gone to his funeral.'

'But when did he die?' I asked. I'd been talking to him only on Saturday at Sandown Park Races.

'Seems he was found dead early yesterday morning,' she said. 'Heart attack, apparently. Very sudden.'

'The funeral is mighty sudden too,' I said, 'if he only died yesterday.'

'Jewish,' she said by way of explanation. 'Quick burial is part of their culture, and usually within twenty-four hours. Something to do with the heat in Israel.'

She was a mine of information, Mrs McDowd. The heat in England in April isn't quite as intense as that in a Jerusalem summer but, I suppose, traditions are traditions.

And I'd never realized that Jolyon Roberts had been Jewish. But why would I?

'Are you sure it was a heart attack?' I asked her.

Never mind the chief inspector's suspicious mind, I thought, mine was now in overdrive.

'That's what I heard from Mr Gregory,' said Mrs McDowd. 'He was quite shocked by it. Seems he'd only been talking to Colonel Roberts on Monday afternoon.'

'I thought Mr Gregory was away for a long weekend.'

'He was meant to be,' she said. 'But he came back on Monday. Something urgent cropped up.'

'OK,' I said, 'I'll call Mr Patrick on his mobile.'

'The funeral service is at three,' she said.

I looked at my watch. It was well past two thirty.

'I won't call him until afterwards,' I said. 'Where is it?'

'Golders Green,' she said. 'At the Jewish cemetery, in the family plot.'

I disconnected and sat on the bed for a while, thinking.

Herb Kovak had accessed the Roberts Family Trust file, and the Bulgarian investment details, and, within a week of doing so, he'd been murdered. I'd sent an innocent-looking e-mail to a man in Bulgaria about the same development and, four days later, someone turned up on my doorstep trying to kill me.

And now, Jolyon Roberts, with his questions and doubts about the whole Bulgarian project, conveniently dies of a heart attack the day after speaking to Gregory about it, as I had told him he should.

Was I going crazy, or was a pattern beginning to appear?

A hundred million euros of EU money was a lot of cash.

Was it enough to murder for? Was it enough to murder three times for?

*

I decided to call Detective Chief Inspector Tomlinson, if only to try and get some more information about the death of Jolyon Roberts.

'Are you suggesting that this Colonel Roberts was murdered?' he asked in a sceptical tone.

Suddenly the whole idea appeared less plausible.

'I don't know,' I said. 'But I'd love to hear what the pathologist said.'

'Assuming there was an autopsy.'

'Surely there would be,' I said. 'I thought all sudden deaths were subject to post mortems.'

'But why do you believe he was murdered?'

'I'm probably wrong,' I said.

'Tell me anyway,' the chief inspector said with a degree of encouragement. 'And I promise not to laugh.'

'Murder is pretty uncommon, right?'

'I've seen more than my fair share on Merseyside.'

'But, generally,' I said, 'for us non-homicide detectives, I'd say it was a pretty rare thing to know a murder victim. Wouldn't you agree?'

'OK, I agree. Murder is uncommon.'

'Well,' I said, 'if I'm right and Colonel Roberts was murdered, then I've known two murder victims, and both of them have been killed within the past two weeks, and I nearly became the third.' I paused.

'Go on,' he said.

'So, I looked to see what connection Herb Kovak had with Colonel Roberts, and also with myself.'

'Yes?' he said with greater eagerness.

'Lyall and Black, for one thing,' I said. 'Herb Kovak

and I work for the firm and Colonel Roberts was a client, although not a client that Herb or I would usually have contacted.' I paused. 'But Herb accessed the Roberts file just ten days before he died, in particular looking at the details of a Bulgarian investment that the Roberts Family Trust had made. I saw the record of him having done so on a company computer.'

'And what is significant about that?' the detective asked.

'Colonel Roberts approached me just a week ago over his concerns about that very same investment.'

'Why did he approach you in particular?'

'I'm not really sure,' I said. 'He knew I worked for Lyall and Black and he met me at the races on Tuesday and again on Wednesday. It was a chance meeting the first time but I'm sure it was on purpose the second day. He was worried that the factory he had invested in hadn't actually been built as he had been told it had, but he didn't want a full enquiry as he was worried that he'd been duped and didn't want the whole world to know. So he asked me to quietly have a look and check that all was well with the investment.'

'And did you?' he asked.

'I did a little bit of digging, but I told him on Saturday that I couldn't go searching behind the backs of others at the firm and he should speak to his investment manager about it.'

'Who is?' he asked.

'Gregory Black,' I said. 'Colonel Roberts spoke to him on Monday, only the day before he died.'

'But it's quite a jump to think that he was murdered because of it. And are you telling me you suspect Gregory Black of killing him?'

'No, of course not,' I said. 'Gregory Black may have an explosive temper but he's hardly a murderer.'

Or was he? Could I really tell what went on in his head? Or in anyone else's head for that matter? But Gregory a murderer? Surely not.

'But that's not all,' I said. 'I sent an e-mail to someone in Bulgaria last Friday, and a would-be assassin turned up at my door on Tuesday afternoon.'

'OK,' he said, now firmly interested. 'I'll try and find out if there was an autopsy carried out on this Colonel Roberts. Where did you say he lived?'

'Hampstead,' I said. 'He only died yesterday and he's being buried in Golders Green Cemetery even as we speak.'

'That's very quick,' he said.

'Apparently it's a Jewish tradition to bury the dead as quickly as possible.'

'At least it's not a cremation,' he said. 'No chance of a second look at the body if it's cremated. And I speak from experience.' He laughed.

What a strange occupation, I thought, daily dealings with violent death and its fallout.

'You will let me know the results?' I asked.

'If I can,' he said. 'I'll call you if I get anything.'

'I'm not at home. And my mobile doesn't work where I am.'

'And where is that?'

I was a little reluctant to tell him. The fewer the people who knew, the safer I'd feel. But he was the police, and he had provided me with an unshakeable alibi when I was arrested for attempted murder.

'I'm in a village called Woodmancote,' I said. 'It's near Cheltenham racecourse. It's where my mother lives.' I gave him my mother's telephone number.

'Cheltenham is a long way from your office,' he said in a tone that seemed to ask a question.

'I know. I know,' I said. 'I ran away. Superintendent Yering was unable to provide me with any protection and I felt very vulnerable, so I didn't go home.'

'I can't say I really blame you,' he said.

'So how about you giving me a bodyguard?' I asked. 'Preferably one bristling with guns, and with evil intent towards assassins.'

'I'll see what I can do,' he said. 'Especially if it does turn out that Colonel Roberts was murdered.'

'And another thing,' I said, deciding to get my requests in quickly as the chief inspector seemed to be in a generous mood. 'Can you find out whether Billy Searle has started talking to the Wiltshire Police? And what he's told them.'

'Do you think he has something to do with all this as well?'

'No, I don't,' I said. 'I happen to know where Billy's money was invested because I manage his portfolio, and it was nowhere near Bulgaria. I'm just interested to know what he's told the police. After all, I was arrested on suspicion of trying to kill him.'

'I'll try,' he said. 'But some of these rural detectives can be reluctant to discuss their cases with officers from other forces.'

'Just remind them it was me who gave them the information that Billy Searle owed someone a hundred thousand, and it was you that stopped them from looking bloody foolish by charging me with attempted murder when I had a cast-iron alibi.'

'OK. OK. I said I'd try.'

When I went downstairs, my mother and Claudia were in full flow with wedding plans.

'It was about time he asked you to marry him,' she said to Claudia while looking at me.

'But he didn't,' Claudia replied. 'I asked him.'

My mother was quite taken aback and even rendered speechless for a few seconds. She had always been a stickler for tradition.

'How very unusual,' she said finally. 'But Nicholas always was a funny boy.'

Jan Setter had called me strange.

Was I really funny, or strange?

I didn't think so.

To me I was 'normal', but I suppose everyone thinks they are 'normal', and yet we are all so different. There was actually no such thing as 'normal'.

'Now, darlings,' my mother said, changing the subject, 'would you like some late lunch? I've a shepherd's pie in the oven.'

'Mum,' I said, 'it's gone three o'clock.'

'So?' she replied. 'I thought you might be hungry when you arrived.'

Surprisingly, I was, and I could tell from Claudia's eager look that she was too. I had been so busy trying to make the journey smooth and jerk-free, to keep Claudia as comfortable as possible, that I hadn't even thought of stopping for food.

Consequently the three of us sat down to a very late lunch of shepherd's pie and broccoli, with my mother insisting that I had a second helping.

I called Patrick on his mobile at twenty to six, late enough for the funeral to be over, but early enough for it still to be in the working day.

Claudia was upstairs having a rest and my mother was busying herself by the stove, preparing yet another high-fat, high-protein, chicken casserole for our dinner. I sat on the chintz sofa in the lounge area, facing her, but at the furthest point of the room.

'Ah, yes. Nicholas,' Patrick said, seemingly slightly flustered. 'Mrs McDowd told me you'd called. Sorry I wasn't able to speak to you earlier.'

'And I am sorry to hear about Colonel Roberts,' I said.

'Yes, what a dreadful thing. He was only sixty-two as well. Enjoy life while you've got it, that's what I say. You never know when the Grim Reaper will catch you up.'

Yes, I thought. But I'd outrun him once down Lichfield Grove.

'Have you spoken to Gregory?' I asked, getting to the point of the call.

'Yes, I have,' he said. 'He is still very angry with you.'

'But, why?' I asked.

'Why do you think?' he said crossly. 'For getting arrested and being splashed all over the papers and the television. He believes you brought the firm into disrepute.'

'But, Patrick, his anger is completely misplaced, and he is wrong. It wasn't my fault that I was arrested. The police jumped to a conclusion and it was an incorrect one.'

'Yes,' he said. 'But you did give them reason to draw it.'

'I did not,' I said, getting quite angry myself. 'It was that idiot Billy Searle who shouted out about murder. I did absolutely nothing wrong.'

My mother glanced over at me from the kitchen area.

'Gregory says there is no smoke without fire. He still thinks you must have had something to do with it.'

'Well, in that case, Gregory is more of an idiot than I thought.' My raised voice caused my mother to stand and look at me from across the room, and with a furrowed brow. I paused to calm myself down. I then spoke much more quietly. 'Am I being fired? Because if I am, I'll be taking Lyall and Black to court.'

He did not reply, and I stayed silent. I could hear his breathing.

'You had better come in to the office tomorrow,' he said at last. 'I will tell Gregory to hold his tongue.'

'Thank you,' I said. 'But I may not make it in tomorrow. Claudia is not very well and I'll probably work from home using the remote-access system. I hope to see you on Friday.'

'Right,' he said, sounding slightly relieved that he had at least another day to dampen the erupting Gregory volcano. 'I'll see you on Friday.'

He hung up and I sat for a while wondering about my future, if I still had one with a gun-toting assassin on the loose.

'What was all that about?' my mother asked with concern.

'Oh, nothing, Mum,' I said. 'Just a little problem at work. Nothing to worry about.'

But I did worry about it.

I had really enjoyed working for Lyall & Black over the last five years, but the role of an independent financial adviser was one that necessitated absolute trust, both of the client and of one's colleagues. What sort of future did I have in a firm where one of the senior partners believed me to be involved in an attempted murder and, at the same time, I wondered if he had been involved in a successful one?

The three of us sat at my mother's dining table for dinner, and I ate and drank too much for my own good.

'What's happened to your cat?' I asked, noticing its absence from under the table.

'It's not my cat,' my mother said. 'He's just an irregular visitor and I haven't seen him for days. He'll probably be back sometime soon.'

No doubt when fillet steak was back on the menu, I thought.

Claudia and I went up to bed early for us, around ten o'clock.

'You are such a clever thing,' Claudia said to me as we snuggled up together under the duvet.

'In what way?' I asked.

'Insisting we came here,' she said. 'If we'd gone home I would have felt pressured to cook or clean, or do something useful. Here I can relax completely, my phone doesn't even ring, and your mother is such a dear.'

I smiled in the darkness. Now that was a turn-up.

'But we can't stay here very long,' I said seriously.

'Why not?' she asked.

'Because, if she goes on feeding me as she's done today, I'll end up with a waistline like Homer Simpson's.'

We giggled uncontrollably.

Since we'd left the hospital that morning, neither of us had mentioned anything about the cancer, or the upcoming chemo treatments. It was as if we had left all our troubles behind, in London.

But they were about to come looking for us.

*

I dreamed that I was riding in a race but, like all dreams, it was inconsistent and erratic. One second I was on a horse, the next on an ostrich, or in a car. However, one part of the dream was unvarying: whatever we were riding I was always racing against Gregory. And he was ever-smiling, and aiming a gun with a silencer at my head.

I woke up with a jerk, breathing fast, ready to run.

I relaxed, and lay there in the dark listening to Claudia's rhythmic breathing beside me.

Did I really think that Gregory Black was involved in fraud and murder?

I didn't know, but I was sure interested to hear the results of the post mortem examination on Jolyon Roberts, if there had been one.

I drifted back to sleep but only fitfully, waking often to listen for sounds that shouldn't have been there. Woodmancote was much quieter without traffic, and much darker without streetlamps, than our home in Lichfield Grove but, nevertheless, I slept badly and was wide awake long before the sun lit up the bedroom window soon after six o'clock.

I got up quietly and padded silently downstairs in bare feet with my computer. I had been seriously neglecting my clients over the past two weeks and, if I didn't pull my finger out soon, I'd have no job worthy of the name at Lyall & Black to cry about even if I was fired.

I logged on to the internet.

I had forty-three unread e-mails including a fresh

one from Jan Setter telling me how fantastic the first night of the Florence Nightingale show had been and how crazy I was to have missed it. It was timed at 5.50 a.m. this morning and the show in London hadn't finished until ten thirty last night, not to mention how late the after-show party had gone on. Did she never sleep, or had she sent it as soon as she'd arrived home?

I e-mailed back to her and said how pleased I was she had enjoyed it and how I hoped it would make her lots of money.

Then I went onto the daily newspaper websites to read the reviews. All but one were pretty encouraging, so maybe the show might make some money. Backing shows and films was always a risky business. I usually told my clients that it was far more of a gamble than they would have on the stock market but, as with most risky investments, the potential gains were greater too. But they had to be prepared to lose *all* their money.

One of my clients never expected any financial return from such investments, he just revelled in rubbing shoulders with the stars at the first-night functions, and taking all his friends to see 'his' show in the best seats. 'I know I might lose it all,' he would say, 'but, if I do, I'll enjoy every minute while I'm losing it. And you never know, I might just make a fortune.'

And he had done precisely that the previous year.

At my suggestion, he had backed a small independent film company to make an obscure and irreverent comedy based around the first transportation of convicts from England to Australia in 1787. To everyone's surprise, not least my client's, the film had been a huge international hit. At the box office worldwide it had earned back over two hundred times its production cost, as well as receiving an Oscar nomination for its young star who played the title role in *Bruce: The First Australian*.

But the successes were few, and the disasters many.

It took me over two hours just to answer my outstanding e-mails, by which time I could hear movement above and, presently, my mother came downstairs in her dressing gown.

'Hello, dear,' she said. 'You're up early.'

'I've been down here over two hours,' I said. 'I have work to do.'

'Yes, dear,' she said. 'Don't we all. Now, what would you like for breakfast? I have some bacon and local eggs, and Mr Ayers, my butcher, has made me some wonderful sausages. How many would you like?'

'Just a coffee and a slice of toast would be lovely,' I said.

It was like King Canute trying to hold back the tide.

'Don't be ridiculous,' she said, already placing a frying pan on the stove. 'You've got to have a proper breakfast. What sort of mother would I be if I didn't feed you?'

I sighed. Perhaps Claudia and I would go out for a drive at lunchtime.

I took her up a cup of tea while the sausages and bacon were sizzling in the pan.

'Morning, gorgeous,' I said, pulling open the curtains. 'How are you feeling today?'

'Still a bit sore,' she said, sitting up. 'But better than yesterday.'

'Good,' I said. 'Time to get up. Delia Smith downstairs is cooking breakfast.'

'Mmm, I can smell it,' she said, laughing. 'Now don't you expect that every morning when we're married.'

'What?' I said in mock horror. 'No cooked breakfasts! The wedding's off!'

'We haven't even fixed a date for it yet,' she said.

'Before or after the hair loss?' I asked seriously.

She thought for a moment. 'After it grows back. Give me time to get used to this engagement business first.'

'After it is, then,' I said. I leaned down and kissed her. 'Don't be long or Mr Ayers's sausages will get cold.'

She dived back under the covers and put a pillow over her head. 'I'm staying here.'

'Hiding won't help,' I said, laughing, and leaving her alone.

My mother hadn't lied, the sausages were excellent, but, as always with her meals, they were too big and too numerous, and then there was the mountain of bacon and the scrambled eggs on fried bread, not forgetting the mushrooms and grilled tomatoes on the side.

I felt totally bloated by the time I sat down again at my computer to check through my client files using the firm's remote-access facility.

Claudia, meanwhile, had managed to extract herself from her bed, coming down to join us in a bathrobe, but she ate just a small bowl of muesli and a little sliced fruit. And had grinned at me as she did so. It really wasn't fair.

I spent the morning briefly looking through all the files for my fifty or so personal clients, to check on the reminder tags, ensuring that I hadn't missed reinvesting the proceeds of maturing bonds, or suchlike.

What I really needed to do was to study all the recent stock movements. It was something that I should be doing every day in order to maintain a 'feel' for the markets, to try and be, if not one step ahead, at least in tune with market trends. Not that Lyall & Black invested directly in individual stocks. That proportion of our clients' money put into equities was almost exclusively invested through unit trusts or investment funds that had a broad range of different shares within them. It was a way of spreading risk, of placing one's eggs in many baskets at the same time. But it was still important for me to have a feel for the markets in order to advise my clients which of the hundreds of trusts and funds to buy into.

And, over the past week or so, I had been guilty of serious dereliction of my duty in the study department.

I used my mother's landline to check on my voicemail. There was one new message and it was from Sherri asking me to call her at Herb's flat.

'Hi,' I said when she answered. 'Is everything all right?'

'Fine,' she replied, sounding totally fed up. 'Least I suppose it's fine. Monday in Liverpool was a bit of an ordeal.'

'I'm sorry,' I said.

'Yeah,' she said. 'Well, it's over, anyway.' She sighed audibly down the phone. 'I'm going home tomorrow morning. I'm on a flight at ten forty-five to Chicago. I just called to say goodbye.'

'Thanks,' I said. 'I'm glad you did.'

'A few letters have arrived here for Herb and I had a phone call from his gym, something about Herb not paying them and they want his locker back. Hold on, I've got their number somewhere.' I could hear her rummaging in the background. 'Here it is. Somewhere called the Slim Fit Gym.' She read out the telephone number and I jotted it down on the back of the rental-car agreement.

'Don't you worry,' I said. 'Leave the letters on the desk, I'll deal with them, and I'll call the gym. You look after yourself. I hope you have a safe trip home. I'll let you know about the funeral and such when I know myself.'

'The police said it could be weeks away. That's why I'm going back. I'll lose my job if I stay here much longer.'

Life could be a bugger.

I called the Slim Fit Gym.

'Mr Kovak's direct debit has been cancelled,' someone said. 'So we want his locker back.'

'He died,' I said. 'So take it back.'

'But there's a padlock on it,' the person said.

'Don't you have a spare key?' I asked.

'It was Mr Kovak's own padlock.'

'Can't you cut it off?' I said, somewhat impatiently.

'No.' The person was getting quite agitated 'We must have the key.'

I remembered the one that was pinned to the notice-board above Herb's desk.

'OK, OK,' I said. 'I'll bring it in next week.'

They didn't like it but it was too bad. However, they did insist on having my contact details. I hated giving out my mobile number so I gave them the office one instead.

I disconnected and leaned back in the chair, stretching.

'Do you fancy going out?' Claudia said, coming over and rubbing my shoulders. 'It's a lovely day out there.'

My studying would have to wait.

'That would be nice,' I said, turning round on the chair. 'But are you sure you're feeling up to it?'

'Absolutely,' she said. 'I'm feeling much better today. But let's take the car. I'm not yet ready to yomp around the countryside. Why don't we go to a pub for lunch?' She winked at me.

'Great idea,' I agreed. I stood up and went into the kitchen area where my mother was fussing with the dishwasher. 'Mum,' I said to her, 'Claudia and I thought we might drive to a pub for lunch. Do you want to come?'

'Oh,' she said. 'I have some nice pork chops from Mr Ayers for lunch.'

'Won't they do for this evening?' I said.

'I've got a roast leg of lamb for us tonight.'

Mr Ayers had obviously been busy.

'Leave the chops in the fridge,' I said. 'Give yourself a rest. Let's all go out for lunch.'

And we did, with me looking over the hedge for my would-be assassin as the three of us climbed into the nondescript blue saloon. But, of course, he wasn't there and we made it safely to a local country pub with a big GOOD FOOD sign outside. Claudia and my mother both ordered a glass of white wine and a poached salmon salad, while I just had a Diet Coke and a bag of roasted peanuts.

'But, darling,' my mother complained bitterly, 'you must have a proper lunch, or you'll fade away.'

'Mother, dear,' I said. 'I've done nothing but eat since we arrived. I think fading away is the least of my worries.' But she didn't like it, and I could already feel an extra-large portion of lamb coming on for dinner.

The phone was ringing when we arrived back at the cottage and my mother rushed in to answer it.

'It's for you,' she said, handing over the phone to me.

'Hello,' I said.

'It was definitely a heart attack,' said Chief Inspector Tomlinson down the line. 'While he was swimming in his own pool. Then he drowned as a result. A full post mortem was carried out at the Royal Free Hospital on Tuesday afternoon. Seems Colonel Roberts had a history of heart problems.'

'Oh,' I said. 'Such are the perils of early-morning swimming.'

'It was late-night swimming, apparently, and on his own. And he'd been drinking. Stupid fool. His blood alcohol level was more than twice that for drunk driving.'

'But he wasn't driving,' I said.

'No,' said the detective, 'but he was swimming and, in my experience, alcohol and water don't mix.' He laughed at his own joke, and I found it slightly irritating. But it reminded me of Jolyon Roberts doing just the same thing during our meeting in the Chasers Bar at Sandown Park Races.

'Hold on a minute,' I said, suddenly remembering something else from that meeting. 'Colonel Roberts told me, categorically, that he didn't drink alcohol. And that he never had.'

14

'I'll get back to you,' said Chief Inspector Tomlinson suddenly. 'I need to call in a few favours.'

He hung up, and I was cross I hadn't asked him about Billy Searle. But it would wait.

The phone rang again in my hand.

'Hello,' I said, answering it. 'Did you forget something?'

'Sorry?' said a female voice. 'Is that you, Mr Nicholas?'

'Mrs McDowd,' I said. 'How lovely to hear from you.'

There was a slight pause at the other end as Mrs McDowd worked out that I was being sarcastic.

'I have a message from Mr Patrick,' she said.

'How did you get this number?' I asked.

'He wants you to –' she started, but I interrupted her.

'Mrs McDowd,' I said again loudly. 'How did you get this number?'

'It was on caller-ID when you called in this morning,' she said.

That was rather careless, I thought, for someone meant to be in hiding.

'Anyway,' she said. 'I know that number. You're staying with your mother. How is she?'

Bloody Mrs McDowd, I thought. How does she know so much about me?

'She's fine, thank you,' I said, biting my tongue. 'Now, what does Mr Patrick want?'

'He wants you to call him in the morning before you come into the office. Something about arranging a meeting between you and Mr Gregory.'

'Did he say what the meeting was about?' I asked.

'No,' she said, but I bet she knew. Mrs McDowd knew everything.

'Please tell Mr Patrick that I won't be in the office very early tomorrow.'

'I've already told him that,' she said. 'Not with you being down in Gloucestershire.'

Who else had she told, I wondered.

In particular, had she told Mr Gregory?

I spent much of the afternoon catching up on the changing price of derivatives and futures, and on how a recent fall in the Dow Jones index in the United States had affected markets in the Far East more than those in Europe, and on fluctuations in the value of gold in pounds as a result of changes in the cost of a barrel of oil in dollars.

It was like a balancing act.

Some economies grew and others contracted; stock markets moved at different paces or in opposite ways; some currencies went up and others went down. The trick to winning in the great global financial game was to invest in the things about to go up in real value, while selling those about to go down. Then there were hedge funds and short selling, both designed to make you money when the values went in the wrong direction.

But it was all a bit like gambling with a bookmaker. For you to win, he had to lose. So it was in the markets – there were winners and losers. The winners had big houses and the losers went bust, losing their big houses to the banks, which then sold them to the winners.

The money went round and round but it did not always end up with the same people.

And then there were the fraudsters, those who tried to load the odds in their favour through insider dealing or market manipulation.

Once upon a time insider dealing had been seen as a perk of the job for stockbrokers and company directors, cashing in on prior knowledge of profits and mergers by buying or selling stock before the facts were known to others. Nowadays the courts send them to jail for doing what everyone used to do, and quite rightly too.

But there are always those who think they can beat the system, and many of them do, because betting on a certainty was like having a licence to print money.

Herb Kovak had said to Mrs McDowd that he liked to bet on certainties.

She'd told me.

Chief Inspector Tomlinson called back at five o'clock.

'He'd definitely been drinking,' he said. 'I've seen the full autopsy report. There's no mistake. They tested both his blood and the aqueous humour in his eye. And the stomach contained whisky residue.'

'How easy is it to force someone to drink whisky?' I asked.

'My, my,' he said. 'Now who has the suspicious mind?'

'It's just too convenient,' I said.

'But how could you give someone a heart attack?' he asked, his slightly sarcastic tone clearly indicating that he didn't believe me.

'Hold his drunken head under the surface of his own swimming pool,' I said. 'Either he drowns straight away or, as he has a history of heart problems, he panics, has a heart attack and then drowns.'

'But why the alcohol?' he asked.

'To add confusion,' I said. 'When you knew he'd been drinking, you instinctively believed he had been a stupid fool, and you probably thought he half deserved to die for it.'

'True,' he said. 'I did. But you are only speculating. There's no evidence of foul play.'

'No,' I agreed. 'And what there was has conveniently been buried in Golders Green Cemetery.'

He laughed. 'Story of my life.'

'What about Billy Searle?' I asked. 'What did you find out?'

'He's wide awake and talking,' he said. 'But he's not saying anything.'

'Nothing?'

'Pretty much. He refuses to say if he knew the person

268

who knocked him off his bike. Says it was an accident. And he denies owing anyone any money.'

I wasn't surprised. If it was a bookmaker, and Billy was involved in some betting scandal, he was hardly likely to admit it. It would be tantamount to handing in his jockey's licence for good.

'Well, thanks for finding out for me,' I said. 'Any news on the gunman?'

'Nothing as yet.'

'Didn't you get any response from the video?'

'Masses,' he said. 'Too much, really. The Met and us are sifting through it all, and cross-referencing with the criminal records bureau.'

That was what worried me the most. If he were a professional hit-man he was unlikely to have a criminal record, so he would never turn up from their cross-reference.

'So how about that bodyguard you promised me?' I asked. 'I can't stay down here for long as it's too far from London, but I don't fancy going home with our friend still out there.'

'I'll talk to my Super,' he said.

'Thanks,' I said, 'And please make it soon.'

We disconnected and I looked at my watch. It was quarter past five. Time to finish for the day.

I leaned back in the chair and pushed the 'get mail' button for a final check on my e-mails. One arrived from Gregory Black.

I sat forward quickly and opened it.

'Nicholas,' he had written, 'Patrick has asked me to write to you to apologize for my outburst of last Friday. So I am sorry. I can also assure you there will be no repetition of my actions when you return to this office after your stay with your mother. Yours, Gregory Black.'

Wow, I thought. My threat of court action had really put the cat amongst the pigeons. I could imagine Gregory absolutely hating having to write that e-mail with Patrick standing over him on one side, and almost certainly with Andrew Mellor, the company's lawyer, on the other, advising them both on employment law.

I may have received a grudging apology from Gregory, but he would resent it for ever. And it wouldn't make my future at the firm any easier.

I also didn't like the fact that Gregory knew that I was staying with my mother.

Mrs McDowd not only wanted to know everything about everyone, she also liked them to know she knew it, by spreading the information. The whole office would now be aware that I was in Gloucestershire, and probably half of Lombard Street too.

At about seven thirty my mother insisted I open a bottle of champagne to properly celebrate Claudia's and my engagement.

'I put one in my old fridge last night,' she said, 'so it should be nice and cold.'

And it was.

I retrieved the bottle and poured three glasses of the golden bubbly liquid, then we each, in turn, made a toast.

'To a long and happy marriage to my Claudia,' I said, and we drank.

'To long life and good health,' Claudia said, looking at me. We drank again.

'To masses of grandchildren,' my mother said, and we all drank once more.

Claudia and I held hands. We knew without saying what we were each thinking. Oh yes, please, to all three of the above. But, with cancer, it was all so scary and unpredictable.

'Have you told your father yet?' my mother asked.

'No,' I said. 'You're the only person that knows.' Not even Mrs McDowd, I thought, knew this little secret.

'Aren't you going to tell him?' Mum asked.

'Eventually,' I said. 'But I haven't spoken much to him recently.'

'Stupid man,' she said.

I knew she blamed him for the break-up of their marriage but, in truth, it had been as much her fault as his. But I didn't want to get into all that again.

'I'll call him tomorrow,' I said. 'Let's enjoy our own company here tonight.'

'I'll drink to that,' said Claudia, raising her glass. So we did.

I thought about my father.

Seven years ago, when my parents had finally divorced and the big house had been sold, he'd taken his share of the money and used it to buy a boring bungalow in Weymouth, overlooking the sea. I'd only been there a couple of times since, although I'd seen him a few times in London for various functions.

We hadn't been very close to start with, and we were drifting further apart day by day. But I don't think it was something that bothered either of us particularly. He hadn't even called me when I'd been arrested and my face had been splashed all over the papers, and on the TV. Perhaps my impending marriage, and the possibility of grandchildren, might help to revitalize our relationship, but I doubted it.

Claudia laid the dining table as my mother busied herself with saucepans of potatoes and carrots, and the lamb roasted away gently in the oven. I, meanwhile, poured us all more champagne and let them get on with it, leaning up against the worktop and enjoying the last of the evening sunshine as it shone brightly through the west-facing kitchen window.

'Bugger,' my mother said.

'What's wrong?' I asked.

'The cooker's gone off,' she said.

'Is it a power cut?'

She tried a light switch, clicking it up and down. Nothing happened.

'Bloody electricity company,' she said. 'I'll call them straight away.'

She rummaged in a drawer for a card and then picked up the phone.

'That's funny,' she said, 'the phone's dead too.'

'Doesn't it need power?' Claudia asked from over by the table. 'Our cordless one does.'

'I'm not using the cordless,' my mother said. 'This is the wired-in landline.'

Oh, shit!

There was a heavy knock on the front door.

'I'll get it,' said Claudia, turning away.

The power was off, the telephone was dead, there was a knock on the front door, and the hairs on the back of my neck were suddenly standing bolt upright.

'Don't touch it,' I shouted at Claudia.

She turned to look at me but she still moved towards the danger. 'Why ever not?' she said.

'Claudia,' I shouted again, 'get away from the door.'

I was already half-way towards her when the knock was repeated. And still Claudia moved towards it.

I grabbed her just as she was reaching for the handle.

'What on earth are you doing?' she said loudly. 'Answer the bloody door.'

'No,' I said quietly.

'Why ever not?' she demanded.

'Keep your voice down,' I hissed at her.

'Why?' she said, but much quieter, with concern. She could probably read the fear in my face.

'Please. Just go over to the kitchen area.' I looked over at my mother, who was staring at us, still holding the useless telephone in her hand.

Something about the urgency of my voice finally got through to Claudia and she went over to join my mother.

They both suddenly looked rather frightened.

I went into the small cloakroom next to the front door and peeked through a minute gap in the net curtains at the person standing outside.

He had on a grey/green anorak with the collar turned up and, this time, he was wearing a dark blue baseball cap, but there was no doubt, it was the same man that I had last seen in the grainy video from Mr Patel's newsagents, the same man who had gunned down Herb Kovak at Aintree, and the same man who had shot at me in Lichfield Grove.

Bugger, I thought, echoing my mother.

I went back into the big room.

The front door had locked automatically when it was closed, with a lock a bit like a Yale latch. It was quite strong, but was it strong enough?

I went quickly across to the kitchen and locked the back door as well, turning the key slowly to keep the noise to a minimum, and sliding across the bolt at the top.

Both my mother and Claudia watched my every step.

We heard the man rattle the front door and they both instinctively crouched down below the worktop.

'Who is it?' whispered my mother.

I'd have to tell them.

'Darlings,' I whispered. 'He's a very dangerous man, and he's trying to kill me.'

Claudia's eyes opened so wide I thought they would pop out of her head. My mother, however, thought I was joking and began to laugh.

'I'm being serious,' I said cutting her off in mid

guffaw. 'It's the same man who killed Herb Kovak at Aintree Races.'

This time they both looked more frightened than ever. And I was, too.

'Call the police,' Claudia said, then she remembered. 'Oh, my God, he's cut the phone line.'

And the electricity.

The broadband connection would have failed with the power, and our mobiles didn't have any signal here.

We were on our own.

'Upstairs,' I said quietly but firmly. 'Both of you. Now. Lock yourselves in the bathroom, sit on the floor, and don't come out until I tell you to.'

Claudia hesitated a moment, but then she nodded and took my mother by the hand. They started to go but then turned back. 'But what are you going to do?' Claudia asked, with huge fear in her face.

'Try to keep him out,' I said. 'Now, go on, go!'

They disappeared up the boxed-in staircase and I heard the bathroom door being shut and locked above me.

And if he did get in and kill me, I thought, perhaps he'd leave them alone and go away, job done. As it was, with all three of us down here, I was sure he would have killed us all.

I looked around for some sort of weapon.

A loaded shotgun would have been nice, but my mother had about as much interest in country sports as I did in origami.

I heard the back door being tried and I instinctively ducked away from it.

The sun went down, the last of its orange rays disappearing from the kitchen window. And it began to get dark, especially indoors with no electric lights to brighten the gathering gloom.

I looked round in desperation for something to use as a weapon. An umbrella stood in a large china pot near the front door, and a walking stick. I grabbed the walking stick but it was a collapsible model, for ease of packing. So I opted for the umbrella, one of those big golf umbrellas with a heavy wooden handle. It wasn't much but it was all there was. How I wished the cottage still had a proper open fire with a big, heavy, metal poker, but my mother had replaced it with one of those gas things with fake coals.

But, at least, I had one advantage over my assailant in so far as I could see him much more easily than he could see me.

It was still quite light outside and I watched him through the windows as he went right round the house. At one point he came close to the kitchen window, cupping his hands round his face and up against the glass in order to peer in. I made sure I was standing to the side of the window, in a dark corner, where he would have had no chance of spotting me.

Perhaps he would go away, I thought.

He didn't.

The sound of breaking glass put paid to any hope I may have had that this was going to end simply and without violence.

My mother's windows were old, in keeping with the

age of her cottage. They were a version of the old leaded lights, small panes of glass held together by a lattice framework of metal strips.

The gunman had broken just one of the little panes in one of the kitchen windows, but it was enough for him to put his gloved hand through the opening and unlatch the whole thing. I watched him do it in the fading light, and the window swung open outwards.

Where could I hide?

Without doubt the best place to be was in the bathroom upstairs with the door locked but I had no intention of joining Claudia and my mother there. I was sure that that would lead, in the end, to the deaths of all three of us.

So, where else was there to hide?

Nowhere.

I concluded that hiding was, in fact, my least-favoured option. It would simply give the advantage to the gunman, who could take his time, all night if necessary, and, eventually, he would undoubtedly find me and then I, too, would get a couple of bullets in my heart and another in my face, just as poor Herb had.

So, if I wasn't going to hide, and I certainly wasn't going to merely stand and wait to be killed, the only other option was to attack, and attack hard and fast.

He started to climb through the window, his gun with its long black silencer entering first.

I stood just to the side of the window and raised the umbrella, holding it by the pointed end so that I could swing the heavy wooden handle.

I used all my strength and brought the handle down hard onto the gun. I had actually been aiming for his wrist but he pulled it back a fraction just at the last second.

The gun went off, the bullet ricocheting off the granite worktop below the window with a loud zing before burying itself in the wall opposite. But the blow had also knocked the gun from the man's grasp. It clattered to the floor, sliding across the stone-quarry tiles and out of sight under my mother's old fridge. That evened things up a bit, I thought, but I would have loved to have been able to grab the gun and turn it on its owner.

'*Ebi se!*' the man said explosively.

I didn't know what he meant, and it sadly didn't stop him coming through the window.

I raised the umbrella for another strike but he was wise to me now and he grabbed it as it descended and tore it from my grasp, tossing it aside as he stepped right through the open window, crouching on the worktop.

I rushed at him but he was ready, pushing me aside with ease so that I stumbled across the kitchen towards the sink.

I turned quickly but the man had already jumped down to the floor. I watched him as he looked around and then withdrew a large carving knife from the wooden block next to my mother's stove. Now why hadn't I thought of that?

I moved quickly to my right, putting the dining table between him and me. If he couldn't reach me, he couldn't stab me either.

There followed a sort of ballet with him moving one way or the other, and me mirroring him, always keeping the table between us. Once we ran round and round the table three or four times with me watching carefully for him to change direction. He pulled out chairs to try to slow me down, but I was quick. I may not be as fit as I was as a jockey but I was still no slouch in the running department. It had fared me well in Lichfield Grove and was doing so again here.

But, for how long?

He only needed to get lucky once.

He changed his tactics, using one of the chairs to climb up onto the table, and then he came straight at me across it.

I turned and ran for the stairs, pulling open the latch door, and bounding up the steps two or three at a time. I could hear him behind me and he was gaining.

Where could I go? I was running out of options.

Panic began to rise in my throat. I didn't want to die.

I turned to face him. At least I would see it coming and I'd be able to make some effort to get away from the thrust of the knife.

He stood at the top of the stairs with me just four feet away in front of him. He advanced a step and I retreated a step, then we both repeated the drill, but my back was now up against the wall. I had no further to go.

He came a step closer to me and I readied myself for his strike, although what I would do when it came, I didn't know.

Die, probably.

Claudia stepped out of the bathroom, just down the corridor to his right.

'Fuck off, you bastard,' she shouted at him with full fortissimo. 'Leave him alone.' She then slammed the bathroom door shut again and locked it.

He turned momentarily towards the noise and I leapt at him, wrapping my right arm round his neck with my forearm across his throat while, at the same time, I tried to gouge his eyes out with the fingers of my left hand.

I squeezed his neck with all my strength.

But it was not enough.

The man was considerably taller and stronger than I and, in spite of my best grip, he simply began to turn himself round to face me. And with both of my arms held up round his head, my abdomen would be totally defenceless to a thrust of the knife.

What had that spinal specialist told me?

'Whatever you do,' he'd said, 'don't get into a fight.'

He'd said nothing about falling down stairs.

I hung on to the man's neck as if my life depended on it, which it probably did, and then I dived head first down the narrow boxed-in stairway, taking the man down with me. It was a crazy thing to do, especially for someone who had precious little holding his head to his body. But it was my only chance.

I twisted as we fell so that I landed on top of the man, his head taking the full force of the heavy contact with the wall where the stairway turned through ninety degrees half-way down. We slithered on to the bottom of the wooden stairs coming to a halt still locked together by my right arm, which I was still pulling as tightly as I could round his neck. We were lying partially through the lever-latch doorway, our legs still on the stairs, with our heads and torsos sticking out into the room below.

Even for me on top, and using the man's body to break my fall, the first impact with the wall had been enough to drive the air from my lungs, but at least my head hadn't fallen off with it.

I pulled my arm from under his neck and jumped to my feet ready to continue the fight, but there was no need. The man lay limply, face down, where he'd come to rest.

I went quickly to fetch my mother's collapsible walking stick, and then I used it to retrieve the gun from beneath her fridge, hooking it out with the handle.

If the man moved so much as an eyebrow, I thought, I'd shoot him.

I stood over him for what felt like a very long time, pointing the gun at his head and watching for any movement.

But the man didn't move. Not even to breathe.

Nevertheless, I still didn't trust him not to jump up and kill me, so I kept the gun pointing at him all the time.

'Claudia,' I shouted as loudly as I could. 'Claudia, I need your help.'

I heard the bathroom door being unlocked and then footsteps on the floorboards above my head.

'Has he gone?' Claudia asked from the top of the

stairs. It was so dark that she couldn't even see the man lying right beneath her.

'I think he might be dead,' I said. 'But I'm taking no chances, and it's getting so dark I can hardly see him.'

'I've got a torch by my bed,' my mother said in a matter-of-fact tone.

I heard her walk along the corridor to her room then she came back shining the torch brightly down the stairwell.

'Oh, my God!' Claudia said, looking down.

In the torchlight we could see that the man's head was lying almost flat against his right shoulder in a most unnatural position. The man's neck was clearly broken, just as mine had once been.

But, on this occasion, there were no friendly paramedics to apply an immobilizing collar, no one to save his life with prompt and gentle care as there had been for me at Cheltenham racecourse all those years ago.

This man's broken neck had bumped on down to the bottom of a wooden stairway, all the time being wrenched to one side by my arm.

And it had killed him.

15

'What the hell do we do now?' Claudia said from the top of the stairs.

'Call the police,' I said from the bottom.

'How?'

'I'll take the car and find somewhere with a signal,' I said.

But there was no way Claudia and my mother were allowing me to go off in the car, leaving them alone in the house with the gunman. Dead or not, they were still very frightened of him, and I can't say I blamed them.

'Pack up our things,' I said to Claudia. 'Mum, pack an overnight bag. No, take enough for a few days. We're going somewhere else.'

'But why?' my mother asked.

'Because someone sent this man here to kill me and, when they find out that he hasn't succeeded, that someone might send another to try again.'

Neither of them asked the obvious question – why was the man trying to kill me? Instead they both quickly went together to pack, taking the torch with them, and leaving me standing in the dark.

In spite of being pretty certain the man was indeed dead, I didn't stop listening, holding the gun ready in case he made a miraculous recovery.

I found I was shaking.

I took several deep breaths but the shaking continued. Perhaps it was from fear, or relief, or maybe it was a reaction to the sudden realization that I had killed a man. Probably a bit of all three.

The shaking continued for several minutes and I became totally exhausted by it. I wanted to sit down, and I felt slightly sick.

'We're packed,' Claudia said from upstairs, the torchlight again shining down the stairway.

'Good,' I said. 'Pass the things down to me.'

I stepped carefully onto the first few stairs, next to the man's legs, and reached up as Claudia handed down our bags and my mother's suitcase.

Next, I guided each of them down in turn, making sure they stepped only on the wood and not on the man.

'Oh, my God. Oh, my God,' Claudia said, repeating it over and over again as she came nervously down the stairs, pressing herself against the side while, at the same time, holding her hands up to ensure she wouldn't touch the man by mistake.

My mother was, surprisingly, much more stoical, waltzing down the stairs as if there was nothing there. In fact, I suspected that she would've liked to have given the corpse a sharp kick for ruining her roast dinner.

The three of us went out to the car, loaded the stuff, and drove away down the rutted lane, leaving the dead man alone in the dark house.

*

I drove into Cheltenham and called the police, but I didn't dial the emergency number. Instead, I called Chief Inspector Tomlinson on his mobile.

'The man who killed Herb Kovak,' I said, 'is lying dead at the bottom of my mother's stairway.'

There was the slightest of pauses.

'How tiresome of him,' the chief inspector said. 'Did he just lie down there and die?'

'No,' I said. 'He broke his neck falling down the stairs.'

'Was he pushed?' he asked, once again demonstrating his suspicious mind.

'Helped,' I said. 'We fell down the stairs together. He came off worse. But he was trying to stab me with a carving knife at the time.'

'What happened to his gun?' he asked.

'He lost it under the fridge,' I said.

'Hmm,' he said. 'And have you told the local constabulary?'

'No,' I said. 'I thought you could do that. And you can also tell them he was a foreigner.'

'How do you know?'

'He said something I didn't understand.'

'And where are you now?' he asked.

'In Cheltenham,' I said. 'The gunman cut the power and the telephone wires. I've had to leave to make a call on my mobile. There's no signal at the cottage.'

'Is anyone still at the cottage?'

'Only the dead man,' I said. 'I have Claudia and my mother with me in the car.'

'So are you going back there now?' he asked.

'No,' I said firmly. 'Whoever sent this man could send another.'

'So where are you going?' he asked, not questioning my decision.

'I don't know yet,' I said. 'I'll call you when I do.'

'Who knew you were at your mother's place?' he asked, always the detective.

'Everyone in my office,' I said. And whomever else Mrs McDowd had told, I thought.

'Right,' he said. 'I'll call the Gloucestershire Police but they'll definitely want to talk to you, and to Claudia and your mother. They may even want you back at the cottage.'

'Tell them I'll call them there in two hours,' I said.

'But you said the line had been cut.'

'Then get it fixed,' I said. 'And get the power back on. Tell them I think my mother has left the stove on. I don't want the place burning down when the power's reconnected. And also tell them I've left the back door unlocked so they won't have to break the front door down to get in.'

'OK,' he said. 'I'll tell them.' He paused. 'Is the gun still under the fridge?'

'No,' I said. 'I retrieved it.'

'So where is it now?'

I had so wanted to bring it with me, to give myself the armed protection that I'd been denied by the police.

'It's outside the front door,' I said. 'In a bush.'

'Right,' he said, sounding slightly relieved. 'I'll tell

the Gloucestershire force that too. Save them hunting for it, and you.'

'Good,' I said.

It had been the right decision to leave the gun behind. I could still claim the moral high ground.

I hung up and switched off my phone. I would call the police on *my* terms, and I also didn't want anyone being able to track my movements from the phone signal.

'Do you really think we're still in danger?' Claudia asked from next to me.

'I don't know,' I said, 'but I'm not taking any chances.'

'Who knew we were there?' she asked.

'Everyone at the office, I expect,' I said. 'Mrs McDowd definitely knew, and she'd have told everyone else.'

And Detective Chief Inspector Tomlinson had known as well.

I'd told him myself.

It was my mother who finally asked the big question.

'Why was that man trying to kill you?' she said calmly from the back seat.

We were on the road between Cirencester and Swindon.

I'd made one more stop in Cheltenham, at one of the few remaining public phone boxes. I hadn't wanted to use my mobile for fear that someone could trace who I was calling. We were going where no one would find us.

'I'm not totally sure, but it may be because I am a witness to him killing a man at Aintree Races,' I said. 'And it wasn't the first time he'd tried.'

Neither my mother nor Claudia said anything. They were waiting for me to go on.

'He was waiting outside our house in Lichfield Grove when I got back there on Tuesday afternoon,' I said. 'Luckily, I could run faster than him.'

'Is that why we came to Woodmancote?' Claudia asked, 'instead of going home.'

'It sure is,' I said. 'But I didn't realize that Woodmancote wasn't safe either. Not until it was too late. I won't make that mistake again.'

'But what about the police?' my mother asked. 'Surely we must go to the police. They will look after us.'

But how much did I trust the police? I didn't know that either. They hadn't given me any protection when I'd asked for it, and that omission had almost cost us our lives. No, I thought, I'd trust my own instincts. The police seemed more interested in solving murders than preventing them.

'I have been to the police,' I said, driving on through the darkness. 'But it will be *me* who will look after you.'

And I would also find out who was trying to have me killed, and the real reason why.

'Well, lover-boy,' Jan Setter said, 'when I asked you to come and stay, I didn't exactly mean you to bring your girlfriend and your mother with you!'

288

We laughed.

We were sitting at her kitchen table in Lambourn drinking coffee, the said girlfriend and mother having been safely tucked up in two of Jan's many spare bedrooms.

'I didn't know where else to go,' I said to her.

I had briefly thought about going to my father's bungalow in Weymouth but he had only two double bedrooms and, amusing as the thought had been, I could hardly expect my parents to share a bed, not after seven years of divorce, and I certainly wasn't sleeping with the old bugger.

'So what's all this about?' Jan asked finally.

All I had said to her on the phone from Cheltenham had been that I was desperate and could she help by putting us up for a night or two.

'How desperate?' she had asked calmly.

'Life or death,' I'd said. 'Complete secrecy.'

She had asked nothing further but had simply said 'come', and she'd asked no questions when we'd arrived, not until after my traumatized mother and fiancée had been safely ushered up to bed. As it had with me, the shock and fear had manifested itself in them after the event.

In all the years I had known Jan, both as her former jockey and, more recently, as her financial adviser, I had never known her to be flustered or panicked by anything. She was the steady head I needed in this crisis.

But how much did I tell her?

Would she even believe me?

'I know this is going to sound rather overly dramatic,' I said, 'but someone is trying to kill me.'

'What's her name?' Jan asked with a laugh.

'I'm being serious, Jan,' I said. 'Tonight a man came to my mother's cottage to murder me. He had a gun. I promise you, we are extremely fortunate to be alive. The same man has now tried to kill me twice.'

'Let's hope it isn't third time lucky.'

'He won't get a third time.'

'How can you be sure?' she asked.

'Because he's dead. The last time I saw him he was lying on the floor of my mother's sitting room with his neck broken.'

She stared at me. 'You are being serious, aren't you?'

I nodded. 'Very.'

'Have you called the police?'

'Yes,' I said. 'But I need to call them again.' I looked at my watch. It had been at least two hours since I'd spoken to Chief Inspector Tomlinson. But they could wait a little longer.

'So why come here?' she asked. 'Why not go straight to the police?'

'I need somewhere to hide where no one can find me.'

Not even the police, I thought.

'But, if the man's dead, why do you still need to hide?' she asked.

'Because he was a hired killer and I am worried that whoever hired him will simply hire another.'

I could tell from the look on Jan's face that her credulity had reached its limit.

'It's true, I assure you,' I said. 'I'm not making it up, and I think it's all to do with stealing a hundred million euros from the European Union. Now that really is big money. And what's the going rate for having someone killed these days? Twenty thousand? A hundred grand, maybe? Or even half a million? That's still only a half of one per cent of the take. Cheap at twice the price.'

'But what have *you* got to do with stealing a hundred million euros?' she asked.

'Nothing,' I said. 'But I may have asked the wrong question to those that have. And I suspect that somebody believes I need to be permanently removed before I ask some more questions and bring the whole scheme tumbling down round their ears.'

'So what are you going to do?' she said.

'Ask the questions quickly,' I said, grinning at her. 'And then keep my head down.'

Someone answered after just one ring when I called my mother's cottage. I was sitting in Jan's office and using her mobile phone, and I had carefully withheld the number from caller-ID. I hoped it was enough to keep it secret.

'Hello,' I said.

'Is that Nicholas Foxton?' came a man's voice in reply.

'It is,' I said. 'To whom am I talking?'

'Detective Chief Inspector Flight,' he said. 'Gloucestershire Police.'

Not another detective chief inspector, I thought. What's the collective noun for detective chief inspectors? It was a posse of police, so maybe it's an evidence of detective chief inspectors.

'Where are you, Mr Foxton?' asked this particular chief inspector.

'Somewhere safe,' I said.

'And where is that?' he asked again.

I ignored him. 'Who was the man who tried to kill me?' I asked.

'Mr Foxton,' he said. 'I need you to come to a police station to be interviewed. Tonight.'

He was persistent, I'd give him that.

'Have you spoken to DCI Tomlinson from Mersey-side Police?' I asked. 'Or Superintendent Yering from the Metropolitan Police Armed Response Team?'

'No,' he said. 'Not personally.'

'Then I suggest you do,' I said.

'Mr Foxton,' he said. 'You are in danger of obstructing the police in the course of their duties. Now, please, tell me where you are.'

'No,' I said. 'Did you watch the television news on Tuesday? The dead man in my mother's cottage is the same man as in the video. And I think he was foreign. He said something I didn't understand. Something like "*ebi se*".'

'Mr Foxton.' Detective Chief Inspector Flight was getting quite worked up. 'I must insist you tell me where you are.'

'And I must insist you speak to DCI Tomlinson or Superintendent Yering.'

I hung up.

That didn't go too well, I thought. Too bad. But I was definitely not going to any police station to be interviewed tonight, or any other night if I could help it. People could get shot at police stations. Ask Lee Harvey Oswald.

I heard Jan leave the house at a quarter to seven in the morning to supervise the exercising of her horses on the gallops. She had asked if I wanted to accompany her up onto the downs to watch, but I had declined, not because I didn't want to, but because I didn't want anyone to recognize me and hence know where I was staying.

It may have been eight years since I was a regular in Lambourn, but there were plenty who had been here longer than that, even amongst Jan's staff, and most would have known me by sight.

I realized it was highly unlikely that news of my whereabouts would then get back to hostile ears, but I didn't want to take any unnecessary risks.

I got up as quietly as I could but Claudia was already awake.

'Don't go,' she said.

I snuggled down again next to her, under the covers.

'When will this all end?' she asked.

'Soon,' I said, but I really had no idea when.

'I was so frightened last night,' she said with tears in her eyes. 'I really thought he was going to kill you.'

I'd thought it too.

'But he didn't,' I said. 'So everything's all right.' I was trying to sound encouraging, even if I was not so sure inside.

'So why have we come here?' she asked. 'Why can't we go home now?'

'There's just a few things I have to do before we can go home,' I said, sitting up on the side of the bed. 'And I don't want to take any chances if we don't need to.'

'I think we should go to the police,' she said.

'I spoke to them last night after you went to bed. They agreed that it was better for us to stay here for a couple of days while they carry out their investigations.'

At least the first bit was true.

'So what is it that you have to do?' she asked.

'Well, first, I have to go to Oxford,' I said. 'And I'm going to do that right now.' I stood up and started to dress.

'I'll come with you,' Claudia said, throwing the duvet to one side and sitting up.

'No,' I said firmly. 'You stay here with Jan and my mother. You need to recover fully from your operation. And I won't be long. You'll be quite safe here.'

I think she was secretly relieved, as she lay down again and pulled the duvet back over her.

'Why are you going?' she asked.

'To see a young man at the university,' I said. 'I want

to ask him some questions about a factory, or rather, about the lack of a factory.'

I stopped on the outskirts of Oxford and turned on my mobile phone to call Detective Chief Inspector Tomlinson.

'DCI Flight of Gloucestershire Police is not happy with you,' he said. 'Not happy at all.'

'Too bad,' I said.

'He's applied for a warrant for your arrest on suspicion of manslaughter.'

'But that's ridiculous,' I said.

'Maybe it is,' he agreed, 'but he's really pissed off. I do think it might be better if you go and see him.'

'Not if he's going to arrest me.' I didn't relish spending another day in a police cell. 'Anyway,' I said. 'I have things to do first.'

'Not investigating again, are you?' said the professional detective. 'I've told you to leave that to the police.'

'But what are you going to investigate?' I said. 'It is me, not you, that believes Colonel Jolyon Roberts was murdered, but there is no evidence for that belief. In fact, quite the reverse. The evidence indicates that he died of natural causes, helped by a dose of stupidity. The police see no crime, so there is no investigation.'

'So what do you want me to do?' he asked.

'Speak to Flight,' I said. 'Get him off my back. Tell him there's no way I'll see him if he's going to arrest me.'

'I'll try,' he said. 'But I still think you ought to at least talk to him.'

'Get me his number,' I said. 'Then I'll call him.'

'How can I contact you?' he asked.

'Leave a message on this phone. I'll pick it up. Flight can do the same.'

'Anything else?' he asked.

'Yes,' I said. 'Can you find out if the dead man in my mother's cottage was Bulgarian?'

I thought about also asking him to get the fraud squad to initiate an investigation into the Balscott factory project but, as I knew from previous experience with a former client, fraud investigations involving foreign investments started with months and months of delving into paperwork before there was any prospect of an arrest. Add to that the complexities of the European Union grants system, and it would take years.

And I'd be dead and buried long before that.

I disconnected from DCI Tomlinson but the phone rang again in my hand almost immediately.

'This is your voicemail,' said an impersonal female voice when I answered. 'You have two new messages.'

One of them was from DCI Flight and, as the other chief inspector had said, he didn't sound very happy. I ignored it.

The other was from Patrick Lyall, who also wasn't pleased with me, in particular because I had left a message on his mobile saying that I wouldn't be coming into the office today.

'Nicholas,' Patrick's voice said, 'I am sorry that you

have decided not to be in the office once again. I think we need to have a talk about your commitment to the firm. I will be writing to you today, formally warning you as to your future conduct. Please would you call me and tell me where to have the letter delivered.'

It sounded to me as if the company lawyer had been advising him again on employment law – written warnings and all that.

I ignored him too.

Did I, in fact, have any future in the firm? And did I really care?

Keble College was on the north side of the city near the Oxford University Museum of Natural History. I parked in Museum Road and walked back to the college.

'Sorry, sir,' said a man in a smart blue jersey intercepting me in the entrance archway. 'The college is closed to the public. Trinity has begun.'

'Trinity?' I asked.

'Trinity term,' he said. 'The students are here.'

It hadn't even crossed my mind they wouldn't be.

'Exactly,' I said to him. 'I've come to see one of the students.'

'Which one?' he asked politely but firmly. He was obviously used to repelling visitors who had no good cause to be there.

'Benjamin Roberts,' I said.

'And is Mr Roberts expecting you?' he asked.

'No,' I said. 'It's a surprise visit.'

He looked at his watch, and I looked at mine. It was just past ten o'clock.

'It might be a bit early for Mr Roberts,' he said. 'I heard he was partying rather late last evening. But I'll try and call him. What name shall I say?'

'Smith,' I said. 'John Smith.'

The porter looked at me somewhat sceptically.

'I get that reaction all the time,' I said. 'Unimaginative parents.'

He nodded, as if making up his mind, and then disappeared into the porter's lodge.

I waited patiently under the arch.

Presently, the porter reappeared. 'Mr Roberts asks if you could come back later, around one o'clock.'

'Could you please call Mr Roberts again and tell him I'm from the Balscott Lighting Factory and I need to see him now.'

Benjamin Roberts appeared in three minutes flat with his long dark hair still unbrushed, bags under his eyes, and with no socks beneath his black leather shoes. He was tall, probably near six-foot four or five, and he towered over me at just five-foot eight.

'Mr Smith?' he asked. I nodded. 'Jarvis here tells me you're from the Balscott factory.'

We were still standing in the entrance archway with students passing us continually in both directions, and with Jarvis, the porter, hovering nearby.

'Is there anywhere quiet we could go and talk?' I asked.

He turned to the porter. 'Thank you, Jarvis, I'll be taking Mr Smith up to the Dining Hall for a while.'

'All visitors have to be signed in,' Jarvis said rather officiously.

Benjamin Roberts went into the lodge for a moment and then reappeared.

'Bloody rules,' he said. 'They treat us like kids.'

We walked along a gravel path down the side of a building and then up some wide steps to the college dining hall, an impressively tall space with three lines of refectory tables and benches running along its full length.

Some catering staff at the far end of the hall were laying up for lunch but Benjamin and I sat down close to the door, across one of the tables from each other.

'Now,' he said, 'what's all this about?'

'Benjamin –' I said, starting.

'Ben,' he interrupted.

'Sorry, Ben,' I said, corrected. 'I was a friend of your uncle Jolyon.'

He looked down at his hands on the table. 'Such a shame,' he said. 'Uncle Jolyon was fun. I'll miss him.' He looked up again at me. 'But what have you to do with the factory?'

'Your uncle Jolyon told me that you'd recently been to Bulgaria.'

'Yes,' he said slowly. 'A group of us from the university skiing club went to Borovets during the Easter vac. It was very good value and great snow. You should try it.'

Not with my neck, I thought.

'But your uncle also said you went to see the factory.'

'There isn't any factory, is there?' he said.

'You tell me,' I said. 'You're the one that went to see it.'

He didn't answer but sat looking at me across the table.

'Who are you?' he said. 'Is Smith your real name?'

'No,' I admitted, 'it is not.'

'So, who are you?' he asked, standing up, and with a degree of menace in his voice. 'And what are you after?'

'I'm not after anything,' I said defensively, looking up at him. 'Except to be left alone.'

'Then why are you here? If you want to be left alone, why don't you just go away?'

'I would, but someone is trying to kill me,' I said, this time without looking up at his face. It was hurting my neck. 'Now, will you please sit down.'

He slowly lowered his huge frame back down onto the bench. 'Who is trying to kill you?' he asked in a tone that indicated disbelief. 'And why?'

'I don't know who,' I said. 'Not yet. But I think I may know why. Your uncle approached me because he was worried that the family's investment in the Bulgarian factory project was a scam. He had been shown photographs of the factory buildings, but you had then told him that they didn't actually exist. So he asked me to look into it, to check that, in his words, it wasn't a rotten egg of an investment.'

He smiled at the use of the words. They were clearly familiar to him.

'And,' I went on, 'I think that it is, indeed, a rotten egg of an investment. Your family money was the key to everything because the private finance for the factory triggered the public funding for all the houses. Someone has been defrauding the European Union out of a hundred million euros by obtaining grants towards the cost of building a light-bulb factory and hundreds of homes that don't actually exist, and never will. And that same someone is trying to kill me before I can prove it, and before I find out who they are.'

I paused and Ben Roberts sat staring at me in silence.

'And,' I said, going on, 'I believe your uncle may have been murdered for the same reason.'

16

'Uncle Jolyon wasn't murdered, he died of a heart attack,' Ben Roberts said unequivocally. 'At least, he had a heart attack and then he drowned.'

Ben looked down again at the table in front of him. Jolyon Roberts had died only four days previously. It was still very recent – very raw.

'Did you know that he was drunk when he drowned?' I asked.

'He couldn't have been,' Ben said, looking up at me.

'The post mortem showed he was.'

'But that's impossible.'

'Why? Because he didn't drink?'

'Never,' Ben said. 'He might have a tiny sip of champagne occasionally, you know, at a wedding for a toast, that sort of thing, but otherwise he never touched any alcohol.'

'Did he ever drink whisky?' I asked. 'Late at night, maybe?'

'Not that I was aware of,' Ben said. 'And I very much doubt it. I tried to get him to have a beer at my twenty-first birthday party but I had no chance. He said that he didn't like booze, so it was no hardship not to have it.'

'Was he teetotal because of his heart condition?' I asked.

'Heart condition?' Ben said. 'Whatever gave you the impression Uncle J had a heart condition? His heart was as strong as an ox. Or, at least we all thought it was until last Monday.'

Perhaps Ben hadn't known about his uncle's heart condition, I thought. After all, it's not the sort of thing people usually advertise about themselves.

'Tell me about your trip to Bulgaria,' I said. 'When you went to see the factory.'

'There's absolutely nothing there,' he said. 'Nothing at all. And the locals know nothing about it. They've never even heard of any plans to build a factory, let alone the houses.'

'Are you sure you were in the right place?' I asked.

He glanced at me with a look that could only be described as one of contempt.

'Of course I'm sure,' he said. 'I took all the details with me so that I would be able find it. My family are so proud of what the Trust does to help those less fortunate than ourselves. That's why I was so keen for the skiing club to go to Bulgaria in the first place, and especially to Borovets. It was close enough so I could spend a day going to see the factory if I wanted.'

'Did anyone know you were going to the factory?' I asked.

'No,' he said. 'I wasn't absolutely sure that I would. It depended on the snow and the weather. To be honest, I'd much rather ski than visit factories but, on one day, the cloud was right down on the slopes so I went, but the factory wasn't there.'

'Where was it meant to be?' I asked.

'Close to a village called Gorni, south of Sofia. But, when I saw the site, it was nothing more than a toxic waste dump left over from the mass industrialization of the country during the Soviet era.'

'So what have you done about it?' I asked. 'Your family has invested a lot of money into the project.'

'Yeah, and lost it all too.' He sounded resigned to the loss.

'Aren't you even going to try to get it back?'

'I don't expect so,' Ben said. 'My father is worried that the family name will be discredited. What he means is that we will be shown up to have been bloody fools – and fools that were easily separated from their money. He is furious about it, but mostly because he was talked into it by Uncle Jolyon and some financial adviser chap.'

'Gregory Black?' I asked.

'He's the one,' he said.

'So your father says to forget it? Forget five million pounds, just like that?'

'It's only money,' he said almost flippantly. 'And money is fairly easy to replace. It's not like one's family reputation. It can take many generations to repair damage to one's family's standing, and sometimes it can never be restored.'

It sounded to me that he was quoting his father.

'But it's not possible to replace your Uncle Jolyon,' I said.

'That's surely all the more reason to forget about

304

the whole thing. If the stress of this factory business gave Uncle J his heart attack, then we should unquestionably let sleeping dogs lie. Otherwise our foolishness will be shown to have cost the family far more than mere money.'

'But I believe your uncle was murdered,' I said. 'Don't you want justice?'

'Would that bring him back?' he said angrily. 'No, of course it wouldn't. And, anyway, I believe that you are wrong. In fact, I believe you are just here to cause my family trouble.' He stood up quickly, bunching his fists. 'What is it you're really after? Do you want money? Is that it? Money or you'll go to the papers?'

This could get very nasty, and very quickly, I thought.

I didn't move but just sat still on the bench, not even looking up at him.

'I don't want your money,' I said calmly.

But what did I want?

Did I really care if some clever Eurocrat in Brussels and a Bulgarian property entrepreneur were conspiring to steal a hundred million euros from the European Union, with or without the help of Gregory Black? Or did I care that the Roberts Family Trust had been duped out of five million pounds?

No, I decided. I didn't care about either of those things.

And was I really bothered whether Jolyon Roberts had died of natural causes, or if he'd been murdered?

No, I suppose I didn't even care about that. He had been a nice enough man, and I was sorry he was dead, but it didn't make any real difference to me how he'd died.

But I did care that someone had killed Herb Kovak, and I cared very much more that they were trying to kill me too.

'So what exactly do you want?' Ben Roberts asked belligerently from somewhere above my eye-line.

'I want what is right,' I said. Whatever that meant.

And, I thought, I want to live a long and happy life with my future wife.

I looked up at his face. 'What is it that *you* want?' I asked back. He didn't answer and I went on looking at him. 'Your uncle told me you wanted to change the world.'

He laughed. 'Uncle J was always saying that.'

'And is it true?' I asked.

He thought for a moment.

'It's true that I want to be a politician,' he said. 'And all politicians hope to be in power. To be in a position to make the changes they believe in, otherwise there'd be no point.' He paused. 'So, yes, I suppose I do want to change the world. And for the better.'

'For the better, as *you* see it,' I said.

'Obviously.'

'So,' I said, 'is it for the better that you value your family's reputation ahead of doing what is right by your late uncle?'

He sat down again and stared at me.

'What's your real name?' he asked.

'Foxton,' I said. 'Nicholas Foxton. I am a financial

adviser with Lyall and Black, the same firm where Gregory Black works.'

'Well, Mr Nicholas Foxton, financial adviser, what is it that *you* really want?' he asked. 'And why have you come here?'

'I need to find out more about your family's investment in the Bulgarian project,' I said. 'I simply don't have enough information to take my concerns to the authorities. They'd probably laugh at me. All I have are some copies of the original transaction report, some e-mails between someone in Brussels and a man in Bulgaria, and a sackful of suspicion. And, now that your uncle is dead, I can't ask *him*.'

'So why don't you go and ask Gregory Black?' he said.

'Because I'm not altogether sure that I trust him.' In fact, I was sure I didn't.

'OK. I'll speak to my father about it,' Ben said. 'But, I can tell you now, he won't like it, and he probably won't talk to you.'

'Ask him anyway,' I said.

'How do I contact you?' he asked.

'Leave a message on my mobile.' I gave him the number, which he stored on his own phone.

'Please speak to him soon.'

'I'm going home tonight for the weekend,' Ben said. 'I'll try to find the right moment to speak to him on Sunday afternoon. He's always at his most relaxed after a good Sunday lunch.'

I hoped it would be soon enough.

*

When I returned to Jan's place in Lambourn at four thirty, I found her, Claudia and my mother sitting round the kitchen table and they were already hard at the vino.

'Bit early, isn't it?' I said, looking at my watch and declining the offered glass of Chardonnay.

'Early?' Claudia said with a giggle. 'We started at lunchtime.'

The others giggled with her.

'Are you sure it's wise to drink so soon after surgery?' I asked. 'Especially on top of your painkillers.'

'Don't be such a killjoy,' Jan said amid more sniggering.

What a fine state of affairs, I thought. I was trying to keep us alive and my mother and fiancée were drunk.

'So what have you done today, other than drinking?' I asked.

'Nothing,' Jan said. 'We've been talking, that's all.'

'I thought you'd be at the races,' I said to her.

'No runners today,' she said. 'But I've got to go now to evening stables.' She stood up with a slight wobble and giggled again. 'Oops, I think I've had a bit too much.'

A lot too much, I thought. But what the hell, it was Friday afternoon, and it had been quite a week.

I left them refilling their glasses and went upstairs to fetch my computer. I then used Jan's broadband to connect to the internet, and checked my e-mails. As always, there were the usual collection from fund managers, but nestling amongst them was one from

Patrick Lyall. It was timed at 3.50 p.m. He had clearly become fed up waiting for me to return his call telling him where to send the letter. I could almost feel the anger as I read it.

'Nicholas,' he had written, 'As you have obviously decided not to reply to my telephone call asking for your whereabouts, I have no option but to deliver the attached letter to you by e-mail. I find the whole situation most unsatisfactory. I hope that you soon come to your senses and start giving the firm the priority it deserves. Patrick.'

I clicked on the attachment. It was a letter from the lawyer, Andrew Mellor, acting on behalf of Lyall & Black. There were no niceties, and the letter was very much to the point.

Mr Foxton,

In accordance with the Employment Act 2008, I am writing to inform you that your employer, Lyall and Black and Co. Ltd, hereby give notice that they consider your recent behaviour to be far below the standard expected from an employee in your position. Consequently, Lyall and Black and Co. Ltd hereby issue you with a formal warning as to your future conduct. Furthermore, and in keeping with the statutory requirements as laid down in the Act, you are requested and required to attend a disciplinary meeting with Patrick Lyall and Gregory Black at the company offices in Lombard Street,

London, at nine o'clock on the Monday morning
following the date of this letter.
Yours sincerely,
Andrew Mellor, LLB

It sounded to me that, this time, I really was about to be fired.

Strangely, I didn't seem to care any more. Perhaps that policeman at Aintree had been right all along – becoming a financial adviser had been a bit of a comedown from the thrill of being a jump jockey.

Maybe it was time for me to look for more excitement in my life?

Like being shot at? Or stabbed?

I think not. I'd had enough of that.

On Saturday morning I left the three women nursing their hangovers while I went to visit Billy Searle in the Great Western Hospital in Swindon.

'So who knocked you off your bike?' I asked him.

'Don't you bloody start,' he said. 'The fuzz have been asking me nothing else but that since I woke up.'

'So why don't you tell them?' I said.

'Are you effing stupid or something?' he said. 'I'd rather go on living, thank you very much.'

'So it wasn't an accident?' I said.

'I didn't say that. It might have been.'

'Now who's being effing stupid?' I said.

He stuck two fingers up at me and said nothing.

We were in a single room, hidden away at the far end of one of the wards. It had taken me three separate requests to find him as well as a security escort that had only departed after Billy had vouched for me as his friend, not foe.

'How much longer are you going to be here?' I asked him. He clearly wasn't going anywhere soon as he was firmly attached to the bed by a weights contraption that was pulling on his right leg.

'About another week,' he said. 'At least, that's what they tell me. They need to apply something called a fixator to my leg but they can't do that until the traction has pulled everything straight. Then I'll be able to get up.'

'I thought they pinned and plated broken legs these days.'

'I did too,' he said. 'But the doc here says that this is the best way, and who was I to argue?' He grinned. Both he and I knew that Billy Searle argued all the time. 'Anyway, I was effing unconscious at the time.'

'They thought you were going to die,' I said.

'No bloody chance,' he replied, still grinning.

'And *I* was arrested for your attempted murder.'

'Yeah,' he said. 'So I heard. Serves you right.'

'What for?' I said.

He laughed. 'For being such a boring bastard.'

Was I really boring?

'I'm sorry.'

'You were much more fun as a jock,' Billy said. 'Do you remember that time we all got thrown out of that effing hotel in Torquay after your big win at Newton Abbot?'

I smiled. I remembered it well. 'It was all your fault,' I said. 'You poured champagne into their grand piano.'

'Yeah, well, so maybe I did,' he said. 'But it was a crap piano anyway. And it was you throwing those pot plants around that did for us in the end.'

It was true, I thought. The plants had come out of their pots and the earth had spread all over the new carpet. The hotel manager had not been at all pleased. We had been politely asked to leave, and never to come back, or else he would call the police.

Billy and I laughed together at the memory.

'Those were the days,' he said. 'Carefree and bloody stupid we were.'

'But such fun,' I said, still laughing.

For both of us, it seemed, fun had been on the wane recently.

'So who do you owe a hundred grand to?' I asked. The laughter died in Billy's throat. But he didn't answer. 'Was it the same guy who tried to kill you?'

He still didn't answer. He just looked at me.

'Or was he just trying to give you a gentle reminder to pay up, a reminder that went too far?'

'Did the bloody cops tell you to ask me that?' he said crossly.

'No, of course not,' I said. 'They don't even know I'm here.'

'So why are you so bloody interested in me all of a

sudden?' The bonhomie of just a couple of minutes previously had disappeared completely.

'Billy. I'm just trying to help you,' I said.

'I don't need your fucking help,' he said explosively, just as he'd done outside the Weighing Room at Cheltenham.

'That's what you said to me once before, and you ended up in here. Next time, it might be the morgue.'

He lay back against the hospital pillows and said nothing.

'All right,' I said. 'If you won't tell me who, at least tell me why you owe someone a hundred thousand. Then I can properly advise you about your financial dealings.'

'I can't,' he said, staring at the ceiling. 'Even if I didn't end up dead, which I probably would, I'd have no bloody job left.'

'Against the Rules of Racing,' I quoted, somewhat self-righteously.

He turned his head and gave me a sideways look.

'Actually, no. At least not that time. That's what's so bloody ironic.'

He paused.

'What's ironic?' I prompted.

'Are you sure you're not working for the fuzz?'

'I swear on a bottle of champagne in a grand piano,' I said with a smile.

'And some separated effing pot plants?' he asked, smiling also.

'Them too,' I said, placing my right hand over my heart.

He thought for a while longer, as if still debating whether or not to tell me.

'I won a race I should have lost,' he said finally.

'What do you mean, a race you should have lost?'

'I told him I'd lose, but then I went and bloody won it,' he said.

'That was rather careless of you.'

'No, not really,' he said. 'I did it on purpose. I was so fed up with that bastard Vickers overtaking me in the championship, I was trying to win on everything I rode. Fat lot of good it did me. I've come bloody second yet again.'

'So who was it that you told you'd lose the race?'

He thought for a moment.

'Sorry, mate,' he said. 'I can't tell you that. My effing life wouldn't be worth tuppence.'

'Is he a bookie?' I asked.

'No,' he said with certainty. 'He's a bloody nob.'

I expect, to Billy, anyone who spoke the Queen's English without a liberal scattering of swear words would be classed as a 'nob'.

'Which nob in particular?' I asked.

'I'm not saying,' he said. 'But even if I did you wouldn't effing believe it.'

'And does this nob still want his hundred thousand?'

'I expect so,' he said. 'That's what he claims he lost because I won the race. But I haven't actually talked to him since this little caper. Perhaps I'll tell him to bugger off. A broken leg must be worth a hundred grand at least.'

'Tell him you'll enlighten the cops as to the identity of your attacker if he doesn't leave you alone.'

'Don't be bloody naïve,' he said. 'These sort of guys don't mess about. Telling him that would get me killed for sure.'

'Sounds to me like you're in trouble if you do say who attacked you, and also if you don't.'

'You are so right,' he said. 'Once you say *yes* to them the first time, you're bloody hooked for life. They've got you by the balls, and there's no way out.' He leaned his head back against the white pillows and I thought there were tears in his eyes.

'Billy,' I said. 'There never will be a way out unless you fight back.'

'Well, count me out,' he said adamantly without moving. 'I am not going to be first over the top to be shot down. I value my jockey's licence.'

'So how often have you stopped one?' I asked.

'Too bloody often,' he said.

I was surprised. Billy didn't have a reputation as being a fixer.

'About ten times altogether, I suppose,' he said. 'Spread over the past three years or so. But I decided there would be no more when Frank Miller broke his leg in December, and I finally had the chance to be Champion Jockey.'

'But then young Mark Vickers pops up to beat you.'

'The bastard,' he said with feeling. 'It's not bloody fair.'

Life wasn't fair, I thought. Ask anyone with cancer.

Jan Setter had already left for Uttoxeter Races by the time I arrived back at her house at noon. I would have loved to have gone with her but I was worried that my enemies might have seen us together and worked out where I was staying.

Claudia was beginning to think I was becoming paranoid, but I would rather be paranoid than dead. And I only had to mention the dead gunman for her to agree to almost anything.

'But how much longer do we need to stay here?' she asked. 'I want to go home.'

'I do too, my darling,' I said. 'We will go home just as soon as it is safe.'

I had asked Jan over breakfast how much longer we could stay.

'How long do you need?' she'd asked.

'I don't know. Another few days at least.'

'I'll need you out by next Friday at the latest,' she'd said. 'I've got my sister and her family coming for the weekend.'

By next Friday we would have been here for eight nights.

'I sincerely hope it won't be as long as that,' I'd said. But, in truth, I had no real idea when it might be safe to go home.

'That's a shame,' Jan had said. 'I'm quite enjoying

316

the company. I get so bored here on my own since my divorce.'

I logged on to the internet and checked my e-mails. There were none – it had to be the weekend. With the exception of dealings on foreign markets, which could extend the working week for a few hours at either end, all financial services in the UK usually went to sleep at five o'clock on a Friday afternoon and awoke again at eight on Monday morning, as if the weekend had never been.

Except, of course, for interest, which was charged daily on loans whatever day of the week it was.

I used online banking to check on my personal accounts.

Things might be going to get quite tight if I did lose my job at Lyall & Black. I had managed to save quite well over the previous five years but much of it had been used to pay off the debts that I'd run up as a student.

While I might regularly handle investments for others of hundreds of thousands, or even millions of pounds, my own nest egg was much more modest.

Historically, the stock market has always outperformed fixed-interest investments such as bank accounts, certificates of deposit, and government bonds. However, stock markets are very susceptible to even minor changes in investor confidence and can fluctuate quite dramatically, especially downwards. For long-term investment, say over ten or twenty years or more, the stock market is considered to be the best but, if you need your money out sooner, the risk that the market may go down suddenly just before you need it would be too great, and more lower-risk assets may be better. Consequently, as an investor gets older, and the time for buying a pension becomes nearer, the balance tends to move away from high-risk stocks and further towards the 'safer' bonds.

In my case, with my expected pension requirement still a long way over the horizon, my savings were almost totally in equities. I would ride the stock market roller-coaster, but hope and expect the underlying trend to be upwards.

If I did get fired from my job, I might need to live off my savings for a while. And then what would I do? Billy had accused me of being boring but it wasn't me that was boring, I decided, it was my job. I needed more excitement in my life, more adrenalin rushing through my veins, but not necessarily due to having a silenced pistol pointed at me.

But what could I do? I was trained and qualified only to be a financial adviser. But what I wanted to be most was a jockey, or a rodeo-rider, or a free-fall sky-diving instructor, or a crocodile fighter, or . . .

Bugger my dodgy neck.

My mother interrupted my depressing thoughts by asking me what I wanted for lunch.

'What have we got?' I asked.

'Jan said we can use whatever we want from the fridge, or from the larder.'

'So what is there?' I said.

'Come and have a look.'

In truth, there wasn't very much to choose from,

just a few low-calorie frozen meals for one in the freezer, with more bare shelves than anything in the larder. Old Mother Hubbard would have felt quite at home.

'Time to go shopping,' I said.

So the three of us piled into the unremarkable blue hire car and went to a huge supermarket on the outskirts of Newbury in order to fill the empty spaces in Jan's fridge and larder. It was the least we could do as uninvited guests.

While Claudia and my mother went from aisle to aisle loading two large trolleys with mountains of food, I was banished by them to the clothing section.

I browsed through the rails of shirts and trousers, jackets and suits, but, sadly, this particular supermarket didn't stock bulletproof vests.

17

Sunday was, indeed, a day of rest.

The trip to the supermarket had almost been too much for Claudia, who was still far from well after her surgery.

'Don't try and do too much too soon,' Mr Tomic, the surgeon, had said. 'Plenty of rest is needed to allow the abdominal wall to mend.'

He hadn't mentioned anything about running up stairs, shouting at gunmen, or food shopping, but he probably wouldn't have approved of any of them.

'You stay in bed today,' I said to Claudia. 'I'll fetch you some breakfast.'

She smiled and closed her eyes again as I went out.

Jan was already downstairs making toast.

'My God,' she said, going into the larder, 'we've even got marmalade!' She turned round and grinned at me. 'I can't remember when I last had so much food in here. I'm completely useless at cooking. All I can do is heat things up in the microwave. But you really shouldn't have bought so much.'

'Consider it our rent,' I said.

'You don't have to pay rent, lover-boy,' she said, coming back out of the larder and opening the marmalade. 'You can pay me in kind.' She laughed. 'Except I now know I have no chance of that.'

'I'm sorry,' I said.

'Don't be,' she said. 'I think Claudia is really lovely. You're a lucky man.' She paused and breathed deeply. 'And I suppose I'd better stop calling you lover-boy.'

There were tears in her eyes. I went over to her and gave her a hug. There was nothing to say, so I didn't speak, I just held her tightly until the moment had passed.

'Life can be so random,' she said, stepping back from me. 'When I was married to Stuart all I wanted was to divorce him and keep half his fortune. Well, I've done that but – and I know this sounds crazy – I miss him. I even miss the godawful rows we used to have. Now, with Maria away at university in London, I'm just a rich, lonely old spinster.'

'But you must have masses of friends,' I said.

She looked at me as she spread the marmalade on her toast. 'I have plenty of acquaintances, but no real friends. Racing is so competitive that I find it difficult to make any true friends with racing people. Of course, I know lots of them round here, other trainers and such, and I see them at the races, but I'm not a member of the village dinner-party set. All my friends were Stuart's friends and, when he went, they went too.'

'Well it's high time you met some more,' I said, trying to lighten the mood.

She laughed again, but only briefly. 'That's not as

simple as it sounds, and finding someone to satisfy one's needs is far from straightforward, I can tell you. You chaps have it made.'

'In what way?' I asked.

'If a man wants sex, he can just go and buy it from some girl on a street corner, or in some lap-dancing club,' she said. 'It's not so easy for a middle-aged woman.'

I stood there slightly dumbstruck. I had always treated her advances as a bit of a joke. I hadn't realized the degree of her desperation.

'Oh, Jan!' I said. 'I'm so sorry.'

'I don't want your pity,' she said, quickly turning away from me and taking the marmalade back into the larder.

No, I thought, she wanted my body.

I took a cup of coffee and some muesli up to Claudia.

'You took your time,' she said, sitting up in bed.

'Sorry. I was talking to Jan.'

'Isn't she lovely?' Claudia said. 'We had a long chat yesterday morning, while you were out.'

'What did you talk about?' I asked.

'Life in general,' she said obliquely. 'Stuff like that.'

'Did you tell her about ... you know?'

Why was the word *cancer* so difficult to use?

'I started to but then your mother came in, and I'm still not sure it's time to tell her yet.'

'But when will it be time?' I said. 'Now seems as good a time as any.'

'I suppose you're right,' she said. 'I just feel . . .' She stopped.

'What?' I said.

'I suppose I feel a failure. And I don't want her to be disappointed in me.'

'Don't be daft,' I said. 'She loves you.'

'Only because she thinks I'm her pathway to grand-children.'

'That's not true,' I said, but I did wonder if she was right.

'And she won't love me if I marry you and then we find I can't have any babies. She will then see me not as a pathway but as an obstacle.'

She was almost in tears.

'Darling,' I said, 'please don't upset yourself. OK. If you don't want to, we won't tell her. Not yet.'

But we would have to tell her if, and when, Claudia's hair started falling out.

The rest of Sunday seemed to drag on interminably with me forever wondering how Ben Roberts was faring with his father. But, as I was still reluctant to leave my mobile phone switched on, I would have no way of knowing anyway.

My mother, with Jan helping, cooked roast beef for lunch with all the trimmings, the wonderful smells even enticing Claudia downstairs in her dressing gown.

'I can't tell you how long it's been since I had a proper Sunday lunch in this house,' Jan said as we all sat down at the kitchen table. 'Not since Stuart left, that's for sure. He used to do the cooking.' She laughed. 'Can't you stay for ever?'

The lunch was accompanied by a couple of bottles of the supermarket's finest claret, of which I had just one small glass. Someone had to keep their wits about them. I left the ladies to sleep it off on the deep sofas in the drawing room, while I again went to make some calls from Jan's office.

First I used her landline to remotely access my voicemail. There were four new messages. All were from Chief Inspector Flight, and each one threatened me with arrest if I didn't come forward immediately to speak to him. He read out a number where he could always be reached, and I wrote it down on the notepad beside the telephone.

But there was no message from Ben Roberts. Perhaps he hadn't yet found the right moment to speak to his father.

Next, I called DCI Tomlinson's mobile, taking care to dial 141 first to withhold Jan's number from caller-ID.

He answered at the fourth ring, but he sounded as if I'd woken him from a Sunday-afternoon slumber.

'Sorry,' I said. 'I thought you'd have your phone off if you weren't working.'

'I am working,' he said. 'I'm in my office. Just having forty winks on my desk. I was up half the night.'

'Partying?' I asked.

'Something like that,' he said. 'Or what goes for partying round these parts. An abused girlfriend finally had too much and stabbed her boyfriend to death.'

'Nice.'

'No,' he said, 'not really. She stabbed him about thirty times with a screwdriver. He bled to death. It was not a pretty sight, and especially not at four in the morning when I should have been tucked up in my bed.'

'Sorry,' I said.

'Thanks,' he replied. 'But it's sadly too common round here, especially after they've been drinking. I rarely get a full night's sleep on a Saturday.'

I decided against adding 'homicide detective' to my list of possible future careers.

'Do you have any news for me?' I asked.

'What sort of news?' he asked back.

'Anything,' I said. 'How about the dead man? Was he Bulgarian?'

'We don't know yet. His image and fingerprints haven't turned up on anything. Still waiting for the DNA analysis. But I can tell you one thing.'

'Yes?' I said eagerly.

'The forensic boys have been working overtime and they tell me the gun matches.'

'Matches what?' I asked.

'The gun found in the bush outside your mother's cottage was definitely the same gun that killed Herb Kovak, and they're pretty sure the same gun was also used to shoot at you in Finchley. They can't be a hundred per cent certain without the bullets.'

The image of the line of policemen crawling up Lichfield Grove on their hands and knees came into my mind. They obviously hadn't found anything.

'Does that mean that Chief Inspector Flight is now off my back?'

'I wouldn't exactly say that,' he said. 'He's still hopping mad.'

'Yes,' I said. 'I know. He's left messages on my phone.'

'Speak to him,' Tomlinson said. 'That's probably all he wants. He may think you're playing with him.'

'Does he still want to arrest me?' I asked.

'I don't know. Ask him.'

We disconnected.

I looked at the number on the notepad and thought about calling DCI Flight. Ignoring him would only make him madder, and then he might use more of his energies trying to find *me* than discovering the identity of his corpse. But I wasn't going to call him from here. Dialling 141 might be enough to prevent the number appearing on caller-ID but I was sure the police could still obtain it from the telephone company if they really wanted to.

But I'd called Chief Inspector Tomlinson using Jan's phone. What was the difference?

It was a matter of trust, I thought. I trusted Chief Inspector Tomlinson not to go to the trouble of finding where I was from the call. But I didn't trust DCI Flight.

So, at about five o'clock, I drove into the outskirts of Swindon and stopped in a pub car park before switching on my mobile and calling the Gloucestershire detective.

'DCI Flight,' he said crisply, answering at the first ring.

'This is Nicholas Foxton,' I said.

'Ah,' he said. 'And about time too.'

'Have you spoken to DCI Tomlinson and Superintendent Yering?' I asked.

'Yes,' he said slowly. 'I have.'

'Good,' I said. 'So who was the man at my mother's cottage?'

'Mr Foxton,' he replied curtly. 'It is *me* who needs to ask *you* some questions, not the other way round.'

'Ask away,' I said.

'What happened at your mother's cottage last Thursday evening?'

'A man with a gun broke in, we had a fight, and he fell down the stairs and broke his neck.'

'Is that all?' he asked.

'Isn't that enough?' I asked sarcastically. 'Oh yes, and he was trying to stab me at the time he fell down the stairs.'

'We found a knife under the body,' he said. 'But why did he need one? What happened to his gun?'

'It was under the fridge,' I said.

He paused.

'And how did it get under the fridge?'

'I hit it with an umbrella.'

This time there was a lengthy pause from the other end.

'Are you being serious, Mr Foxton?' he asked.

'Very,' I said. 'The man cut the power and the telephone. He then broke a pane of glass in the kitchen to get in and, as he was climbing through the window, I hit him with a golf umbrella. He dropped the gun, which slid under the fridge. He then took a knife from the block and tried to stab me. I managed to get upstairs but the man followed. As he was attacking me, we struggled and both of us fell down the stairs. He came off worse. End of story.'

There was another pause, another lengthy pause, almost as if the chief inspector had not been listening to me.

'Hold on,' I said suddenly. 'I'll call you back.'

I hung up, switched my phone off, and quickly drove the car out of the pub car park and down the road towards the city centre. After about half a mile, a police car with blue flashing lights drove past me, going fast in the opposite direction. Now was that just a coincidence, I wondered.

I went right round a roundabout and drove back to the pub, but I didn't go in. I drove straight past without even slowing down. The police car, still with its blue flashers on, had stopped so that it was completely blocking the pub car park entrance, and two uniformed policemen were getting out of it.

Was that also a coincidence? No, I decided, it was not.

I obviously hadn't needed to ask DCI Flight if he still wanted to arrest me. I'd just seen the answer.

I drove north along the A419 dual carriageway towards Cirencester, in the opposite direction to Lambourn, and pulled over near the village of Cricklade.

I turned my phone on again, and pressed redial.

DCI Flight answered immediately.

'Trust,' I said. 'That's what you need.'

'Give yourself up,' he said.

'But I've done nothing wrong.'

'Then you have nothing to fear.'

I hung up and switched off my phone. Then I started the car and made my way back to Lambourn, being careful not to speed or in any way attract the attention of any passing policeman.

Dammit, I thought. All I didn't need was an overly interfering detective who was more interested in catching me than in anything else. 'Give yourself up' indeed. Who did he think I was, Lord Lucan?

I caught the train from Newbury to Paddington just after seven o'clock on Monday morning, leaving the blue hire car in the station car park.

As the train slowed to a stop in Reading, I turned on my phone and called my voicemail.

'You have two new messages,' said the familiar female voice.

The first was from DCI Flight promising not to arrest me if I came to Cheltenham Police Station to be interviewed.

Why did I not believe him?

The second was from Ben Roberts.

'Mr Foxton, I have spoken with my father,' his voice said. 'He is not willing to meet with you or to discuss the matter further. I must also ask that you do not contact me again. I'm sorry.'

He didn't actually sound very sorry and I wondered if his father had been standing next to him as he had made the call.

My investigating wasn't exactly going very well. Where did I go from here?

I turned off my phone and sat back in my seat as the train rushed along the metal towards London. I watched absent-mindedly through the window as the Berkshire countryside gradually gave way to suburbs, and then to the big city itself, and I wondered what the day would bring.

I had to admit that I was nervous about the disciplinary meeting with Patrick and Gregory.

Lyall & Black had been my life for five years and I had begun to really make my mark. I had brought some high-profile, high-worth clients to the firm and some of my recommendations for investment, especially in film and theatre, had become standard advice across the company.

Over the next few years I might have expected to have expanded my own client base while giving up most of the responsibility of acting as one of Patrick's assistants. I might even have hoped to be offered a full senior partner position when Patrick and Gregory retired, and that would be only five or six years away. That was where the real money was to be made, and when my modest nest egg might start expanding rapidly. Providing, of course, that I was good enough to maintain the confidence of the clients.

However, I was now in danger of missing out completely.

But why? What had I done wrong?

It wasn't me who was defrauding the European Union of a hundred million euros, so why was it me who was attending a disciplinary meeting?

Perhaps the only thing I had done incorrectly was to not go straight to Patrick, or to Jessica Winter, the Compliance Officer, as soon as Mr Roberts had expressed his concerns over Gregory and the Bulgarian factory project. I should never have tried to investigate things behind their backs.

And I would rectify that mistake today.

I caught the Circle Line tube from Paddington to Moorgate and then walked from there towards Lombard Street.

As I walked down Prince's Street, alongside the high imposing walls of the Bank of England, I suddenly started to feel uneasy, the hairs again standing up on the back of my neck.

For the past four days, I had been so careful not to let anyone know where I was staying, yet here I was walking to a prearranged appointment at the offices of Lyall & Black. Furthermore, the appointment was for a meeting with one of those I believed was responsible for trying to kill me.

I really didn't fancy finding another gunman waiting for me in the street outside my office building.

I slowed to a halt on the pavement with people hurrying past me in each direction, late for their work. I was less than a hundred yards away from Lombard Street.

It was as near as I got.

I turned round and retraced my path back up Prince's Street to London Wall, where I went into a coffee shop and ordered a cappuccino.

Perhaps Claudia was right and I was becoming paranoid.

I looked at my watch. It was ten to nine. Patrick and Gregory would be expecting me in ten minutes.

What should I do?

My instinct at my mother's cottage had been absolutely right when I had prevented Claudia from opening the front door to the gunman. But I desperately needed to talk to someone about my suspicions, to set in motion a proper investigation into the Bulgarian affair. Surely then I would be safe, as killing me would then be too late. If Ben Roberts's father wouldn't talk to me, who else should I speak to? It had to be Patrick, if not to save my job, to at least to save my life.

I turned on my mobile phone and rang the office number.

'Lyall and Black,' answered Mrs McDowd. 'Can I help you?'

'Hello, Mrs McDowd,' I said. 'It's Mr Nicholas here. Can I speak to Mr Patrick, please?'

'He's in the meeting room with Mr Gregory and Andrew Mellor,' she said. 'I'll put you through.'

Patrick came on the line. 'Hello,' he said.

'Patrick,' I said. 'Please don't say anything. It's Nicholas. I need to talk to you alone,' I said. 'And without Gregory knowing.'

'Hold on a minute,' he said. 'I'll go to my office.'

There were some clicks on the line and then Patrick came back on.

'What's this all about?' he asked quite crossly. 'You are due to be here now for a disciplinary meeting.'

'I'm sorry,' I said, 'but I won't be coming to the meeting.'

'Nicholas,' he said formally, 'I must insist that you come into the office right now. Where are you?'

Where should I say?

'I'm at home,' I said. 'Claudia still isn't well.'

'I'm sorry,' he said, not sounding it. 'But this meeting is very important.'

So was Claudia, I thought.

'Where can I speak to you in private?' I asked.

'Here,' he said firmly and loudly. 'I will speak to you here, in the office, at the disciplinary meeting.'

'I'm sorry,' I said, 'but I will not be coming to the office today.'

'Listen to me,' he said. 'If you don't come into the

office today, there seems little point in you coming back at all.' He paused. 'Do I make myself clear?'

'Yes,' I said. 'I'll see what I can do.'

'Yes,' he said with ill-disguised anger. 'You do that.' He hung up.

I could imagine him going straight back into the meeting room and telling Gregory and Andrew that I wasn't coming. I was just glad I hadn't told him the truth about where I was.

I caught the Tube from Moorgate Station, but not back to Paddington. Instead I took the Northern Line to Hendon Central, walked down Seymour Way to number 45 and let myself into Herb Kovak's flat.

Sherri had gone home to America the previous Friday and there were already a few letters lying on the mat. I picked them up and added them to the pile that she had left on the desk.

I sat down on Herb's desk chair and opened his mail.

Amongst other things there were some utility bills and a letter from a building society complaining that the direct debit had been cancelled and they hadn't received the preceding month's interest on Herb's mortgage. It reminded me of the gym that also hadn't been paid due to the bank cancelling the direct debit. I wondered how many others there would be.

There was so much to deal with, and the worst of it was not the domestic bills, troublesome as they were, it was the never-ending stream of demands from the twenty-two credit card companies. About half of them had sent their next statements and not only were the previous month's balances still outstanding, overdue and generating interest, but there were more charges on the accounts.

The American gamblers were still gambling, and still losing. But how could I stop them if I didn't know who they were?

There must come a time, I thought, when the credit card accounts reached their credit limit. That should bring it all to a stop, but at what cost?

I used Herb's landline telephone to call the building society and let them know why the direct debit had been stopped. They were so sorry to hear of Mr Kovak's death but, of course, that did not mean they would stop accruing the interest on the loan. Did they not know the real meaning of mortgage? The 'mort' bit referred to death, like the 'mort' as in mortuary and mortality. A mortgage was originally a pledge to repay the loan outstanding on one's death, not on the never-never thereafter.

Next I called the utility companies and tried to arrange for the gas, electricity and phone to be cut off. I made the mistake of telling them that I wasn't Herb Kovak himself, that he was dead, and I was his executor. They all needed documentary proof that I was acting on Mr Kovak's behalf and, anyway, they needed the bills paid first. I pointed out that if I didn't pay the bills they would cut the services off anyway. It didn't help.

I collected the credit card statements and the other

things together and put them in a large white envelope that I found in Herb's desk. What I really needed was a solicitor to get things moving on the job of obtaining probate. At least I would then be able to cancel the credit cards, but probably not before they were paid off as well. This apartment would also have to be sold, and if the scale of the outstanding interest payment in the building society's letter was anything to go by, there may not be enough capital remaining after paying off the mortgage to cover the other bills. Perhaps I might need to make Herb's estate bankrupt.

All in all, it was not such a fine legacy.

I knew Patrick lived in Weybridge. I knew it because Claudia and I had been to his house for dinner a few times, and also the firm's annual summer party the previous year had been held in his expansive garden.

I also knew that his journey from home to work involved being dropped at Weybridge Station by his wife, catching a train to Waterloo, and then squeezing onto the Waterloo and City tube line to Bank. Everyone in the office knew because Patrick was not adverse to complaining loudly about public transport or, for that matter, his wife's driving, especially if it had made him late for work.

I assumed his return journey would be the same but in the opposite direction, and I planned to join him for some of it.

He usually left the office between six o'clock and

half past but I was at Waterloo waiting by five in case he was early. Even so, I still very nearly missed him.

The main problem was that there were at least six trains an hour to Weybridge and they seemingly could leave from any of the nineteen platforms.

I waited on the mainline station concourse opposite the bank of escalators that rose from the Underground lines beneath. During the peak evening rush hour, two of the three escalators were used for up-traffic and these, together with the stairs alongside, disgorged thousands of commuters every minute onto the concourse, all of them hurrying for their trains.

By twenty-five past six my eyes were so punch-drunk from scanning so many faces that my brain took several long seconds to register that I had fleetingly glimpsed a familiar one and, by then, he had become lost again in the crowd walking away from me.

I chased after, trying to spot him again while also attempting to search the overhead departure boards for trains to Weybridge.

I followed someone right across the concourse towards platform 1 and only realized it wasn't Patrick when he turned into one of the food outlets.

Dammit, I thought. I had wasted precious minutes.

I turned back and looked carefully at the departure boards.

There was a train for Basingstoke, via Weybridge, leaving from platform 13 in two minutes. I would have to take the gamble that Patrick was on it. I rushed right back across the station, thrust my ticket into the grey automatic barrier and ran down the platform.

I leapt aboard the train just seconds before the doors slammed shut. But I hadn't foreseen that it would be so crowded, with more people standing in the aisles than actually sitting in the seats. As the train pulled out of Waterloo Station I began to make my apologies and work my way along the congested carriages.

Eventually, after annoying at least half the train's occupants, and thinking that Patrick must have caught a different one, I spotted him sitting in the relatively empty first-class section. Where else? He was reading an evening newspaper and he hadn't noticed me coming towards him. He didn't even look up as I made my way through a sliding glass door and sat down on the empty seat next to him.

'Hello, Patrick,' I said.

If he was surprised to see me, he didn't particularly show it.

'Hello, Nicholas,' he said calmly, folding his paper in half. 'I was wondering when you would turn up.'

'Yes,' I said. 'I'm sorry about this but I needed to talk to you without Gregory knowing, or listening.'

'What about?' he asked.

'Colonel Jolyon Roberts,' I said quietly, conscious of the other passengers.

He raised his eyebrows a little. 'What about him?'

'He spoke to me nearly two weeks ago at Cheltenham Races and again at Sandown a week last Saturday.'

'You know he died last week?' Patrick asked.

'Yes,' I said. 'I do know. Terrible. I spoke to you after his funeral.'

'Of course you did,' Patrick said. 'He had a heart problem apparently.'

'So I've heard.'

'So, tell me, what did he speak to you about?'

'He was worried about an investment that the Roberts Family Trust had made in a light-bulb factory in Bulgaria.'

'In what way was he worried about it?' Patrick asked.

'Mr Roberts's nephew had evidently been to the site where the factory should be and there was nothing there. Nothing except a toxic waste dump.'

'Perhaps it hasn't been built yet. Or the nephew was in the wrong place.'

'That's what I thought,' I said. 'But apparently Gregory had shown photos of the factory to Mr Roberts, and the nephew is adamant that he was in the right place.'

'You have spoken to the nephew?' Patrick asked.

'Yes, I have,' I said. 'I spoke to him on Friday.'

'And have you approached Gregory about it?'

'No,' I said. 'Gregory was so angry with me last week for all that Billy Searle business that I didn't like to.'

'How about Jessica?' he asked.

'No, not her either. I know I should have done, but I haven't had the chance.'

The train pulled into Surbiton Station and two of the passengers in the first-class section stood up and departed.

'So why are you telling me?' Patrick asked as the train resumed its journey. 'The Roberts Family Trust is a client of Gregory's. You need to speak to him, or to Jessica.'

'I know,' I said. 'I just hoped you could look into it for me.'

He laughed. 'You're not frightened of Gregory, are you?'

'Yes,' I said.

And I was, very frightened indeed.

'Is this what all this being away from the office has been about?'

'Yes,' I said again.

He turned in his seat and looked at me. 'You are a strange man at times, Nicholas. Do you realize that you have placed your whole career on the line here?'

I nodded.

'Gregory and I agreed at the disciplinary meeting this morning, the one you were supposed to attend, that we would demand your resignation from Lyall and Black forthwith.'

So I *was* being fired.

'However,' he went on, 'Andrew Mellor advised us that we were obliged to hear your side of any story before we made such a precipitous decision. So no final conclusion was reached.'

'Thank you,' I said.

'So will you be in the office tomorrow so we can sort all this out?'

'I can't be sure of that,' I said. 'I would much rather

340

you started an internal enquiry into the Bulgarian investment before I returned.'

'You really are afraid of Gregory,' he said with a chuckle. 'His bark is worse than his bite.'

Maybe, I thought, but his bark had been pretty ferocious. And I also wasn't too keen on his hired help.

'Patrick,' I said seriously. 'I have reason to think that a multimillion-euro fraud is going on here, and that Gregory may be mixed up in it. Yes, I am frightened and I feel I have good reason to be.'

'Like what?' he said.

'I know it sounds unlikely but I believe that the Bulgaria business may have something to do with why Herb was killed.'

'But that's ridiculous,' he said. 'Next you'll be accusing Gregory of murder.'

I said nothing but just sat there looking at him.

'Oh, come on, Nicholas,' he said. 'That's madness.'

'Madness it may be,' I said. 'But I'm not coming into the office until I'm certain that I'd be safe.'

He thought for a moment.

'Come home with me now and we'll sort this out tonight. We can call Gregory from there.'

The train pulled into Esher Station.

Esher was the station for Sandown Park racecourse. Had it really been only nine days since I had alighted here to go to speak to Jolyon Roberts?

And two days later Jolyon Roberts was dead.

'No,' I said, jumping up. 'I'll call you tomorrow morning in the office.'

I rushed through the glass dividing door and then stepped out onto the platform just before the train's doors closed shut behind me.

I didn't want Patrick telling Gregory where I was – not tonight, nor on any other night.

18

By the time I made it back to Lambourn, all three of the ladies were in bed and the house was in darkness save for a single light left on for me in the kitchen. It was only fair, and I had called from a public phone box at Paddington to tell them not to wait up.

I realized I was hungry.

I looked at the clock hanging above the Aga. It was ten to eleven at night and I'd had nothing to eat since a hurried slice of toast at six o'clock in the morning. All day my stomach had been so wound up with worry that I hadn't even thought about food. My mother would not have been pleased.

I raided Jan's fridge and made myself a thick cheese sandwich.

I then sat eating it at the kitchen table, washing it down with a glass of orange juice.

It had been a good day, I decided. I still just had a job and I had finally spoken to Patrick about my concerns. Whether or not he believed me was another matter. But surely he was duty-bound to start an investigation and bring Jessica Winter into the loop, whatever he might think of my cloak-and-dagger tactics.

But would I then be any safer?

If Gregory, or whoever, was trying to kill me in order

to prevent an investigation into the fraud being started, then surely I should be out of danger once it had, because killing me then would only reinforce the need for the investigation to continue. Unless, of course, he felt he had nothing more to lose and killed me out of revenge for uncovering his scheme.

Either way, I was going to lie low for a few more days yet.

Tuesday dawned bright and sunny, which matched my temperament. Talking to Patrick had set my mind more at ease and I really felt I was getting somewhere at last.

In spite of being the final one to bed, I was the first up and downstairs, making myself an instant coffee by the time Jan appeared.

'Are you sure you don't want to come up on the Downs to watch the horses?' she said. 'It's a beautiful day for a change.'

I thought about it.

'I can lend you a hat and sunglasses,' she added with a laugh. 'As a disguise.'

'OK,' I said. 'I'd love to. I'll just take some tea up to Claudia.'

'There's plenty of time,' Jan said. 'First lot doesn't pull out until seven thirty and, even then, I give them a good head start. Be ready by about seven forty-five. We have breakfast afterwards.'

I glanced up at the clock. It was only five to seven.

344

'Right,' I said. 'I'll be ready.'

I took the tea and coffee up to our room and sat on the bed.

'Morning, sleepyhead,' I said to Claudia, gently shaking her shoulder. 'Time to wake up.'

She rolled over onto her back and yawned. 'What time is it?'

'Seven,' I said. 'And it's a beautiful morning so I'm going up on the Downs with Jan to watch the horses work.'

'Can I come too?' Claudia asked.

'I'd love you to,' I said. 'But how are you feeling?'

'Better every day,' she replied. 'I just wish . . .' She tailed off.

'I know, I know,' I said. 'But everything will be just fine. You'll see.'

I leaned down and gave her a hug and a kiss.

'I do so hope you're right,' she said.

This cancerous Sword of Damocles seemed to cast a shadow over our every waking moment. We were living in limbo and, as far as I was concerned, the sooner she started the chemotherapy the better. These weeks of doing nothing just seemed to invite the cancer to grow within her.

To my mind, there was nothing more revitalizing to the soul than a bright sunny, spring morning on the gallops. My only sadness was that I was watching the horses work from inside Jan's Land Rover rather than from the saddle.

God, how I still ached to ride, to sit again astride half a ton of Thoroughbred racehorse, and to gallop once more at full pelt with the wind in my face.

I watched with envy as Jan's stable staff brought the horses up the hill towards us side-by-side in pairs, some racing flat out and others at half or three-quarter pace. Just to hear the sound of their hooves thudding into the turf was enough to give me goosebumps, and to raise my pulse.

How cruel had been my neck injury to rob me of such delight.

But I supposed I shouldn't be too downhearted. At least my broken neck hadn't killed me, unlike someone else I could think of.

I didn't wear Jan's offered sunglasses, but I did don one of her ex-husband's old trilbies with the brim pulled firmly down and with my coat collar turned up. And I was careful not to get too close to the horses. I could easily recognize some of Jan's long-serving stable staff and I was still wary of them seeing me, if only to prevent DCI Flight from turning up with his hand-cuffs.

Claudia had no such qualms and walked across the grass to be nearer the horses.

Standing there, I watched her in the sunshine as she shook her hair out of a woolly hat and let it blow free in the wind.

How strange things had been over the previous few weeks. I had thought I was losing her to another man, and now I feared losing her to an illness. There was no doubt that the cancer had brought us closer together. I loved her more now than I had ever done. I would stay alive for her, I promised myself. And she must live for me.

She turned towards me and waved, her long hair blown in streaks across her face. In spite of it, I could tell she was laughing with joy, living for the moment.

I waved back.

In two or three weeks' time all that gorgeous hair would start to fall out, and she would absolutely hate it, but, I suppose, it was a relatively small price to pay for more life, and more love.

After lunch, I took the car out to call Chief Inspector Tomlinson. In the light of the episode at the Swindon pub, I decided that calling-on-the-move was the best policy, hence I started to dial the chief inspector's number as I was travelling at seventy miles an hour eastwards along the M4 motorway between Newbury and Reading. But the phone rang in my hand before I had a chance to complete the number.

'Nicholas Foxton,' I said, answering.

'Hello, Mr Foxton, it's Ben Roberts.'

'Yes, Ben,' I said. 'How can I help?'

'My father has changed his mind. He'd now like to talk to you.'

'Great,' I said. 'When and where?'

'He wonders if you would like come to Cheltenham Races tomorrow evening as his guest. It's the Hunter

Chase evening meeting and he's hired a private box. He says he would like to talk to you at the end of the evening's racing.'

'Will you be there?' I asked.

'I will to start with but I'll have to leave early to get back to Oxford for a club dinner.'

'Can I get back to you?' I said. 'I need to talk to my fiancée.'

'Bring her with you,' he said immediately. 'It's a buffet supper, not a sit-down, so numbers are not a problem. And I'll be leaving before the pudding so there'll be plenty of that left, anyway.' He laughed.

I couldn't help but like Ben Roberts.

'OK,' I said. 'I'd love to.'

'One or two?' he asked.

'One definitely, two maybe.'

'I'll tell my dad. He'll be pleased,' he said. 'We'll be there by five o'clock. See you then.'

We hung up.

I wondered if it was sensible to go back to Cheltenham. It was DCI Flight's home patch and the racecourse would be full of Gloucestershire policemen. But why should I worry? After all, I hadn't done anything wrong.

Next I called Chief Inspector Tomlinson.

'Where are you?' the chief inspector asked. 'There's lots of noise on the line.'

'I'm on the motorway,' I said. 'And this car isn't very well sound-insulated.'

'Which motorway?' he asked.

'Does it matter?' I said evasively.

'Are you using a hands-free system?' he asked.

I didn't answer.

'OK,' he said. 'I'll take that as a no.'

'So what are you going to do about it, arrest me for using a mobile phone while driving?'

'No,' he said. 'I'll just try and keep the call short. What do you want?'

'I want a meeting with you and Superintendent Yering,' I said. 'And DCI Flight, I suppose, if he wants to be there. As long as he doesn't arrest me.'

'Where do you want this meeting?'

'That's up to you,' I said. 'But arrange it for Thursday if you can.'

'What's the meeting for?' he asked.

'So I can tell you why I think Herb Kovak was killed and why our dead gunman was also trying to kill me.'

'What's wrong with today?' he said. 'Or tomorrow?'

'There's someone else I want to talk to first.'

'Who?' he said.

'Just someone.'

'I told you to leave the investigating to us,' said the chief inspector sternly.

'I intend to,' I said. 'That's why I want the meeting with you and the superintendent.'

But I also wanted to learn more about the Bulgarian investment before it.

'OK,' he said. 'I'll fix it. How do I contact you?'

'Leave a message on this number, or I'll call you again tomorrow.'

I disconnected.

I left the motorway at the Reading junction, went round the interchange and joined the westbound carriageway to go back towards Newbury.

I called the office and Mrs McDowd answered.

'Hello, Mrs McDowd,' I said. 'Mr Nicholas here. Can I speak to Mr Patrick, please?'

'You're a very naughty boy,' she said in her best headmistressy voice. 'You mustn't upset Mr Gregory so. His heart can't take it.'

I didn't reply. As far as I was concerned, the sooner his heart gave out the better.

I waited as she put me through.

'Hello, Nicholas,' said Patrick. 'Where are you?'

Why, I wondered, was everyone so obsessed with my whereabouts?

'In Reading,' I said. 'Have you spoken to Jessica?'

'Not yet. I've been reviewing the file myself this morning. I intend to discuss the matter with Gregory this afternoon.'

'Mind your back,' I said.

'Be serious,' Patrick said.

'I promise you I am being serious, very serious,' I replied. 'If I were you, I'd speak to Jessica first and then both of you talk to Gregory.'

'I'll see,' Patrick said.

Patrick and Gregory had been partners for a very long time and I reckoned that Patrick might need quite a lot of convincing that his friend was up to no good. I suppose I couldn't really blame him for checking things himself before he brought in the Compliance Officer.

'You might need someone who can read Bulgarian,' I said.

'Leave it to me,' Patrick replied decisively.

'OK,' I said. 'I will. But I'll call you again tomorrow to see how you're getting on.'

I hung up and glanced in the rear-view mirror. There were no signs of any flashing blue lights, nor of any eager unmarked police cars. I drove on sedately, back to Lambourn.

'I want to go home,' my mother said, meeting me in Jan's kitchen as I walked in from the car.

'And you will,' I said. 'Just as soon as I'm sure it's safe.'

'But I want to go home now.'

'Soon,' I said.

'No!' she stated in determined fashion, putting her hands on her hips. 'Now.'

'Why?' I asked.

'We've been here long enough,' she said. 'And I'm worried about my cat.'

'I didn't think it was *your* cat.'

'He's not, but I'm worried about him nonetheless. And I've got a WI meeting tomorrow night and I don't want to miss it.'

Don't mess with the Women's Institute. Tony Blair, for one, had discovered that.

'All right,' I said. 'I promise I'll take you home tomorrow.'

She wasn't very happy but, short of ordering herself a taxi, there wasn't much she could do. Tomorrow would have to do. I'd take her before I went on to the races.

And there was more unrest in the ranks from Claudia.

'I want to go home,' she said when I went up to our bedroom. She was standing by the bed packing her things into her suitcase.

'Have you been talking to my mother?' I asked.

'Maybe,' she said.

I thought there was no 'maybe' about it.

'Darling,' I said. 'I've arranged a meeting with the police on Thursday to sort everything out. We can go home after it.'

'Why can't you have this meeting tonight or tomorrow?'

'Because I have to talk to someone first and I'm seeing them at Cheltenham Races tomorrow evening.'

She stopped packing and sat down on the bed.

'I don't understand it. If the man who was trying to kill you was himself killed then why are we still hiding?'

'There may be others,' I said. 'And I don't want to take any unnecessary risks. You're far too precious to me.'

I sat down on the bed next to her and gave her a hug.

'But I'm bored here,' she said. 'And I've run out of clean knickers.'

Ah-ha, I thought, the true reason reveals itself.

'I'll tell you what,' I said. 'I've promised Mum I'll

take her back to her cottage tomorrow so why don't I take us all out to dinner tonight, then we'll go back to Woodmancote with Mum around lunchtime, and you can either stay there or come with me to the races in the evening. What do you say?'

'I'm not going to the races.'

'OK,' I said, 'that's fine. You can stay at Mum's cottage.'

'Oh, all right,' she said in a resigned tone. 'Where shall we go for dinner tonight?'

'Some nice quiet pub with good food.'

And preferably where I wouldn't be recognized by any Lambourn locals.

On Jan's recommendation, we went to the Bear Hotel in Hungerford for a sumptuous dinner in their Brasserie, washed down with a bottle of fine wine.

'I'll miss you,' Jan said over coffee. 'It's been great having the house full again. Please can you all come back for Christmas?'

My mother and Claudia toasted her kindness with large snifters of brandy and it seemed to have done the trick as I drove a happy car-load back to Lambourn, and to bed.

'Will the police still be there?' Claudia asked as I drove the last few miles to Woodmancote.

It was the question I had been wondering about ever since I'd agreed to bring my mother home.

'I don't care if they are,' my mother said loudly from

the back seat. 'I'm just so looking forward to being home again.'

'If they are,' I said, 'I'll pretend to be a taxi driver just delivering you two.' I dug in my pocket and gave Claudia a twenty-pound note. 'Here. Give me this and I'll drive away after I've unloaded your stuff. Then I'll call you later, from the races.'

'But they might recognize you,' Claudia said.

'I'll just have to take that chance.'

What I was more worried about was arriving to find the whole place sealed up as a crime scene, with 'Police – Do Not Cross' tape across the porch, and padlocks on the doors.

I needn't have worried. We arrived to find no tape, no padlocks, and no police guard.

The only external signs that anything was different was a new dangling wire that connected the corner of the building to a telegraph pole in the lane – the hasty repair of the cut telephone wire.

My mother let us in through the front door using her key.

It was all, remarkably, just the same as before with no visible evidence to show that a ferocious life-or-death struggle had gone on here less than a week previously. However, none of us could resist staring at the foot of the stairwell, at the place where we had last seen the gunman. There was no white-chalk-drawn outline of a body, or any other such comic-book indication of where the man had lain. Indeed, there was nothing at all to signify that anyone had violently died there.

The police had even secured the kitchen window, fixing a piece of plywood over the broken window pane.

'Fine,' said my mother, trying to show that things were back to normal and that she wasn't as uneasy as she sounded. 'Who'd like a cup of tea?'

'Lovely,' said Claudia, also betraying a nervousness in her voice.

I couldn't blame them. Being once again in that cottage suddenly brought the memory of the terrifying evening back into vivid focus, and none of us had quite realized the effect it would have.

'What time are you leaving for the races?' Claudia asked.

I looked at my watch. It was just past three o'clock and the first of the six races was at half past five.

'In about an hour and a half or so,' I said.

'And what time is your WI meeting?' she asked my mother.

'Seven thirty,' she said. 'But I usually go round to Joan's beforehand. We go to the meetings together.'

'So what time do you leave here?' Claudia asked patiently.

'About six,' she said. 'Joan and I usually have a sherry or two before we leave. Gives us a bit of courage for the meeting.' She giggled like a schoolgirl.

'And what time does it end?' Claudia asked.

'I'm usually home by ten, ten thirty at the very latest.'

'I really don't fancy being here on my own all evening,' Claudia said. 'I've changed my mind. I'm coming to the races.'

19

In the end, Claudia and I dropped my mother off at Joan's house at a quarter to five on our way to Cheltenham Races. It seemed she didn't particularly want to be on her own in the cottage either, which didn't bode well for the morning, when Claudia and I planned to return to London.

'Who is it we are going to see?' Claudia asked as we turned into the racecourse car park.

'A man called Shenington,' I said. 'Viscount Shenington. And he's hired a private box.'

'Very posh,' she replied, making a face.

We might be glad of the box, I thought as we climbed out of the car. The brief sunny interlude of yesterday morning was a distant memory and another weather front had moved in from the west, bringing a return to the thick clouds and rain that had characterized the weather for the majority of the last week. Evening meetings like this one at Cheltenham, with no floodlighting, relied on long bright summer evenings. I reckoned the last race on this particular dank miserable evening might be run in near-total darkness.

'And who is this Viscount exactly?' Claudia asked as we walked to the entrance huddled together under her minute umbrella.

'He's a racehorse owner and the senior trustee of the Roberts Family Trust. They're clients of Lyall and Black.'

'Oh,' she said, seemingly losing interest. Was my job really that boring? 'So why do you need to talk to this man before you see the police?'

I had purposely not told Claudia anything about my suspicions concerning the Bulgarian factory and housing project. She had far too many of her own problems to contend with, without having mine added on top.

'The Trust,' I said, 'has made an investment in something which I think is a front for fraud. I need to learn more about it before I speak to the police. I just have some questions to ask him, that's all.'

'Will it take long?' she asked.

'He wants to speak to me after the racing.'

'Oh,' she said again, this time sounding disappointed. 'So we're here till the bitter end.'

'I'm afraid so,' I said. 'But he has invited us to his box for the whole time, and there'll be food and drink available.'

That cheered her a bit, and she perked up a lot more when she discovered that the box in question was a magnificent glass-fronted affair at the top of the grandstand with a wonderful view over the racecourse.

It was also dry and warm.

Even though we were hardly late at ten past five, the box was already full of guests, none of whom I recognized.

I was just beginning to think we must be in the

wrong place when Ben Roberts came through the door, instinctively ducking his head as he did so.

'Ah, Mr Foxton,' he said, marching over to me with outstretched hand.

'Ben,' I replied. 'How nice to see you again. Can I introduce my fiancée, Claudia?'

'Great,' said Ben, shaking her hand and smiling. 'I'm Ben Roberts.'

Claudia smiled back.

'Come and meet my father.'

He led the way across the room to a group of men standing in the far corner. It was pretty obvious which one of them was Ben's father. He towered above the others by a good five or six inches. The 'tall' gene was clearly alive and well in all the Roberts family.

'Dad,' said Ben during a lull in the men's conversation, 'this is Mr Foxton and Claudia, his fiancée. My father, Viscount Shenington.'

'Delighted to meet you,' I said, offering my hand.

He looked down at me and slowly put forward his hand to shake. It was hardly the most friendly of welcomes, but I hadn't really expected anything else. I knew that even though he was prepared to speak to me, he didn't truly want to.

'Good evening, Mr Foxton,' he said. 'Good of you to come.' He turned slightly towards Claudia. 'And you too, my dear.'

That wouldn't go down too well, I thought. My father always called Claudia 'my dear' and she hated it, claiming that he was an arrogant old git who shouldn't be so patronizing.

'Have a drink,' Shenington said. 'And some food.' He waved a hand towards the impressive buffet table. 'We'll speak later.'

He went back to his former conversations.

'Good,' said Ben with considerably more warmth. 'What would you both like to drink? Champagne?'

'Lovely,' Claudia said.

'Fruit juice for me, please,' I said. 'I'm driving.'

'Yeah, me too,' said Ben, holding up a glass of orange liquid. 'But I'll get a proper skinful later at the Boat Club dinner.'

'Rowing?' I asked.

'Absolutely. Tonight's our home celebration for beating the hated enemy.'

'The hated enemy?' said Claudia.

'Cambridge,' Ben said, smiling broadly. 'In the Boat Race. Beat them by half a length. Dead easy!'

'Were you in the crew?' I asked.

'Certainly was,' he said, pulling himself up to his full six-foot-plus-plus. 'Number four – in the engine room.'

'Well done,' I said, meaning it. 'Are you trying for the Olympics next?'

'No. Not for me. I was good, but not that good. It's time to retire gracefully and get my life back. These last few weeks I've really enjoyed not having to be on the river every morning at dawn, and in all weathers. Now I'm just working hard for my finals.'

'And then what?' I asked. 'Politics?'

'That's the plan,' he said. 'A special adviser and political researcher for the party, at least for a while. Then Parliament.'

Then the world, I thought.

'Commons or Lords?' I asked.

'Commons,' he said with a laugh. 'The power house. There's no place left in the Lords for the likes of us, not any more. And I wouldn't want it even if there was.'

Ben himself was a walking 'power house', and his enthusiasm was infectious. I was sure he'd go far.

'Good luck,' I said to him. 'I personally can't think of anything worse than being a politician. Everyone I know seems to hate them.'

'No, they don't,' he said sharply. 'All they hate is that it's other people who are the politicians, when they want the power for themselves.'

I wasn't going to argue with him, and not least because I had a feeling I would lose, and lose badly. If Ben told me the grass was blue and the sky was green, I'd probably believe him. Except that, this particular evening, the sky wasn't green or blue, it was dark grey.

Claudia and I took our drinks out onto the private balcony and I briefly turned on my phone to check my voicemail. There was a new message from Chief Inspector Tomlinson.

'The meeting is fixed for tomorrow morning, Thursday,' his voice said. 'Eleven a.m. at Paddington Green Police Station.'

Not back in their holding cells, I hoped. I'd had my fill of those.

From our vantage point on the box balcony Claudia and I looked down at the few brave souls rushing around in the rain beneath us.

'It's such a shame,' Claudia said. 'The weather makes or breaks an event like this. Everyone gets so wet.'

'It's worse for the jockeys,' I said. 'They'll not just get wet, they'll get completely covered in mud kicked up from the horses ahead of them. On days like this, being a front-runner is the only sensible option. At least you can then see where you're going, and where the fences are. However, the down side is that, if your horse falls, the rest trample over you as you lie on the ground.'

'At least they're getting paid,' she said.

'Not tonight, they're not. All the races are for amateur riders only.'

'Then they're mad,' she said.

I laughed. 'Not at all. For some of them, tonight is the best evening of their whole year. They've been working hard all winter to qualify their horses for this one meeting, and a bit of dampness isn't going to spoil their party.'

'Well,' said Claudia, 'I'd definitely want a big fee to ride in this rain.'

Not me, I thought. I'd happily do it for nothing. In fact, I'd pay to be able to join them, and handsomely.

'Amateur jockeys do it just for the love of the sport,' I said. 'Indeed, the very word "amateur" comes from the Latin word "*amator*", meaning "lover".'

'You're my *amator*,' she said quietly, turning towards me and cuddling up with her arms inside my coat.

'Not now, darling,' I said. 'And not here. I'm working, remember.'

'Shame,' she said, letting me go. 'Your job is *so* boring.'

That seemed to be the unanimous conclusion.

Claudia and I braved the damp conditions to go down to the parade ring after the second race. We went to support Jan, who had a runner in the third.

'Not much chance, I'm afraid,' Jan said as she emerged from the Weighing Room with a small saddle over her arm. 'The horse is fine but the owner insists his son should ride it and he's only eighteen. He's still just a boy and this mare needs to be held up to the last. She gets lazy if she's in front too soon.'

'But *I* was only eighteen when I rode my first winner for you,' I reminded her.

'Yes,' she replied. 'But you were good, very good. This boy is barely average.' She rushed off towards the saddling boxes to prepare the horse.

Claudia and I waited under cover in front of the Weighing Room and, presently, Jan's mare came into the parade ring, closely followed by her and the horse's owner.

I scanned my soggy racecard to see who it was and, instead, noticed that one of the other runners in the race was owned by our host, Viscount Shenington. I looked around the parade ring and spotted him and some of his other guests huddling under large golf umbrellas at the far end. They were talking to the horse's trainer, the gossip, Martin Gifford.

The jockeys were called from the changing room and the eager mob streamed out onto the grass, their brightly coloured silks in stark contrast to the gathering gloom of the day.

Claudia and I decided to stay down where we were for the race rather than to go back up to the grandstand box. We could watch all the action on the big-screen television, and we wouldn't have to get wet coming down again if Jan's horse won. And also, I thought, I didn't really want to have to talk to Martin Gifford, who would surely go up to the box with his owner to watch their horse run.

But, on that score, I was sadly wrong.

Martin Gifford came to stand on the Weighing-Room terrace right next to me to watch the race on the television.

'Hi, Foxy,' he said. 'Penny for your thoughts?' He seemed to have recovered from, or forgotten, our little spat at Sandown. 'What a horrid day.'

'Yes,' I agreed.

'I'm quite surprised you're here for the hunter chasers,' he said. 'I wouldn't be if I didn't have this damn runner. I tried to talk the owner out of running it but he insisted. It should win, though.'

Now what was I to make of that? Martin Gifford made a habit of saying his horses had no chance, and then they went on to win. I knew that from the last meeting at Cheltenham, when both his horses had won after he'd told me they wouldn't. But was the reverse also true? Was this horse, in fact, a useless no-hoper? Did I even care? I wasn't going to back it either way.

I looked again at my racecard. A rating was printed alongside the details for each horse as a guide to punters. The higher the rating the better the horse was supposed to be, but, of course, it didn't always work out that way. Martin's horse certainly had a high rating for what was otherwise a moderate field of runners. Perhaps he really was telling the truth. I glanced up at an approximate-odds indicator and the public clearly agreed with him. The horse was starting as a very short-priced favourite.

We watched on the television as the horses jumped off very slowly from the start, which was at the far end of the finishing straight. With more than two complete circuits in the three-and-a-half-mile race, and in heavy ground, no one was really prepared to make the running and the fifteen horses had hardly broken into a gallop by the time they reached the first fence.

'Come on, you bugger,' said Martin next to me. 'I could really do with this one winning. Perhaps then the bloody owner will pay me some of his training fees.'

I turned my head towards him slightly. Maybe Martin could be useful after all.

'Slow payer, is he?' I asked.

'Bloody right,' said Martin without taking his eyes from the screen. 'But not so much slow, more like dead stop. I've even threatened to apply to Weatherbys to have the ownership of his horses transferred to me. He owes me a bloody fortune.'

Weatherbys was the company that administered all of British racing, and through which all racehorse registrations were held.

'How many horses does he have?' I asked.

'Too many,' he said. 'Twelve altogether, I think, but only six are with me, thank God, including one he used to jointly own with his brother. He hasn't paid me anything now for months. I tell you, I'm getting desperate.'

'But you'll get your money in the end, surely.'

'I don't know,' he said. 'Shenington claims he hasn't got it. Says he's nearly bankrupt.'

How interesting, I thought. The Roberts Family Trust, it seems, could happily lose five million pounds on an investment in Bulgaria, but the senior trustee couldn't pay his training fees because he was broke.

And how about hiring a private box for this meeting? It wasn't the sort of behaviour I would have expected from someone flirting with the bankruptcy courts. Not unless, of course, he had wanted to maintain a façade of affluence and respectability. Maybe the other guests were his creditors. Perhaps it was not so surprising that Martin hadn't been invited up there to watch the race.

'But Lord Shenington must have pots of money,' I said.

'Apparently, that's not so,' said Martin. 'Seems his father, the old Earl, still keeps his fingers very tightly on the family purse strings. And what money Shenington did have of his own, he's lost.'

'Lost?' I said.

'Gambling,' Martin said. 'On the horses, and at the casino tables. Addicted to it, evidently.'

'And how do you know this?' I asked with a degree of scepticism.

'Shenington told me so himself. Even used it as his excuse for not paying my bills.'

'So why are you still running his horses?' I asked. 'Did he pay the entry fee for this race?'

'No, of course not,' he said. 'I paid it.'

'You're mad,' I said.

'He has promised me all the prize money if it wins.'

We both watched on the screen as the horses swung past the grandstands for the first time. The daylight was now so dismal that, in spite of the different silks, it wasn't easy to spot which horse was which, but they were all racing closely packed and there was still a long way to go. All of them remained in with a chance of the prize money, but that wouldn't be much, I thought, just a few thousand pounds at most. I looked at the race conditions in the racecard. The prize to the winner was just over four thousand, and a month's training fees for six horses would be at least double that. The win would hardly pay off much of what Martin was owed, even if Shenington kept his promise, which somehow I doubted.

By the time the runners passed the grandstand for the second time, their number had been reduced by fallers from fifteen to twelve, and those twelve were no longer closely bunched but spread out over more than a furlong. And if it had been difficult to tell them apart last time round, it was almost impossible to do so now as they raced towards the television camera, each jockey with a uniform mud-splattered brown frontage. Only when the horses swung away onto their final circuit was it feasible to tell them apart by the coloured patterns on the backs of the silks.

Both Jan's and Martin's horses were still in the leading group, although even those appeared tired and leaden-footed as they reached the highest point of the course and then swung left-handed down the hill towards the finishing straight. Three and a half miles was a very, very long way in such heavy going.

Just as Jan had feared, the young jockey on her horse took the lead too soon. Even on the screen, it was clear to see that the horse didn't enjoy being on her own in front and the mare started to falter and weave about, almost coming to a complete stop just before the last fence. She would probably have refused to jump altogether if another horse hadn't galloped past and given her a lead to hop over the obstacle with almost zero forward motion, not that the other horse seemed that keen to win the race either.

That horse, too, swung from side to side as the jockey kept looking round, as if he was wondering where all the other horses had gone. The answer was that most of them had pulled up on their way down the hill, figuring, quite rightly, that they didn't have any chance of winning.

Only three of the original fifteen starters actually

crossed the finishing line with Martin Gifford's horse home first. Jan's mare was second, finishing at a walk and some twenty lengths behind the winner, and then one of the others finally staggered up the hill to be third, and a very long way last.

The rain eased a little and Claudia and I made our way over to the white plastic rails that ran across between the parade ring and the unsaddling enclosure, to watch the exhausted horses come in.

Jan wasn't very pleased. 'She could have won that,' she said, referring to her mare. 'I told the stupid little arse not to hit the front too soon. Certainly not until after the last, I told him, and then what does he do? God help me.' Martin Gifford, meanwhile, was beaming from ear to ear, which was more than could be said for his horse's owner.

Viscount Shenington looked fit to explode with fury, and he gave the victorious rider such a look that I wondered if this young man, like Billy Searle before him, had also won a race which he'd previously agreed to lose, not that he'd had much choice in the matter. Short of pulling up during the run-in, or purposely falling off, he'd had no alternative but to win.

And Lord Shenington was certainly a 'nob'.

Perhaps I would look at the records to see if Billy had ever ridden any of Shenington's horses.

'I'm freezing,' said Jan, coming over to us again after the horses had been led away. 'Either of you two fancy a Whisky Mac to warm up? I'm buying.'

As the rain began to fall heavily once again, the

three of us scampered over to the Arkle Bar on the lower level of the grandstand.

'How well do you know Viscount Shenington?' I asked Jan as we sipped our mixture of Scotch whisky and ginger wine.

'I know of him, of course,' she said. 'But not well enough to speak to.'

'We're guests in his box,' Claudia said.

'Are you, indeed?' Jan said. 'He does seem to have quite a lot of clout in racing, and his father is a long-standing member of the Jockey Club.'

'He's a client of the firm's,' I said. 'But not one of mine.'

She smiled at me. She was *my* client, she was saying but without using the words, and don't forget it.

'Do you know if he's got any financial troubles?' I asked her.

'How would I know anything about his finances?' she said. 'You're the specialist in that department.'

True, I thought, but he wasn't my client, and I could hardly ask Gregory.

We watched the fourth race on a television in the bar, the winner again coming in exhausted and smothered in thick mud.

'They ought to do something when the going's as heavy as this,' Jan said.

'Do what?' Claudia asked.

'Make the races shorter, or reduce the weights.'

'You can't realistically reduce the weights,' I said. 'Half of them are carrying overweight already.' Most

369

amateur jockeys were taller and heavier than the professionals.

'The races should be made shorter, then. Most of these poor horses are finishing half dead. Three and a half miles is too far in this mud.'

She was right, of course, but how could the clerk of the course predict the course conditions when planning the races several months in advance?

'Right,' said Jan decisively, finishing her drink, 'I've had enough of this misery. I'm going home.'

'Can't we go too?' Claudia asked, shivering.

'Not yet,' I said. 'I've still got to talk to Viscount Shenington.'

Claudia looked far from happy.

'I'm sure Jan would take you back to Mum's place, if you'd like,' I said. 'It's only a mile or so down the road from here.'

'No problem,' said Jan.

'Here,' I said, taking my mother's house key from my pocket. 'I'll be back by ten and I'll collect Mum from Joan's on the way.'

Claudia took the key, but slowly as if nervous.

'Jan will see you into the cottage,' I said, trying to be reassuring. 'Then lock yourself in, and only open the door to me.'

Suddenly, she wasn't so sure about going back to the cottage on her own, but I could see that she was very cold, and she was also not yet fully recovered from her operation. If the truth were told, I would be much happier if she went with Jan as I could then concentrate on what I had to ask Shenington, and be quick about it.

'OK,' she said. 'But please don't be long.'

'I won't,' I said. 'I promise.'

Shenington's box was much emptier when I went back up there before the fifth race, and there was no sign of Ben.

'He's had to go back to Oxford,' explained his father as I removed my Barbour and hung it on a hook by the door, the rainwater running down the waxed material and dripping off the sleeves onto the carpet. 'He said to say goodbye.'

'Thank you,' I said. 'He's a very nice young man. You should be proud of him.'

'Yes, thank you,' he replied. 'But he can also be a bit idealistic at times.'

'Isn't that a good thing in the young?' I said.

'Not always,' he replied, staring at the wall above my head. 'We all have to live in the real world. To Ben, everything is either right or wrong, black or white. There's no middle ground, no compromise, and little or no tolerance of other people's failings.'

It was quite a statement, I thought, and one clearly born out of a certain degree of conflict between father and son. Perhaps Ben didn't easily tolerate his father's addiction to gambling.

Shenington seemed to almost snap out of a trance.

'Where's your lady?' he asked, looking around.

371

'She was cold,' I said. 'A friend has given her a lift to my mother's house. I'll pick her up later. I'm sorry.'

'I don't blame her,' he said. 'It's a cold night, and many of my guests have already gone. The rest will probably go before the last race.'

I ventured out onto the balcony and peered through the gloom as yet another long-distance hunter chase became a test of stamina for the tired and dirty participants. At least this one promised to give the crowd an exciting finish, that was until one of the two leaders slipped while landing over the last fence and deposited its hapless rider onto the grass with a sickening thump. I watched as the miserable jockey sat up holding his arm in the classic 'broken-collarbone' pose, the bane of every rider's life.

I realized that it was at a point not very far from where the jockey was sitting that my own life had changed for ever some eight years previously. How different things might have been if I'd landed on my outstretched arm that day as he had just done, and not on my head; if I'd only broken my collarbone instead of my neck.

As Shenington had predicted, almost all his remaining guests departed after the race, saying their goodbyes and preparing for the dash to their cars in the rain.

Finally, there was just Viscount Shenington, myself, and two other men in rather drab suits remaining. Even the catering staff seemed to have disappeared.

Suddenly I felt uneasy.

But my concern was far too late.

One of the two men stood by the door to ensure no one could come in, while the other advanced towards me. And he had a gun in his gloved hand, together with the ubiquitous silencer.

'Mr Foxton, you are an extraordinarily difficult man to kill,' Shenington said, smiling slightly. 'You usually don't turn up when you're expected, and yet you came here so sweetly, like a lamb to the slaughter.'

He almost laughed.

I didn't.

This time I'd been bloody careless.

20

'What do you want?' I asked, trying to keep the fear out of my voice.

'I want you dead,' Viscount Shenington said. 'So you can stop spreading your silly rumour that my brother was murdered.'

'But he was, wasn't he?' I said.

'That is something you are not going to have to worry about any more,' Shenington said.

'How could you have killed your own brother?' I asked. 'And for what? Money?'

'My brother had no idea what it was like to be desperate for money. He was always so bloody self-righteous.'

'Honest, you mean.'

'Don't give me all that claptrap,' he said. 'Everyone's on the make. I just want my share.'

'And is your share a hundred million euros?' I asked.

'Shut up,' he said loudly.

Why should I? Maybe I should shout as loudly as I could, to attract attention.

I took a deep breath and the cry for help began in my throat. But that was as far as it got. The man with the gun punched me very hard in my lower abdomen, driving the air from my lungs and leaving me lying in a heap on the floor, gasping for breath. And then, just for good measure, the same man kicked me in the face, splitting my lip and sending my blood in a fine spray onto the carpet.

'Not in here, you fool,' Shenington said to him sharply.

That was slightly encouraging, I thought, through the haze in my brain. At least they weren't going to kill me here. It might have been rather incriminating to leave a dead body in the corner of the box amongst the empty champagne bottles.

'It won't do you any good,' I said through my bleeding mouth, my own voice sounding strange even to me. 'The police know I'm here.'

'I somehow doubt that,' Shenington replied. 'My information is that you've also been avoiding them over the past week.'

'My fiancée knows I'm here,' I said.

'Yes, so she does. When I've dealt with you, I'll deal with her too.'

I thought about saying that Jan Setter also knew I was here, but that might have placed her in mortal danger as well.

I kept quiet. I'd opened my big mouth enough already.

I could hear the public address system outside. The last race had started.

'Now,' said Shenington to the men. 'Take him down now while the race is running.'

The two men came over and hauled me to my feet.

'Where are you taking me?' I asked.

'To your death,' Shenington said with aplomb. 'But not here, obviously. Somewhere dark and quiet.'

'Can't we –'

It was as far as I got. The man on my right, the one without the gun who had been standing by the door, suddenly punched me again in my stomach. This time I didn't fall to the floor, but only because the two men were holding me up by my arms. My guts felt like they were on fire and I was worried that some major damage may have been done to my insides.

'No more speak,' said the man who had punched me. English was clearly not his strong point.

'No more speak' seemed a good plan, at least for the time being, so I kept quiet as the two men walked me past my coat, through the door, across the corridor, and into one of the deserted catering stations. The three of us descended to the ground in one of the caterer's lifts. There was no sign of Shenington. I wasn't sure whether that was good or bad. I suppose two against one was marginally better than three to one but, on the down side, I'd have little or no chance of reasoning with these two heavies. Although I doubt if I'd have had any chance anyway, had Shenington been there with us.

The lift stopped and I was marched out of it, and then across the wet tarmac towards the north exit and the racecourse car parks beyond. The facilities at Cheltenham were really designed for the Steeplechase Festival in March, when more than sixty thousand would flock into the course every day. The car parks were therefore huge but, on a night like this with only a small fraction of the crowd, most of them were deserted and, at this time of the evening, they would be dark and quiet.

'Somewhere dark and quiet,' Shenington had said.

I came to the conclusion that my last, brief journey would likely come to an abrupt end in a far corner of the racecourse car park. I tried my best to slow down but I was being frog-marched forward. I also tried to sit down, but they were having none of that. They gripped my arms even tighter and forced me on.

I'd have to shout for help, I thought, and chance another punch, but the commentator's voice was booming out through the public address, so would anyone hear me? There were only a very few people about, hurrying to go home with their heads bowed down and their collars turned up against the rain. Most of the remaining crowd were sensibly under cover watching the race. Only a fool would stand about down here in the wet.

'Horse!' a voice called loudly off to my right in warning. 'Loose horse!'

There is no doubt that horses have a homing instinct. Ask any trainer who has had a horse get loose and lost on the gallops. More often than not, the horse is found happily standing back in the stable yard, in its own box, and is usually home before the search party.

Horses that are reluctant to race, or those that might get loose due to falling, often dive back towards the place where they came out onto the course, as if they were trying to get home, or at least back to the race-course stables.

This particular loose horse came galloping down the horse-walk and attempted to negotiate the ninety-degree turn to get back into the parade ring. A combination of too sharp a bend and too much momentum, coupled with the wet surface, meant that the horse's legs slipped out from beneath it and it fell, crashing through the white plastic railings and sliding across the ground towards the three of us, its legs thrashing about wildly as it tried to regain its footing.

The men on either side of me instinctively took a step backwards away from the sharp flailing horse-shoes, slightly relaxing their hold on my arms as they did so. But I stepped forward boldly, out of their clutches, and caught the horse by the reins. In one movement, as the animal managed to stand up, I swung myself onto its back and into the saddle.

I needed no second invitation. I kicked the astonished horse in the belly and we galloped back the way it had come, down the horse-walk towards the race-course.

'Hey, stop!' shouted an official who was standing in my way, waving his arms about. I glanced behind me. The two men were in pursuit and one was reaching into his pocket. I had no doubt he was going for his gun.

The official realized at the very last second that I wasn't going to stop and he flung himself aside. I kicked the horse again, and crouched as low as I could to provide the smallest target for the gunman.

I looked ahead. Even though the last race of the day was still in progress, out on the racecourse was definitely the safest place for me to be. Another official saw the horse galloping back towards him and he tugged frantically at the movable rail, closing it across the end of the horse-walk.

But I wasn't stopping. Stopping meant dying and I'd promised myself I wouldn't do that.

A rider communicates with his mount in a variety of ways. Pulling on the reins, either together or separately, is an obvious one, and cajoling with the voice or kicking with the feet are others. But the most powerful messages between horse and jockey are transmitted by the shifting of weight. Sit back and a horse will slow and stop, but shift the weight forward over his shoulders and the same horse will run like the wind.

I gathered my feet into the stirrup irons, stood up, shortened the reins, and crouched forward over the horse's withers. The animal beneath me fully understood the 'go' message. Riding a horse was like riding a bike – once learned, never forgotten.

As we neared the end of the horse-walk I made no move to slow down. In fact, I did quite the opposite. I kicked the horse hard in the belly once more. The animal received the new message loud and clear, and he knew what to do. I shifted my weight slightly again, asking him to lengthen his stride and to jump, and to jump high.

We sailed over the rail with ease, and over the official as well, who'd had the good sense to duck down.

The horse pecked slightly on landing, almost going down on its knees and, for a moment, I feared he was going to fall, but I pulled his head up with the reins and he quickly recovered his balance.

Left or right?

Left, I decided, pulling that way on that reins, away from the grandstand and towards the safe wide-open spaces of the racecourse.

The other horses were coming up the finishing straight towards me, but I was well to the side of them, on what would have been the hurdle course at any other meeting.

My mount tried to turn, to run with the others, but I steered him away and galloped down to the far end of the finishing straight before stopping and looking back.

What remained of the daylight was disappearing rapidly and the grandstand lights appeared unnaturally bright. It was difficult to tell if the two heavies were giving chase but I had to assume they were, joined possibly by Viscount Shenington himself. He must be keener now than ever to remove me permanently from the scene.

I turned the horse again and cantered up the hill, towards the farthest point on the racecourse away from the stands and the enclosures.

What did I do now?

The nondescript blue hire car would be waiting for me in the racecourse car park, but the problem was that its keys, together with my mobile phone and my wallet, were in the pockets of my Barbour, which I presumed was still inconveniently hanging by the door in Shenington's box.

I watched as a vehicle turned onto the racecourse from close by where I had emerged from the horse-walk. I could see the headlights bumping up and down slightly as it worked its way along the grass in the direction that I had come.

Another vehicle followed it onto the grass but turned the other way.

Both vehicles then moved forward slowly, driving round the course. If I stayed where I was then the two of them would close on me in a pincer movement.

But who was in the vehicles? Was it Shenington and his cronies, or would it be the police, or the racecourse security guards? I imagined that the trainer of the horse I was riding would be far from pleased to have discovered that his charge had been horse-napped, and was currently running about the racecourse in the dark.

But I couldn't stay where I was, that was for sure. Not without being seen or captured. And I had absolutely no intention of allowing a vehicle to come up close to me unless, and until, I knew for certain that Shenington and his heavies were not in it.

At Cheltenham, the racecourse, unlike those in America, was not a simple oval track, but was in fact two complete racecourses laid one on top of the other, and with an extra loop down one end. In addition the centre was used for cross-country races. There was no way that these two vehicles would be able to corner me on their own, not unless I was careless, and I had been quite careless enough for one day.

I waited to see which part of the racecourse the car

would choose to move along and then simply rode the horse down the other bit. By this time, the last of the daylight had faded away completely and there was no way the occupants of the vehicle would be able to see me unless I was actually in the arc of the headlights.

However, I watched with some dismay as three more vehicles turned out onto the racecourse, two turning straight towards me and the third starting the long anticlockwise sweep round the course. And worse, in the glow of their lights, I could see some figures walking, spreading out across the centre of the track in search of the horse, or of me.

They couldn't all be Shenington's men. Some of them must be the good guys, the cavalry coming to my rescue. But which ones? I simply couldn't afford to get it wrong.

I decided that my present position was hopeless, and it would be only a matter of time before I would be seen by either someone in the vehicles, or one of those on foot. I trotted the horse over to the very edge of the racecourse property looking for an exit, but the need to keep out the ticket dodgers had resulted in a robust five-foot-high chain-link fence being erected along the whole length.

I supposed I could have tied the horse to the fence and climbed over but the location of the deserted horse would then have given away the fact that I had gone and where, and I feared I would have had Shenington and his mob still on my tail. And I somehow felt safer on the horse because I could outrun those on foot, gun or no gun.

'With that neck, I wouldn't ride a bike, let alone a horse,' the spinal specialist had said to me all those years ago. Yet here I was on horseback galloping around in the dark, but I felt completely safe and at home. I just had to make sure I didn't fall off.

I cantered the horse right along the fence in the hope there might have been a gate. Five feet was too high for any horse to jump, let alone a tired-out hunter chaser that should have been warm in his stable by this time of night. Not that a gate would help much. It would probably be locked and I couldn't ask the horse to jump it in the dark.

The pincer arms of the search parties were moving closer together and, if I didn't move away pretty soon, I was in danger of being caught in their trap. I kicked the horse hard and galloped back along the perimeter fence all the way down to the far northern end of the racecourse and into the extra loop, taking my chances that the horse wouldn't stumble or put his foot in a rabbit hole.

I was still looking unsuccessfully for an exit through the fence. And I was beginning to think that my only option might be to double right round and try to find a way out through the car parks, but the lines of searchers were getting closer, and the opportunities for doing that were being closed off by the minute.

The chain-link fence finally gave way to a hedge,

though not a nice low jumpable hedge but a high impenetrable jungle of hawthorn and blackberry. I trotted on along its length and finally found a gap in the undergrowth. The horse and I went through the gap and into the field that was used as a helicopter landing area during the Festival meeting.

I doubled back, putting the hedge between me and my pursuers. By this time it was an almost completely black night and I didn't now have the reflected light from the vehicle headlamps to help me. The horse and I moved steadily forward at the walk, the blind leading the blind. The animal beneath me must have been as confused as I was as to where we were going but he had been trained well and responded easily to my every command.

'Come on, boy,' I said quietly into his ear. 'Good boy.'

I could see the lights from the houses in Prestbury village. The hedge must be thinner straight ahead.

Suddenly, I thought I heard a man cough. I gently pulled the reins and the horse stopped and stood silently. I listened intently in the darkness.

Had I been mistaken?

The man coughed again. Then he called out, but in a language I didn't recognize. He was on the other side of the hedge, but I couldn't tell exactly how far away. A second man answered, again in a foreign tongue, and he was certainly further away still.

The men had to be Shenington's heavies.

I held my breath and prayed that the horse wouldn't make a noise or jangle the bit in his mouth.

I strained to listen to their conversation and thought I might have heard the nearest man moving, but I was far from sure.

The rain came to my aid.

It had been easing somewhat but now it returned with a vengeance, falling in heavy drops that ran down my neck. But I didn't care. The noise of the rain may have prevented me from hearing anything further of the men's conversation, but, more importantly, it would also mean that they would be unable to hear me moving on.

I made some fairly gentle clicking noises and gently nudged the horse in the ribs with my foot. 'Walk on,' I said to him in his ear.

We eventually came upon a gate, and it wasn't locked.

I dismounted and led the horse through, closing the gate behind us.

A light suddenly came on, flooding the area with brightness and momentarily startling the horse, which whipped round, pulling the reins from my fingers.

Dammit!

'Here, boy,' I said in as calming a voice as I could muster. 'Good boy. Come on.' I held out my hand towards the terrified animal, which tossed his head up and down and neighed loudly. 'Good boy,' I repeated, as I moved towards where he stood quivering by the gate. When I was close enough, I lunged forward and grabbed the reins once more, but not before the horse had neighed loudly a couple of times more.

Had the men heard? Or seen the light?

The light in question was attached to the gable-end of a wooden barn and had a motion sensor below it – a security light.

I looked around. We were in a farmyard with more buildings beyond the barn.

I heard a whizzing sound close to my right.

The sound instantly gave me goosebumps on my arms and made the hairs on my neck stand upright. I knew that noise. I knew it because I'd heard it before in Lichfield Grove. It was the sound of a bullet passing by, and much too close for comfort. A second whizzed past and embedded itself into the wooden planking just a few inches from my face. And I could hear shouting, foreign-language shouting. Time to move, I thought, and quickly.

I pulled the horse forward and we ran around the corner of the barn away from the direction of the shouting. Another bullet whizzed past me and disappeared into the night.

I had intended leaving the horse tied up somewhere, while I made my way to safety alone, but my plans had just changed. If the men were close enough to shoot at me, they would be close enough to catch me if I was on foot. I needed the speed of the horse to escape.

I put my left shoe into the stirrup iron and pulled myself back up into the saddle, gathered the reins, and set off again. More security lights came on as I cantered the horse through the farmyard but the horse was happier now with someone on his back, and he didn't react once. We went right across the brightly lit farmyard and then down a long drive that curved away into the darkness. Soon I could see headlights moving quickly from right to left ahead of us, as a car moved along the Winchcombe road at the end of the drive.

We had now left the security lights well behind, but I had to take a chance in the dark as I kicked the horse forwards as fast as I dared.

I neared the road. Which way should I turn?

I knew that I ought to go to the right towards Prestbury village and Cheltenham. I knew it because I should be on my way to Cheltenham Police Station. I'd be safe there, and DCI Flight would finally get his interview.

I even worked out the best route in my head.

I had grown up in Prestbury village and I knew intimately all the short cuts from there to Cheltenham town centre. I had used them either on foot or on my bicycle for half my life. And I knew all the deserted back-roads and the quiet way through Pittville Park, past the Pump Room that gave Cheltenham its spa status, across the Tommy Taylor's recreation area, and down past the allotments off Gardner's Lane where I had often played as a kid with my school friends. Wherever possible I would keep the horse off the hard surfaces and on the grass, all the way to Swindon Road, not far from the old Cheltenham Maternity Hospital where, nearly thirty years ago, I had been brought screaming into the world.

I could then trot the horse past the railway station

and down the wide, tree-lined avenues around Christ Church to my destination on Lansdown Road.

Yes, I thought, I really ought to turn right towards the police station.

Instead, I turned left towards Woodmancote, and Claudia.

How could I have been so stupid to have told Shenington that she had gone to my mother's? If he had been the one who sent the broken-neck gunman there to kill me, and I had no doubt that it had been, he would know exactly where to find my mother's cottage. It would only be a matter of time before he worked out that he could get to me by attacking Claudia.

I just hoped I would get there first.

Fortunately, at this time on a wet Wednesday, the road was quiet. Only on a couple of occasions did I have to pull off onto the wide grass verges as cars came sweeping past. Neither of them even slowed down. Other than that, I kept to the road. It was much too dangerous for the horse even to walk along the verges at night with the many hidden drainage ditches.

However, the noise of the metal horseshoes clickety-clacking on the tarmac as we cantered along suddenly sounded alarmingly loud in the night air. Which was safer, I wondered, speed or stealth? That same question had been taxing military strategists ever since armies had been invented.

I opted for speed, but I did slow to a walk as we reached the edge of Southam village and, as much as I could, I used the grass there to minimize the noise.

Even though it was late, and still raining, the sound of a horse at such an hour, especially one moving at speed, might bring people out of their houses to investigate, and there was no way I wanted to have to stop and explain what I was doing, not yet.

The horse and I went right through the village of Southam without attracting any unwelcome attention, other than a curious look or two from a cat out on its nocturnal hunt for food.

Southam to Woodmancote was less than a mile and I trotted the horse down the centre of the road using the dotted white line for guidance. At long last the rain was beginning to stop, not that it made much difference to me, I was completely soaked to the skin, and cold with it.

I skirted round the edge of the village towards the lane where my mother lived.

The lane was actually the fourth arm of a cross-roads junction and I was just approaching it from straight ahead when a car came along the other road and turned right into it. The car had to be going to my mother's cottage as it was the only house down there.

I kicked the horse forward and followed, keeping to the grass to deaden the noise of the hooves.

Half-way down the lane I slid off the horse's back and tied him to a tree, moving forward silently but quickly on foot. I stayed close to the hedge as I came round the last turn.

I could now see the cottage and Shenington was standing to one side of it as I looked, by the front

389

door, his face brightly lit by the outside light. I crept closer across the grass, towards the gravel drive.

'Viscount Shenington,' he was saying loudly. 'We met earlier at the races.'

'What do you want?' I could hear Claudia shouting back from inside.

'I'm returning Mr Foxton's coat,' Shenington said. 'He must have left it in my box by mistake.' He was holding my coat out in front of him.

Don't open the door, I willed Claudia. PLEASE – DON'T OPEN THE DOOR.

She did, of course. I could hear her turning the lock.

Once Shenington was inside I would have no chance. He could simply put a knife to Claudia's neck, or a gun to her temple, and I would do exactly as he wanted. A lamb to the slaughter it would certainly be.

My only chance was to act decisively, and to act now.

As the front door swung open I ran for him, crunching across the gravel. He turned slightly towards the noise but I was on him before he had a chance to react.

At school, despite my moderate size, I'd been a regular member of the first XV rugby team, and primarily for my tackling.

I caught Shenington just above the knees in a full-blown flying rugby tackle that literally lifted him off his feet.

The two of us crashed to the ground together, the whiplash causing his upper body and head to take most of the impact.

Shenington was in his mid to late sixties and I was

less than half his age, and I had the strength brought on by desperation and anger.

He really had no chance.

I jumped up quickly and I sat on him, twisting my fingers in his hair and forcing his head down into a rain-filled puddle on the drive. How did he like it, I wondered, having *his* face held under water?

Claudia stood, shocked and staring, in the doorway.

'Nick,' she wailed. 'Stop it. Stop it. Stop it. You'll drown him.'

'This is the man who has been trying to kill me,' I said, not releasing my grip.

'That doesn't mean you can kill *him*,' she said.

I reluctantly let go of his hair and rolled him over onto his back. His lips were blue and I couldn't tell if he was breathing or not. I didn't care. One thing was for sure. There was absolutely no way I was going to put my mouth over his to breathe air into his lungs. Even the thought of it made me feel sick.

'He's got a gun,' Claudia said suddenly, the fear clearly apparent again in her voice.

He'd been lying on it.

I leaned down and picked it up by the barrel.

I left Shenington where he lay and went inside to call Cheltenham Police Station.

'Can I please speak to DCI Flight?' I said to the officer who answered. 'I want to give myself up.'

'What have you done?' he said.

'Ask DCI Flight,' I replied. 'He's the one who wants me.'

'He's not here at the moment,' the officer said. 'Some bloody lunatic has stolen a horse up at the racecourse and every spare man is out looking for him.'

'Ah, I might just be able to help you there,' I said. 'The horse in question is tied up outside my mother's house in Woodmancote.'

'What!' he said.

'The horse is right outside where I'm standing now,' I repeated.

'How the hell did it get there?'

'I rode him,' I said. 'I think I'm the bloody lunatic that everyone is looking for.'

21

Detective Chief Inspector Flight was far from amused. He, personally, had spent more than an hour trudging across the dark, muddy racecourse looking for the horse while wearing his best leather shoes and, if that wasn't bad enough, he was also soaked to the skin. As he explained to me at length and rather loudly, his coat was meant to have been waterproof but, on that count, it seemed to have failed rather badly.

'I'm tempted to put you in a cell and throw away the key,' he said.

We were in one of the interview rooms at Cheltenham Police Station.

'How is Viscount Shenington?' I asked, ignoring his remark.

'Still alive,' he said. 'But only just. They're working on him at the hospital. The ambulance paramedics got him breathing again but it seems his heart is now the problem.'

Just like his brother.

'And the doctor is also saying that, even if he does survive, his brain is likely to have been permanently damaged due to being starved of oxygen for so long.'

Shame, I thought. Not!

'You say that you simply rugby-tackled him and

you didn't see that his nose and mouth were lying in the water?'

'That's right,' I said. 'I just thought he was winded by the fall. Only after I'd checked that Claudia was all right did I discover he was face-down in a puddle. Then, of course, I rolled him over onto his back.'

'Did you not then think of applying artificial respiration?' he asked.

I just looked at him.

'No,' he said. 'I can see the problem.'

'Exactly,' I said. 'The man had come there to kill me. Why would I try and save him? So that he could have another go?'

'Some people might argue that you were negligent.'

'Let them,' I said. 'Whatever happened to Shenington was his own fault. You saw the gun. He wasn't there making a social call.'

He looked up at the clock on the wall. It showed that it was well after midnight.

'We'll have to continue this in the morning,' he said, yawning.

'I have to be at Paddington Green by eleven,' I said.

'So do I,' Flight replied. 'We can talk on the way.'

The meeting at Paddington Green Police Station lasted for more than two hours. In addition to me, there were four senior police officers present, Detective Chief Inspectors Tomlinson and Flight, a detective inspector from the City of London Police Economic Crime Department – the Fraud Squad – and Superintendent Yering, who chaired the meeting by virtue of his superior rank.

At his request, I started slowly from the beginning, outlining the events in chronological order from the day Herb Kovak had been gunned down at Aintree, right through to those of the previous evening at Cheltenham racecourse, and at my mother's cottage in Woodmancote. However, I decided not to include the finer details of how I had forced Shenington's head down into the puddle on the gravel driveway.

'Viscount Shenington,' I said, 'seems to have been desperate for money due to his gambling losses and clearly provided the five million pounds from the Roberts Family Trust in order to trigger the grants from the European Union. It appears that he even gave his brother the impression that he had needed to be convinced to make the investment.'

'Perhaps he did to start with,' said DCI Flight, 'until he discovered the availability of the grants.'

'Maybe,' I said. 'But I think it's far more likely that the idea for stealing the EU grants came first and Shenington was simply brought in as the necessary provider of the priming money.'

'So he wasn't the only one involved?' Tomlinson said.

'Not at all,' I said. 'I've seen e-mails between a Uri Joram in the office of the European Commission in Brussels, and a Dimitar Petrov in Bulgaria.'

'How did you see them?' Tomlinson interrupted.

'On Gregory Black's computer,' I said. 'He was copied in on their correspondence.'

'And who is Gregory Black?' asked the detective inspector from the Fraud Squad.

'He's one of the senior partners at Lyall and Black, the firm of financial advisers where I work.' Or where I used to work.

'And what do you think he has to do with this?' he asked.

'I'm only guessing, but I believe that Gregory Black probably found Shenington for Joram and Petrov. They would have needed someone with five million pounds to invest to trigger the much larger sum from the EU. Shenington was a client of Gregory's and who could be better, a man who controlled a wealthy family trust but was himself broke and in dire need of lots of ready money to pay his gambling debts. And Gregory would have known that. Financial advisers are aware of all their clients' most intimate financial secrets.'

'But what has all this to do with the death of Herbert Kovak?' asked DCI Tomlinson. That was *his* major concern.

'Herb Kovak had accessed the file with the e-mails between Joram and Petrov just a few days before he was killed. And Gregory Black would have known he had, because Herb's name appeared on the recently accessed list. I saw it there. Perhaps Herb had asked some difficult questions about the project, questions that got him killed.'

I could see that I was losing them.

'Remember,' I said, 'we are talking about a huge amount of money here. A hundred million euros. Even split four ways, it's a handsome sum, and worth a bit of protecting.'

I could see them doing the simple maths in their heads.

'And,' I went on, 'in the last week or so, every time Gregory Black knew where I was, someone tried to kill me there. I now think that Shenington only changed his mind about wanting to talk to me, then asked me to the races because I hadn't been turning up at my office. He as good as admitted it yesterday. He said I was a difficult man to kill because I usually didn't turn up when I was expected. Well, I was expected at a meeting with Gregory Black on Monday morning, and I'm now certain that I would have been killed if I'd gone to it. I probably wouldn't have even reached the office front door. I'd have been shot down in the street. Murdered in a public place, just like Herb Kovak was at Aintree.'

'I think it's time I spoke again to Mr Gregory Black,' said DCI Tomlinson. 'I remember him from my previous encounter.'

Yes, I thought, and I bet he remembers you.

There followed a brief discussion as to who had the proper jurisdiction to arrest, and on suspicion of what charges. Finally, it was agreed that the honour would fall to DI Batten, the detective inspector from the Fraud Squad – after all, the City of London was his patch. However, we all wanted to be present and a total of three police cars made the trip across London to 64 Lombard Street where we were joined by a fourth from the uniformed branch.

It was quarter past two by the time we arrived at my office. Gregory should be just back from his usual substantial lunch at the restaurant on the corner. I hoped he'd made the most of it. There would be no more *foie gras* and *filet mignon en croûte* where he was going.

'Can I help you?' Mrs McDowd asked as the policemen entered. Then she saw me with them. 'Oh, Mr Nicholas, are these men with you?'

DI Batten ignored her. 'Can you tell me where I might find Mr Gregory Black?' he said rather grandly.

'I'll call him,' she said nervously, clearly slightly troubled by the mass of people crowding into her reception area.

'No,' said DI Batten, 'just tell me where he is.'

At that point Gregory walked down the corridor.

'There he is,' said Mrs McDowd, pointing.

The detective inspector wasted no time.

'Gregory Black,' he said, taking hold of Gregory by the arm, 'I arrest you on suspicion of conspiracy to defraud, and also on suspicion of conspiracy to murder. You do not have to say anything, but it may harm your defence if you do not mention when questioned something which you later rely on in court. Anything you do say may be given in evidence.'

Gregory was stunned. 'But that's ridiculous,' he said. 'I've done nothing of the sort.'

Then he saw me.

'Is this your doing?' he demanded, thrusting his face belligerently towards mine. 'Some kind of sick joke?'

'Murder is never a joke,' said DI Batten. 'Take him away.'

Two uniformed officers moved forward and hand-cuffed Gregory, who was still loudly protesting his innocence. The policemen ignored his pleas and led him out of the glass door and into the lift.

I knew all too well what that felt like.

'What the hell's going on?' Patrick had appeared in the reception, obviously summoned by the noise. 'What are these men doing here?'

'It seems they are here to arrest Mr Gregory,' said the unflappable Mrs McDowd.

'Arrest Gregory? But that's ridiculous. What for?'

'Conspiracy to defraud, and conspiracy to murder,' DI Batten said.

'Fraud? Murder? Who has he murdered?' Patrick demanded, turning towards the policeman.

'No one,' said DI Batten. 'Mr Black has been arrested on suspicion of *conspiracy* to murder.'

Patrick wasn't to be deterred.

'So who, then, is he suspected of conspiring to murder?'

'Me,' I said, stepping forward.

Patrick said nothing. He just stared at me.

Later in the afternoon, life in the offices of Lyall & Black at 64 Lombard Street returned to some sort of normality, if having one of the senior partners arrested for conspiracy to defraud and murder could ever be considered normal.

I went into my office for the first time in almost two weeks to find that Rory had moved himself into Herb's desk by the window. Diana was still where she had always been.

'By rights that should have been Diana's,' I said to Rory. 'She's the more senior.'

'She had yours until half an hour ago,' Rory replied with a sneer. 'Patrick said you weren't coming back.' His tone implied that he was sorry I had.

Diana, meanwhile, remained silently resentful as I opened the window to let in some of the warm spring day. Perhaps the weather had changed for the better as well.

Maybe Diana wouldn't have to wait too much longer to get back to my desk, anyway. That was, if my desk remained at all. At the moment, I couldn't see Lyall & Black surviving as a firm beyond next week. Once news of a fraud investigation got out, our clients would desert us quicker than rats off a sinking ship. Everything in financial services comes down to client confidence, and confidence in a firm involved in fraud would be close to absolute zero.

The quickest way to create a run on a bank was to publicly warn that there might be one. Depositors would quickly lose confidence in the institution and would queue round the block to get their money back. But, of course, no bank leaves cash lying around in its vaults just in case of such an eventuality. The money will have been lent out to other customers as mortgages and business loans. Hence the bank can't pay. As word spreads that the bank is in trouble, even more depositors come looking for their money and the whole crisis self-perpetuates, and then crashes down like a house of cards. The bank's credibility, which might have taken several hundred years to establish, can be destroyed in as little as a day. As it had been with Northern Rock in the UK and IndyMac in the US, and so would be with us but, in our case, there would be no government bail-out.

Yes, indeed, we had all better start looking for new positions by another firm's window, but what chance would we have with a reference from Lyall & Black? Not much.

There were nearly a hundred unanswered e-mails for me on the company server, plus twenty-eight messages on my office voicemail, including quite a few from irate clients with whom I had missed meetings. There were also two from the Slim Fit Gym reminding me again that they wanted Herb's locker back.

'Where's the key?' I asked Rory.

'What key?' he said.

'The key that was pinned to Herb's desk.'

'Still on it, I expect,' Rory said. 'I swapped the whole desk cubicle.'

I went over to one of the empty cubicles and checked. The key was still pinned to the board. I took it off and put it in my pocket.

I sat down again at my desk and started going

through the mass of e-mails but without really taking in any of the information contained in them. My heart simply wasn't in this job any more.

If and when Claudia beat this cancer, we would do something different, something together.

Something more exciting. But maybe something a little less dangerous.

'I'm going out,' I said to Rory and Diana, as if they cared.

As I walked down the corridor I had to step over some big tied-up polythene bags stacked full of files and computers. The Fraud Squad was busily packing up the stuff from Gregory's office. I was quite surprised they hadn't thrown us all out of the building to pack up the whole firm. That would come later, no doubt, when they had discovered a little more.

The receptionist at the Slim Fit Gym was really pleased to see me.

'To be honest,' she said in a broad Welsh accent, 'it's beginning to smell a bit, especially today in this warm weather. It's upsetting some of our other clients. There must be some dreadfully sweaty clothes in there.'

The key from Herb's desk fitted neatly into the hefty padlock on the locker, and I swung open the door.

The receptionist and I leaned back. It smelled more than a just a bit.

There was a dark blue holdall in the locker with a pair of off-white training shoes placed on top, and I think it was the shoes, rather than the clothes inside, that were the culprits as far as the smell was concerned. Perhaps Herb had suffered from some sort of foot fungal problem that had spread to his shoes, and then they had clearly festered badly over the last three weeks. But whatever the cause, the smell was pretty rank.

'Sorry about this,' I said. 'I'll get rid of it all.'

I tucked the offending shoes into the holdall on top of the clothes and left the receptionist tut-tutting about having to disinfect all the lockers.

I walked back towards Lombard Street and dumped the whole thing, together with all the contents, into a City-of-London-crested street litter bin. I didn't think Mrs McDowd would be very happy if I took that smell back into the office.

I had walked nearly a hundred yards further on when I suddenly turned round and retraced my steps. I had searched everything else of Herb's. Why not that holdall?

Neatly stacked, in a zipped-up compartment beneath the clothes, was over a hundred and eighty thousand pounds wrapped in clear-plastic sandwich-bags, three thousand in twenty-pound notes to each bag. There was also a list of ninety-seven names and addresses, all of them in America.

Good old Herb. As meticulous as ever.

'Mr Patrick would like to see you,' Mrs McDowd said to me as I skipped through the door with the bag of loot over my shoulder. 'In his office, right now.'

Patrick was not alone. Jessica Winter was also there.

'Ah, Nicholas,' said Patrick. 'Come and sit down.' I sat in the spare chair next to the open window. 'Jessica and I have been looking at how things stand. We need to implement a damage-limitation exercise. To seek to maintain the confidence of our clients, and to assure them that it's "business as usual" at Lyall and Black.'

'And is it "business as usual"?' I asked.

'Of course,' he said. 'Why wouldn't it be?'

I thought that was pretty obvious. Members of the Fraud Squad were still in the room next door bagging up evidence.

'No,' Patrick went on, 'we mustn't let this little setback disrupt our work. I will write to all of Gregory's clients telling them that, for the time being, I will be looking after their portfolios. It will just mean we all have to work a little harder for a while.'

But for how long, I wondered.

The maximum sentence for conspiracy to murder was life imprisonment.

'So how about the Bulgarian business?' I asked.

'Jessica and I have just been looking at it,' Patrick said. 'Or what is left to look at after those damn police have been in here taking stuff away.'

'And?' I asked.

'It's rather inconclusive,' Jessica said.

'What's inconclusive?' I asked, somewhat surprised.

'There seems to be no evidence to show if the original investment was obtained by fraudulent means, or whether there was any purposeful deception by anyone in this firm,' Jessica said.

She's covering her back, I thought.

'But how about the European Union grants?' I said.

'They are not our business,' Patrick said sharply. 'Neither Gregory individually, nor Lyall and Black as a firm, can be held responsible for the actions of people in Brussels, those who may have issued EU grants without due diligence. The only matter that affects this firm is the original Roberts Family Trust investment, and then only if we were knowingly negligent in brokering it. As far as we can establish, the investment idea was put forward by the senior trustee of the trust.'

I had to admit, it was a persuasive argument, especially as Viscount Shenington was unlikely to be in any state to refute it. Perhaps I had been a tad premature in writing off the future of Lyall & Black.

But that didn't explain what had happened to Herb Kovak, and it didn't explain Shenington's comment about me being difficult to kill, and not turning up where I was expected. The only place I'd been expected had been the offices of Lyall & Black, and the only people who had known where I'd been expected had been the firm's staff. Gregory must have at least discussed the matter of my murder with Shenington. That alone would have been enough to convict him.

'What about the photographs that Gregory showed to Colonel Roberts?' I said. 'The ones that purported to prove that the factory and houses had already been built.'

'Gregory told me this morning that he'd been sent those by the developer in Bulgaria, and in good faith,' said Patrick. 'He'd had no reason to doubt their authenticity.'

'Not until Jolyon Roberts asked about them,' I said. 'What did he do then?'

'Gregory told me that Colonel Roberts didn't exactly say that he questioned whether the photos were accurate or not. In fact, Gregory said that Roberts kept contradicting himself and changing his mind throughout their final telephone conversation, and he kept apologizing all the time for wasting Gregory's time. In the end, Gregory wasn't quite sure what to think.'

I could believe it. Jolyon Roberts had done exactly the same with me at Cheltenham. I thought it strange that a man who had clearly been so decisive on the battlefield could have been so befuddled and incoherent when it came to accusing a friend of lying, and of stealing from him. I suppose it was all about honour, and not losing face.

'Thank you, Jessica,' Patrick said. 'You can be getting back to your office now.'

Jessica stood up and left. I remained where I was.

'Now, Nicholas,' said Patrick when the door was shut, 'I have decided to overlook your rather strange behaviour over the past three weeks and to wipe the slate clean. Your job is still yours if you want it. To be honest, I don't know how we would manage at the moment if you weren't here.'

So was that a vote of confidence in my ability, I wondered, or a decision born simply out of necessity?

'Thank you,' I said. 'I'll think about it.'

'Don't take too long about it,' Patrick said. 'It's time to put other things out of your mind and get back to work.'

'I'm still not happy about things,' I said. 'Especially the fraud.'

'Suspected fraud,' he corrected. 'If you ask me, it is a shame you ever went to see Roberts's nephew in Oxford.'

'Maybe,' I said.

'Well go now and get on with your work, I have things to do.'

It was a dismissal, so I stood up and went back to my desk.

I was still greatly troubled by Patrick's and Jessica's seeming brush-off of such a serious situation.

Herb had accessed the file and then he was killed.

Shenington and his gunmen knew more about my movements than they could have done without someone in the firm passing on the information.

Something wasn't right. I could tell because the hairs on my neck refused to lie down. Something definitely wasn't right. Not right at all.

I took out a sheet of paper from a drawer and wrote out again a copy of the note I had found in Herb's coat pocket.

YOU SHOULD HAVE DONE WHAT YOU WERE TOLD. YOU MAY SAY YOU REGRET IT, BUT YOU WON'T BE REGRETTING IT FOR LONG.

I wrote it out in capital letters using a black ball-point pen so that it looked identical to the original.

I picked up my mobile phone and the note, and went down the corridor. I walked into Patrick's office, closing the door behind me.

'Yes?' he asked, showing some surprise at my unannounced entrance.

I stood in front of his desk looking down at him as if it was the first time I had ever seen him properly.

'What did you tell Herb to do?' I asked him quietly.

'What do you mean?' he replied with a quizzical expression.

'You told him that he should have done what he was told,' I said.

I laid the note down on the table, facing him, so that he could read the words.

'What was it you told Herb to do?'

'Nicholas,' he said, looking up at me and betraying a slight nervousness in his voice, 'I don't know what you're talking about.'

'Yes, you do,' I said with some menace. 'It was *you* all along, not Gregory. *You* devised the fraud, *you* found Shenington to put up the five million from his family trust, and *you* saw to it that you weren't found out.'

'I don't know what you're talking about,' he said again, but his eyes showed me he did.

'And *you* had Herb killed,' I said. 'You even wrote this note to him as a sort of apology. Everyone liked Herb, including you. But he had to die, didn't he? Because he had accessed the Roberts file and he'd worked out what was going on. What did you do?

Offer him a piece of the action? Try and buy his silence? But Herb wasn't having any of that, was he? Herb was going to go to the authorities, wasn't he? So he had to die.'

Patrick sat in his chair looking up at me. He said nothing.

'And it was *you* that tried to have me killed as well,' I said. 'You sent the gunman to my house in Finchley and then, when that didn't work, you sent him to my mother's cottage to kill me there.'

He remained in his chair staring at me through his oversized glasses.

'But that didn't work either,' I said. 'So you arranged for me to come here on Monday for a meeting with you and Gregory.' I laughed. 'A meeting with my maker, more like. But I didn't come, although you tried hard to convince me to. Then I saw you on the train and you said, "Come home with me now and we'll sort this out tonight". But I'd have been dead if I had, wouldn't I?' I paused and stared back at him. He still said nothing. 'So then Shenington changed his mind about talking to me and invited me to be his guest at the races in order to complete the job.'

'Nicholas,' Patrick said, finally finding his voice, 'what is all this nonsense?'

'It's not nonsense,' I said. 'I never told you that I'd been to see Mr Roberts's nephew in Oxford. In fact, I'd purposely *not* told you because I didn't want anyone knowing my movements. I just told you that I'd spoken to him. For all you knew, it could have been on the telephone. But Shenington told you that I went to Oxford to meet his son, didn't he? And you repeated it to me just now.'

'You have no proof,' he said, changing his tune.

'Did you know that you can get fingerprints from paper?' I asked, picking up the note carefully by the corner.

He wasn't to know that the original had already been tested by the Merseyside Police forensic department and found to have only my and Herb's prints on it.

His shoulders sagged just a fraction and he looked down at the desk.

'What did Herb say he regretted?' I asked.

'He said he regretted finding out,' Patrick said wistfully with a sigh. 'I was careless. I stupidly left a document under the flap of the photocopier. Herb found it.'

'So what did you tell him to do?' I asked for a third time.

'To accept what he'd been offered,' he said, looking up at me. 'But he wanted more. Much more. It was too much.'

Herb had clearly not been as much of a saint as I'd made out.

'So you had him killed.'

He nodded. 'Herb was a fool,' he said. 'He should have accepted my offer. It was very generous, and you can have the same – a million euros.'

'You make me sick,' I said.

'Two million,' he said quickly. 'It would make you a rich man.'

'Blood money,' I said. 'Is that the going rate these days for covering up fraud, and murder?'

'Look,' he said. 'I'm sorry about Herb. I liked him and I argued against having him killed, but the others insisted.'

'Others?' I said. 'You must mean Uri Joram and Dimitar Petrov.'

He stared at me with his mouth open.

'Oh yes,' I said. 'The police know all about Joram and Petrov because I told them. I told them everything.'

'You bastard,' he said with feeling. 'I wish Petrov had killed you at the same time he shot Herb Kovak.'

Throughout the encounter I'd been holding my mobile phone in my left hand. It was one of those fancy new do-anything smartphones, and one of its functions was the ability to act as a voice-memo recorder.

I'd recorded every word that had been said.

I pushed the buttons and played back the last bit. Patrick sat very still in his executive leather chair listening and staring at me with a mixture of hatred and resignation in his eyes.

'I wish Petrov had killed you at the same time he shot Herb Kovak.'

It sounded rather metallic out of the telephone's tiny speaker, but there was no doubting that it was Patrick Lyall's voice.

'You bastard,' he said again.

I folded the note, turned away from him, and walked

back along the corridor to my desk to call Chief Inspector Tomlinson. But I'd only just picked up the telephone when there was a piercing scream from outside the building.

I stuck my head out through the window.

Patrick was lying face up in the middle of the road, and there was already a small pool of blood spreading out around his head.

He had taken the quick way down from our fourth-floor offices.

Straight down.

And it had been the death of him.

Epilogue

Six weeks later Claudia and I went to Herb Kovak's funeral at Hendon Crematorium, the Liverpool coroner finally having given his permission.

There were just five mourners, including the two of us.

Sherri had returned from Chicago and would be taking Herb's ashes back to the States with her. The previous day, she and I had attended the solicitor's offices of Parc Bean & Co., just off Fleet Street, to swear affidavits in order for the court to confirm a Deed of Variance to Herb's will, making her, his twin sister, rather than me, the sole beneficiary of his estate. It would surely have been what he would have wanted. I, however, was to remain as his executor in order to complete the sale of his flat, and to do the other things that were still outstanding.

I had written to all the American names I had found in Herb's dark blue holdall informing them of his untimely death, and that their little scheme to use his credit card accounts for their internet gambling had died with him. I'd told them that they shouldn't worry about me going to the authorities and they wouldn't be hearing from me again. But I also told them that I had no expectation of hearing from them either, even if they had paid Herb in advance more than they had subsequently lost. Then I'd used the cash from the holdall to pay off all the credit card balances, and used my letter from the coroner to close the accounts.

Detective Chief Inspector Tomlinson had come down from Merseyside for the funeral service and he sat in front of Claudia and me in the chapel wearing the same ill-fitting suit he'd worn when I'd first met him in the offices of Lyall & Black. That had been less than three months ago but it felt like a lifetime.

Lyall & Black and Co. Ltd was no more.

Gregory Black had been quickly released by the police but he had taken early retirement. Without Patrick, he hadn't had the incentive to carry on, and he had heeded his heart doctor's advice to put his feet up in his Surrey garden.

I, meanwhile, had quit before I was fired, walking out of 64 Lombard Street for the last time before the paramedics had even had a chance to scrape Patrick's lifeless corpse from the pavement.

I still didn't know what I would do, so I was currently living off my savings, and looking after Claudia.

We stood up to sing the hymn 'The Lord's My Shepherd' and I took her hand in mine.

The last six weeks had been very difficult for her. She had undergone two sessions of chemotherapy, each for three days, and three weeks apart.

Her hair had fallen out in handfuls immediately after the second treatment and, by now, she was completely bald. Today, as usual, she was wearing a headscarf, mostly to prevent other people from staring at her. Strangely, it had not been the loss of hair on her head that had upset her the most, but the loss of her lovely long eyelashes with it.

However, Mr Tomic, the oncologist, was pleased with her progress and reckoned that the two sessions were enough. As he'd said, 'We don't want to jeopardize your fertility now, do we?'

On that count we would just have to wait and see. With cancer, there were never any guarantees.

The fifth mourner at the funeral was Mrs McDowd, who had arrived just before the undertakers had carried in the plain oak coffin. I wondered how she had known about the funeral but, of course, Mrs McDowd knew about everything.

I stood out at the front to utter a few words about Herb, as it somehow seemed wrong to allow him to go for ever without at least marking his passing.

I tried hard to visualize in my head the features of the man lying in the wooden box beside me. The unravelling of the enigmas of his life had seemingly brought us closer together and, in a strange way, he had become more of a friend to me after his death than he ever had before it.

I didn't really know what I should say so I made some banal comments about his love of life, and his wish to help others less fortunate than himself, but without actually pointing out that the others he helped were law-breaking American internet gamblers and poker players.

In all, the service took less than twenty minutes. Sherri sobbed quietly and the rest of us stood in silence as the priest pushed a hidden button, and the electrically operated red curtains closed round my colleague, my friend, my free-spending greedy friend.

Then the five of us went outside into the warm June sunshine.

Claudia and Mrs McDowd consoled Sherri while the chief inspector and I moved a little distance away.

'The European Union have started an internal enquiry,' he said, 'into the whole Bulgarian light-bulb factory affair.'

'Any arrests?' I asked.

'Not yet,' he said. 'And between you and me, I don't think there will be. There didn't seem to be the slightest urgency at the meeting I had with the administrator from the European Court of Auditors. He seemed to think that a hundred million euros was hardly big enough to worry about. I ask you. A hundred million euros could build us a new hospital in Liverpool, or several new schools.'

'Any news on Shenington?' I asked him.

'No change,' he said. 'And I doubt if there will be. The medics are now saying he has entered what they call a "persistent vegetative state". It's a sort of half-coma, half-awake condition.'

'What's the prognosis?'

'They say he's unlikely ever to make any improvement, and he'll certainly never stand trial. In cases of severe brain damage like this, if patients show no change for a whole year, the doctors usually recommend to their families that artificial nutrition should be withdrawn, to let them die.'

Ben Roberts would clearly have some difficult decisions to make in the months ahead. And I also wondered what effect the actions of his father might have on his planned life in politics. He would surely now become the Earl of Balscott rather earlier than he might have expected.

'Have you managed to identify the dead gunman as Dimitar Petrov?' I asked.

'We're still working on it,' he said. 'It seems that both Dimitar and Petrov are very common names in Bulgaria.'

'Can't Uri Joram in Brussels help you?'

'Apparently he denies any knowledge of anything,' he said. 'Claims his e-mail address must have been used by others.'

'Why am I not surprised?' I said. 'How about Shenington's heavies at Cheltenham?'

'Not a sniff,' he said. 'I expect they vanished into the night as soon as their boss ended up in hospital.'

It reminded me of Billy Searle, who was now, in fact, out of hospital, recuperating at home with the fixator on his broken leg. Officially, he was still denying any knowledge of who had knocked him off his bicycle, but he had confirmed to me privately that the 'nob' responsible had indeed been Viscount Shenington. 'I'm so glad the effing bastard got what was coming to him,' had been his exact words when I'd told him of Shenington's medical condition. And he had giggled uncontrollably, and repeatedly punched the air.

The chief inspector and I rejoined the others.

'Rosemary says she's lost her job,' said Claudia, sounding affronted on her behalf.

'Everyone at Lyall and Black has,' said Rosemary McDowd with bitterness.

Her tone also implied an accusation, and I took it to be towards me. Why was it, I wondered, that the blame often fell, not on the wrongdoer, but on the person who exposed them?

It wasn't me who Mrs McDowd should blame for the demise of Lyall & Black. It was Patrick Lyall, and maybe Gregory Black too, for not being sufficiently diligent in his management of the Roberts Family Trust.

And I surely had more right to be angry with her than vice versa.

After all, it had been she who had told Patrick that I'd been staying at my mother's house, which had then allowed him and Shenington to send a gunman there to try to kill me.

'So what are you going to do now?' I asked her.

'I have absolutely no idea,' she said flatly. 'How about you?'

'I thought I might try my hand at working in the movies, or in the theatre,' I said. 'I've written to a few companies offering my services as a funding specialist, to help them find the production money for films and plays. I think it looks quite interesting.'

'But isn't that a bit of a gamble?' she said.

I smiled at her.

With ovarian cancer, life itself was a bit of a gamble. Heads you win, tails you die.